C000175660

Endorsements

These stories are gripping. In part due to the dramatic period of history in which they are set, but especially due to the engaging way Christine Farenhorst tells them. Not every story has a "happy ending," so to speak, and many of them conclude in an open-ended manner. And yet it is these very characteristics that give free reign to the reader's imagination long after each story is over. Jesus Christ is near to his own, even in the midst of enormous uncertainty and suffering, and Farenhorst shows how this plays out in the lives of her characters. What a comfort to know that Christ is near to us as well!

R. Andrew Compton
Asst. Prof. of Old Testament
Mid-America Reformed Seminary

The short story "I Was a Stranger" is, by itself, reason enough to pick up this collection. The hero of this WW II story isn't a resistance fighter or soldier, and the bravery involved isn't big or bold. But quiet heroics are heroics still, and what Christine has crafted here is a story to inspire all of us called to everyday, on-going faithfulness.

This is a story - and a book! - dads will want to share with their daughters! The very best stories should be read out loud, and what Christine has crafted here will make for great road-trip reading for the whole family. So, kick back in the passenger seat, shut all the screens off, and share with your spouse and kids what life was like during and just after the Great Wars.

Jon Dykstra
Editor
Reformed Perspective

The book you are holding in your hand, is my opinion, the high-water mark of Christine's accomplishments. Set in the time frame of World War II or shortly thereafter, Hidden deals with a number of fictional but very believable scenarios - scenarios in which the characters must navigate the ethical aftermaths of a very dark period of history. The actual beauty of this book is that she has captured a very real component of the Christian Faith with which many will identify. That component is the way in which the Sovereignty of God often comes into play into the lives of people in the most unexpected ways bringing about unanticipated results under very trying circumstances.

After acclimating to the Dutch names and some of the Dutch terminology, the stories began to carry my mind and imagination in much the same way a smooth-running river moves a wayward tree branch from headwater to mouth. The journey is well worth the effort.

Heinz G. Dschankilic,
Former Publisher
Joshua Press

HIDDEN

HIDDEN

Stories of War and Peace

Christine Farenhorst

Dedication

To: David
Spurgeon
and
Martyn Lloyd-Jones

as they sought to demonstrate
providence,
sweetness and
zeal

The LORD is my light and my salvation;
whom shall I fear?
The LORD is the stronghold of my life;
of whom shall I be afraid?
When evildoers assail me
to eat up my flesh,
my adversaries and foes,
it is they who stumble and fall.
Though an army encamp against me,
my heart shall not fear;
though war arise against me,
yet I will be confident.
One thing have I asked of the LORD,
that will I seek after:
that I may dwell in the house of the LORD
all the days of my life,
to gaze upon the beauty of the LORD
and to inquire in his temple.

For he will hide me in his shelter

in the day of trouble;
he will conceal me under the cover of his tent;
he will lift me high upon a rock.
And now my head shall be lifted up
above my enemies all around me,
and I will offer in his tent
sacrifices with shouts of joy;
I will sing and make melody to the LORD.

Psalm 27:1-6

Table of Contents

Preface

David said "Some trust in chariots and some in horses: but we will remember the name of the Lord our God." (Ps. 20:7)

It's easy to trust in missiles, man-power and all the expertise that we think has revolutionized and modernized today's society. These things epitomize today's chariots and horses, and most people feel these things will lead to power, success and peace. A century has passed since WW I ended, that war referred to as the war to end all wars; and it's almost three quarters of a century since the close of WW II. Yet in spite of man's so-called advancements, wars have not ceased. We see violence around the globe on our internet screen, read of it in our daily newspapers, and, if we are honest, feel it in our hearts

Martyn Lloyd-Jones, in his 'Studies in the Sermon on the Mount' both asks and responds to the innate questions: "Why are there wars in the world? Why is there this constant international tension? What is the matter with the world? Why war and all the unhappiness and turmoil and discord amongst men? There is only one answer to these questions - sin. Nothing else; just sin."

Should we consequently cower in fear? Should we rise up and fight? Just what should our response be? Spurgeon answered that question well when he commented,

How angry are my enemies and especially the arch-enemy! Shall I stretch forth my hand and fight my foes? No, my hand is better employed in doing service for my Lord. Besides there is no need, for my God will use His far-reaching arm, and He will deal with them far better than I could if I were to try. "Vengeance is mine; I will repay, saith the Lord." He will with His own right hand of power and wisdom save me, and what more can I desire?

The stories related in this book, although set against the backdrop of the "Great Wars," speak not only of external, physical struggles but also of internal, spiritual struggles and of God's armor - an armor we should all constantly wear.

May you be blessed as you read these stories. Although the main characters (and some towns) are fictional, the times and events in which the characters are placed are factual. For example, in 'I Have Called You by Name', 'I Was a Stranger 'and 'Forming Adam', the extreme contempt and hatred after the Second World War of those who had been occupied, for those who had sympathized with Nazis is graphically portrayed. In 'I Have a Sonne', the physical and emotional difficulties faced by individuals in Holland as they strove to survive, especially during the hunger winter of '44, are depicted. The urge to emigrate to newer and greener pastures after the disastrous war years was felt by many war survivors. This is seen in 'The Drawing' and in 'The Fallen Lines'. The story 'When You Open Your Hand', gives insight into the lives of some of the German civilians in rural Germany during the war years. In 'The End of a Thing', a mother's love overcomes the trauma of war. The First World War story, 'Any Fool Can Sing in the Day', accurately portrays the advance of Germany's troops into Belgium and describes the havoc and fear that the Huns' advance heaped on the villages and towns they took over.

Some of the occurrences in these stories are based on anecdotes, some on fact, and some on fiction. May you be nudged by all them, nudged into remembering that Jesus accomplished the victory over sin and death and hell - so that we might have peace everlasting.

Christine Farenhorst

1: I Have Called You by Name

But now thus says the LORD, he who created you, O Jacob, he who formed you, O Israel: "Fear not, for I have redeemed you; I have called you by name, you are mine. When you pass through the waters, I will be with you; and through the rivers, they shall not overwhelm you; when you walk through fire you shall not be burned, and the flame shall not consume you. For I am the LORD your God, the Holy One of Israel, your Savior (Is. 43:1-3a).

Grey morning light fell through the half-open curtain of a clean but shabby room, vaguely outlining the form of a man stretched out on a cot. It was early, not quite five o'clock. Half awake, half asleep, he stirred. In their stalls behind the thin slats that separated his dingy quarters from the stable, cows shifted about noisily. Slowly Job, for that was the man's name, opened his eyes. Shadows of elm trees bending in the wind in the outside yard, cast strange shapes onto the wall. He lay still, quietly contemplating the swaying forms for a few minutes. Then he coughed. The phlegmatic sound mingled with that of the village clock striking five. Abruptly sitting up, Job pushed the blanket aside, swinging bony legs over the edge of the bed. His socks, pants, shirt and coveralls lay in a heap on a rattan chair next to the cot. He dressed quickly, then walked over to the water bucket next to the dresser. Splashing water on his face, he sputtered a bit before reaching for the towel hanging on a wooden peg beside the door.

He had dreamt – dreamt of the past and of the future. It was not his wont to dream and as he dried his face, rough with stubble, he pondered on it. Mechanically he lit the gas stove, and placed a round-bellied kettle on top of the burner. Through the gap in the curtained window he could see that it was going to be a dull day. It was drizzling slightly but steadily. The wind kept moving the trees back and forth, branches lifting up and down, not wildly but without stopping. He stood immobile, staring out at the yard, until the kettle, puffing steam through its spout, drew him back into the room. Turning away from the window, he lifted it off the stove and poured the boiling water into a brown teapot, poured it over top of the dregs of yesterday's drink. It wouldn't be much, but it would be hot, and he needed a little something hot in his belly before going out.

After finishing the tea, which he drank sitting on the edge of his bed, Job pulled his jacket off the back of the rattan chair. Slipping it on, he rose and walked towards the door. Reaching it, he stood still for a moment before taking hold of the handle. Chill air embraced him when the door opened and as he stepped out, but he did not shrink from its touch. Shutting the wooden frame behind him, he began his stride down the sand path leading away from the farm house. Moistened by the rain, the sand received his footfall with a steady crunch. Eventually reaching the end of the path, he turned left onto a bigger road leading towards the village. Job had trudged the way so often in both sun and rain, that he could walk it blindfolded. It took him about fifteen minutes to reach the village of Kerkhorst. There was no way to by-pass the small community in order to reach the cemetery on its other side. Initially, when he had first returned from the concentration camp, people had frequently stopped him in the streets, albeit with some trepidation.

"Hello, Job. Good to have you back."

Although not impolite, he had not responded with a great many words. Village folk, in turn, had not really had too much to say to him. After all, his sort of sorrow was not the kind that loosened tongues, that made for idle chit-chat. It had been several years now – years in which people had become so accustomed to regularly seeing him walk through the village towards the graveyard that they had dubbed him 'cemetery Job'.

Hardly anyone was about. It was too early in the morning, although the yellow warmth of lamps behind some curtains gently intimated that a number of families were rising and that everyday activities were beginning. The walls of the stone houses glistened and shone with the ongoing drizzle. Lights of a heavy truck suddenly loomed ahead. The vehicle passed with a swish, heavy on the little puddles between the cobblestones. A shower of water swept past Job but it did not slow him down. The collar of his jacket up, his step purposeful, he soon left the village, as well as the main street, behind him. The cemetery, just to the south of the village, lay waiting. He opened the black, iron gate and slipped through alongside a rusty creak, letting it clank shut behind him.

Most people thought Job came to the cemetery to visit his wife's grave. Some even speculated that perhaps he tried to literally converse with her, alerting dominee to this possibility. But the minister, after speaking with Job, had merely smiled at the gossipers, telling them that they had nothing to worry about, that Job's eternal welfare was quite safe. The truth was that Job did come to the cemetery to talk, to converse, as it were. But it was not his wife with whom he spoke – it was God. For it was prayer that drew him to the solitary plot of soil that housed the last remains of so many whom he had known; and it was prayer that he now made as he stood in the drizzle. Why it was that he felt comfortable here, he hardly knew himself as he made his way between headstones and slowly stepped through the rain-soaked grass. He did perceive that by staying in his room back at his squalid quarters at farmer Niets, he would not have the opportunity to worship as openly and as long as he did here. For back there it would be, *'Up, Job, time to get up! Cows waiting to be milked*!' But farmer Niets, who employed Job, and whose father had employed Job's father before him, had a healthy respect for, or rather a fear of, grief. And if he thought that Job came to bewail the sad providence of his widowerhood and to remember the ills of warfare, then so be it. Job had not enlightened him as to the whys and wherefores. Because he worked hard each day and earned the frugal, post-war wage paid out to him each month without complaining, the farmer permitted this eccentricity, even took pride in it when speaking with others of his hired hand.

Job pulled a somewhat crumpled letter out of his jacket pocket, smoothing it in his hands.

"Lord," he began, "dear Father, Creator of heaven and earth, please listen to me this morning. Read, please Father, the words of this letter which I received just this last week by the hand of Liesbet, my sister. It came to her house, and was not forwarded to the farm. Read it because You know everything and You are in control of everything and this I confess."

Rain spattered on the thin, blue vellum. It left blotches on the paper. Job folded it up again and put it back into his pocket. He walked about as he spoke, as he prayed. "It was hard to come back, Lord, to this place and to find out that Els was gone – gone from our home; gone as a mother; gone as a wife. You alone know what went on in her heart. Perhaps what she did was correct. Perhaps...."

He stopped and wiped his face and then whispered, "It was very hard."

He halted again and lifting his face, contemplated the dark clouds above his head.

"But it was even more difficult," he went on, "to come back and to find out that ... well, that pieces of Your Word seemed to be missing... missing from a lot of households here."

The drizzle fell on his stubble and he rubbed his chin.

"You have heard me say this so often but yet again I intercede for Your body the church. And especially for my children, Lord... my children."

He stopped and coughed.

"I think I would like to be here," he went on, "when you come back, Lord; when you will roll back the clouds like a scroll; and when the trumpet will sound."

He turned his face downward again, towards the earth, towards the grey tombstones by his feet.

"I know that my physical body will soon lay here because the doctor left nothing unsaid at the last visit. And that doesn't matter. But I don't want...."

He stopped again. His right hand stroked the pocket holding the letter.

"You see, Lord, I'm not sure about what to do about Sofia and Aafke Roos."

He stopped again and turned, facing a black stone on which was written in italic script:

Els Deken, 1906 - 1945, wife of Job Deken, and mother of Sofia and Aafke Roos.

"She was a good wife, Lord," Job continued his prayer, "You know she was a good wife. But no matter. That is all in the past and it seems to me that it would be good for the girls to get away from the past and from this present. And I confess that You have shown me the way and that You will also give me the courage to do what is right."

A sparrow sang out through the drizzle and Job smiled.

"Yes, sing, little bird," he said, "Sing, because God has created you to sing and so you should."

That evening, after the farm work was done, Job made his way into the village once more, this time to his sister's house. Liesbet and her husband owned a small grocery store which also sold yarn, needles, thread and certain farming necessities. The backyard of their home held a carpentry shop in which his brother-in-law, Harro, fashioned brooms, rakes, shovels and other such implements. Their business had thrived during the war, and they also owned, to a certain degree, Job thought with a wry smile even as he knocked at the front door, his two daughters. Aafke Roos opened the door. Aafke Roos was his youngest and a dark-haired beauty. She was twenty. Behind her stood Sofia, his oldest daughter, a brown-haired, serious, twenty-two-year-old young woman and one whose eyes reflected the tenderness and compassionate love in which she held her father.

"Father, do come in," Aafke Roos called out enthusiastically, as she stepped aside to make way for him to enter the foyer.

Liesbet was nowhere to be seen.

"Tante Liesbet's out helping Oom Harro in the carpentry shop," Sofia answered his unspoken question, "So we can have a nice visit without...."

She stopped and blushed.

"That was unkind of me," she went on, "Tante Liesbet and Oom Harro were good to take us in after mother... well, after she died. And they are good to keep us here now. Only I wish...."

She stopped again, ill at ease. Job smiled at her.

"It's all right, child," he said, "I know."

"Well, I'm glad I'm here," Aafke Roos put in, even as she hung her father's jacket on a peg on the wall, "because I'm sure we couldn't live on the farm where you are now. It stinks."

"Aafke Roos!"

Sofia's eyes flashed as she spoke. Job sighed. It was not that he minded Aafke Roos' words, but he did mind that she was of a rather impetuous and selfish nature; that she often paid no heed to what someone else felt or needed.

"So," he said, sitting himself down on a chair by the table in the small kitchen, "and how are you both?"

"Just fine, father," Sofia answered, regarding him with a look of worry, noting that he was getting thinner each time she saw him, and that he had dark circles under his eyes.

"Well, that's good."

He leaned his elbows on the table, resting his head on his hands, waiting a short moment before he spoke again.

"Girls," he began, "I want to take advantage of this private time to speak with you seriously about the future, about the very near future actually."

"If you mean that Tante Liesbet has asked you if I could work in her shop this summer instead of being hired out again as a drudge to farmer Ten Kate, then I hope you'll say 'yes', father," Aafke Roos threw out.

"No," Job responded, regarding his youngest daughter as she sat across from him, eyebrows lifted, "that's not what I mean."

Sofia leaned against the stove, waiting for the water to boil for the tea. Next to the red teapot stood three cups, and as she waited, Sofia carefully meted out several pieces of *speculaas*, spiced biscuit, onto a dish. Her silhouette appeared remarkably like that of her mother, Job reflected with some degree of pain, her mother who had always cared passionately for those around her.

"Well, then," Aafke Roos pouted, "what do you mean."

He coughed before he was able to respond and even then it was so slowly and with such evident difficulty that Sofia eyed him with growing concern.

"I have received a letter from a friend in Canada. A friend whom neither of you know. He is someone I met a number of years ago...."

He stopped and Sofia, leaving her place at the counter, came over. She put her arms about his shoulders and kissed the top of his balding head.

"Is the letter from someone in the camp, father?" she asked softly.

"Yes," he said, "someone I met in the camp."

Aafke Roos looked down. She shied away from emotion when it did not concern herself.

"You don't have to speak, father, if it troubles you so," Sofia said.

"No, I must speak of it," Job responded, lifting his head out of the crook of his hands, "for it concerns you both. And I do believe," he added, looking at each of them in turn, "that there is providence for your future here. Yes, I do believe that."

He reached into his pants right pocket and took out the letter. Both girls were quiet, eyes on the blue paper. He lay it on the kitchen table and smoothed it with his rough, work-worn hands.

"I have thought long and hard, girls," he said, "and you must listen to me carefully and not interrupt while I am reading."

"Yes, father," Sofia answered.

Aafke Roos said nothing, but looked doubtful.

"My dear friend, Job," Job started to read, *"You will be surprised to hear from me after several years of silence. But several years are really of little consequence between true friends. I hope that this letter finds you in good health. We had so many talks, you and I, and I think without elaborating, you will know what I mean by 'good health'.*

Aafke Roos shrugged ever so slightly at these words, but she said nothing.

"You will remember that I told you that I had a son, a son who immigrated to Canada just before the war. You might also remember that I told you that this son bought a farm, a dairy farm, in Ontario. And now, even as Abraham looked for a godly wife for his son Isaac, so I send this letter as an Eliezer of sorts to see if one of your daughters can be a Rebecca for my child."

Sofia's hands tightened on the shoulders of her father and Aafke Roos' eyes grew round with shock.

"Enclosed you will find money for boat fare from Rotterdam to Montreal. I will make sure that I meet...."

At this point Aafke Roos could no longer restrain herself.

"Surely, father," she spouted out, "surely you are not serious about this."

"Yes," her father said, "I am. And I have already written back that...."

"Well, I won't go," Aafke Roos said, "I just won't go and that's all there is to it. You can send Sofia if you like, but I...."

"You what?" Job interrupted, "What exactly is it that you will do, Aafke Roos? Live on here off your Tante Liesbet's and Oom Harro's charity?"

The kettle whistled and Sofia walked back to the counter and poured water into the red teapot. Then she automatically carried the plate with the cookies to the kitchen table.

"Have a cookie, father," she said.

"I won't eat," he said, "until I know your mind, Sofia."

"I don't know, father," she answered, "This takes me totally by surprise and, ... well, I don't know your friend or his son, you see. So I can't really give you an honest reply."

"No," he countered, "but you know me, your father. And if I assure you that my friend is a good man and that his son is a good son, then perhaps your mind and your heart can trust that all is well."

"But you, father," she responded, sitting down next to him, "if such a thing were truly to happen, you would stay here, in Holland, and I cannot bear the thought that...."

Here she left off speaking. He nodded. This was the part with which he struggled himself.

"Is he a rich man?" Aafke Roos asked in the quiet that ensued, "Because to send the fare just like that... It must be very expensive, a trip across the ocean, and... Well, he must be rich then, mustn't he?"

She looked very pretty, cheeks flushed with sudden excitement. Anyone, it occurred to Sofia as she looked at her sister, would desire her as bride. For a moment Sofia was overcome with jealousy, with a desire to look like her sister. Aafke Roos grinned at them, displaying perfect teeth, and then she yawned.

"You know," she said, as she stretched, "I think I will consider it after all. Willem De Mas has told me about Canada. He says it's a very big country with lots of opportunity for all sorts of people. He thinks that he might go there someday. But he also says it costs...."

"I've told you that you were not to speak with Willem De Mas anymore."

It came out a little sharper than Sofia intended.

"I can speak with whomever I like," Aafke Roos shot back, "and besides, can I help it if I meet him in the street? You don't want me to be rude, do you?"

The back door opened and they could hear Tante Liesbet and Oom Harro coming in. Job stood up.

"Oh, father," Sofia said, "you haven't touched your tea yet."

"I'll have a cup next time," Job answered, "but now it's time to go. Perhaps you shouldn't yet speak about...."

Sofia nodded, but Aafke Roos said, "Why not? If one of us goes, they'll have to know sooner or later, won't they?"

"Know what?" Tante Liesbet said, the kitchen doorway a frame for her bulk.

But Job did not stay to inform his sister. After a quick glance at his daughters, he passed his sister without a word and disappeared into the evening.

Over the next few weeks, there was a great deal of speculation in the village as to which of the two daughters would leave for North America, for Canada. For Aafke Roos, as soon as her father had left, had recounted the whole matter to Tante Liesbet. Tante Liesbet, never one for secrets had consequently informed the butcher, the baker, and all the members of her women's society. The two girls were not popular in the village and were a rather solitary pair most of the time. But almost everyone agreed that Aafke Roos should go. After all, it was argued that she was the prettiest of the two girls, and that she had been endowed with a bold streak that might stand her in good stead in a new country. Sofia, they said, should stay in Kerkhorst and take care of her father in his old age, and wasn't Job getting old? Throughout all this gossip, Job continued to work at the farm. He rose early, milked, cleaned, and did whatever farmer Niets required. It was spring and there was much to be done.

On a sunny afternoon during the early days of May, Sofia walked over to the farm. She found her father in the stable, putting straw into the stalls. When he saw her, he stopped working and put down his pitchfork.

"Is everything all right?"

"Yes, father."

Sofia stood quietly, a blue scarf tied over her straight brown hair. He walked towards the stable door and beckoned that she should follow. A few minutes later they were seated at the wooden table in his room. As she did each time she visited her father, Sofia repressed a sigh. It was so poor, so dark, and so lonely in this place.

"What is the matter, my Sofia."

Her father was facing her across the table. Reaching over, he took her hand into his own and smiled.

"Nothing really," she answered, "although I was for a moment remembering the house where we lived before... before the war. I was thinking how different it all was at that time. But," she continued with a small smile, "I know you don't want to hear about that and I won't go on about it."

She stopped and stared down at their hands. Her father spoke gently.

"There are many things, my Sofia," he said, "to which we do not know the answer. And to which we may never know the answer, not now and perhaps not in the afterlife either."

"But you ought to have..." she retaliated rather lamely and then halted her flow of words again.

"I ought to have what?" he said, "And what ought anyone to have really, when it comes to that?"

"I wonder about... about mother," she went on, "about why...."

The words twisted about in her mind and would not come out properly.

"Your mother loved you Sofia."

Job was looking out the window now and he had let go of his daughter's hand. Sofia sighed and changed the subject. It was always so when she tried to broach the matter that weighed most heavily upon her. With her finger she traced a crack in the not too steady table, and went on.

"I do think that I have to tell you that I'm not at all sure that what you are asking me, or both of us," she corrected herself, "is the right thing to ask."

"The right thing to ask?" he repeated, turning his gaze back on his daughter.

"Yes, the right thing to ask, father. You see, if I went to Canada, then who would look in on you, or look after you if you became...."

She halted amid her flow of rapid words and then went on.

"Or, for that matter, who would look after Aafke Roos? And if she went, well...."

Here Sofia hesitated again but regarded her father with a knowing look. He nodded and waited for her to continue.

"Aafke Roos is not... well, she is not always reliable in what she says or does. She is easily influenced or manipulated by others. Sometimes she, ... she lies. So... so I think that neither of us should go, even though I fully trust your judgment, father. I truly do and...."

"So you are willing to go?"

"Willing to do as you ask? Well, yes – in my heart I am. Even though, father, it is a strange path you ask me to walk. One that I cannot fathom."

Sofia shook her head in wonderment before continuing.

"But physically, no, I cannot go. I don't think it is possible for me to go for the reasons I just gave you."

He nodded and reached for her hand again, stroking it as he spoke.

"I was hoping that you would be willing, Sofia. There is this, you see, which I haven't told you yet. And that is this – that I have, with the help of Mr. Van Geest, the notary public, purchased a passage for both of you.

"For both of us? But...."

"Yes, for both of you in the middle of June."

"The middle of June? But father, that is very soon, and ...father, there is still yourself – you would be left here all alone."

She threw out the words vehemently and he smiled and looked at her intently.

24

"Will I be alone, Sofia?"

She was silent for a long moment and slowly withdrew her hand from her father's.

"No, not in the way that you mean, but," she went on, her defenses up again, "but you certainly don't know that Aafke...."

She halted. He smiled at her.

"Don't I know that, my dear girl? She does want to go, but for different reasons than you yourself will go."

"But father...."

Sofia didn't know how to respond.

"Both of us?" she again repeated in a questioning manner and then faltered, "but the money... You said there was only money for the passage of one person."

"No I did not say that," he responded calmly, "I just read there was money for boat passage. And remember, where there is food to feed one, as my mother always said, there surely is food to feed two."

"But we are not talking about food but about a sum of money," Sofia responded, a trifle irritated. "And," she went on, "next month... that is very soon, father. And, really, what if Aafke Roos doesn't want to go?"

"She does want to go," Job said, "She informed me that she was willing to go two days after I first proposed the idea."

"Two days? But she never said anything to me. She never...."

"No, and I'm not surprised," Job answered, "but she is willing. I do assure you of that."

Sofia stood up, scraping her chair back rather noisily over the wooden floor.

"Seriously, father," she said, "what about you? You will have neither myself nor Aafke Roos if we go. And what if... I mean, Canada is so very far away."

"There is always your Tante Liesbet," he smiled, "and I'm sure that in spite of her... her desire to control and always have the last word, that she would take good care of me should that be necessary."

"You are ill, aren't you, father?"

Sofia did not look at him as she spoke, hand on the back of her chair, a shadow darkening her face as she studied the floor.

"We are all ill, child," he responded, "and sooner or later we will all die of the same disease – a disease called time."

"But what if I never see you again, father?"

She threw out the words with great force, great force that ended in a sob.

"That," he answered, "is a question to which you very well know the answer, my Sofia."

It was only later, on the way home, that Sofia thought of the second problem which a double passage would engender – the fact that only one of them could marry the son. And what would happen to the other?

Surprisingly, Tante Liesbet put up very little opposition to both of the girls leaving. This made Sofia ashamed to a certain degree, as she had been convinced that Tante Liesbet had counted on one of them staying with her and Oom Harro to help in the store. They had no children of their own.

"I think it costs more than three hundred guilders for the passage of one," Tante Liesbet had initially calculated out loud, "And where did my brother get the money? And couldn't we use it as well in the store and haven't we always treated you girls as our own? I ask you, 'Why leave Holland?'"

Sofia had chosen not to respond and Aafke Roos had only half-listened. Then dominee had visited Tante Liesbet. And when Sofia had informed Tante Liesbet that both of them would be going to Canada, she had made no protestations, she had only smiled a thin smile and had helped them begin to pack.

Aafke Roos, now that she had openly made up her mind to leave, became rather enthusiastic. There was a whole world out there, she told Sofia, that she had never seen and it was a world, she was sure, which would be delighted to see her. Tante Liesbet, usually not chary with her vocabulary, grew quieter as the days sped by but did nothing to interfere with plans. She even made sure both girls had a warm coat, decent underwear, and several new frocks. As a matter of fact, Tante Liesbet seemed to have grown a heart, Sofia thought as she, with a small twinge of conscience, watched the older woman as she bustled about the shop, commenting to customers that she felt as if she was losing two daughters. Most people commiserated very little. Sofia and Aafke Roos were not much sought after in the small farming community.

It was Mr. Van Geest, the notary public, who escorted the girls to Rotterdam in mid-June. Job had arranged that the man escort his two daughters to the boat. Tante Liesbet and Oom Harro were only too glad to be spared the traveling and embraced the girls while the entire neighborhood watched from behind their curtains, before they stepped into a waiting taxi with Mr. Van Geest. Sofia sighed with relief when the car doors closed. They slowly drove down the main street, out of Kerkhorst, and past the sand path that turned towards the Niets' farm. Pressing her face against the car window, Sofia fancied she could see father's face at the window, but knew that he would be in the barn. Father had said goodbye to them the night before, and she forced herself to think of other things.

Wasn't it a good and bright day in which to travel? Mr. Van Geest was a short, rather thin man, and he studiously tried to make conversation for the first ten minutes of the journey. When neither Sofia nor Aafke Roos responded to his comments, he gave up and they traveled on quietly. At only one point did Sofia almost begin to weep. It was when they passed the ruins of their old home – the skeleton remainder of the house in which they had spent the first years of their lives. For a moment Sofia saw herself and Aafke Roos playing in the yard, saw the children they had been, and pictured her mother standing at the backdoor smiling. And then she imagined the crowd of people as they had mobbed the place, as they had dragged mother outside, as they.... And here her mind stopped. People had whispered, had talked behind her back. Aafke Roos and herself had been visiting the dominee that day and they had stayed, and stayed, and stayed, until Tante Liesbet....

Mr. Van Geest was noticeably nervous about the whole business of being responsible for two young women. In Rotterdam he paid the taxi driver, meticulously meting out the exact change down to the last penny. For the next twenty minutes, he carefully maneuvered Sofia and Aafke Roos through the crowds packed onto the quay.

"Be sure to hold onto your purses," he said every thirty seconds, "there are bound to be pickpockets about."

"Don't worry," Sofia answered, lugging a heavy brown suitcase which Mr. Van Geest had offered to carry but which offer she had turned down, "we will be fine. We have one another and all we need to do is get on board and find our cabins."

"Yes, but," Mr. Van Geest began, bumping into yet another person and almost losing his tight grip on Aafke Roos' arm, "it's so busy and there are bound to be people who will try and take advantage of two young girls."

Aafke Roos snickered and Sofia shot her a baleful look.

"Mr. Van Geest," she said, stopping and putting her suitcase down, "you really don't have to stay. Look, people are boarding. I see a great many walking up the gangplank onto the boat. Why don't you stay here? The truth is that you can watch us board from this vantage point. That way you can tell father you waved to us as we stood on deck. You can let him know we made it and that we were healthy and happy when you left us."

Mr. Van Geest looked relieved.

"It might be the thing to do," he commented, "but...."

"No buts," Sofia countered, "Aafke Roos and I are very thankful that you took the time to take us all this way, aren't we, Aafke Roos?"

"Yes," Aafke Roos said, all the while searching the crowds as if she were looking for someone, "we certainly are grateful to you, Mr. Van Geest. But Sofia is right. We will be fine now. We'll have no trouble getting on board and the ship will take us to Canada. We can't get lost once we're on board now, can we."

"Well, then, I'll say goodbye," Mr. Van Geest smiled.

He extended his hand. Both girls shook it. Then Mr. Van Geest reached into his vest pocket and took out a yellow envelope.

"Your father asked me to give this to you, Sofia" he said, "before you boarded, and now I've fulfilled that duty."

Sofia took the envelope from him. Aafke Rose stared at it but made no motion to take it from her.

"Thank you once again, dear Mr. Van Geest. And please tell my father I send him a kiss."

Impulsively Sofia leaned forward and kissed the little man on the cheek. He blushed but looked pleased. Aafke Roos looked embarrassed. Then Sofia took Aafke Roos' arm and with one more wave at Mr. Van Geest, they walked away, heavy suitcases dangling awkwardly from their hands.

Much later, as the large passenger boat was pulling away from the dock, and the sisters stood next to one another waving at the crowd of people left behind on the quay, Sofia's first tears fell. It was not only her father she was leaving, but also her fatherland. Someone in the background began singing 'Wilhelmus van Naussau', the Dutch national anthem. Others joined in and although she tried to sing along, Sofia could not because of weeping.

"Cheer up, Sofia," Aafke Roos said brightly, "Think of the adventure of the whole thing. Think of the good times we'll have on board and of all the people we'll meet."

Fresh wind blew on their cheeks and seagulls flew around the boat, screeching as the waves hit the side of the ship. The girls stood side by side for a long time, gazing at the disappearing harbor, until Sofia began to feel slightly queasy.

"I'm going to the cabin. I don't think I feel that well," she said softly.

"Well, I'm staying out a bit longer. You'll soon feel better. Have a bit of a lie-down and make sure you let me have the top bunk."

Making her way down several stairs and through narrow, tight corridors, Sofia eventually found the cabin to which they had been shown earlier. It was not large and left very little room in which to maneuver. There were two sets of bunk beds and with relief Sofia saw that their suitcases were standing neatly against the side of one of these. A woman with a young child sat on the edge of the other bunk.

"Hello."

Sofia responded with a greeting as well and noted that the woman seemed to have a friendly manner about her and that the little girl smiled shyly.

"I'm Sofia. What's your name?"

The child responded softly.

"Alie."

"Hello, Alie. I'm so glad you will be sharing our cabin."

"My name is Emma," the mother said, standing up and extending her hand.

Sofia took it and then, feeling the ship pitch a bit, felt her stomach churn.

"I'm afraid," she apologized, letting go of Emma's hand, "that I'll have to lay down a bit until I get my sea legs."

"Oh, that's all right," Emma responded, "Here, let me help you move the suitcase so that you can make yourself comfortable. And don't mind us. We'll be quiet, won't we Alie?"

The little girl nodded and then grinned at Sofia. Sofia smiled back at her and then, feeling slightly lightheaded, sat down on the edge of her bunk. She lay her purse on the floor and put the yellow envelope on top of her purse. Then slowly sinking down, she put her face on the pillow.

"Are you all right?"

"I think I will be. A little rest will do me a world of good."

"Let me help you take your shoes off. That always improves things."

Emma bent over and undid the brown laces of Sofia's sturdy shoes, pulling them off and slipping them under the bed.

"That should feel better. It always makes me feel better. And why don't you crawl under the blanket. Just have a snooze before supper."

The thought of food made Sofia's stomach churn even more. She tried to smile but could hardly manage it. Emma's arm aided her into a half sitting position and with a bit of help she felt her feet slide under the covers. How wonderful it was to lie down. She wondered how father was, and she missed him with a fierce pain. Her eyes shut.

Then she remembered the envelope. Would father have sent her a letter?

"The envelope," she murmured, "can you give me the envelope, Emma?"

"Envelope? Oh, you mean this yellow one by your purse?"

"Umh.

Emma reached down, picked up the envelope, and placed it in Sofia's hands. It seemed for a moment as if she was holding her father's hand. Sofia smiled and smiling fell asleep.

Later, much later, she awoke. It was dark in the cabin. Everything was quiet except for the unfamiliar groaning of the motor. It took a few minutes before Sofia recalled exactly where she was. The boat swayed gently and the envelope was still between her fingers. Moonlight shone through the porthole and in the vague dimness of the night she could see Aafke Roos' dress draped over the nearby sink. So that meant Aafke Roos was here, sleeping above her in the top bunk and that she was safe. Sofia turned over and put the yellow envelope under her pillow. Tomorrow she would open it and see what father had sent her. Tomorrow she would do many things.

In the days that followed, however, Sofia was not able to do much. She was not blessed with sea-legs, as Harold, the steward, remarked as he cleaned the cabin floor each day. Every motion that the ship made, her stomach made as well. It was no matter that Aafke Roos and Emma, as well as little Alie, brought her tea, dry biscuits and other food designed to be easy on the digestive system. There was little that stayed in. Each day Harold came in and cheerfully mopped the floor and each day he told her she would soon be feeling better. Days passed. Aafke Roos, breezing in and out of the cabin, excitedly regaled her with stories about the dolphins that jumped in and out of the water early every morning as the people from the garbage disposal unit dumped all the waste into the ocean.

"The fish follow the boat for scraps," she said, "and it's so exciting. William says...."

"William?" Sofia questioned as she half-opened her eyes.

"He's one of the crew-members," Aafke Roos quickly responded, not looking directly at Sofia, "and he knows a lot. He was explaining to a group of us about the dolphins."

"Oh."

"And you know, a lot of people are sea-sick, so you don't have to feel as if you're the only one. Half of the people on deck carry little paper bags in case they have to vomit."

"I'll soon feel better," Sofia said, closing her eyes again, not convinced, although she had walked about the cabin that morning and had truly felt a bit better.

"Sure you will," Aafke said, and then went on to ask, "You know the envelope Mr. Van Geest gave you, where is it?"

"I have it safe," Sofia answered, opening her eyes again.

It was still under her pillow, but for some reason she did not want Aafke Roos to have it before she herself had a chance to open it and read it. She had not had the energy to do so yet, but soon, perhaps later today, she would open the envelope.

"I wonder what's in it?" Aafke Roos continued, "if you tell me where it is, I'll open it and we can both...."

"I really don't feel up to it," Sofia countered weakly, "maybe later."

Aafke Roos shrugged.

"OK, later. Well, I'm going back on deck. I do love the wind and the splash of the waves. When the hull pushes the waves into an arc, you get a lovely feeling of ... well, of being part of the water."

As soon as her sister was gone, Sofia reached under her pillow and took out the envelope. Emma Liefkind and Alie were gone. They spent most of their time with Arie Liefkind. Men and women were separated for the trip across the ocean. The small family Liefkind, after reaching Montreal, would be on their way to Manitoba, to work on a farm until they could save enough money to buy their own place. Pulling herself up, Sofia sat quietly for a moment. Then, after adjusting her pillow, she slid open the envelope with her thumb nail. Feeling slightly guilty, after all she had been dishonest with her sister, she took out a piece of paper. Drawing up her knees, she unfolded the paper, stroking it straight with her right hand. It was a letter – a letter dated April 1945.

My dear husband:

The children, or actually they are young women now, are asleep and I have a little time. But when you read this, it is very likely that I shall no longer be living – living in the sense, that is, of being here on this earth.

Sofia, stopped and stared at the porthole. Her mother must have written this letter. She recognized the writing. Her heart pounded and she swallowed audibly.

You have been a wonderful friend, a fine husband, and a good father. And I thank God for the days and weeks and years you have been in my life.

I cannot bear the thought that you should think ill of me in any way. So I am writing this letter to you to set your mind at ease with regard to my death – for I am almost certain that I shall die shortly.

Let me backtrack a little. You are well aware that my upbringing was one without God. That it was only in my teenage years that I came to know and believe. God used dominee to help me see that God was my Father and that Jesus was my Savior. I know this so clearly and that is why I can tell you, without any reservation, my dear husband, that I am not afraid to die. Well, maybe a little of the actual physical... but let me continue.

Even though I was converted, by the grace of God, through the pastoral care of our dominee, Liesbet, my sister, was not. Perhaps outwardly she conformed to the mode of church attendance when she met and married Harro, but inwardly she did not know God. Desire for material things had her in its grip even from childhood onward. Perhaps coming from a poor background, this is to some degree understandable, and that she reveled in owning and operating a store was always obvious. And now in this dark hunger winter, when goods are next to impossible to come by, she has just confessed to me that she has been fraternizing with the enemy – and that she has made a deal with one of the Nazi officers here in Kerkhorst. Not only that, she has involved Aafke Roos, our youngest daughter. Liesbet compiled a list of names of those whom she suspects to be in the underground and through Aafke Roos passed these names on to the officer in exchange for black market favors. What finger of conscience suddenly prompted her remorse and her confession to me? I do not know. But yesterday she came to me here in our home and begged me to help her and Aafke Roos. Aafke Roos, she stressed, had little idea of what she was doing and was merely excited by the adventure and thrill of it all. Perhaps Liesbet is truly repentant; or, and that is more likely, she is consumed by fear of reprisal by the Dutch underground. There are hopes, very actual hopes, here in Kerkhorst that the war will be over soon. God knows! In any case, she begged for my help. I asked if she had knelt down and repented before God, and I offered to pray with her. But she merely shook her head. Then, beginning to weep, and incoherent with emotion, she showed me a note that had been thrown through her window just yesterday. The note warned her that she would not live long – that her days were numbered. Liesbet pleaded with me to go to the leader of the underground and ask for mercy. This I plan to do, and then I shall take this letter and the two girls, to dominee.

My dear Job, I thank God for you. I thank Him for the many years that you have loved and cherished me and the girls. Actually, for all I know, you could already be in the heaven I have longed for so desperately at times in these cold and somber months. But there are the girls

– Sofia and Aafke Roos...

The letter, rather abruptly, stopped here. Sofia stroked the page. She could see her mother in front of her – her mother who had always been ready to help and listen. What exactly had happened? She reached into the envelope and took out another paper – a paper that appeared to be typewritten. Slowly she unfolded it and laid it on top of her mother's letter. And she read on.

On this last day of April 1945, I verify that Els Deken, wife of Job Deken came to visit me bringing her two daughters, Sofia and Aafke Roos. She asked if my wife and I would care for the girls for a few days as she had reason to believe it would not be safe for them at her place of residence.

When I questioned her with regard to why she thought this, she answered that she could only tell me if I would promise not to tell anyone on pain of death. I shook my head at such language, but she was very agitated and because she had always been a good and faithful parishioner, I did promise her.

"I have," she began, "just confessed to a crime I did not commit. Whether rightly or wrongly, I have done this."

"What crime?" I asked, puzzled.

We were in the study. My wife had taken the girls into the kitchen for some tea.

"The crime of treason," she answered very quietly, her hands gripping the edges of the chair in which she was sitting.

"Treason?" I repeated.

And then Els Deken proceeded to relate to me that her sister, she was afraid, was a Christian in name only and that she feared for her eternal welfare. She hoped, she said, that this would change in time and then explained how her sister had compromised both her store and her life by underhanded dealings with the Nazis. And she told me how her sister had compiled a list with names of underground members and had given them to the SS. When I said that I did not understand why, in consequence to this, she wanted my wife and myself to take care of her children, she began to weep.

"I have just been to see a member of the underground," she cried, "and I have told him that it was I and not my sister who made up the list of suspect members. And I confessed that it was I and not my sister who gave this list to the Nazis. And I begged him to tell all the other members to hide, to run and to leave this area before it was too late."

"What did he say?" I asked her.

"He hit me," she said, stopping her weeping and I noted, at this point that her cheek was beginning to bruise"And then," she went on, "he warned me that there would be satisfaction."

It was quiet then in my study. It was difficult for me to grasp the situation quickly, and to give Els wise advice.

"You should not have lied," I said at length.

"Better that I should lie," she answered, *"then that Liesbet should die in her sins without confessing them to God. Liesbet would... Liesbet would...."*

And then she fell to weeping again.

"You should stay here tonight," I offered, *"No one would think of you as being here. Please, Els, you would be most welcome."*

But she shook her head.

"I do not want to put the lives of you or your wife in jeopardy. And I want the children to be safe. They would be the safest," she added, *"away from myself right now."*

We let the girls stay, of course, and Els left again as quickly as she had come. She did not come back the next day, or the next. We kept the girls, answering their questions as best we could, saying that their mother had some important business and that she would come back when this had been attended to.

The war was over a few days later. And then, a group of people, heady with victory, went over to the house, the Deken house. They dragged Els outside, and then threw some petrol inside, before setting the whole place ablaze. They shaved Els' head, (I was not there, but heard it later). Then they painted a swastika on her bald head with red lead, the paint they use on ships in port, and she was driven through town on a farm wagon. My wife, who was in town, came running home to tell me and we kept the girls inside, kept them inside the whole day. Els died that same day, whether from grief or because of the hunger winter's deprivation, I do not know. I do not know. And her death is partly on my head, because even though I was not there with the mob, I should have spoken out.

The dominee's letter, or note, ended here and Sofia lay back on her pillow, her eyes swimming with tears. She had not known the extent of her mother's involvement. There had been some name-calling by children following them down the street now and then.

"Slut! Whore! Nazi-lover!"

But those incidences had stopped as time went on. But the scorn of a number of the villagers, the icy stares of many women and the disapproving looks of a number of men, these had not stopped. But she had not known what it was exactly that mother had been accused of, although she had guessed that perhaps mother had, for the sake of food, sold herself. No one had spoken to her, and, as far as she knew, no one had spoken to Aafke Roos. And Aafke Roos, what had she thought? After all, she had been involved. Why had dominee not told her these things after mother had died? Why had he kept quiet? Was it because mother had made him promise not to tell? Was it still to protect Tante Liesbet? But surely such a promise would have become void upon mother's death. Even if people believed that mother had fraternized with, had sold herself to the enemy, surely they would have known that the children.... Her thoughts, jumbled and ran amuck. And Tante Liesbet – what about Tante Liesbet? She had, after all, been mother's main concern, the reason that she had lied, had opened herself to scorn and ridicule and death. This was, of course, the reason why Tante Liesbet had been so kind in the end. She had worried that the truth would out. Sofia stretched out her legs and sighed. The papers slid sideways. She grabbed them with her left hand and crumpled them. Should she let Aafke Roos read this? The envelope lay empty. She smoothed the papers and slid them back into the yellow jacket. But then she saw that there was another white envelope at the bottom of the yellow envelope.

She reached for the last item slowly, carefully, propping herself up again, tucking her knees back under her chin. The envelope was thick. She opened it in rather a daze. Money fell out. It was Canadian money, not Dutch currency. Mechanically she counted five bills – five one hundred-dollar bills. And then a small note in her father's writing at the bottom:

Dearest daughter: Enclosed you will find some money. No doubt you will be surprised at the sum. It was given to me by your Tante Liesbet so that you might have a bit of a start in Canada. Perhaps, and I say this without any rancor, she and Oom Harro feel that the better you settle in that country, the less chance there is that you will come back to haunt them.

You have, by this time, I am sure, read the letter your mother wrote as well as the dominee's accounting. It will take time for you to absorb all this information. Just remember that in God's providence nothing happens by chance.

There is one more thing which I want to say to you – and that is this, that you need not concern yourself with the matter of recognition upon arrival in Montreal. Does a bridegroom not always know his bride?

I am weary now and this packet must go with Mr. Van Geest who will be here shortly.

May God keep you until we meet again in Jerusalem,
-Your father

Sofia pushed the money back into the envelope, and the envelope back into the yellow jacket of the other envelope. Then she put everything under her pillow. Sliding down, she curled up into a ball. Pulling the blanket over her head, she cried for a long time – cried for her mother, for her father, for Aafke Roos and Tante Liesbet, and for herself – and finally she fell asleep. It was evening when she awoke. Emma was sitting on the edge of her bunk reading. The cabin light glowed faintly and Sofia sighed audibly. Emma looked at her and smiled.

"Feeling a bit better, Sofia?"

"Well...."

Sofia dangled the word, remembering with a sickening feeling all the knowledge that was stored under her pillow and now filed away in her heart as well.

"You know, Sofia," Emma went on, "I don't know if I ought to tell you this, especially when you are still sick and weak, but...."

She stopped and looked down at her book. Alie was soundly asleep on the top bunk.

"What?" Sofia asked.

"Well, your sister. She is often, no, not often but always, in the company of a young man. They spend all their time together. I think he is also from your village and ... Well, he doesn't seem to me to be the type of young man you'd want her to be with."

"Do you know his name?"

"No, I don't."

Their conversation was interrupted by Aafke Roos' entrance into the cabin. She literally flew in and the smell of the ocean seemed to fly in with her.

"Hello, Emma. Hello, sister. Awake are you? Shall I get you some tea? I'm sure I can get some from the steward. I just saw him down the hallway."

Emma stood up, shut her book and stretched.

"If you don't mind," she said, "I think I'll go and find Arie and say goodnight. Maybe you can keep an eye on Alie?"

She walked past Aafke Roos, opened the door and disappeared.

Aafke Roos stepped up to the porthole and looked out into the dark.

"You know we're approaching Quebec City and then we go on to Montreal. We're almost there, Sofia. We'll be docking tomorrow."

"Yes, I know."

Sofia sat up, swung her feet over the edge of the bunk and reached for her housecoat.

"Do you have to go to the bathroom? Shall I help you?"

Aafke Roos was solicitous, helpful, and something ached inside Sofia as she looked at her younger sister.

"I think I can manage by myself. But when I come back, Aafke Roos, I'd like to talk. Maybe you can stay here and not go out anymore this evening?"

"Sure."

A few minutes later, when Sofia returned, Aafke Roos was still standing by the porthole. Sofia sat down on her bunk, patted the place next to her and asked her sister to come and sit by her side. Aafke Roos obliged.

"You know," Sofia began carefully, "I've not been able to be with you the last while and I hope you've not been lonely."

"Oh, no," Aafke Roos responded, "I've enjoyed every minute on the boat. You needn't worry about that."

"I think that when we sail down the St. Lawrence tomorrow, I'll be well enough to have you show me around."

Aafke Roos looked startled.

"Show you around?"

"Well, I've not been very far away from this bunk the whole time we've been at sea, and I thought that maybe you...."

"Actually," Aafke Roos answered slowly, as if she were thinking deeply, "it might be wise for you to rest as long as you can tomorrow, Sofia. It'll be fairly hectic on the decks. Once we dock lots of people will be walking about, trying to get on land. You may as well stay down as long as you can."

"I see," Sofia said, softly but distinctly, "Well, then perhaps I can read you a letter now from our mother – a letter that was in the yellow envelope that Mr. Van Geest gave me just before we boarded. Do you remember?"

"Yes, of course I remember. But I don't think I want to hear you read that to me just right now. Maybe after... well, after we're settled ... settled in our new home. Because," she went on quickly, "because you're so weak at this point, Sofia, and I'm sure that reading something from mother would not be good for you at all."

"Oh," Sofia answered, vainly searching for more words, for better words.

"I'm actually very tired too," Aafke Roos went on, "I think I'll turn in for the night and not go out any more."

Partially relieved that her sister would be where she could keep an eye on her, Sofia nodded.

"That's fine, but there's one more thing."

"What?"

"Well, have you been seeing someone? Someone from Kerkhorst here on the ship? Emma says...."

"Emma's an old gossip. I've seen her watching me while she was hanging about the railing on the deck and spying on me out of the corner of her eye. Don't listen to what she says, Sofia. I don't think she likes me very much."

"Why wouldn't she like you, Aafke Roos?"

"Well, because I'm young and ... well, I'm pretty and she's an old fuddy-duddy and she's jealous."

"She's not the jealous sort, Aafke Roos, and she's happily married."

Aafke Roos shrugged her shoulders and stood up.

"Well, I still say she hasn't liked me from the very beginning of the trip, so there you are and now I'm going to get ready for bed."

Sofia sighed. Once they got off the ship and once she had Aafke Roos with her for full days, she would be able to exercise the kind of oversight that she ought to have exercised this whole time. It was only later in bed, much later, as Sofia pondered the contents of the letters and the events of the day, that she realized that Aafke Roos had not answered her question as to whether or not she had been seeing anyone from Kerkhorst on board the ship. Tomorrow, tomorrow she would speak with her sister again. Then she fell to wondering about which picture of Aafke Roos her father had sent on to his friend. She did not recall that her father had actually possessed a picture of either herself or of Aafke Roos. Well, no matter. Then she pondered the fact that once Aafke Roos was settled and married, that she would not be able to stay on in her sister's home. Perhaps the money, which would have to be divided between the two of them, would help. It surely would buy some time to look around in this new country. Her skills, however, lay mainly in keeping house. That is what she had done for Tante Liesbet these last years and that is what she enjoyed. Perhaps she could persuade father to immigrate as well, although she knew full well in her heart of hearts that soon her father would immigrate to a new and better place than this country Canada. Oh, how could she have left her father? How could she had done it? And the tears coursed down her cheeks again until she recalled with clarity how her father had spoken with her and how sincerely he had wanted her to go with Aafke Roos.

Morning dawned without Sofia having slept. At least she thought she had not slept. But when Emma yawned and called out good-morning to her, she also informed Sofia in the same breath that Aafke Roos seemed to have risen early for her bed was empty.

"Empty?"

"Yes," Emma answered, "and it almost looks as if it has not been slept in at all."

"But she went to bed after we spoke last night. I know she did."

"Well, all I can tell you is that she is gone right now."

"But where would she be?"

"Well, she's probably sitting down at the early breakfast table. Lots of folks are excited about landing at Montreal today. I know that we are."

Emma dressed quickly and left with Alie to find Arie. Sofia, still shaky and weak, took longer. She pulled her suitcase out from under the bed and carefully removed a white, linen summer dress. It was new and she smiled as she remembered how her father had been particularly pleased with it.

"You'll have to wear that the first day in Canada," he had said, and so she would.

A few minutes after she was dressed, the steward knocked at the cabin door and upon her calling out 'Come in', he entered, cheerful as always.

"Well, don't you look well today," he said, full of admiration and smiles. "We're close to the Montreal harbor and it would do you a world of good to go on deck for a breath of fresh air. Would you like me to walk you up to the deck?"

"No," Sofia smiled, "but thanks, Harold. I think I'll try it on my own."

He whistled in answer and began to mop the floor.

Sofia walked out of the cabin slowly. She actually felt good. The miserable, sick feeling in her stomach had totally disappeared and as she climbed the stairs to the first deck, she rejoiced in the sweet wind that tousled her hair and tickled her cheeks. There were a great many people crowding the railing. She edged out a place for herself and stared with interest at the shore line dotted with white houses and red roofs. What a large country this was! How very different than Holland. She wondered if Aafke Roos was standing at the railing as well. She probably was and very likely would be on the second deck, not the first. She wished her father could see this! He would most certainly enjoy it. Then, feeling that she was, after all, not as strong as she thought, she walked away from the railing over to a deck chair. A number of them were unoccupied, as most of the passengers were enthralled by the Quebec landscape. Seating herself, she sighed deeply. The sun shone, and with her feet up, Sofia fell into the sleep that had eluded her most of the night.

It was a few hours later when Sofia awoke. They were in port. People bustled about. Men, women and children passed in front of the deck chair. Between their moving bodies she could see land – land that was not moving. Slowly she sat up. They had arrived, had arrived safely without mishap. She got up and made her way back to the cabin. Emma was smoothing out her bed. Alie was patiently standing by her side.

"Oh, good. You're back. I was afraid I was not going to be able to say goodbye."

"Have you seen Aafke Roos?"

Emma turned, looking slightly uncomfortable, Sofia thought.

"Aafke Roos? Haven't you seen her then? She told me that she had spoken with you and that you had given her permission to go ashore with...."

"With whom?"

Sofia's voice sounded squeaky to herself.

"With the young man from Kerkhorst – a family friend, she said."

"What was his name?"

"William, I think it was."

"William," Sofia repeated, "William De Mas?"

"Yes," Emma answered, "that was the name she gave. And she said that you knew. That is to say, she said that she had said goodbye to you and that she was on her way to Alberta, to an uncle of William's."

Woodenly Sofia turned towards her bunk. She bent down and reached under her pillow for the yellow envelope. But as she swept the white bed sheet with her right hand, she felt nothing.

"It's gone," she said.

"What's gone, dear?"

Emma had come to stand next to her.

"My envelope. You know...."

"Yes, I remember that you had it with you when you first came in. I gave it to you."

"Yes, but it's gone," Sofia repeated, bending over again and searching under the pillow one more time.

Emma cleared her throat.

"I think that Aafke Roos had it with her when I saw her last. No, I don't just think so, I know so. She was carrying it along with both suitcases."

Sofia sat down on the edge of her bunk.

"There was money in that envelope," she said, "and some letters. And you say she took both suitcases?"

She looked up at Emma.

"Now I have nothing," she said, "what shall I do, Emma?"

"She gave me this letter for you. But she said.... That is to say, I was given to understand that someone was meeting you here, Sofia?"

"Not me," Sofia whispered, "not me, Emma. Someone was supposed to meet Aafke Roos here though. She was the one. She was the one whose...."

She stopped.

"I have nothing now," she repeated, "no money, no clothes, nothing... really. And my father...."

"Listen," Emma said, "Here's the letter. It might explain everything. She's probably waiting for you somewhere. I'll go up on deck and ask Arie what we should do. He'll know."

When the cabin door shut behind Emma and Alie, Sofia unfolded the letter which Emma had handed her. At first the words blurred and she could not properly read what Aafke Roos had written. But then, blinking away her tears, she was able to focus on Aafke Roos' rather untidy script.

Sofia: I know that when you read this you will be shocked, and, I suppose worried. Yes, I took the envelope and the money as well. The money is actually mine, you know. Tante Liesbet and I earned it several years ago. I'm sure that, having read mother's epistle, you probably wouldn't even want this money, so I'm doing you a favor by taking it off your hands. As for the information contained in the envelope, I think I feel more comfortable with burning it. It could possibly fall into the wrong hands and some people might hold it against me. Also, I think that even without the money you will be fine, financially I mean, because it seems to me that anyone willing to fork over several hundred dollars to bring two girls across the ocean has got to have a well-padded bank account. Just between you and me though, it might be that consequently, not having married up to this point, he might look like a loser – like someone with whom you wouldn't want to spend the rest of your life. Oh well, it will be yourself who will have to look at him — not me! And it will be yourself who will have to listen to his voice -- not me! And you really don't have to worry about me. Will De Mas has promised to marry me as soon as we get settled in Alberta. I'll write Tante Liesbet – I promised her I would – and you can always get my address from her.
-Aafke Roos

Emma came back in just as Sofia was crumpling the paper in her hand into a wad.

"I can't find Arie. But I think we ought to go up on the deck again. I just didn't want to leave you alone any longer. Was there any helpful information in the letter?"

Sofia shook her head.

"Well, let's go outside. I'm sure I'll find Arie and we'll figure something out, honey."

Slowly Sofia stood up and Alie took her hand.

"Don't be sad, Sofia. I love you."

Sofia smiled as Emma took her other hand.

"There you are. Surrounded by love. Now let's go up to the first deck."

Once on the deck, Emma carefully deposited Sofia by the first lifeboat.

"Stand here, honey, by the rail and this lifeboat and I'll go and find Arie. Don't move. I'll be back shortly."

Obediently Sofia stood quite still. She was in somewhat of a daze. The water around the boat was quiet. It almost looked like glass.

"Excuse me."

The voice was kind. Sofia turned to find that a man had come to stand next to her, a tall, blond-haired man. As a matter of fact, his hair was so blond it almost appeared white. He looked down at her and his eyes pierced through her own enabling him to see, she felt, her very insides. His mouth was firm. He laid his right hand upon her right hand. She did not pull away.

"Sofia."

It was not a question. It was a statement."

"Yes," she said, not answering but assenting.

After all, she was Sofia and she felt very certain at that precise moment that if the man knew her name, that this was good.

"My father told me that you were coming," he continued, "and I knew it had to be you because of the white linen dress you are wearing."

"My dress?" she faltered, repeating, "My dress? So there was no picture of ...? You know me because of the dress?"

He said nothing but just looked at her intently and she gazed back. It appeared, in some strange way, that she had always known him and that he had always known her. Suddenly she smiled at him.

"Come," he said, offering his arm.

She took his proffered arm without hesitation and he went on to say, "I hope you like cows and bees, because we have both milk and honey on our farm."

As they made their way across the deck, Emma, Arie and Alie met them.

"Sofia! I've found Arie," Emma exclaimed, "Where are you going? And who is this gentleman?"

"He is...," Sofia answered, and then stopped.

"John Shepherd," her escort supplemented with a smile, "I'm the bridegroom, and I have come to take my bride home."

2: Any Fool Can Sing in the Day

For to me to live is Christ and to die is gain (Phil. 1:21).

In the early 1900s when I was a small boy, a lad of some nine or ten summers, growing up in the southern part of the Netherlands, I remember well a day that I stood leaning on the wooden railing of the bridge that spanned the entrance to our farm. Father was busy pitching hay into the barn. The barn was an old structure with sizable cracks in its walls which let in sunlight during the warm season, as well as rain and snow during winter. Father and grandfather were both men who thoughtfully turned over a 'stuiver', a nickel, several times before inevitably deciding to deposit it into the iron box in the front room instead of spending it. Consequently, cracks in the barn as well as holes in the roof, went unfixed until they became emergencies. The day I remember was a dark day, a September day, which threatened rain. I had just come home from school and dreaded going inside. Mother had been sick for a long time and I knew that she would not be sitting in her chair, waiting to ask me what Master Deernis had been teaching that day. So I dawdled and hung about on the bridge, throwing a few stones into the water, watching the circles that spread out into the black of the river, and hoping that my father would not take heed of my presence. But he did.

"Paulus Vlam," he said, and his voice pricked me like his pitchfork.

I turned to look at him.

"Come here, boy!"

I dropped the stones into my pocket, picked up my schoolbooks and sauntered over.

"What were you doing?"

"Oh, nothing!"

"Nothing? "he said, as if it were a sin to even pronounce the word.

He kept pitching the hay as he spoke and from behind a stack, my brother Peter's face appeared. He stuck out his tongue at me and disappeared again. Peter was my twin. He was the older of us two having been born before me by a good half hour. We were not alike, Peter and myself. Whereas I was small and dark-haired, he was tall and blond like my father. My eyes were dark brown, but his were as green and vibrant as an oak leaf in the rain. Awkward and unable to even muck out a stable to the satisfaction of my father and grandfather, I was the antipode to Peter who throve on feeding and milking cows, eagerly talked of the quality of udders and teats and knew the names of all the important bulls in the surrounding county. My father was proud of him, that was a fact, and my grandfather doted on him and that was a double fact.

"Well?"

My father now stood directly over me, pitchfork in hand, waiting for me to say what I had been doing and why I had been doing it. I regretted not having gone in directly, as I usually did and stared at my shoes. That was a mistake for nothing irritated my father so much as the appearance of indolence.

"Go inside the barn and help your brother."

I moved towards the barn but for once my brother intervened.

"Let Paulus go inside, father," he said from behind the haystack, "I know that mother is waiting for him."

Father indicated with his head that I should move and move quickly. I ran towards the house as fast as I could, running as the crow flies, almost tripping over the white geese waddling across the yard. Downy, white feathers flew. Cackling filled the air, but I was inside now and did not stop until I had reached the living room. To my surprise I found my mother sitting up, a warm blanket wrapped around her, with great-aunt Nellie presiding over the teapot.

"Hello," I said.

Great-aunt Nellie was grandfather's sister. She lived with us and shared his view that I had been born for trouble and would, no doubt, sooner or later drag the entire family into dishonor.

"Shoes," said great-aunt, and I immediately bent over double to undo the laces of my brown shoes before taking them off.

"Hello, Paulus," said mother, "and how was your day with Master Deernis?"

She asked the question as I retreated back to the door, deposited the shoes on a mat, and then returned to come and stand by her whom I loved better than anything.

"It was good. I learned...."

"Hands," said great-aunt, staring pointedly at the grime on my fingers.

I turned once more and trotted on my stocking feet into the good-sized anteroom where we ate all our meals and which also served as a kitchen. Next to the stove was a round bowl with water and I washed my hands and dried them on the small towel hanging next to it on a rack. When I returned to the living room my mother's eyes had shut and great-aunt was anxiously standing by her side.

"Out," she said to me, and again, "out, you clumsy lout of a boy."

Mother opened her eyes and smiled.

"He's not a clumsy lout," she said, "He's my clever son whom I love and he shall stay and tell me all about his day."

"Tut, Anna," said great-aunt, sighing with some relief, "you always do run on so with emotions. No wonder you're ill six days out of seven and puny-looking. You draw all your strength from your heart and not from your body."

Mother sighed and sat up straight.

"No doubt one morning I'll wake up and be a cow. That should satisfy this household."

I grinned, but great-aunt clucked as she poured me a cup of tea. Not considering mother's statement worthy of reply, she disappeared into the kitchen. I sat down next to mother and studied her face. She looked pale and there were dark circles under her eyes.

"Have you spit up today?"

I whispered this but great-aunt heard it.

"Yes, she did," she called out from the kitchen, "and nearly a cupful it was. Going to cost your father a pretty penny to fetch the doctor again."

My heart thumped within my chest and I anxiously considered mother. She smiled reassuringly and held out her hand. I put mine within hers and for a few blissful moments we sat silently as the fire crackled in the hearth and the small wax light under the teapot flickered.

"Master Deernis gave me a star for spelling today."

This time I whispered very softly and right into mother's ear.

She smiled and stroked my hair, whispering back conspiratorially, "I'm so very proud of you, my Paulus. Sing me a song!"

I sang. I always sang for my mother. Some of the tunes and words I knew she had taught me and others I made up. Singing made me come alive; singing made me forget my problems; and singing made me happy. Afterwards, for some unaccountable reason, I began to cry, my face in her lap. Perhaps some part inside me knew that it was the last time we would sit thus, side by side. For the next day when I came home from school, she was gone, my mother. Not gone to a hospital, where there might have been some chance of recuperation from the consumption that had been eating her the last year and a half, but gone for always to that place where the dead go — go and do not return.

Father Roothaer buried my mother. Mother had not been Roman Catholic, as father and grandfather were. Indeed, it had required a special dispensation for father to marry her. As she had been a girl who stood to inherit a fortune her money had erased any prejudice against Protestants which the family might have harbored. It was with greedy intent, sweet words and intense courting, that father had won her hand. I was not there when all this happened but have listened to village folk talk and knew it to be true. Because mother had not been a church member, her coffin was put into the earth outside the church cemetery. I was angry over this, so angry that a few weeks later I defaced the cemetery gate with a can of whitewash. No one ever found out, and it did not change matters any. So then I resolved to hate God, at least the God Father Roothaer represented. Indeed, if such a divinity did not love my mother enough to let her be buried in the cemetery, how could I love Him?

I cried much the first year after mother's death, but life went on. Peter and I continued our studies in the village with Master Deernis along with the other village children. There was one incident that year which stands out in my mind. My mother had had a box of chocolates given to her when she was ill. It had been brought to her by a cousin, a distant cousin from Belgium who visited us. He had only come for a few hours and had left before either Peter or I had come home from school. Belgium is well-known for its chocolates and I can still see before me the creamy whiteness and the rich brownness of the candies. They were encased in a black box with gold lettering inscribed on it. That box stood on mother's night table next to her bed. She offered me one that same evening but father, with one authoritative look, forbad me to accept. I understood this to mean that chocolates held some medicative power which would strengthen mother. So I put my hand behind my back and said, 'No, thank you, mother'. As it was, I chanced upon the box one day about six months after she died, when I was hiding in the large closet in the great bedroom. Great-aunt Nellie was after me for she was bound and determined that I had broken a vase, which I had not, and I knew that even if I told her the truth she would not believe me. She constantly lectured me on what she referred to as my 'lazy way of life'. True, I didn't help out much in the barn and in the stalls, but I did my share of housework by fetching water, feeding the chickens, collecting the eggs and weeding the vegetable garden. As I sat down in the closet I saw the box. It was standing on a shelf hidden behind my mother's dresses which were still hanging there. I smelled her familiar smell and a great longing came over me to feel mother's arms around me once more. I took the box down and opened it. Only two chocolates were missing. The rest were all still lying neatly in their paper jackets, waiting. What where they waiting for? I touched them with my index finger, traced their smooth outline and sniffed them. But I had no desire to eat them. Later, when I heard great-aunt go outside, I hid the box under the mattress in my bed.

It so happened that a few months later I was playing with Jackie Piek during recess. Jackie was called 'runt' by all the schoolchildren because he was, as his nickname implied, very small. His father was a dirt-farmer and owned not even one cow although he kept a few goats and chickens. To supplement his income, he occasionally day-labored on area farms — ours as well. Jackie's mother was sick. As such I identified with him. Had not my own mother been sick for a long time and had I not felt pain as Jackie must now feel it? But while we were tossing a ball back and forth between us, two older boys kicked it away. Neither Jackie nor I had the gumption to go after it, so we sat down companionably on the curb bordering the schoolyard.

"How's your mother?" I queried and was not surprised to have him break out in sobs.

Had I not done that myself last year whenever anyone mentioned mother? Feeling genuine compassion a sudden, luminous idea struck me.

'I have some medicine," I said, "which might help your mother."

He stopped blubbering and looked at me, a green streak of mucus across his cheek as he rubbed his nose.

"What medicine?"

"Well, it's a box of candies called chocolates, and if she eats them...."

I stopped, considering if I should after all, give them to Jackie.

"What's chocolates?"

"You don't know what chocolates are?"

Jackie shook his head vigorously and eyed me as if I were a doctor of great renown. This tickled my ego. Renewed in my role as doctor and protector, I told him that chocolates were sweet medicine, especially made for ailing mothers, and that we had some left over from when my mother was sick.

"But she died," Jackie answered, looking at me rather dubiously.

A wave of anger swept over me and I considered hitting him for that statement. But it was true. She had died and I could not really blame him for doubting the efficacy of what I had to offer.

"She did not eat enough chocolates," I replied.

"Oh," said Jackie and looked down at the pavement.

Then he looked up again.

"What'll it cost me to get them?"

"I'll give them to you."

He sighed deeply, gazing up at me, half in disbelief and half in adoration.

"Will you really?"

I nodded and then shook his hand to affirm that I meant it.

"I'll meet you on the side-road by the knotted oak after school. Just wait for me and I'll bring them to you."

Jackie nodded.

The meeting transpired without a hitch. I smuggled the chocolates out of the house under my jacket and met Jackie at the agreed upon spot. He took the box, told me he would say ten Hail Mary's for me, and ran off. I shrugged and walked back home thinking all the while that mother would have been happy to have her chocolates eaten by another sick woman. For such had been her nature that she had often given away baskets of food to the poor in the neighborhood, something which had irritated father and grandfather to no end. I began to sing. I had not sung for a long while. The birds in the willows at the side of the road sang with me and I laughed in my song, for were not things going rather well again. Mr. Deernis had spoken to me that afternoon, saying that he would visit father soon to suggest that I be allowed to study longer than the usual time period for farm boys in the area. I loved studying, even as Peter loved farming. Peter never looked at a book twice and could not abide the classroom. The truth was that we did not get along very well. Peter was always with father and grandfather and I had always been with mother. But now mother was gone. My song stopped and I kicked a pebble into oblivion.

That evening as we sat together around the table under the low and blackened beams of the wooden ceiling, eating the stack of bread which great-aunt Nellie had buttered sparingly, there was a knock at the door. It was easy to hear. The rapping fell through silence. We were not permitted to speak while we ate, and the only sound in our kitchen was that of our forks clicking against the tin plates and that of the water boiling in the copper kettle on the stove.

"Now who would be out at this time," great-aunt said as she got up.

I rather suspected it was Master Deernis and wished that he had chosen a more auspicious time to call. Father and grandfather liked to eat heartily and then push back from the table, pull their hats over their eyes and nap before beginning the evening chores. But it was not Master Deernis who had come, but Jackie's father. Twisting his cap round and round in his rough hands, he stood awkwardly in the doorway.

"Yes, Jan," grandfather said, not too unkindly, "what is it?"

"Jackie," Jan Piek said, "came home with a box of candy. He said Paulus gave it to him. But I thought I would ask... just in case."

Father stood up. He looked at me.

"Well, boy?"

I stared at my half-eaten slice of bread and at the bowl of steaming milk behind it waiting for me to cup my hands around its smooth form. I had been hungry but suddenly I fought the urge to vomit. Father repeated his words with a little more emphasis.

"Well, boy!"

I looked up at him and he saw the truth written all over my face. But since he was not disposed to be humiliated in front of a day-laborer such as Jan Piek, he smiled.

"I think the boy made a mistake," he said, "and he'll go with you to fetch the box home. Won't you, Paulus?"

I nodded quietly, got up, left the table and went to the door to put on my shoes.

Jan Piek didn't say a word as we trudged the roads back to his house. Jackie stood at the door as we plodded up the thin lane. A goat bleated next to a sparse vegetable patch. Jackie walked towards us, gingerly holding the box. Handing it back, he said nothing and avoided looking at me.

"I'm sorry, Jackie," was all I could manage.

And then I turned and began the stretch back to my home. But at the knotted oak my feet suddenly turned to lead, refusing to carry me further. I sat down and contemplated the box. What would my father do with it? He did not care for the taste of chocolates himself. I had heard him say often enough that they had been 'a waste of good money'. The idea that he might have wanted to keep them as a souvenir in mother's memory did not hold water. He never spoke of mother, had actually never done so, and of late there had been talk of a widow — an older woman who ran a farm by herself some ten kilometers south of us. I had seen her once. Two of her bottom teeth were missing. She certainly wouldn't be able to chew the chocolates although maybe she could suck them. The idea was repellent to me. No, my father was surely selfish in wanting to keep mother's box. Slowly undoing one of my shoelaces, I stood up again and continued my way home. Just before the bridge entrance to our farm I began to run. Father and grandfather were walking towards the barn. On the bridge I tripped. The chocolates fell into the river. As I lay down flat, face down, I could see the box drift past through the planking. My father reached me first. His hand, hard like the shovel I had never been able to manipulate, pulled me up on my feet. My right knee was bleeding. The shoelace, my only defense, lay silent.

"You wretched boy!"

It was the first time my father had ever used such denigrating language on me. I closed my eyes and began to heave, fully expecting to be pulled into the barn for a thrashing. But the grip on my shoulder loosened, let go and I stood free. And then I heard a voice. It was Master Deernis.

"Had an accident, Paulus?"

Opening my eyes, I saw my teacher standing in front of me on the bridge. His bicycle, black and shiny, leaned against the bridge railing. Anxiously scanning my face, his presence reassured me. My father's voice came again.

"Go to the house, Paulus and get cleaned up."

The threatening tone used a minute earlier was gone. I obeyed, casting a backward glance at Master Deernis, who winked at me. Inside, great-aunt Nellie grumbled about, cleaning my knee none too gently, saying all the while that she expected that I would grow up to disgrace the entire Vlam family. Then she sent me to bed. The next morning, much to my surprise, I learned that Master Deernis' visit had been favorably received by both my father and my grandfather. I was allowed to continue my studies in the village whereas, after the summer, Peter was to stay home to immerse himself in farming. The chocolates were never mentioned again and Mrs. Piek died the following year.

In 1913, the year I turned seventeen, Mr. Deernis said that he could teach me nothing else, and that as I was fluent in Dutch, English, French, Latin and bookkeeping, he judged I would make a fine secretary for someone. Shortly afterwards, early one afternoon following the midday meal, my grandfather called me into the front room. He was an old man now, my grandfather. Always an imposing, strong figure with his flowing white beard, bushy eyebrows and piercing grey eyes, he gazed intently at me across the table in the front room, making me feel both uneasy and inadequate. It was he who ran the farm despite his great age and it was he who decided whether or not a cow was to be sold or a field ploughed. He had never, in my remembrance, ever shown me any affection or asked for my opinion on a matter. My father was much like him. Neither of them was sentimental about anything except *stuivers* and *dubbeltjes*, nickels and dimes. Since the death of my mother, however, I would sometimes catch my father gazing at me when he perceived that I was busy with something else and seemingly unaware of his presence. Yet if I ventured a quick smile or stared back, he turned away and then it was as if there had been nothing.

"You have finished your education," grandfather began and drummed his great, bony fingers on the table top.

I nodded and waited, knowing better than to make conversation.

"It's time, therefore," he continued, "for you to venture out into the world."

I nodded again for it seemed to me that nothing would please me more than to leave the farm and discover what lay beyond it and our village.

"It troubles me to say what I am about to say," the old man continued, "but I must do so. I have been aware for years and years that you are not true-born."

I was confused and at a loss as to what he meant. But I replied nothing.

"Your mother," he went on, never taking his gaze off me, "played the harlot. The man you know as your father is not your father."

Now I could not stop the words that came to my mouth.

"I am a twin," I said with great agitation, "Peter is my brother. Mother was my mother and father...."

"No," he said quietly, "although you are right on one count. Your mother was your mother. But the man you call father is not your father and Peter is only your half...."

I paled, clenched my hands into fists and did not let him finish.

"Stop it! You are proposing an impossibility!" I cried, "We were born in the same hour, Peter and I, so...."

"It is possible," he interrupted, unperturbed, "that twins in the womb of a woman can have two fathers. It so happened that the month Peter was conceived, and yes, he is indeed true-born, that your mother's cousin visited her. He was uncommonly friendly...."

For the second time I did not let him finish but stood up so violently that I knocked down my chair in the process. I was about to walk around the table to punch him when my father stepped out of the shadows of the curtained window niche.

"It is true, boy," he said.

It came to me now, how often my father called me boy and not son. My stomach churned and I stood still, unable to move. Grandfather, who had never taken his eyes off me, continued.

"We talked and after some thought decided it would be unkind to place you in an institution after your mother died, especially because your half-brother Peter was not, as yet, informed of the circumstances of your birth. When Master Deernis proposed to continue teaching you, we came to the conclusion that an education would serve you well."

I heard their voices, my father's and grandfather's, but did not really comprehend what they were saying. I saw, as if at a distance, that grandfather walked over to his cabinet and got out the money box. I had never seen it before, had only heard Peter mention it. From the box Grandfather removed a linen bag tied about with a cord.

"There are one hundred guilders in this bag," he said, placing it on the table, "and I am giving them to you to start you off on the right foot."

I blinked and felt as if I were living a nightmare and then heard myself reply.

"Have no fear, I will leave! But I will leave by myself and walk by myself on both my right and my left foot. And you can keep your stinking money to buy another cow or pig or field or wife. But let it never be said that I took...."

And then I began to weep. But I would not stay to have them see me weep, so I ran out the door upstairs to the loft I shared with Peter. He was in the barn doing chores and although we never exchanged much except trivialities, I felt slightly uneasy about leaving without saying goodbye to him, for it was dreadfully clear to me that I must go immediately. Gathering clothes into a bundle and wrapping my blanket about them, I concocted a backpack of sorts. Then, after I saw father and grandfather head for the barn as if this afternoon was one like any other, I scrounged around the kitchen for some food to take along. Great-aunt Nellie was napping in her room. It was spring and a warm day. If there was any mercy in this horrid moment of time, that was it. I was not likely to catch cold as I traveled away from the only home I had ever known.

Our little village lay very close to the border of Belgium and this is where I resolved to go. Indeed, the farther I walked the more I thought that I should like to meet this maligned cousin of my mother whose name grandfather had so degraded in order to get rid of me. I would very much like to see for myself what sort of fellow he was. Albert, I recalled after I had been on the road for a while, Albert Degrelle was his name and he came from a town called Geel just south of the border. That first night I found a place to sleep under the bushes at the side of the road. In some strange way one part of me was glad that perhaps father was not my real father. However, another part of me did not believe a word grandfather had said.

My mother had been a good wife, a faithful wife. Never had she belittled or spoken ill of anyone. She had worked hard when she was able and, although she had never gone to church, she had always minded me to pray to the Lord Jesus. She had told me stories about when she was a little girl, and sometimes, when it stormed violently outside, she related Bible stories. Peter would never stop to listen to her. My mother loved Peter, of that I am certain, but I believe she was resigned to the fact that she did not have any influence over him. I was her child and Peter was father's. Mother had not had any living relatives but this one cousin, this Albert Degrelle. I'd never asked her any questions about him. Now I regretted the fact that I had not done so. Mother had also owned a Bible. I had not taken it. Since the chocolate incident, a lock had been put on the door of the great bedroom. Consequently, I had not been able to take, with the exception of myself, anything that had belonged to her. Still, in hindsight I wished that I had tried the bedroom door. Perhaps I might have been able to pick the lock. The Bible would have been something and mother always said it held a great many songs. Father, grandfather and great-aunt Nellie never went to church and surely would not have missed that Bible. They unfailingly, however, made the sign of the cross before they ate and once, when grandfather fell from the hayloft and lay unconscious for an hour, I saw great-aunt say her rosary. But all three mocked the priest and called him a money-grabber who was out for their wealth.

"Just before I die," grandfather had said, "I'll pay the man to light some candles and say some prayers for me. That ought to do it."

I tossed and turned under the bushes that night, trying to forget home and everything that had happened. Between their branches I peeked up at the stars. Gazing at the vastness of the heavens made me feel puny and unimportant. For a moment both a sense of awe and a feeling of fear and aloneness gripped my heart. But the overriding feeling of relief that I was not subject to the ridicule and mockery of Peter, father, grandfather and great-aunt Nellie anymore, prevailed. Yawning, I knew they would be glad I was gone. It shouldn't be too hard to find the town of Geel. I sleepily fantasized that cousin Albert would be overjoyed to see me; that he would be very sad to hear about mother's death; and that he would ask me to stay with him. Pushing away all the ugly insinuations grandfather had put into my brain, I fell asleep.

The singing of birds awoke me early the next morning. Not in a hurry and walking at a leisurely pace, I enjoyed all the freshness the spring countryside offered. For some reason I was not worried about money, food or shelter. Perhaps I did not care. When I was hungry, I turned aside into farm lane-ways, asking if I might do odd jobs for farmers. On the whole, even though work was scarce, there was hardly anyone who refused to share a meal with a hungry, growing boy. Farm wives, clucking at my skinny arms and legs, usually gave me parcels of cheese and bread to tuck into my pack. Northeast Belgium, into which I had passed, was poor. Its people grew potatoes, heather and fir trees but little else. And then, at dusk one day, I arrived singing and whistling my heart out, in the quiet, little town of Geel.

On the outskirts, Geel seemed a friendly little place. Streets crisscrossed randomly, and small houses with picket fences ranged side by side. An old man sauntered along the main street, a dog at his side. People sat on benches in small gardens, seemingly doing nothing but soaking up evening sunshine. A few children played ball on the road and a wagon, in the distance, rumbled along peaceably. Surely cousin Albert, coming from such a sleepy hollow, would be a friendly man, a good man. I approached the greybeard and put cousin Albert's name in his ear.

"Who?"

The old man bent forward while the dog wagged his tail.

"Albert Degrelle. Do you know an Albert Degrelle?" I repeated, and had to do so again for the third time.

"No," he said, "can't say that I know someone by that name. But you might ask Madame Comte. She knows a lot of people."

He pointed to a woman who was walking rather rapidly ahead of us through town. I thanked him and followed the woman, almost running to catch up with her. The children stopping their ball playing and eyed me with wonder.

"Madame! Madame!"

She looked over her shoulder, saw me trailing her and stopped.

"Yes?"

"I am looking for a man by the name of Albert — Albert Degrelle. He is my mother's cousin. Would you happen to know where he is?"

"Albert Degrelle?"

A frown of concentration came to her face. She was a handsome woman, middle-aged, with a kind look about her.

"Yes, I know where he is."

She studied my person and I smiled at her to show I had only good intentions. She smiled back and asked me what my name was.

"Paulus Vlam, Madame."

"Vlam?"

"Yes, Madame."

"Well, Paulus Vlam, I am on my way home and will be walking past his... past where he is. Why don't you walk with me?"

Madame Comte lived on the southern outskirts of Geel. She asked me a great many questions as we were walking and I answered them as truthfully as I could. What, after all, had I to conceal save the hideous lies which grandfather had concocted just before I left. At length we came to a cemetery. Turning, she put her hand on its gate and I, following close on her heels, thought she was taking a short-cut to her house. The iron gate creaked and suddenly a sense of foreboding overcame me. It was not a short-cut. Madame Comte stopped and pointed.

"Here lies your mother's cousin, Albert Degrelle, Paulus."

There between a great many other gravestones, stood a stone cross. Newer than its surrounding markers, it stood straight and smooth.

Albert Degrelle — 1840 -1909
Asleep until the last day

I mouthed the words silently and then read them again. I could feel no grief for Albert Degrelle for I had not known him. But I did feel great grief for the plans I had made — plans dead and buried right in front of me. At a loss as to what to do and where to go, I dully stared at the gravestone.

"Your cousin was a kind man."

Madame Comte spoke solicitously. I did not answer. What was it to me now that he had been kind? He was gone and of no more use to me. He could not now say, 'Stay with me, Paulus. For I have always wanted a clever boy like yourself to live with me.' The woman touched my arm.

"I would consider it a kindness if you would stop the night with me. I live a little way further out of town. A kilometer or so more down the road."

I nodded mutely and followed her, slamming the iron gate shut behind us, leaving Albert's bones and my hopes for a new home buried in the cemetery. The songs I had sung that morning shriveled within my breast.

Madame Comte, taking pity on my silence, began to tell me about Geel. It was a town which centuries ago had established an unusual skill. The families in Geel took in mentally disabled people to live with them. Many local people had someone in their home who was abnormal and each family cared for that person as normally as his or her condition would allow. Perhaps, I reflected, as Madame Comte told me this, that this was why she was taking me home. Perhaps she thought I was abnormal. But what was normal?

"Your cousin, as well, took care of a number of people," she said, and went on to describe several handicapped people whom cousin Albert had, apparently, helped.

I confess that I did not respond much to the details in her accounts. The matter that kept jumping out at me with every step I took was the fact that cousin Albert was gone and that he could not now help me. But Madame Comte was not deterred by my silence and continued her story telling.

"It all began," she continued later in her cottage, as she placed a bowl of steaming potatoes in front of me, "in the fifteenth century. I'm surprised that your Master Deernis did not teach you this. Pilgrims flocked here to the tomb of a refugee Irish princess who was said to have cured her father's insanity by her own death. From that time on God's unfortunates, for that is what they are, were treated here in a humane and considerate way, in contrast to the brutal and rough treatment that medieval people usually gave the insane."

"Oh," I replied and did not know what else to say.

My own future nagged at me. What was I to do?

"You know, Paulus," Madame Comte said, sitting down across from me at the table, "from the little you have told me about yourself, you are well qualified to work with books and such matters as clerks do. Is that not right?"

I nodded and dug my fork into a yellow potato although, truth be told, I had no appetite at all.

"Well," she said, "I happen to know that a Father Christophe in Louvain is looking for a clerk to help him in the library of the University there. The road is straightforward from Geel to Louvain.

You can walk there, find Father Christophe, and tell him that Madame Comte recommends you help him."

With these last words she smiled broadly, as if to say that approval by her would make Father Christophe think that I was the answer to his prayers. Not that I was much acquainted with prayer. I had, as a matter of fact, kept my eyes wide open when Madame Comte had prayed the Lord's Prayer before serving up the potatoes. But I smiled back at my hostess and instantly clung to the idea of becoming a clerk for this Father Christophe as if it were a lifebuoy. And early the next morning, carrying bread and cheese in my backpack, set out for Louvain.

"And if things do not happen to work out," Madame Comte said, just before waving me off down the road, "come back here, Paulus. There are always open doors in Geel."

Everywhere on the road I passed peasants tilling their fields. Browned by the sun, they paused in their work to see me tramping alongside their road. I waved and, without fail, they waved back before returning to their labor. Wayside shrines were numerous and often I saw peasant women kneeling before Maria figures in stone grottos, candles burning as they offered their prayers. I scoffed at their ignorance. It seemed to me that praying to statues displayed a lack of knowledge. Master Deernis had been an atheist. How he had ever become a teacher in a predominantly Catholic village such as ours had always been a mystery to me. Perhaps there had been no one else available.

"It is true," he had said to me, "that religion satisfies that need in humans which looks for mercy and comfort, that part which must worship. But the sane and educated man can satisfy that need through accumulating knowledge."

I listened. I had no great love for religion aside from the fact that my mother had told me a few Bible stories and had encouraged me to pray to Jesus. But Jesus was as far removed from me as Buddha or Mohammed, both of whom, according to my teacher, had also been good men.

"All men reach out to something, Paulus," Master Deernis had expostulated, "and what satisfies one may not satisfy another."

I believed everything Master Deernis told me, mainly because he had cared enough about me to teach me and because his acceptance of myself gave me a certain measure of security.

As I continued to pass through a great many picturesque, little villages, the fine weather and the very act of steady walking restored my confidence. I began singing again. Children generally followed me as I passed by their homes. Sometimes I sat down at a well and ate sparingly of the provisions Madame Comte had given me, before taking a drink of water. The provisions had to last until I reached Louvain. But if I sat too long in one spot, my thoughts became somber. What if Father Christophe did not need anyone after all? What if he took an instant dislike to me? And then I rose and went on walking, lifting my backpack onto my shoulders and kicking my worries away as the pebbles flew under my feet.

At length I arrived at Louvain. It was almost evening and the sun's last rays slanted across the fields behind me. Louvain was a fine-looking place at dusk. Small houses, crouched side by side, hugged the outskirts of the town. As I entered and explored the main boulevards, I also came upon many stately, larger homes. Trees, huge trees, grew everywhere providing both shade and beauty. Many of the high walls separating individual gardens were covered with wisteria blossoms and the faint scent of them filled the air. I asked a group of children rolling a hoop whether they knew where Father Christophe lived. Most shook their heads and went on playing. But when I persevered and asked if they then perhaps knew where the university was, several pointed in the direction of a group of buildings further down the road.

It did not take me long to reach the buildings. The sun was rapidly sinking. A number of people strolled about the square directly in front of the university. Hesitantly I approached a man who, lost in thought, held a book very close to his face— no doubt because it was almost getting too dark to read.

"Excuse me," I ventured.

He stopped and regarded me with a bland expression.

"Yes?"

"Would you happen to know," I went on in halting French, "Father Christophe?"

"Father Christophe?"

I nodded, almost afraid to hear the answer. But the man smiled.

"He lives just around the corner. If you walk towards that road there, and turn left, his is the first house to your right."

I almost danced a jig.

"Thank you, sir."

He smiled again and put the book back up to his face. Turning, I quickly paced towards the road to which he had pointed. Turning left, I stopped to consider the first house at my right. It was a cream-bricked house with its persiennes drawn, as if there was no one home. The big, double front doors were imposing. I fumbled in my pack for the small note Madame Comte had given me at the last moment.

"Here," she had said, "just in case he does not believe that you have met me."

The bell-cord pulled easily and I heard its peel clang hollowly inside. Moments later a girl opened the door. She was dressed in a simple, blue dress over which she wore a white apron. A small child of some three or four years old clung to her hand.

"Yes, how can I help you?"

"I am looking for Father Christophe."

She was pretty, this girl. I was seventeen years old now and had an eye for such matters. The boy peeped at me from behind his mother's skirt. At least that was what I presumed — that she was his mother.

"Father Christophe is at his prayers," she answered.

I was at a loss as to what to say to that and stood quietly for a moment.

"Does he pray long?" I asked then.

"That depends," she answered with an impish grin.

"On what?"

"On whether or not he feels he has sinned a great deal today."

"Oh."

"Would you like to wait for him in the kitchen?"

I nodded and she stood aside to let me enter, closing the door behind me.

The kitchen was large. Pewter utensils hung from the ceiling, a cast-iron stove stood under them, and a table in the center was covered with a linen tablecloth and flower arrangements. It was a clean and tidy place; one over which great-aunt Nellie would have rejoiced. A row of wooden cupboards lined the wall, and a rack filled with sparkling dishes stood in an alcove under a window. Several pies cooled in the sill and the smell of them made my saliva run. The girl eyed me for a moment and I fancied she could read my thoughts so clear was her gaze.

"Have you had your supper?"

The truth was that Madame Comte's provisions had run out that morning and my belly was rumbling. The little boy sat down on the floor and, although watching me out of the corner of his eye, began playing with a wooden train.

"No, I haven't."

"Well then, sit down and I'll cut you a piece of pie."

Although she spoke perfect French, I detected an accent.

"Are you from Louvain?"

"No," she answered, "I'm from England actually. And you?"

"From Holland," I answered, hoping she wouldn't question me further as I did not know what exactly I would recount regarding my past life. Not that I did not intend to tell Father Christophe the truth. I certainly did. But if he did not ask certain questions, then I surely would not bring up information voluntarily.

"Here's a piece of apple pie, then," she said, "They always say that Dutch people like apple pie."

Well, that was a safe enough topic. I lauded the pie for melting in my mouth, for being a taste of heaven on earth, and being as sweet as its baker. She blushed in a most becoming manner.

"Maggie!"

The voice was sharp and instantly brought me to my feet, my mouth full of pie. A black-robed man stood in the doorway, a frown on his face. He had prominent eyes, a pointed black beard and high cheekbones.

"Father Emile!"

The girl, whose name was obviously Maggie, was uneasy. I could tell by the way she stood and by the way the child had immediately hidden behind her skirts.

"And who is this young man?"

"My name is Paulus Vlam, sir."

I spoke with more assurance than I felt. He did not reply but gazed at me as though I were an intruder and in no way welcome.

"He is here to see Father Christophe."

Maggie spoke softly but clearly and I saw that her hand reassuringly stroked the boy's head as she did so.

"Mmh."

There was a noise in the hallway and suddenly another priest stepped around Father Emile into the kitchen. Unlike him, he was clean-shaven and smiling.

"Did I hear my name mentioned?"

I immediately rather liked Father Christophe who seemed to exude friendliness.

"Apparently this fellow is here to see you."

Father Emile's voice bristled like the brush great-aunt Nellie had used to scour her potato pan. It grated on my skin.

"I see."

Father Christophe turned to look at me.

"Can I help you in some way, son?"

Maggie turned around and began to pay attention to some cutlery in the sink. The small boy sat down in her shadow. I wished that

Father Emile would go about his business as well but he did not move and hung about the doorway like a cloud waiting to rain.

"Yes, please. I've come from Geel."

At the name of the town Father Christophe drew in his breath.

"Geel?"

"Yes," I repeated, "from Geel. And a Madame Comte has given me a note for you."

I judged, at this point, that it was better to begin with the note. If I talked, Father Emile would hear every word and somehow, I did not like that. Father Christophe took the note, which was a trifle the worse for the wear, from my hand. He read it quickly. Then he sat down, gesturing with his right hand that I should sit as well.

"So you are a young scholar, lad," he said.

"Well," I replied, taking care to be modest, "I've taken some languages and am able to keep books...."

My voice trailed off and I looked at him expectantly. He cupped his chin in his hand and read the note again.

"My sister seems to have taken a liking to you," he said.

"Your sister?"

I had not known that Madame Comte was sending me to her brother.

"Yes," he answered, "my dear sister, who is a mother to many unfortunates in this world."

I did not know if I considered myself an unfortunate or if that was what he meant, but replied nothing.

"So, this is what I will do, young man," he said, looking at me and putting out his hand as if he expected me to shake it, "I will take you on conditionally for a few weeks and see what kind of stuff you are made of. How does that suit you?"

"Very well, sir."

I took his hand and we shook. Father Emile coughed into his sleeve.

"Shouldn't you run that past the board of directors at the university?" he said.

"No," Father Christophe answered decidedly, "this is a decision that, in the long run, mostly concerns me. I will gauge the lad and will find out soon enough if he will do."

Father Emile disappeared down the hall and Maggie cut a piece of apple pie for Father Christophe as well and soon we ate companionably side by side. Then he showed me a place where I might sleep — a small attic with a cot under a skylight.

"What do you think? Can you manage here?" he asked.

I nodded happily.

"Tomorrow then, at eight," he said, "I shall expect you to be up and ready so that I can introduce you to the university library."

And that is how I came to be Father Christophe's clerk, that early summer of the year 1913.

From that time on, I arose around seven each morning, bathed outside at a water pump and then had breakfast served to me by Maggie. The child, whose name was Abel, always sat next to me as I ate. He watched me, smiled if I happened to look at him and sought in all manner of ways to attract my attention. But in those first months, I did not pay him much mind. I was obsessed by the fact that I must meet Father Christophe in his room at the library by exactly eight o'clock and not be late. Making sure my appearance was neat and that my nails were clean, I tried to make a good impression on all those who visited the library. Father Christophe was an able teacher. Always kind and friendly, he also remained somewhat aloof. Perhaps it was about the matter of religion. I had told him during the course of the summer, that I was an atheist. Although he seemed somewhat surprised by the disclosure, he did not comment much. One thing was certain — he loved books with a passion and had me cataloguing, shelving and rearranging the greater part of each day. After a while, when I was not under his constant supervision any more but working much on my own, I found that I had begun to like the work. Dusting off jackets, repairing old and torn pages and signing out books and manuscripts to students — all these things gave me a sense of security and importance. The students called me Master Vlam. On the whole they were courteous and jolly and I became a part of the community. To and from my way to work, I sang. I could not contain myself. Life was good again. Would not mother have been proud of me?

"How was your day?"

Unfailingly, each late afternoon, Maggie asked that question. I grew to expect it. She would serve me a cup of tea and sit down as I expounded on the volumes I had signed out that day, on the repair work I had done and on the fact that Father Christophe had left me in charge for several hours while he worked in his office. Abel, or Abba, as Maggie sometimes affectionately called him, would usually stand at my knee and patiently listen along, although for a child of five he could not have comprehended much. He was a solitary, happy child. Content to play in the kitchen with the few toys that Maggie had obtained for him, I rarely saw him cry or behave in any manner that was contrary to what Maggie required of him. During that fall, the fall of 1913, it so happened one day that Maggie was not in the kitchen when I came in from work. Abel was sitting at the table, drawing a picture on a piece of paper.

"Where's your mother?"

"She's sick?"

"What is the matter with her?"

"She has a pain in her stomach."

I suddenly realized that I actually had no idea where exactly the rooms were which Maggie and Abel occupied. Nor had I ever asked her where the father of the boy was.

"Does she need help?"

Abel shook his head.

"She just wants to sleep," he said.

That evening I foraged about the kitchen for a meal for myself, Father Christopher and Father Emile. Abel followed me about, directing me whenever I seemed lost for a certain item.

"No, Paulus, look in this cupboard," he said, and "the bread is kept in this container."

As we sat down together for our evening repast, I seated Abel between myself and Father Christophe. Usually the boy ate later with Maggie, after we had been served. But he looked so lonely and clung to me so closely that I did not have the heart to leave him out. Neither Father Christophe nor Father Emile objected but after they had made the sign of the cross over their food, Father Emile directed a rather unkind comment to the child.

"Take care, Abel," he said, "that you do not follow the godless ways of your mother."

I glanced down at Abel to see if he understood what the priest had said to him. Indeed, I had not understood it myself, and was surprised to see that the boy had clenched his fists tightly and was regarding Father Emile with a frown.

"My mother is good," he replied.

"Indeed, she is," I quickly interjected, "but she would want you to eat your food, Abel. So be a good boy, and take a bite of your bread."

Father Emile raised his eyebrows at me and redirected his invective.

"What," he asked, "makes you a judge of good and evil, Paulus? From what I understand, you call yourself an atheist. So what makes you think that...."

He was interrupted by Father Christophe.

"Paulus does his work well, and I think that we, Father Emile, may win by example. And that is all that might be said at the present. Now let us continue our meal in peace."

Abel's small hand crept into mine. Father Emile, directly across the table, gave both of us a cold look and I was suddenly thrown back into my childhood. So it had ever been for me as a boy. So my father and grandfather had stared at me when I ate and when I worked. I smiled down at Abel. He smiled back.

After the meal, Father Christopher and Father Emile both left. I fixed up a tray for Maggie with some warm milk and some buttered bread and told Abel to take it up to their room. He eagerly trotted off but was back again soon enough with the message that his mother said 'Thank you'. As I cleaned up the table, I questioned him.

"Have you no father, Abel?"

He shook his head.

"But I do have a grandfather," he volunteered.

"In England?"

"Yes, but he does not like us for he sent mother to Belgium before I was born because he did not want to see me."

"Oh."

It was all I replied. I could guess the circumstances. From that time on, I made an effort to be kinder to Abel and to pay more attention to him. Sometimes I took him for walks and at other times I read to him. And so my first year in Louvain passed.

Maggie was a few years older than I was. She was twenty-one years to my eighteen years. It was that following spring, or perhaps early that summer, that I began to love her in that way that men love women when they want to marry them. She cared for me too. This I instinctively felt for whenever I caught her looking at me, she blushed. Abel was the great bond between us. That is to say, we both wanted the best for the little boy. I began teaching him to read. Maggie was grateful. It was a wonderful summer. To me the grass was greener, the sky bluer and the sun brighter than I had ever known them to be. I sang much. Abel began to sing as well, imitating and becoming reasonably able to carry a tune.

"Why are you not Catholic, Paulus?" Maggie once began in a hesitant voice.

"Because my mother was not. She was Protestant. But I am neither Catholic nor Protestant."

Her face lit up when I mentioned that my mother had been a Protestant.

"My father," she said, "is an elder in the church of England. He ...."

She stopped.

"I know," I responded, putting my hand on her arm, "you needn't say. Abel once told me that your father sent you to Belgium when...."

"Yes," she said, and again, "Yes."

And then we talked of something else.

And then, the first week of July, Father Christophe called me into his office.

"Sit down, Paulus."

He looked very agitated and I turned over in my mind whether or not I had been remiss in my work, if I had been sloppy about something or if he perhaps questioned my intentions towards Maggie. If so, I could put his mind at rest. My intentions were honorable.

"The Crown Prince of Austria has been assassinated," he said, "at Sarajevo!"

"Who is the Crown Prince of Austria?" I asked, "And why...?"

I had never heard of Sarajevo and had no idea where it was. And Austria was not half as real to me as Louvain was at this precise moment in time.

"It means that we might have war, Paulus."

He stood up and walked towards the window. I did not follow his line of thought and as the sun pooled into a beam by my feet, thought Father Christophe was exaggerating.

"There will be a High Mass sung for the soul of...."

He stopped, turned and regarded me. His eyes softened.

"You have no idea, do you, Paulus, of the repercussions?"

I shook my head. Indeed, I did not. But his demeanor was beginning to worry me.

"It means," Father Christophe went on, "that France and England will be at odds with Germany and Russia."

"Oh."

I fear I did not sound intelligent. It had been languages that I had studied with Master Deernis and, although he had professed to be an atheist, he had never initiated me into the art of politics. War was a word outside my vocabulary.

"I fear that Russia will mobilize her troops before the end of this month. Sooner or later, Paulus, this incident in Sarajevo will touch us. Germany will want to reach out and attack France."

He paused and I regarded him blankly.

"Belgium," he went on softly, "is in the way."

I sat quietly, prepared to digest what he said but unable to swallow his words.

A week or so later, a requiem High Mass was sung at the Louvain Cathedral for the repose of the murdered prince. I knew Father Christophe would not order me to attend, but I went out of curiosity. The entire church was draped in black velvet. It was a thoroughly somber atmosphere and I chafed as I sat in the pew, knowing that the sun shone outside and that Maggie and Abel were out for a walk. A black catafalque displayed Austrian arms and candles blazed everywhere. I smelled the wax and recalled my mother's death. It was not a memory on which I cared to dwell. The choir sang, each member morosely mouthing high notes without joy. Then everyone partook of the Mass. I believe I was the only one who did not. And I wondered if they were all mourning the murdered prince, the Crown Prince of Austria, who was surely buried by now. And how could they mourn one whom they did not know.

Maggie, who was in many ways more world-wise than I was, said that I was not to worry.

"Belgium is neutral," she postulated while scrubbing pots and pans, "and besides that, England is her ally. Germany knows that England would never stand by and see an ally threatened. Don't worry, Paulus. Father Christophe sees bears where there are only rabbits."

Abel climbed onto my lap and asked for a story and I was only too happy to oblige. In a way, I was reliving my childhood through him, giving him what I myself had never had from my father — attention and love. The boy was six years old now. I had taught him his letters and was proud of him, each day discovering a new facet of what it meant to receive unconditional love. For that is what Abel had for me

2: Any Fool Can Sing in the Day

— unconditional love. I did not understand the why of it, but lapped it up as readily as a cat goes at a bowl of cream.

But Maggie was wrong and Father Christophe was right. The beginning of the next month brought war.

"*C'est la guerre*," was a phrase which everyone on the street mouthed. It meant, "It is war," and a look of unbelief and incredulity always accompanied the statement.

"What is war?" Abel asked as he ate his breakfast of jam and toast early in August.

Maggie, sitting next to him, wrinkled her forehead.

"It is," she said slowly, repeating herself, "It is a time when people ... No, no, I'm going to say it wrong. You see, Abel, it is hard to explain because it is such a big word. War is a fight not just between two people but between a lot of people."

He chewed as slowly as she was speaking.

"Do we know the people that are fighting?"

"We will," said Father Christophe, who had just come in through the door, "for they will be here soon enough."

Maggie looked worried.

"But England," she added hopefully, "will also come here. They will surely defend Belgian neutrality, don't you think, Father?"

"Ah," he answered gravely, as he headed for the door, "but who will be here first, Maggie, that is the question, is it not? The Germans or the English, if indeed, the English get here at all."

"We are English, aren't we?"

Abel toyed with his bread and brightly looked up at his mother.

"Yes, we are Abel," she answered.

"Well, then we can help, can't we?"

I laughed at the boy.

"You're too small, little Abba," I said, lapsing into his mother's pet name for him, "much too small to carry a gun or to think of such things."

Pushing back my chair, I got up, wiped my mouth on a napkin as I did so, and prepared to follow Father Christophe. I winked at Abel.

2: Any Fool Can Sing in the Day

"I have to go to the university now, but I'll see you tonight and then we'll go for a walk."

Abel grinned and Maggie's grateful eyes met mine for a moment.

Father Christophe was of one mind during the next few weeks. He had me and other workers crate and mark box upon box of books and store them in the basement of the university. Viewing the staggering amount of manuscripts and volumes that were yet on the shelves, he sighed deeply and made the sign of the cross.

"May God forbid that they be...."

Although I loved my work, I had not the dedication that the priest had to these works and often thought to myself that Father Christophe was overreacting. But the truth was that Louvain was now beginning to hear the thunder of guns and that at night red lights flashing in the south reminded us that the city of Liége was being besieged. The rumor that Liége had fallen followed. Maggie packed a suitcase for herself and Abel. Then the Belgian soldiers, although there were not many, began to leave Louvain and we were left alone in the city with only a small civic guard to protect us against the enemy. There were tales. Everyone shared them. Tales of burned and shattered houses; of villages razed to the ground; of women who were raped and of children who were killed; and of drunken soldiers who cared for neither God nor man.

"Will England come soon?" Abel asked each day as the rumble of artillery grew nearer.

He was not allowed to play outside anymore and Maggie looked worried.

And then one day they came, marching, marching and marching — thousands of them. Through the attic skylight Maggie and I could see them approaching miles down the road — that same road I had walked so blithely and unaware the year before. Like a poisonous snake, their file wound towards Louvain. They came in rows of eight men and between their ranks Belgian prisoners limped along rather painfully. One of the first things they did was tear down the Belgian flag from the town hall hoisting up the German flag of black, white and red to take its place. Carts with supplies followed every division — divisions which never seemed to stop.

"Will they stay? "Maggie whispered the words, even though no one would have heard her speak out loud in the attic.

"I don't know," I answered truthfully, "but I do know that you and Abel ought not to be out or be seen by any of them. Do you promise me that you will stay here and hide?"

She nodded. Abel was asleep on my cot. Our plan was that, if the soldiers should come knocking at the door, they were to go out the back way, scale the stone fence and seek shelter in the neighbor's garden shed. We had looked at that shed. It held garden implements, hay and some rough sacks. She and Abel would hide behind the sacks.

We watched the Germans overrun the city for most of that day. They covered the boulevards with methodical precision. Bayonets glinted, drums beat, cymbals clanged and horses trotted. Fifes played and the men sang. They sang like a huge choir that had been trained to instill order and enthusiasm. The words were harsh. I could understand a bit of it here and there, but the guttural sounds which rose triumphantly from a thousand throats mocked the larks.

"What are those things?"

Abel, who had woken up and climbed onto the box between us at the window, pointed to the bayonets.

"They are weapons."

I answered shortly, wishing that the child was still asleep. But he was wide awake and watched the soldiers with increasing interest.

"What kind of weapons?"

"They are like swords," Maggie said, as she put her arm around her son.

"You mean they will cut through people?"

"Yes."

Both of us answered simultaneously and then were quiet. But Abel continued.

"I think that their mothers would not like it if they used them."

Maggie smiled and kissed the top of his head.

"I think you are right, Abba."

The lettering on the belts of the soldiers read '*Gott mit uns*' meaning 'God with us', and I wondered out loud just how many gods there were. But Maggie became angry at this.

"There is only one God, Paulus. And this is not a time to joke about that."

I did not go back to the university for several days. Father Christophe stayed at the school and did not come home. Neither did Father Emile. I rather suspected they were busy carting books off to various secret places together with the other custodians of the library. I finally left the house late one afternoon, leaving strict injunctions for Maggie to stay put or, if necessary, to leave by the back door. I passed a number of soldiers on the way. They did not look friendly. To my dismay, I saw billowing plumes of smoke come from the north-east section of the city. Quickening my pace, I noted both terror and anger in the eyes of all the civilians I passed. Every corner, it seemed, held a platoon of soldiers. Joking and laughing, they eyed me without fear. Perhaps I should not have left Maggie and Abel alone.

"They are rounding up the men of Louvain. Get lost as quickly as you can."

This was whispered to me by a passing lad, a boy of perhaps some twelve years of age. The university lay straight ahead. I could see the marble steps and on them a great many soldiers lounged about. There seemed, as yet, to be no order, no plan on their part to act. I decided to brave the moment and climbed the steps nonchalantly, looking neither to the right nor to the left. No one stopped me. Once inside, I quickly made for the room in which we had been working just a few days earlier. Utter chaos met my eyes as I opened the door. Father Christophe was on the floor, hammering nails into a crate, while several other men were packing boxes. Papers cluttered everywhere and two German officers sat at a desk looking on. One was smoking a cigar and the other was sipping a beer. The doorknob still in my hand, I wondered if I should enter or if I should perhaps leave just as quietly as I had come in. But Father Christophe, looking up, saw me.

"Ah, Paulus," he cried, as if he had been looking for me, which he might well have been. "Ah, Paulus, you must tell these men how important these books are. I know that you can speak a bit of German...."

He left off abruptly and continued to hammer away at the box. The two officers regarded me with interest. The one with the cigar motioned that I should come closer and take a seat opposite them.

"Who are you?" he said, after I had sat down.

"Paulus, sir," I answered, trying to keep my voice steady, "Paulus Vlam."

"Where are you from, Paulus?"

"Holland, sir."

"Holland?"

"Yes."

The man sipping the beer, reflected that his mother was from Holland as well and that the Dutch were a nice people, very closely related to the Germans. I noted that both men were slightly tipsy.

"Why are you here, Paulus?" the other officer asked, drawing heavily on the cigar.

"I came to visit a cousin in Belgium," I answered truthfully.

"What is his name?"

"Albert Degrelle."

"Where is he?"

"He is dead."

They were quiet for a few moments after this and regarded the men who were boxing the books with something akin to pity.

"Watch this," the cigar said and standing up, he walked across the room and picked up a manuscript from the floor. He then, after lighting a match in front of the horrified Father Christophe and the others, began burning the edge of the paper. Father Christophe stood up, and putting his hands together in a supplicating gesture, begged the officer to refrain. But the man laughed, tossing the rapidly disintegrating paper onto the floor. A young clerk, younger than I, jumped up from his place in the corner and ran over to the paper. He stomped on it with his feet, succeeding in putting out the flame. But it was the last thing he did. A revolver shot rang out and in horror I watched the boy, for he was not older than sixteen, crumple up and fall down.

"So Paulus," the other officer took a pull at his beer as if nothing had happened, before he continued, "your cousin is dead. And where will you be going?"

"Home," I answered without hesitation as I stared at the dead body, but it was Maggie I thought of when I said it.

"Fine," he answered, "go back to Holland and it's where I would like to go myself. Go, go, boy, before we burn this entire place down."

I stood up hesitantly, glanced at Father Christophe who was bent over and weeping into his crate. He had forgotten about me. A small pool of blood had collected under the corpse. I turned and walked out stiffly, expecting at any moment to be stopped, to be shot dead. But nothing happened and I made it safely back into the hall. Now I had the street to brave. And yet, that was not true either. I knew that were I to follow the corridor to the right, I would eventually come to a small door which exited into the university garden. Perhaps it would be wiser to take that way out. I walked quickly, but not so quickly as to attract attention. Incredibly I encountered no one. Several times I heard voices coming from rooms I passed. And then there was the door and the garden beyond it. Empty as well, I made straight for the small gate which led to an alley, beyond which lay one of the main streets. Cautiously making my way back, I almost tripped over two bodies. They were men, Red Cross workers, who had been dropped in the alley by whoever had shot them. Crouching over their bodies and ascertaining that they really were dead, I thought that perhaps their uniforms might prove to be helpful later. Or perhaps just their arm bands. Pulling them off, I slipped one over the sleeve of my right arm and the other in my pocket and then went on, never looking back. I made it safely to the house, and from there quietly made my way to the neighbor's shed, checking to see if Maggie and Abel had already presumed upon its relative safety. They had not. Going back to the house, I found them sitting in my attic room.

"We must leave Louvain tonight," I said, and these were the first words that came out of my mouth as I walked into what had been my little haven since I first arrived in Louvain.

"Leave?" puzzled Abel, after he had hugged me, "but where will we go?"

"We'll go to Geel," I answered, "There is a lady there who is a sister to Father Christophe. She is very kind and she will help us."

Maggie said nothing. She indicated with a gesture that their suitcase was ready and asked if I would like to have something to eat first. I nodded and she went downstairs.

"What have you been doing?" I asked Abel.

"Mother has been telling me stories," he said.

"Oh, that's nice. Maybe later you can tell them to me."

He nodded happily and leaned against me, his blond hairs soft against my arm. Looking up to say something, he suddenly saw the cross on my sleeve.

"What's that?"

"It's a Red Cross band," I answered, "people wear it when they help other people who have been hurt."

"Oh," he said, and he frowned in thought, continuing, "have you been helping others, Paulus?"

"No," I answered.

"But now that you are wearing the band, you will," he said with a smile, as if he understood the matter totally.

"Yes," I answered, happy to see him smile.

We left soon afterwards. I had taken several white handkerchiefs with me. They, together with the Red Cross bands, one of which was now also on Maggie's arm, would perhaps see us safely out of Louvain. Smoke was visible everywhere and, as we turned one corner, we could see men, women and children being herded in the direction of the railroad station.

"What will they do with them?" Maggie whispered.

"I don't know," I whispered back.

We managed, somehow, street by street, to get out of Louvain, eventually crawling on our hands and knees through a field towards an old barn.

"Can we stop here for the night?"

Abel was tired. I was not sure in which direction we were traveling. We had taken so many curves and turns to avoid spotlights, that I was disoriented. Perhaps it would be better to wait now until morning, or until tomorrow evening.

"Yes," I answered the boy, "we'll stay here for the night."

The barn rivaled my father's for holes. It was easy to see the moon and the stars as we sat down on the bit of straw that carpeted the floor. Maggie took off her jacket and lay it on top of the straw.

"Here's a good bed for you, Abel," she said.

"Is there a manger?" the boy asked.

"A manger?" I repeated.

"Yes," he said, "like in the story. Don't you know it, Paulus?"

"No," I answered, "is it a Brothers Grimm's fairy tale?"

Abel laughed.

"No, it's a Bible story and mother just told it to me today. Shall I tell it to you, Paulus?"

I looked at his eager face, white in the moonlight, and nodded.

"Well, you see," Abel began, "a long time ago, even before the very world was here...."

He stopped and looked at Maggie.

"That's right, isn't it mother?"

"Yes."

Maggie sat hunched, her arms snug around her knees, gazing up at the stars.

"Well then, at that long time ago, that was when God made a plan to send His Son, the Lord Jesus into the world."

He stopped, again looking to Maggie for confirmation as he added, "And that means Belgium too, doesn't it, mother?"

Maggie nodded at him.

"And do you know why God made this plan?" Abel went on, looking earnestly at me.

I shook my head. Abel was a good story-teller, if only for the fact that his voice had such inflections, such sweet tones that it almost sang.

"Well, He made this plan so that we could go to heaven, you see."

"I don't see," I said a trifle angrily.

After all, the boy was dabbling in myth. That's what Master Deernis would say.

"Well, you see, Paulus, we are very bad, really bad."

I smiled for in my heart I thought that Abel was a good boy. But he frowned and repeated himself.

"We are really bad, Paulus. And God can't abide any badness in heaven. He doesn't like it. So because of the way things are with us, we can't go to heaven. And so the plan was that Jesus would come and be very good in our place. And then the plan was that He would die."

"And what good would dying do?" I said, the memory of the death of three men graphically imprinted on my brain.

Up to that point I had followed Abel's story, but the mention of dying did not sit well with me at all.

"Well," Abel said, thinking deeply, a wrinkle of concentration creasing his forehead while he pulled at the straw pieces that would be his mattress, "Well, you see Paulus, the thing is that Jesus never did anything bad while He was a little boy like me. And later on, when he was a man like you He never did anything bad either. So He was allowed back into heaven when He died."

"But why," I interrupted rather harshly, exasperated and repeating myself to some extent, "would a father plan a death for his son? There is no love in that. Why, Abel?"

Maggie drew in her breath and looked at me strangely. My voice had risen several decibels and I knew she was on edge.

"Sorry," I mumbled.

"Because," Abel continued patiently, and seemingly unperturbed, "without God's plan we couldn't go to heaven. Not mother, not me and not you."

He stopped for a moment and contemplated the space beyond my head before he went on. I continued to listen because I loved the boy.

"So the plan," Abel's childish voice went on, "was to let us get into heaven. Jesus could go back to heaven after He died because He was good. And because He is there, He can open the door for us when we get there. He can open it with His hands, I think. Well, I don't know how to say it, but I understand it inside."

"I don't understand," I said stubbornly.

"Well, it's true" he answered, equally stubborn, "I know it inside myself. I just think I didn't tell it very well."

And then he lay down and closed his eyes. Just like that. And Maggie looked at me.

"It is true, you know, Paulus," she said even as Abel sat up again.

"I know," the child iterated joyfully, "I know how to explain it to you some more, Paulus. Jesus has the cross band on His sleeve. I think that when I come to the door of heaven Jesus will lift me up in His arms with the crossband on it and carry me through the door right into heaven."

And then he lay down and closed his eyes again. I knew about the cross. The sign of the cross that is. But not really the Person of the cross. I shrugged. Why would you die for someone else? Why, indeed!

Abel sat up again.

"I love you, Paulus."

And then he lay down again and this time he stayed down.

The next morning was rather misty. I thought it an auspicious bit of weather, weather that would cover us like a blanket. We ate some of the 'manchets', some of the small loaves of white bread Maggie had brought along in her suitcase and then I went outside to gauge the fields and roads surrounding the barn. It was very early yet. The dew touched my shoes, my pants, and soaked through quickly. But I scarcely noted it as I breathed the air as a dog might, sniffing to the right, to the left and even up in order to ascertain whether or not it was safe to move. I came across a road rather quickly, a dirt road. There was no sign post, no mark which might have indicated to me exactly which area we had wandered into the previous night. Perhaps if I took Maggie and Abel down here, Maggie might know. She had, after all, lived here much longer than I had. I found my way back. Abel was rubbing his eyes.

"I think today will be a good day," he said.

"We'll be off then. There's a road just ahead — a small, dirt road," I told them. "Maybe you'll recall it, or see a landmark that you recognize, Maggie, when we come to it because I have no idea where we are."

Maggie looked serious.

"I've never been good at directions," she said, "but let's go and see."

"Now, Abel," I took the boy's hand as I spoke, carrying one of the suitcases in my other hand, "you must walk very quietly and stay close by my side. Do you understand? And no talking at all."

He nodded, gripping my palm tightly. We came to the road and Maggie was not sure whether to turn right or left. Birds flew up ahead of us out of a thicket and Abel pointed with his free hand, whispering as he did so.

"Let's go where the birds are flying."

I shrugged at Maggie. She laughed silently and that is the way we turned — to the right, in the direction the birds had flown.

For a few hours all was well. I reasoned within myself that since we had not come to any intersection or heard any noise, that we were traveling away from Louvain. The mist had cleared and the sky overhead was blue. Just as I was contemplating the fact that we were very much in the open, a shot rang out ahead.

"Jump into the ditch."

I hissed the words at Maggie and Abel, pulling the boy even as I spoke, into the small hollow next to the road. But it was too late. Two soldiers came running towards us out of a small copse.

"Halt!"

Revolvers glistened in their hands and we had no choice but to put down the suitcases and to raise ours high above our heads. They indicated that we should walk in front of them and so we did.

"Our suitcases..." Maggie began, casting a backward glance over her shoulder, but the soldier behind her pushed her hard and if I had not grabbed her, she would have fallen. Abel whimpered and let go of my hand. But the men behind us did not permit the child to seek out his mother and he had to walk next to me again.

We had only covered a kilometer or so when another shot rang out. Approaching a river, we could see movement in the brush along the opposite edge of water. The guards motioned that we should sit down and they began to exchange German in such rapid tones that I could not follow their words.

"French or English partisans?"

Maggie whispered the words loudly enough so that I understood. Before long one of the soldiers motioned that Maggie stand in front of him and that I should stand in front of his partner. They ignored Abel who stayed on the ground, watching us with his big, brown eyes. I smiled at him, although a smile was difficult to muster at that precise moment. He smiled back and kept his eyes riveted on me. Maggie and her guard walked in front of me. Using her as a shield, he maneuvered her to the river bank, all the while balancing his rifle on her shoulder. The shots stopped. Maggie's face was white and drawn and I felt as if my own was a mask of fear.

"This is not the time," Maggie had said yesterday, "to joke about God."

I looked up into the sky. Was it only a year and a half ago that I had still been studying with Master Deernis? Suddenly I was sorry that I had not closed my eyes for the Lord's Prayer, because staring up into the sky it seemed to me that I was contemplating eternity and that it was unavoidable. All my knowledge was no help at this moment — no help whatsoever. The soldier behind me, shoved me with the butt of his rifle and I took another step through the brush grass, another step closer to the brink of the river.

"The hand of Jesus," Abel had talked about it as if it was a literal hand.

I heard the child's voice as clearly as if he were next to me instead of behind me hidden in the tall grass of the roadside. I wished we had talked more. My mother had tried to teach me how to pray and I had prayed at her knees, a long time ago. A shot rang by us, but it was so far off the mark that the men behind us laughed. Maggie's guard shot back, shot back as he balanced the rifle on her shoulder, and she stood rigid. Another prod — another step forward. How long would it be before the men on the other side would shoot us by mistake? How long would they tolerate the audacity of these Germans? We were only two — two dispensable hostages — and we were likely holding up a regiment of allies waiting to cross the river, waiting to pass on to Louvain and other cities. Maggie turned her head to look at me. She was only a few feet away on my right. She moved her left hand up to touch the cross-band she still wore on her sleeve. The soldier pushed her on. But he pushed too hard and she tripped. In that instant a salvo of shots rang out and the soldier behind her dropped down dead. Instantly the fellow behind me pulled me backwards, pulled me behind some brush. I could not see Maggie who, it seemed to me, had rolled to the side. My guard was afraid and tense. His breathing was heavy in the nape of my neck and his gun pushed hard into my back. After a few minutes he laboriously took off his jacket and gestured that I should put it on and stand up. Pretending not to understand, I raised my eyebrows. Impatiently, he gestured again. Either way, I knew that I was finished. Angry and irritated at my playing for time, he jabbed the butt of his gun into my rib cage. Slowly my arms worked their way into his jacket.

"'*Aufstehen,*— stand," he barked.

So I did. But the moment I stood a little form hurtled itself at my breast.

"Paulus!" it cried.

The soldier, startled by the impact and force of Abel's body, stood up next to me. And the inevitable shots rang out.

"Abba," I replied, but the little child lay dead in my arms. And then I understood that death could be the result of love.

3: The Drawing

With joy you will draw water from the wells of salvation. And you will say in that day: Give thanks to the Lord, call upon His name, make known His deeds among the peoples, proclaim that His name is exalted (Isaiah: 12:3-4).

A t birth a child's affection is instinctively and irrevocably drawn to his father and mother. In due time, however, as a child grows up, he will come to realize that his parents are fallible. So his love is tested. And it is only when the child comes to the realization that only God, and not one's parents can be relied upon totally and that only God, and not one's parents, loves him perfectly, that the child himself can fully and sacrificially love his parents (and others) as they ought to be loved. For it is a great truth that an understanding of even a small fraction of God's unchangeable and enduring love, will reflect clearly and joyfully upon all other relationships. This, in any case, is what I experienced.

By any standards, Katrien Pret, my mother, was a solid, large-boned woman, although by no means an unattractive one. Taller than most, she naturally stood out in a crowd simply because she took up more vertical room. In contrast, her husband, my father Jaap Pret, who was almost a full head shorter than she was, could be described as fairly small and thin. They were a rather striking couple in their own way and did not at all follow the pattern which Martin Luther referred to when he postulated that men have broad and large chests, and small narrow hips, and more understanding than the women, who have but small and narrow breasts, and broad hips, to the end that they should remain at home, sit still, keep house, and bear and bring up children.

My father met my mother in the decade prior to World War II, when he was just beginning to set up a business as cordwainer, or shoemaker, in a small town in northern Holland. The name of the town is not relevant. It was but one town of many and has no bearing on the purpose of this narration. My mother, whose name was then Katrien Kats, hobbled into his small shop one day, as the heel had broken off her shoe just outside his door. He fixed it for her while she waited. Afterwards, he fitted her for a new pair of shoes, which she, in a burst of uncharacteristic audacity, had ordered that same afternoon. Self-conscious, and not very talkative during that hour, perhaps my father fell in love with her feet first. He did ascertain from the few questions he posed, that she lived with and worked for her father, Peter Kats, a local dairy farmer. She, in turn, was quite taken with the courteous, young cobbler. So much so that, during their second meeting, when she picked up her new shoes, she invited him for supper without even thinking of consulting her parents. Catching sight of her blushing cheeks, my father Jaap, who was an orphan and twenty-six at the time, accepted the invitation with alacrity. He consequently visited the dairy farm quite frequently. They were married five years prior to the war and lived, during these honeymoon years, in two sizeable rooms behind the shoe shop. I was born in the second year of their marriage. It was 1937 and by all accounts I was a healthy, nine pound, boy whom they named Peter Jaap – Peter after my mother's father and Jaap after my own father. My father's shoe business flourished in this time, and these years, I gather, were filled with both sweetness and pain. Sweetness because of their love for one another and pain, because my mother suffered two miscarriages. And then, despite her neutrality, the Germans invaded Holland. War broke out. My father joined the underground, aiding in the hiding of Jews and participating in sabotage against the German occupation. He had good reason to fear for his life, consequently disappearing from our lives. I vaguely recall that one day, riding on the back of a bike, holding my arms around my mother's solid midriff, with the wind in my back, we moved to the relative safety of my grandparents' farm. Here my mother resumed her old role of helping out in the barn whenever help was needed. My grandparents were delighted to have both of us live in their home. Life continued, albeit at an uneven pace. The war finally ended and I remember dancing in the village street with everyone crying and laughing simultaneously; but what I remember most vividly is that my father came back home to us – thin, gaunt-eyed, wiry, but alive.

At this juncture, there was some effort on the part of my grandfather Peter, who did have one other daughter, my aunt Hilda, to entice father into working for him. But father was not tempted at all. Although the shoe shop in which he had initially set up trade had been bombed to rubble, and not much else was available in the way of renting store space, he was set on beginning cobbling again. "Let's emigrate," he said to my mother several years after the war. I remember father's statement well, because I was seated at the table drawing a picture, when father made it. Mother's single word response was given in a high-pitched tone of voice; in a voice slightly incredulous.

"Emigrate?"

"Yes."

Father's answer brooked no argument.

"Emigrate to where?"

Mother's voice was still rather high.

"I've heard someone speak of Canada. It's a land of opportunity."

"But..." said mother, and then fell silent, thinking perhaps of the generous Canadian soldiers who had cheered up our entire village and who had brought liberation from the war.

I know that opportunity was what she wanted for me, her only son. And in just those few moments of time she must have concluded, with father, that this country Canada might contain opportunity. She must also have considered the fact that her sister Hilda had become engaged to a young man who was very interested in dairy farming. It was a truth, I think, that helped her become resigned to follow father's inclination. But although the decision to emigrate was made rather quickly, a number of years were eaten up by planning, by weighing the pros and the cons. Meanwhile, as he had done since the war was over, father worked part-time on the farm, while he also spent a few afternoons every week in shoemaking. Grandfather Peter had magnanimously cleared a corner of the barn for this enterprise and, whistling as he worked, father possessed a measure of contentment.

But the desire to immigrate grew and as he whistled, he thought many thoughts. I could see it in his posture, in the words he spoke to me and in the dreamy look in his eyes. Holland was full – too full to house new, young families such as ours; Holland was small – but Canada contained thousands of miles of open land; Holland held few job opportunities – Canada had schools aplenty and I, his son, would be able to become... anything. He would, from time to time, look at me questioningly. Although I was past ten years of age, I had not really, according to my father, shown any particular skills or ambition as yet. Perhaps he was hoping that cordwaining was in my blood as it was in his. But the gift that flowed in my blood was not shoemaking but sketching. From the time that I had been a toddler, I had coveted pencil stubs. On the farm I often went to a special spot behind the barn. Here I sat quietly, my back against the dark barn boards, drawing fields, trees and animals. Once, during the early war years, my father chanced upon me sitting there. He smiled and said that I looked like my mother for I was dark-haired, and tall even at an early age. He went on to say that I was also like her in character – for I expressed myself well with very few words.

"What would you like to be later, Peter?"

"Like you, father."

"What do you mean, son?"

"I mean... I mean," I had hesitated, trying to find the right words.

At that moment I recall being torn between the courtesy of love and my natural inward desire.

"I mean that I want to draw shoes."

Father had smiled broadly, had almost laughed, but had held his laughter back.

"Draw shoes?"

"Yes," I answered positively, adding, just to make sure that I would not be misunderstood, "not make them, but draw them."

"But," puzzled father, standing still in front of me, "I do not think that drawing shoes is a job. Do you know anyone else, Peter, who draws shoes for a living?"

I hung my head. I had been all of five years old.

"No, father."

"Ah, well," father had reconciled, "there is plenty of time yet, and I'm so pleased that you want to be like me."

"Yes," I had nodded happily, and then had added, not feeling guilty at all about the words because he had just iterated them himself, "and like mother."

I was not untruthful. I did very much want to be like father, who was brave and never seemed afraid of anything. But mother was the one who ultimately took care of me and who always admired all of my drawings.

A small tenant house on the farm property had been designated as our family's living quarters after the war. It did well enough, but often father chafed to be gone from the confines of the grandparents' oversight – yearned to have his own place. I, on the other hand, loved the farm and could walk it blindfolded. Because of the war years, I had begun schooling late. I had turned eight in 1945, and had to walk more than half an hour to reach the local village school. Mother brought me the first day, but after that I walked alone and appreciated her insight into letting me become independent. For toys, father had made me stilts on which to balance, making me very tall, and out of some old spools of thread, he fashioned wooden spinning tops. Both these toys delighted me. But the pencil was still my number one favorite implement, my 'sixth finger', as mother laughingly teased, as it was always in my hand.

My mother, during this time, was quite content to be living near her parents and her sister, and did not think much beyond the four walls of her snug home; neither did she, I think, care to imagine beyond the days of the week in which she lived. When she had time, she sat in the field with me and watched me draw, admiring what she termed as 'my skill', wondering out loud where such a talent had come from. She inspected, at intervals, her own large hands, exclaiming that they could never wield such creativity, such direction on paper as my hands could.

"I like your cows," she said one afternoon, as we sat on a hillock in the sunshine, I with a pad and she with her knitting.

"They are not my cows," I answered with a laugh.

"If something is in your head," she remarked thoughtfully, "so that you can reproduce it, or set it on paper, is it then not yours?"

"I don't know," I said, "I don't know, mother."

"Well, God has made us," she said, "and we belong to Him."

My mother had a very strong faith, but she did not often speak about spiritual things. That sentence is perhaps a contradiction in terms, so I will add that I often saw her pray at the kitchen table, hands folded in her lap, eyes closed, lips murmuring softly. She was also the one who read the children's Bible to me and the one who had taught me to kneel in front of my bed before I went to sleep.

"You must pray every night," she said.

"What shall I say?"

"You must praise God, thank Him and tell Him you are sorry for your sins."

"What sins, mother?"

"Well," she had paused a long time, looking at the wall over my head, "well, Peter, you must know something you have done wrong today. Perhaps you became angry for no reason; maybe you didn't pay attention to grandfather or grandmother as you should have. And also, dominee tells us that we were born sinful. I mean," she went on, still looking over my head, "that we are sinful just by being. So it stands to reason that without doing anything we are sinful."

She sighed and then smiled. Her eyes came back to me.

"You too, mother? You are sinful too?"

"Yes, me too."

It was hard to think of mother doing anything wrong. She was so kind, so quiet, and so sweet. I looked at her as we sat by the hillock. The knitting needles moved deftly in her hands. My own hands grasped the pencil I held between my left thumb and forefinger, as I shaved off wood with a penknife to sharpen dull lead, slowly responding to her statement about belonging to God.

"Yes, I think we do belong to God because He made us," I answered thoughtfully, for what she said made sense, and then I went on, "Does that make you feel like you were drawn by Him, mother?"

She laughed at that and almost dropped a stitch.

"I think that God has a lot of erasing to do," she responded by way of answer, "Just look at me, Peter. My legs are too long, and my body is so awkward. I don't know what your father ever saw in me that he chose to marry me."

"But father did not draw you," I persisted, intrigued by the thought, "God did."

"You're a little theologian, Peter," mother smiled, as she rolled up her knitting and put it and her needles into a bag, "and I must get back to the house to make supper."

"I don't think God erases," I went on, speaking to her as she got up, "but He might add to His pictures."

She did not respond. I watched her tall back disappear down the hillock, round the bend and on to our wee house. I loved my mother. She was ever attentive, always listened to my ideas, and was always where I could find her. But the truth was that I did not always feel that way about God. As a matter of fact, in spite of the conversation we just had, I did not think about God very often, even though I knew very well that He was there.

In the long run, the immigration plans sorted out. The time eventually came that we all waved goodbye to friends and family standing on the pier at Rotterdam as we ourselves stood on the deck of a large immigrant ship. I was thirteen – tall, lanky, awkward and on the verge of a great adventure. All our belongings had been packed away into two big, wooden crates. With great care father had stowed away his cobbling equipment – his lasts, (one for the right foot and one for the left), needles, laces, metal plates, leather material, a great wooden table, measuring cord, knives, and other material. Mother, with equal care, had added to the interior of the crates, plates, cups, cutlery, blankets, and essential furniture. Grandmother Kats assisted her, and every now and then, overcome by emotion, one of them would weep. This was because it seemed very clear to both of them that neither would see the other again. The ocean was incredibly vast and the distance to Canada almost immeasurable. "It is for the child. It is for Peter."

My mother repeated this phrase many times. She loved me with a love she could not put into words, and she fathomed that her mother must somehow love her and her sister in this way also. So, when we stood on the deck of the ship, she hand-in-hand with my father, she must have felt in some small measure as if she were perhaps sinning. She intuitively knew that her parents were grieving hard, grieving as if she were, in some measure, dying. She also knew she was the cause of their grieving.

"Look, I see my mother."

Mother leaned her tall frame far over the railing and father firmly took hold of the back of her coat.

"Be careful!"

"Peter!"

My mother suddenly called out my name, prompted, I think, by a momentary need to have her child close by.

"Here I am, mother."

I stood behind her. She let go of father's hand and turning, took hold of my hand, pulling me to the front, pointing to the small figures of my grandparents on the shore.

"Wave to them, Peter."

I waved. They waved back. Letting go of my hand, she turned to father for perhaps the thousandth time and asked the same question she had been asking all along.

"Why are we going, Jaap?"

Mother's voice was doubtful. It wavered. It trembled like a leaf in the wind. Father took her hand back into his own.

"It's a new country, Katrien. It's a wide country. We will have room. Peter can grow and he can go to school and...."

"But," she falteringly interrupted, "but I might never see them again. Father and mother, I mean. Look, they're waving again."

I now, without mother's realizing it, slipped away from them both. Walking backwards, I pushed against the crowd of people behind me. They let me through, happy to have more space to press against the railing. Gradually easing out, I found an empty bench on the deck and sat down. Then I took out pencil and paper from my jacket pocket and began to draw. I drew backs, backs hiding a railing, and backs enveloped above by a magnificent, clear sky. When I was done, I stood on the bench, managing to sketch the ever smaller Dutch coastline as well. In the days that followed, I also drew the captain, the steward, the dining room, people vomiting into little, brown paper bags, waves, seagulls, groups huddling together talking small and big talk, and father peering out over the railing into the horizon.

"What are you looking at, father?"

I was curious. Mother was rarely on deck. She was sick – seasick, I presumed. It appeared to me that father, with whom I bunked in a men's section of the boat, perpetually stood at the railing –

motionless, seemingly intent on the ocean. He turned and smiled at my question.

"I didn't know you were there, Peter."

"Yes, I've been watching you, father" I said, and repeated, "What are you looking at?"

"I'm looking at... at tomorrow. I'm seeing...," father's words came slowly, haltingly, as if he had to pull them out of a deep recess within himself.

"What are you seeing?"

"Well, I'm seeing," father went on, turning his gaze back on the water, "something that you likely don't see when you draw. For you draw what is there. You see a person, a thing, something you can touch – or an area into which you can physically walk. I see what is not there – at least not yet."

"You mean like our new home in Canada?"

"Yes, that and then perhaps other things."

"You mean like you hope your business will do well and then you see lots of people walking into your new shoe shop?"

I probed. I loved to hear father speak. Although he did not do so very often, there were times when he could not stop. But this was not one of those times. He merely nodded, not turning his head but smiling into the horizon.

"Yes, Peter. That's right, I suppose."

I puzzled for a while about what father said and sometimes, as I lay in my bunk in the cabin, I thought about drawing what I could not see. Someone coughed through the darkness of the night, and I imagined what it might be like to draw a cough. But I could not quite develop the idea. The ship lilted slightly to the right, and I felt myself rolling that way. What deeps beneath the ship had so shifted its bulk that the whole mighty vessel moved? I did not know, and I could neither fathom nor draw the thought. I missed mother very much. She did not come out on the deck often but stayed in her cabin. Was she still feeling quite ill? What was she thinking all this time? Could I draw what she might be thinking? It was only two more days before we would be docking in Montreal. I sighed deeply and curled into a ball. Drifting off, I remembered what dominee had said that last Sunday when we were in the 'kerk', in the church, in our village in Holland. People had come to shake our hands, to say goodbye as we stood on the wide stone steps leading up to the heavy oak church door. Dominee had taken special trouble to speak to me.

"Remember the One Who made all the countries of the world, Peter, and you won't have trouble in your new country. Remember the One Who caused the light to shine in the beginning, Peter, and you will have light within you wherever you are to show you the path on which you ought to walk."

I knew that what dominee said was true – even as my eyelids were heavy with sleep. I knew it, not just because Oma Kats always admonished me to listen to what dominee said while I sat in the pew each Sunday, but because I just knew within myself that it was true. But I could not really explain why I believed these truths. They lay in my heart – perhaps like packages waiting to be opened, or perhaps like brushes ready to draw but not dipped in paint yet. Then I fell asleep.

Three days later, the contact man, a Mr. Wim Kooy, met father, mother and me as we got off an evening train in Union Station in Toronto, Ontario. We knew he was our contact man because he was carrying a cardboard sign that read: *"Welcome, Pret family."* Father had been assigned to him by the immigration people back in Holland.

"Welcome to Canada," Mr. Kooy said, even though we had already been in Canada for longer than a day, adding, "How was the trip from Montreal?"

"Fine," father answered.

Mr. Kooy was a rather small, rotund man, shorter than me. Putting down the sign he was carrying, he extended his right hand and we all shook it.

"Wim Kooy."

His voice was solid and his grip was firm. He exuded leadership and confidence. Then, after handing me a chocolate bar from his suit pocket, he led us as we each lugged one of our three heavy suitcases, across the busy train station platform. We followed him through several hallways, up some stairs, and finally, to a car. Lifting up the trunk, he deposited our suitcases into its roomy space as we watched. Moving to the front of the vehicle, opening the passenger door with a flourish, he indicated that I should get in first. I had never before in my life been in a car, but was too tired to exult in this new experience. Working my large frame past the slim front seat gap, I managed to squeeze into the back seat. Mother followed suit. Father was given the privileged front seat. No one spoke. It was late, almost midnight, and weariness and excitement fought within me for attention. Weariness had the upper hand but did not win. My eyelids almost, but not quite, closed. Mr. Kooy took his place behind the steering wheel.

"How do you like Canada so far?" he asked, as he turned the key and started the motor.

He was speaking Dutch now, much to mother's relief. Not waiting for an answer, he showered us with information as he maneuvered the car onto the road.

"I'm taking you directly to your new home. It's just off Yonge Street – a street called Carson Crescent. It's a dead-end street actually – but a decent one. It's in an area right between Willowdale and North York – a good location for a shoe shop, I thought. The rent for the house is next to nothing. We put in some cots for you, made them up, my wife and I, and there's some food in the cupboards, so you'll be able to manage the next few days, I think, until your own things arrive in the crates."

Mr. Kooy continued to talk non-stop as he drove. It was night. It might have been dark outside but for the headlamps of passing cars and the streetlights and the lights in the windows of the many homes we passed. I was very tired. The chocolate bar lay in my lap. I had often heard Oma Kats say that she remembered the Canadian soldiers with fondness because they handed out such good chocolate bars when they came to liberate Holland. Maybe Mr. Kooy wanted to be liked. Maybe the chocolate bars the soldiers had handed out had been chocolate bars like this one. I had been young when the war ended, but not so young that I did not remember the taste of those chocolate bars. Absently I fingered the one in my lap as I looked out. More lights, more lights, and then the car turned sharply to the left onto another street, and then to the right onto a driveway.

"Well, here we are," Mr. Kooy cheerfully announced.

He opened his door and father also opened his. There was a house to the right of the driveway. I could see its shape faintly illumined by the streetlights on the road. There were darkish bricks, some bushes hugging the side, and a small patch of grass between the front of the house and the road. There was also a white picket fence. Mr. Kooy walked to the back of the car. He extricated the suitcases from the trunk as mother and I fumbled our way out of the car. Next Mr. Kooy drew a flashlight from his coat pocket.

"This will help me find the steps to your new front door."

A round, moon-like circle jumped out. It beamed in front of him as he slowly made his way towards what we could now all see was a stone path leading to the front of the house. The path led to a door – a dark, reddish sort of door. Shining the light directly onto the handle, Mr. Kooy dug into his pocket once again, this time producing a key. He inserted it into the lock, turned it, and then pushed open a creaking door.

"Home, sweet home," he called out over his shoulder, "Come on, folks. This is your castle now."

Imperceptibly, next to me on the driveway, I felt mother sigh as she picked up one of the suitcases and began following father up the path.

The creaking door, we discovered once we had stepped through it, led directly into what appeared to be a living area – a living room with a rather musty smell. Once the switches were turned on, undeniably drab and possibly dirty wallpaper, greeted us. Walking ahead of us through the room to a hallway of sorts, Mr. Kooy kept up a dialogue of encouragement.

"Here to the right is a bedroom, and on your left a bedroom as well. The next right is the bathroom. And, as you can see, straight ahead lies the kitchen. As well, and you didn't likely notice it, there was another room right off the living room when we came in. The house is a bit snug, but cozy as can be for a family of three."

It was not at all, I felt with a pang, what our home in Holland had been.

"My wife and I stocked the kitchen with some necessities. Tomorrow morning I'll be by to show you the nearest stores and to fill you in on some other details. But I think it best that you all get to bed now as soon as possible. You must be dead tired."

We had trailed into the kitchen behind him.

"This is a refrigerator," Mr. Kooy announced, standing next to the white appliance and opening its door, "It keeps the food cool and in here, in the top part of the refrigerator, you can freeze things."

In spite of her weariness, mother began to look interested.

"There's running hot and cold water from the tap here," Mr. Kooy went on, after he closed the refrigerator door, walking over to the sink and turning on the tap to prove his words.

"We put some milk in the refrigerator so that you can have some cold cereal for breakfast tomorrow morning. Have you folks ever eaten corn flakes?"

We shook our heads.

"Well, I'm sure you'll love them."

He opened one of the top kitchen cupboards and took out a cardboard box. Bold letters on the box shouted the words, *"Kellogg's Corn Flakes."* Smaller ones near the bottom whispered, *"Deliciously flavored with sugar, malt and salt."*

"Just shake some flakes out of this box into a bowl tomorrow morning, pour some milk on top, and *'voila'*, you'll have yourselves a breakfast."

A few seconds later, Mr. Kooy trotted out the front door, throwing us a friendly wave over his shoulder as he left. Father, mother and I were alone in our new home. As if by common consent, we walked back to the kitchen.

"Perhaps," father said slowly, "perhaps we should, now that we have finally arrived in this new country, first offer up a prayer of thanksgiving to God for bringing us here safely."

Mother nodded and sat down on a grey, vinyl-covered chair. There were three such chairs grouped around a small, rectangular table. Father and I sat down as well. Father took off his hat and placed it on the table. Then he folded his hands next to his hat and cleared his throat. Mother bent her head.

"Dear Lord," father prayed, "Thank You for bringing us to Canada, to Toronto. You know our going out and our coming in. You are our everlasting God and Father whether we are in Holland or in Canada. Please let us sleep safely here tonight, and wake us up to a new day tomorrow in which we may serve You with the talents You have given us."

He paused for a long bit before he went on.

"We ask You also to take care of those family members we left behind in Holland."

Mother swallowed audibly.

"For Jesus' sake, Amen."

We all opened our eyes.

"Mr. Kooy was right," father said, pushing his vinyl chair back with a scraping sound, "We should all go to bed and in the morning we'll see what sort of place this is."

It was a busy sort of place. We all agreed on that the next day. The house that had been rented for us was located on a quiet enough street – Carson Crescent – but that street was right off busy Yonge Street. When we walked to the intersecting corner, we saw a continual stream of cars, although from time to time it seemed that there was a space of empty road in which one might cross to the other side.

"I'll never be able to cross the road," mother declared anxiously to no one in particular.

She was, however, most pleased with the backyard – a yard which was quite deep and which possessed an apple tree, some rose bushes, as well as some yellow flowers growing freely and profusely right in the middle of the lawn. Mother bent down to pick one and Mr. Kooy, who had come back early as he had promised, laughed heartily.

"Those are dandelions, Katrien," he said, "weeds."

"Weeds?"

"Yes, they come up in the spring and people try to get rid of them."

Shamefacedly, mother stood up.

"I didn't know."

"Oh well, there are lots of things to learn. Alice and I will be over this afternoon to take you shopping and you'll be settled in before you know it."

Turning to father, he clapped him on the shoulder and asked if he had investigated the side-room off the living room yet.

"No," father answered.

"Well, let's go and have a look at it together then."

I followed them as they traipsed through the living room towards a door on the left. When Mr. Kooy opened it, a sizeable space was revealed. It held no furniture and the floor was mud.

"I was thinking," Mr. Kooy trumpeted, with his loud voice as he walked up and down the area, "that if you put in a tile floor, and that's not so expensive, that this could be a good workshop. The owner, by the way, won't do it. I checked with him. But he said that it was fine should you want to do it and he might take a bit off the rent. There are two windows," he continued, pointing to the outside walls, "and they should let in lots of light by which you can conduct your business. As well," he enthused, "there is a light bulb."

He pointed overhead, and father and I looked up simultaneously. We saw a fly-encrusted, dirty bulb dangling from the ceiling, as well as multiple spider webs.

"When customers come," Mr. Kooy orated on, "they will have to come through the front door. I don't know if you noticed that there is a back door as well. It gives entrance into the kitchen. You can put a sign on your front lawn advertising your cobbling and note that people should go to the front door. That way they won't have to go through the kitchen and bother Katrien."

Father shrugged half-heartedly. What was the difference? People would still have to walk through the house. But he said nothing. I went and stood next to him feeling empathy, for I could at that moment clearly see father standing at the railing of the ship, looking out into the distance, hoping, dreaming. This what not what he had dreamt.

"We'll go and see a man this afternoon about a tile floor. I'm sure that by the time it's put in, your crates will have arrived and you can go from there."

Father shrugged again. Perhaps, I could see him reflecting, Mr. Kooy was right. Perhaps this was the way they did business in Canada. But I knew there was only so much money he had been allowed to bring into the country. He had talked about it often enough. And this money would keep us afloat for only so long.

"As well, you will need a car."

"A car?!"

I couldn't help it. The suggestion took me by surprise and I shouted out the words with enthusiasm.

"We are going to try and do without a car for a little while," father interjected, "There is someone from church, the dominee wrote us, who will pick us up each Sunday."

"You can't do without a car, Jaap!"

Mr. Kooy gesticulated with his hands as he spoke.

"I know you don't think you have the money for a car, but the bank will be happy to give you a loan if you can produce a small down payment. Besides that, you have a sponsor. That will speak volumes on your behalf."

Father shook his head.

"For now," he said decisively, and I was proud of him as he spoke, even if I was disappointed about not getting a car, "we will do without."

By and by, things settled down. Mother became accustomed to walking to the nearby shopping center. I went along to help carry the grocery bags back for her. We became acquainted with different

107

members of the church community and we were faithfully picked up for services each Sunday. The side-room was tiled, the walls and ceilings of the entire house were scrubbed, the windows sopped with soap and water, and the ceiling fixtures were cleaned. Then the 'kisten', the crates, arrived and once they were unpacked and familiar things were given a place, a more home-like feeling prevailed.

As soon as father had his workshop in order, he put up notices, with the help of some church members, in the nearby shopping centers, and a few customers began to trickle into his workshop. The summer sped by and I was registered by father in a nearby public school. There was no Christian school, although there was talk at church about starting one. I was not at all excited by the prospect of returning to the classroom. I had not enjoyed school in Holland and saw no reason to expect to like it in Canada either. Besides that, already tall for my thirteen years, I hated the thought of being put into grade six with the eleven-year-olds instead grade eight with my own age group where I really belonged. But I had no choice. My English was still scanty. I'd had little contact with other children during the summer, except for those at church. But the children at church were immigrant children, like myself, and I spoke Dutch with them.

Father deposited me at the principal's office on the first day of school. I carried a brown briefcase. I'd used it in Holland to carry my books and it would have to do service in Canada as well. Father and mother agreed that it would be a waste of money to buy something new. I didn't mind. What I did mind was being brought to school by my father. I hated myself for minding, but I did. But father did not stay and after winking broadly at me behind the principal's back, he disappeared quickly. And then, strangely enough, I wished he were back. The principal took me to a classroom, introduced me to the teacher and the children and also left. It actually only took me a few weeks to acclimatize, and then, amazingly, I began to speak English as if it had been my native tongue.

As the summer months wore to a close, mother was also beginning to feel at home. She loved the flowers in the garden and once she had thoroughly cleaned the house we rented, she considered it her home. In September, when I left for school, I anticipated that she would shed a few tears on my first day. But she did not. As a matter of fact, there was a certain new ethereal quality about her that I could not put my finger on.

"You are different, mother."

I spoke to her after school one day as we were having tea.

"I'm going to have a baby, Peter."

I was dumbfounded. Truly I could see by her face that this news was sweetness to her – that she delighted in it. She laughed at the expression on my face.

"You will have a brother or a sister."

Surreptitiously I studied her belly. But it produced in no way a clear picture of what a brother or sister would look like.

"Have you told father?"

She laughed again – laughed as clear as a bell and this was a joyful sound.

"Yes, I have, you goose."

"Well, what did he say?"

"He said that he was very happy about it. That we would have ourselves a little Canadian child."

"A doctor...?"

"Yes, I have a doctor too. Alice Kooy has taken me to see a doctor. She has been very kind, even though..." and here a shadow crossed her face, "... even though she is not a Christian."

"Oh."

It was all I could think of to say. Mrs. Kooy was as cheerful as her husband and as plump as well. She often brought us extras – sometimes cake, sometimes preserves and sometimes a ride to a park.

"When I tried to talk to her about... well, about Jesus, she told me to stop. Not in a nasty manner, but just plainly. She said, 'Stop, Katrien. You're a sweetheart, but I'm fine the way I am. And you're fine the way you are. So let's not get caught up in these things. But I'd love to help you out with the new baby. How exciting!' That's what she said."

Mother looked at me rather helplessly.

"Well," I said, "then you've done all you could. Maybe we could pray for her."

She smiled.

"Yes, Peter. We will do that."

Recalling this now, I don't believe that at the time I really prayed for Mr. and Mrs. Kooy. Maybe this was because I myself had not yet realized how important it was to belong to God.

Perhaps it was the advent of the child that made mother more content each day in her new surroundings. She always spoke to the baby – whether weeding in the garden, cooking in the kitchen, or shopping in the store – no matter where she was, there were always tender words, soft murmurings that I heard when I walked by her side

"The doctor told me today," mother told us one evening at suppertime, "that I was fine and in good shape, even though I am past the age of forty. He said there are often concerns when a woman is past forty and that he was sure I was aware of that. But he said I was doing very well and that I would be monitored regularly."

Mother did worry about one thing though and that was going to the hospital to have the baby. In Holland she'd had me at home, with the help of a midwife and a doctor. But a hospital intimidated her, even though the ladies at church assured her that she had nothing to fret about.

"The Canadian hospitals are very clean," they all vouched with one voice, "and besides that, you get fine meals and good care. They bring the baby when it has to be fed, change the diapers, and you can sleep and rest. Once you get home, that's over. So enjoy it while you can."

"But who will take care of Peter and Jaap?"

"Oh, don't worry. They will manage. They always do."

The minister's wife, who was speaking to mother, winked at me while she said this.

I laughed and mother smiled as well. But inside her heart I knew she did not care for the idea of being away from home at all. Besides that, the birth would take place during the late winter, early on in March. If there was one thing people agreed upon, it was that Canadian winters were harsh. There was lots of snow and it was very cold!

The months passed quietly. The fall with its magnificent display of colors, awed all of us. I sketched many pictures of the trees in the neighborhood, and of the squirrels in the backyard, mother often by my side while I was drawing. Father's business, although slow in starting, did manage to make household ends meet. I was helpful around the house, and did not complain about school. My first report card had come with a number of comments – comments such as: 'Peter's English is improving rapidly', and 'Peter's math work is much ahead of the rest of the class' and, most importantly to me, 'Art work is outstanding'. Oma Kats sent three dozen Dutch diapers from Holland along with a lengthy letter about how she was knitting and crocheting, and that soon she would send a box with many little baby outfits. It made mother feel secure and she often sat in her rocking chair in front of the living room window and watched the snow deplete God's storehouses in the sky. That's what the minister said when he came to visit, and mother relished that phrase. After all, she said, it was God Who was in charge and who was she to worry. The baby moved inside her. She described the first kicks to me as little butterfly kicks, small hiccups of physical activity. Later as they grew into much harder impatient movements, I could actually detect and feel little hands or feet pushing my mother's flesh.

The doctor told mother during one of her visits to him, that her blood pressure was a trifle on the high side. He said it was nothing to worry about, but that a salt-free diet should be begun and a little extra bed-rest in the afternoon would be helpful. Remembering the miscarriages she'd had in the past, mother faithfully obeyed his orders. She ate her eggs without salt, cooked the potatoes without salt, and even stopped eating salted black licorice. As well, she took a nap each day after lunch. Father usually tucked her in, and then went back to work, whistling as he walked through the living room. I faithfully shoveled the sidewalk, often heavy with the ever-increasing amounts of snow, and made sure mother did not have to lift any groceries or heavy objects.

And yet it was a good three weeks prior to the due date that mother began her labor. It was early afternoon, a Saturday, and I was home, and she had just lain down for her sleep. She had been holding her hand to her back most of the morning and grimaced every now and then.

"Indigestion, Peter," she said, as she noted the worried look on my face.

But just a few minutes into her nap time, she called me and told me to fetch father. Together they decided that it was time to call Alice Kooy, who had volunteered to take them to the hospital no matter what time of day or night. She came immediately and father considered me as I stood in front of him.

"Can I come?"

I knew I could not, and actually I did not want to come. But it seemed the right thing to say. Alice was already tucking mother into the back seat of the car, a blanket draped over her legs.

"I'll be back as soon as I can, son."

It struck me that father called me son. He'd never before called me that as far as I could recall, always addressing me as Peter.

"All right, father."

And then they were gone and there was only the snow falling, the white snow from God's storehouses.

Father was home again by early evening. He told me that births in Canadian hospitals were not the same as the home births in Holland.

"They did not allow me in the delivery room," he said, and the irritation that he had not been allowed in was still evident in his voice, "even though I was there when you were born. The nurses told me that they would let me know when the baby was born and pointed the way to the waiting room."

"So you had to leave mother?"

"Yes."

"Was she all right?"

"Yes. I was allowed to kiss her and I told her I would pray for her and she gave me a small smile, just a small one. Your mother is a brave woman, Peter."

"Then what happened, father?"

"Well, less than an hour later, your little sister was born."

"It's a little girl then?"

"Yes, a girl and her name is Johanna."

I had known it would be Johanna if it was a girl. It meant 'gift of God'.

"You saw the baby, father?"

"They didn't immediately let your mother and I see the baby," he responded slowly, "When I first came into her room, the baby wasn't there. Mother had not even held her – not even really seen her. Then the doctor came in."

"Mother's doctor?"

"Yes, and he congratulated us on our daughter and told us that she was receiving a little oxygen because she wasn't quite able to breathe on her own yet."

"Why not, father?"

My heart was beginning to beat fast and faster.

"Because she was premature, was born a little early. You know that she wasn't due for another few weeks."

I nodded gravely.

"So they put Johanna into an incubator. The doctor told us not to worry, because he was sure she would be fine. It was to be expected that she would need some extra care, he said.

"Oh."

It was all I could say. Father went on talking, sitting with his head in his hands at the kitchen table. I had made him some tea but the cup stood untouched. He kept on talking, but it was almost as if I was not there.

"Some time later they wheeled in the incubator and put it next to mother's bed. Together we looked at the perfect body that was Johanna, our little girl. Her tiny eyes were closed, and her round little stomach pumped up and down, up and down, as if everything in the world depended on that motion. And then, after we had looked at her for a long time, the nurse wheeled the incubator away."

I sighed.

"What about mother, father? What did she say?"

"She was very tired. I kissed her and then I came home."

He looked at me at this point and gave me a weary smile.

"I think I'll go to bed, son."

It was the second time that day he had called me son.

"All right, father."

I went to bed early myself that evening but couldn't fall asleep. The shadows of the limbs on the single maple tree in the yard were outlined on my wall. The branches, naked branches without leaves, were like parents without children. Why did I think such strange thoughts? How was mother right now? Was she able to sleep? I know that I myself did fall asleep in the long run, because the next thing I knew was father's hand gently shaking me awake.

"Peter, I have to go back to the hospital."

"Back? Why?"

My voice was scratchy with sleep and I couldn't quite comprehend what he was saying.

"Because they just called. And...."

Here fear gripped me.

"Is mother?"

"No, mother is fine."

His hand stroked my arm.

"It's the baby," he went on slowly, "the baby...."

114

"The baby?" I repeated.

"Yes, she died."

I was silent. I did not know what to say. With my left hand I plucked some yellow wool tufts off the blanket and crumpled them into a wad in my palm.

"I'm not sure when I'll be back."

Father's voice was uncertain. I knew he did not like to leave me alone this late at night and truthfully, I did not want to be alone. In my heart I felt a little foot kick under the flesh of mother's belly. She'd let me put my hand there often enough. That little foot would never, ever walk. Not on earth that is. And father would never make shoes for those little feet.

"It's all right, father."

"If something happens while I'm away, you can call dominee. You know the number."

"Yes, father."

And then a car honked through the privacy of my bedroom.

"That'll be Alice or Wim Kooy. Goodbye, son."

"Goodbye, father."

Later I remembered with regret that I had not passed along greetings to mother, had not sent her a message. In the darkness of the night surrounding me, I tried to think what message I should have given along. But I could not think of any words. There were only pictures – pictures of roses, of snowflakes falling from the great expanse of the sky, of dandelions and other things she loved to see.

"What will you call the baby, mother?"

"Well, if it is a boy like you, then we'll call him John. If it is a girl, Johanna. Both names mean the same thing – 'beloved of God'.

Now the 'beloved of God' had died. Why?! And why?! My finger plucked more tufts of wool off the yellow blanket.

"Don't do that, Peter. You'll wear the blanket thin and then it won't keep you warm."

I heard mother's voice clearly. I got up and went to my parents' room. The cradle, ready for life, stood at the foot of the bed. I carried it over to my father's workshop, placing it near the workbench. Then I shut the door to the workshop. I wished I could have seen the baby.

A few days later that week, I did get my wish – at the funeral home. I viewed a beautiful, well-formed little body in the casket and I stared at my dead sister for a long, long time. Then, in the privacy of my bedroom, I drew her picture. The funeral was held while mother was still in the hospital. Our small church was packed. Every family came to bury my tiny sister, but mother was glaringly absent. Actually, mother stayed in the hospital for a few more weeks. They moved her out of maternity to a different ward, but it was still the hospital. She was diagnosed as disoriented, confused and unable to cope. Father was away to visit her each day and most days when I came home from school, no one was home. I told myself again and again that it did not really matter. After all, I was fourteen years old now and that was that. But it was almost as if father and mother had forgotten me, as if they did not remember that they still had a child.

When mother eventually returned home, she was quiet. Her belly was loose, flabby almost, and her eyes, for the most part, unseeing. She cooked and cleaned but said very few words – only mouthing the necessary 'yesses' and 'nos'. But she did, in the evening, ask me to draw. Father had made me an easel and I would carry it to the front room and sketch. Mother sat in her chair knitting socks for myself and father, seemingly relaxed as she watched me. Perhaps she was recalling the times in Holland when we had sat together out in the fields. It was hard to know as she rarely responded and said very little.

"Give her time," father said, "Please, Peter, give her time."

The second week after she was home, mother startled me with her presence in the hallway of my school when it was time to go home. She gave me no greeting, appearing tall, even as she slouched against the wall, looking alternately from the floor to myself. Some of the children in my class stopped and stared at her; others grinned and pointed; but most just walked past.

"Mother?"

I came over to stand in front of her. She met my gaze for an instant, smiled briefly, took my hand and immediately turned towards the door.

"Wait, mother. I need to get my coat and boots."

She let go of my hand and I moved towards the coat peg that held my winter jacket. After I put it on, I bent down to take off my shoes and put on my boots. Standing next to me, mother was motionless. It made me uncomfortable. After I stood up, I put on my mittens. She again took me by the hand, making a beeline for the door. I let myself be pulled, speaking as we moved.

"Why are you here, mother?"

It did no good. No matter what I said, she would not answer. Directing me past the myriad snowmen lining the sidewalk, snowmen who were melting in the spring thaw, we walked as the crow flies through a jumble of children slipping and sliding about in the schoolyard towards the street that meant home.

Father met us at the door.

"Mother met me at school," I said by way of explanation.

"I see."

Perhaps he did. I did not. But he made no other comment. Mother calmly took off her boots, neatly placed them under the coat rack, took off her coat, hung it up, smiled briefly and headed for the kitchen. There we heard her filling the teakettle with water, as she did each day when I arrived home. Father shook his head slowly, raised his eyebrows at me, and disappeared into his workshop.

The next day mother was waiting for me once more after school. And again the next day and the next. By now, some of the other children were calling me a 'mama's boy', or worse, trailed us out of the hall into the schoolyard, mimicking mother's pronounced slouch, dancing around us until we reached the road. I hated it and began to hate mother as well. I spoke with father.

"Can't you stop her from coming, father?"

"She is worried that you won't come home, Peter."

"Why? You can tell her that I will come. Can't you do that?"

He shook his head at me.

"Why?" I asked again.

But I knew the answer within myself. Mother had lost the baby and she was afraid that she would also lose me. She thought that if she placed herself by the school door, in the school hall, that there would be less chance of ... Of what? I did not know. But this I did know, mother's daily meeting me was far worse than when no one had been home for me.

There was a small tombstone in the graveyard. It was only the width of a ruler and a half and the length of a large book. It had the words *"Johanna Pret – Safe in the Arms of Jesus"* engraved on it. Father, mother and I had gone to look. The ground had been soft enough to inter the minuscule coffin. But there was still snow on the grave.

"She is gone?"

After standing on the path by the grave for a long time, mother spoke the words out loud. I thought it passing strange that she could not associate the grave and the words on the little stone with the fact that Johanna was dead. I did not understand that mother did not grasp that the empty cradle which still stood in father's workshop meant that Johanna would not come to lie in it.

"She is gone?"

I could see her on the ship's deck waving goodbye to my grandparents. The farewell had been difficult for her, but it had been something in which she had participated; it had been something she had seen with her eyes. Perhaps if she had been able to see the child die; perhaps if she had held the child. She had not. I knew she had not from what father had told me. And then I saw father at the ship's railing.

"What do you see, father?"

"I'm seeing something that you likely don't see when you draw. For you see what is there. A person, a thing, or an area into which you can physically walk. I see what is not there – at least not yet."

What was it that mother ought to see in order to let go, in order to hope?

The following Sunday I asked the dominee if I could speak with him after the morning service. Dominee shook hands with people as they came out of church, and when I asked if I could speak with him I felt as if everyone around me was listening, wondering why a fourteen-year-old boy would want to speak to dominee. But the dominee simply smiled and nodded and went on shaking hands. I went and stood by the closet where dominee always hung his toga. But when he was done greeting people, he did not bother to take off his black toga, but just walked past me and indicated I should follow him into the consistory room. I was just a trifle intimidated. After all, I did not know him very well as yet, not as well as I had known the dominee in Holland.

"My mother," I began, and then stopped short.

It was actually not only about mother but also about myself that I wanted to speak. I had lain awake many nights now thinking about Johanna. Mother might miss her and want her, but I had a question.

"Yes," the dominee encouraged.

"Well," I tried again, "how do you know... I mean, where is the baby now?"

"In heaven."

"But how do you know?"

"Because she was one of Jesus' sheep."

"How do you know?"

"Because your parents are both believers in the Lord Jesus. Your mother and your father – they are both sheep. And that makes your little sister the child of sheep – that makes her one of His little lambs."

"Oh."

The dominee had a very matter-of-fact, easy tone of voice. I looked down at my hands before I posed my next question.

"How do you draw heaven?"

The dominee was taken aback. I could see it in his face when I looked up.

"Draw heaven?"

He repeated the words rather weakly.

"Yes, I would like to draw heaven."

"I can't tell you how to do that, Peter."

"Who could?"

"Well," the dominee's voice was hesitant, almost as if he were groping for a handle that he could not see, "heaven is something we hope in, or for... It's a land, but mostly it's being with our Lord and Savior."

My eyes were riveted on his face.

"Can I draw God?"

"No," the dominee's answer was immediate.

"But He has drawn us," I replied slowly, recalling almost verbatim, the conversation I had with mother in the field while drawing cows.

"God has made us," she had said, "and we belong to Him."

"Does that make you feel like you were drawn, mother?"

I remembered that she had laughed at that, had called me a little theologian. The dominee was regarding me with a mixture of surprise and wonder.

"You know, Peter, the word draw means more than putting pencil to paper. Drawing can also mean pulling – as in tugging hard. I'm going to give you a verse to read in the Bible. I'm going to give you a text that might be good for you to memorize – a text in which Jesus talks about drawing."

"Yes?"

"You'll find it in John 6:44. I won't tell you what it says. But I think that it will be good for you to look it up and think about it. Will you do that?"

"John 6:44?" I repeated.

"Yes, that's it."

I nodded and then the minister got up and walked towards the door. He opened it, but before he walked out he stopped, turned and reached out his hand. I was right behind him, took his hand and we shook.

"Have a good Sunday, Peter."

"Thank you, sir."

That afternoon I looked up the text the dominee had given me in my Bible.

"No one," the verse said, *"can come to Me unless the Father Who sent Me draws him. And I will raise him up on the last day."*

I lay down on my bed and drew up my hands under my head. God drew; He pulled; He tugged. That's what dominee said it meant. His drawing then, was not like my drawing at all. I read the text again.

"No one can come to Me unless the Father Who sent Me draws him. And I will raise him up on the last day."

It sounded like God pulled people. Pulled them where? To Me, it said, and the Me was Jesus. And the last day – what was that?! You had Sundays and holidays, and birthdays. But the last day? Well, it must be what it said – the last day of everything. And raised up? I sat up in my bed. I remembered the story of the little girl, the daughter of Jairus, whom Jesus had raised from the dead. That must be what it meant. I wished that Jesus could have done that to Johanna. How surprised everyone would have been – and how happy! Now Johanna would have to wait until that last day. I lay down again, putting my hands back under my head. God the Father drew; He pulled. He pulled people out of the grave – out of death – to Jesus. This was what the text meant. I just knew it. I shut my eyes and felt myself engulfed in something I could not see; and I felt sure of something that I could not put my finger on.

Later that week, I showed mother the crumpled picture I had drawn of Johanna. I had looked at it so often that it had smudge marks. She took it in her lap and smoothed it out.

"You drew this, Peter?"

"Yes," I said, happy that she was responding and then added quickly, "and no."

"Yes and no?"

She smiled in a way that I remembered from before, from before the baby was born. I took a breath.

"Yes," I began haltingly, "I drew Johanna on the paper when I saw her. I drew her on the paper you are holding, mother."

She looked at me, her face a question. Her hands kept smoothing the picture, as if by smoothing it out, something better would emerge.

"But, no," I went on, "I did not draw her out of the grave – out of the little grave where her body lies in the cemetery. God will do that drawing. He draws in a different way than I draw. His drawing is a pulling, mother. God will pull her out of the grave where we buried her."

My words sounded, to my own ears, strange – they sounded rather silly and futile. It was quiet in the living room. Steam rose from the teacups. Father coughed in the workshop. His door was open. He must be able to hear our conversation. Mother studied the picture in her lap intently. Drawing a breath, I went on.

"It says so in the Bible, mother, so it must be true. The dominee gave me a text in John 4," I continued, if a soft voice.

Father coughed again, louder this time. And for some strange reason, I felt as if I were riding a bicycle. I was riding and mother was on the back seat, her arms around my waist, and the wind was in our back. And we were riding towards the safety of a house.

"I did draw the picture in your lap, mother. The picture is Johanna as she was on earth. But God drew her much better than I ever could – and He drew her right into heaven."

Mother looked away from the picture then. And she looked at me with eyes full of tears – but they were clear eyes, eyes that saw me.

"Thank you, for showing me the drawing, Peter," she said, and then she took a sip of her tea.

4: When You Open Your Hand

These all look to You, to give them their food in due season. When You give it to them, they gather it up; when You open Your hand, they are filled with good things. When you hide Your face, they are dismayed; when You take away their breath, they die and return to their dust. When You send forth Your Spirit, they are created, and You renew the face of the ground (Psalm 104:27-30).

Because the road had been dusty and the weather warm for the last few days, and because he'd quite had his fill of quaint villages and lonely lakes, of hillsides and edelweiss, Otto decided it was time to desist from his walking tour. Sightseeing in nearby bustling Munich was appealing. Leaving a well-worn mountain path, he purposefully took a right turn onto a bigger road. An hour or so later, within Munich's city limits, he asked the first passerby where the tourist office might be.

"At the *Hauptbahnhof*, the train station."

The helpful answer was accompanied by a smile and some pointing. Consequently, Otto had no trouble locating either the station or the tourist office. With the help of a friendly attendant and the purchase of a city map, he trekked on to *Marienplatz*, Mary's Square, the heart of Munich.

The square was alive with fountains, fruit stands, and pedestrians. Tables and chairs spilled onto the sidewalk from crowded cafes. Otto took off his backpack by one of these cafes and sank down onto a solid, wooden armchair for a well-deserved rest. He'd been on the road for many days, only stopping for breaks at youth hostels. Stretching his long legs in front of him, he studied the square while he waited for his order.

"You must visit the *Frauenkirche*," he was told by the friendly waiter, as he placed cold beer and some bread on the table.

Eager for conversation, the fellow pointed to the lofty twin towers of a church in the distance, repeating, "*Domkirche zu unserer lieben Frau*" which Otto understood to mean, "The Church of our dear Lady."He was quite proficient in German really. He'd always enjoyed languages - languages and working with his hands. The waiter puttered about, keeping up a running commentary about the weather and other local sights, even as he constantly wiped the surface of the small table around Otto's food with a damp cloth. He noted, with a great deal of curiosity, Otto's right hand resting on the edge of his chair. That is to say, he permitted his eyes to rest for a long moment on the leather glove which fitted snugly around Otto's right hand. Otto followed the waiter's glance.

"An accident?" the man ventured carefully, stopping his cleaning and rearranging the beer stein and bread platter just so in front of Otto, "The young herr has had an accident?"

"*Ja* - yes."

Otto offered no further explanation and pointedly ignoring the man, began studying his newly acquired city map. After waiting a few more seconds, the waiter shrugged and left. Otto took no notice. Taking a long draught of the cold beer, before he took a bite of the crusty bread, he decided that seeing the Frauenkirche might be a worthwhile endeavor before trying to find a hotel for the night.

A half an hour later, quite refreshed, Otto stood up, strapped on his backpack, and began to walk in the direction of the Frauenkirche. He passed the *Rathaus*, the Munich city hall, just as the carillon began to play. People in front of him pointed up and following their gaze, he saw life-size figures – knights jousting in a mock tournament – high up by the bell tower. The spectacle of the bells and the clocks soured his mood. Without knowing it, he clenched his left fist, almost crushing the Munich map. Not giving the figures another glance, he continued on until the next corner brought him face to face with the Frauenkirche.

The Frauenkirche was an overpowering edifice. Its onion-domed twin towers – towers which dwarfed all the other structures in the neighborhood – straddled the roof. For a moment Otto stood transfixed, craning his neck. Then he sprinted up the entrance steps to the big, wooden doors. Pushing the right side open with his left hand, his backpack somehow caught on the door handle. Losing his balance, he stumbled and almost fell inside. A hand caught him under the elbow.

"Be careful."

It was a soft voice and he turned to look into the smiling face of a young woman.

"Thank you."

He blushed and inadvertently put the leather-gloved right hand into his jacket pocket. She let go of his elbow and asked if he was visiting Munich.

"Yes, I'm here to see the sights."

He hated his answer. It was neither bright nor witty, something he suddenly wanted to be.

"Then you've never seen the Frauenkirche before?"

"No."

His blush deepened. Tongue-tied, he stared at the girl. She did not walk on, but stayed by his side. Dark eyes, dark hair and even white teeth all combined to produce a strikingly beautiful picture.

"Will you allow me to show it to you?"

"Are you a guide?"

Perhaps he thought, she was looking for work, for a way to earn some money. But she didn't look like a guide.

"No, I am not. I am just someone who enjoys the magnificent splendor of this place. So may I have the honor of showing it to you?"

"Yes."

It was impossible for his mind to formulate any longer sentence.

"Well then, my name is Emmy Bauer."

She put out her right hand and he shook it awkwardly with his left. She had a very soft warm palm and he became increasingly conscious of the leather glove hidden in his right pocket.

"My name is Otto – Otto Haak."

"Are you from around here, Otto?"

"No, I'm from... well, I'm from...."

She laughed.

"Sounds like you don't know where you're from."

"Well, the thing is, I was born in Holland but I've lived in Germany for a number of years. I was... I was...."

He stopped and she nodded, encouragingly.

"*Was is dein beruf*? What is your trade?"

"I actually have no trade," he answered rather gruffly, "That is to say, I don't have a trade anymore. But I was an apprentice in Hamburg learning the clock trade."

While they were talking, he followed the girl's lead as she walked towards a staircase and began to ascend the steps of one of the towers of the church. The ascent was rather steep and that put an end to their conversation, a fact for which he was thankful. When they reached the top after a lengthy climb, the view was breathtaking. All of Munich stretched out below. The tiny figures of the people milling about on the square, the expanse of immense sky above, as well as the rising Alps behind the city, all made Otto feel small and insignificant.

"It's very impressive," he said to Emmy who was standing next to him, arms over the railing as she gazed out at the horizon.

"I love coming here," she said, "It's both peaceful and powerful and I think of what God sees when He looks down at us."

"God?" he repeated.

"Yes, God. Don't you believe in Him?"

He clenched the right fist in his pocket.

"I don't know."

"Oh," she said.

The wind blew black tendrils of hair about her profile and the setting sun gave the strands a lustrous bluish hue.

Later downstairs, after she had guided him past the rose windows in the sanctuary constructed, as she told him, in 1392; and after she had shown him the black marble grave in memory of Prince Maximilian I, they stood in the back of the church. Otto was enjoying himself immensely, and was glad when Emmy continued her historical discourse.

"There's a legend," she said, pointing to a large casting in a square at Otto's feet, "which tells a story about the architect of the church, Jörg von Halspach. The legend relates that von Halspach accepted a challenge from the devil to build a church without windows."

Looking down, Otto saw a footprint in the casting, a footprint with a small hooked tail at the heel.

"But von Halspach, who, by the way, accepted the devil's challenge, didn't really want to build a church without windows. So he tricked the devil by setting up these columns in the entrance hall."

Patting the large columns at their side, Emmy moved to stand behind them beckoning Otto to join her. Their position hid the windows. Emmy grinned at him and continued her explanation.

"It is said that when the devil first came into the church and stood here where we are standing, the pillars obscured his view of the windows. To him the church really did appear to be windowless. But when he walked on into the church proper he discovered that he had been tricked. Losing his temper, he stamped his foot in anger and that is what you see there."

Otto smiled and walking back to the casting, put his foot on top of the imprint.

"Do you believe in the devil?"

Emmy's voice was curious.

"I told you already, I'm not sure what I believe any more."

Slightly irritated, Otto took his foot off the imprint and turned away.

"I'm sorry," Emmy said.

"What are you sorry about? You don't know...."

He stopped abruptly, knowing he sounded unreasonably rude. Continuing in a calmer voice, he stared past her at the windows.

"I was raised in an orphanage in Rotterdam and through the patronage of some altruistic person, was sent on to Hamburg as apprentice to a clock-maker when I was eighteen. It was fine work and I loved it."

He halted before drawing his right hand out of his pocket.

"But a number of years later, last fall actually, there was an accident. A heavy box fell on my right hand, crushing it. Later there was surgery – reconstructive skin graft surgery. Consequently, there was no chance of my continuing on as apprentice to the clock-maker, even though I did regain some use of the fingers."

Emmy's eyes registered sympathy but she said nothing and her gaze never left his face.

"My employer was generous in paying out a year's stipend – very generous actually. And for the last month or two I've been traveling through Germany, sightseeing and walking and thinking."

"So there is a pillar in your life that hides windows?"

Her voice was soft and coming to stand beside him, she now put her own foot in the casting.

"It is called the *Teufelstritt,* this mark, or the devil's footprint. But I think that often we also make footprints like his because we refuse to see windows."

Although moved by the compassion in her voice, Otto was irritated by her words.

"You don't know," he said, cutting the conversation short, "and you have no idea. I think we'd better be going. It's getting late and there's a guard coming to close the doors."

"My father," said Emmy, as she walked beside him back to the entrance doors, "is looking for someone. He is a farmer and needs help. Why don't you...."

He did not let her finish.

"Didn't you hear what I just told you?"

His voice was louder than it had been.

"My hand was crushed. True, I can manage a number of things, but...."

With the copper, onion-domed towers straining over them, they now stood on the church steps. Emmy took a pencil and a piece of paper out of her pocket. Using her purse as backing, she wrote on the paper.

"Here," she said, giving it to him, "if you change your mind, I think you would like it where we live."

Then she was gone, gone down the steps, down the street, and around the corner, without even once turning her head.

And now here it was fifteen years later, fifteen fruitful years later. Otto had been employed by his father-in-law, a dairy farmer near Munich, for most of that time. He had obtained a work permit. Even though he had often considered returning to his native Holland in the decade preceding World War II, he had never done so. It was not that he was unhappy working on the farm because, truth be told, he had enjoyed learning to work the soil and care for the animals. His injured hand had strengthened, had become accustomed to the farm labor. Neither was he was homesick. But there was something within himself which intuitively felt he had not yet reached that place where he was supposed to be. Working outside in the fields, he often imagined himself walking along a road, a road that wound its way upwards and onwards to some unknown destination. He desired to see what was beyond the bend, beyond the trees and the hills on the horizon. Emmy, however, whose parents and grandparents had lived and died in the area, was not so easily persuaded to leave.

"We are happy here," she flatly stated and smiled at him.

Even when he pointed out to her that the restrictions which the National Socialist German Labor Party imposed on many people were leading from bad to worse times, she shook her head.

"Life's not perfect anywhere."

It was true. Life was not perfect anywhere. It was 1941 and bombs were falling with such regularity that even the cows were no longer alarmed by the sound. Otto had no ties to Holland. He had no relatives who wanted him to move back to his native country. Raised in an orphanage, he possessed no letters, pictures or memories to draw him back across the border.

"But to be drawn back," he thought to himself, "is not the same as being pushed out."

He often pondered deeply as he worked the German soil in the fields around the farm, as he took care of the cows in the stable and curried the horses in their stalls. Why was it that he was in this particular place? Why had he met Emmy at just that time in the Frauenkirche in Munich when she was visiting an aunt whom she only saw about twice a year? Why had she fallen in love with him, a cripple with a crushed hand? He shrugged and kicked a clod of earth as he stood in front of the barndoor, gazing out at the fields of sugar beets, rye, oats and vegetables. His father-in-law, Hermann Bauer, preferred to produce his own fodder. A native German, he was a decent, friendly fellow who had shown nothing but courtesy and affection for the Hollander, the man his daughter had brought home. Was he, Otto Haak, now also a German by virtue of his wife's and his father-in-law's acceptance? He thought not. Did mucking out a German stable and milking German cows make him German? Grinning to himself, he patted a nuzzling heifer with his leather-gloved right hand. Although not limber like his left hand, and certainly not able to perform delicate work, there was no doubt that farming had surely been good for it.

"Moo for me in German," he whispered to the heifer.

Wind blew through the half-open barn door behind him, picking up straw-dust, whirling it about, irritating Otto's nose. He sneezed and turned to close the barn door but continued his pondering. Herta

Bauer, his mother-in-law had some Polish blood, but she was as German a *hausfrau* as he could imagine. Was there a nationality to which he belonged? Truth be told, he did not really feel Dutch. Was there a creed which he confessed? And would such a confession make him a citizen of something? Life was complicated and he sighed. Emmy's family attended the local Lutheran church. Their attendance, however, had become extremely sporadic because Hermann was convinced that the pastor was a Nazi who preached party slogans and not the Bible. Although not devout, Hermann would occasionally pray with the family when they hid in the farmhouse cellar listening to British planes flying overhead towards Munich. Hermann had been disillusioned about Hitler ever since the Nazis had arrested him in 1934 after he had attended a local propaganda meeting.

Standing outside, the wind blowing through his blond hair, Otto recalled vividly what Hermann had told him about that meeting. The speaker on the platform had depicted Jews as dishonest. When Hermann stood up to disagree, he had been asked to step to the front of the hall where the meeting was being held.

"You do business with Jews?"

As if on cue the crowd, goaded by the officer in charge, laughed uproariously. Hermann, angry and prodded by integrity and a desire to defend truth, answered defensively.

"Yes. Yes, I do. And well you all know that Herr Stein, for example, who supplied furniture for many of you for most of your life, was forced to sell his business to the Reich. He was paid only one tenth of what he should have been paid. He was paid 80,000 marks instead of 800,000 marks. He went to the Commandant, Heinrich von Schwer, because he thought the price offered was a mistake, but then he disappeared and who knows where the man is right now. But I do know who owns his business right now!"

"Oh, Herr Bauer! Herr Bauer!!"

The chairman interrupted. A tinge of dismay underlined his exclamation.

"You are the victim of Yiddish tales. Believe me, we know the Jews! Herr Stein inflated his prices because he wanted German money. His Jewish greed was obvious."

"That's not true! Herr Stein was an honest man. Everyone here...."

Hermann was interrupted again.

"Don't let those Jews fool you, Herr Bauer. But now let's get on with business. You may sit down again. We've taken up too much precious time here already with this trivial matter. Let's continue to discuss ways in which good Aryan businessmen can acquire Jewish concerns and property."

After the meeting, on his way back to the farm, Hermann had been arrested by the Gestapo. Although he was neither beaten nor charged with anything, he was jailed. His cell was a tiny cubicle. It held only a bed, a stool, a toilet and a dirty high window through which he could catch bittersweet and tiny glimpses of the sky. It also contained two books – a Bible and a copy of a work by Luther entitled *"Against the Robbing and Murdering Hords of Peasants."* Hermann presumed that the Nazis, knowing him to be Lutheran, had placed Luther's book down for him to read. They wanted him to know and understand that Luther believed that loyalty to the authorities in charge was paramount and that rebels, meaning Jews, should be punished without mercy. Hermann heard other prisoners in neighboring cells crying out in pain. He also often heard cries for mercy followed by gunshots. Having nothing else to do, Hermann read the Bible.

"The Nazis," Hermann told Otto, as he recounted his prison stint, "wrongly supposed that I would begin to believe that God did not want me to question their authority."

The Nazi army chaplain who told Hermann that "too much stubbornness could lead to trouble," beat a hasty retreat after Hermann waved a fist in his face and threatened to throw him out.

"...if the ruler is a Christian," Luther had written, *"the peasants have no case against him...."*

But the truth was that the Nazis were not Christian and after several months of imprisonment, and one severe beating which left Hermann permanently deaf in one ear, he was free to return to the farm.

Each passing year after the 1934 incident saw Hermann become more tight-lipped whenever anyone mentioned his imprisonment. Embittered, he steadfastly refused to say *Heil Hitler*. Instead he gave the old greeting 'Gruss Gott'. It was a greeting almost always intentionally misunderstood by the SS men as the imperative 'Greet God', and not as Hermann meant it as 'May God bless you.' Consequently, soldiers were apt to answer rather profanely, 'Yes, when you see Him'. Hermann had not been rearrested for this lapse of patriotism, but on trips into town he was often detained. The Gestapo, time and time again, made him wait for hours on end for no reason at all. But Emmy always said she was glad that he was not being deported and that waiting, even for hours, was better than being sent to the front. Perhaps the leniency shown was because Heinrich von Schwer, a local boy who had made it to the post of Commandant, had been, at one time, according to his mother-in-law, sweet on Emmy. As things stood, life outside the Bauer farm was ignored as much as possible.

"God is God and He is in heaven and yes, I believe in Him, as you also should." Hermann Bauer responded emphatically to Otto when he once asked him if he believed.

"And," he had continued, "the soil is a gift from Him. If I work it, and get my hands dirty in it, then God will use it to repay me richly. He always has."

True to his own words, Hermann worked hard. Otto, following his example, worked hard also. Consequently, like his father-in-law, he grew to love farming. Emmy stood to inherit. She was an only child. A long time ago, Emmy told him, it used to be German custom to divide property between sons but that custom had died out and it was now the right of the first-born, male or female, to take both land

133

and title. But it remained to be seen if there would be anything left of the farm if the war kept on. There was not much these days that anyone could keep for him or herself. Everyone's major objective right now was simply to have enough food to remain alive. The far north field was shell-pitted. Three cows had died there and several others had miscarried. It was providential really, that Hermann was now deaf in one ear because of his prison term and that Otto had his bad hand. Conscription passed both of them right by.

Otto and Emmy had no children. They had been married in 1927 and although there was still a faint glimmer of hope in Emmy's eyes when she watched her neighbor push a perambulator down the dirt path towards the river for an afternoon stroll, Otto nursed no such dreams. Barren was barren, and when a cow was barren, there was not much you could do about it except butcher the animal. Not that he wanted Emmy butchered. She was a good wife and he loved her dearly. He had done so since he had first laid eyes on her. The only thing he could fault her with was that she seemed to have her eyes open only as far as the fields surrounding their home stretched.

In the fall of 1941 Rudi Ritter, a friend of Hermann who lived in Munich, came and stayed at the farm for a week. He was a polio survivor and limped, thus making him unfit for the German army. Rudi was a cheerful sort of fellow. Pushing his chair back from the kitchen table after lunch one day, he smiled at everyone.

"So what's the difference between Hitler and a dud bomb, Emmy?" he asked.

Emmy stopped her work at the sink and turned, round-eyed.

"I don't know," she said.

"There is no difference," Rudi laughed and slapped himself on the thigh in glee.

Hermann Bauer, mildly perturbed, stood up.

"You do well to keep your jokes to yourself," he said, "It's enough that I'm feeding and housing you without having to worry about the SS breathing down my back."

"Well you might worry," Rudi retorted, "because the Gestapo has begun to seize buildings belonging to the churches. I've just heard from a friend in Münster that they've taken over the nunnery there."

Following his father-in-law's example, Otto stood up as well.

"The nunnery?" he asked, puzzled.

"Yes, they're letting on that it's for people injured in the air raids, that it's going to be a hospital of sorts. But I'm pretty sure it's an anti-religious action."

Rudi stood up as well while he was talking.

"Well, Hermann," he continued, "I'm not one to eat the bread of charity, so what can I to help you this afternoon?"

"Why," Otto continued, ignoring Rudi's question about working, "Why do you say it's anti-religious?"

"Otto, you must surely read the paper sometimes!! Think of the number of occasions that demonstrations by Roman Catholics have taken place in Münster against the Nazis."

It was quiet for a moment. Hermann stood with his hand on the outside door handle, but did not leave. Rudi went on.

"Well, maybe you people don't read the newspapers. I know you certainly rarely venture out to Munich any more or to other cities. And," he paused for a moment, "I also know that you don't attend church anymore."

"At Christmas," Emmy piped up, "last Christmas I...."

Rudi laughed and interrupted her.

"Sure, Emmy. As if that counts. Well, I plan to go to Münster next week to attend services. I hear tell through the grapevine that Count Galen, the Bishop of Münster, is planning something. But I'll tell you right now that the Gestapo has no intention whatsoever of turning that nunnery in Münster into a hospital. My friend saw them tossing rosaries onto the street and children as well as old people from charity homes have been ordered to leave the city."

"Leave?"

Otto repeated the words rather foolishly and later, as he worked outside, contemplated on what he would have done if he had been ordered to leave the orphanage when he was a child. Was a crime worse when it was against a church? Against a child? What made up the church anyway? In the orphanage he had been brought up as a Protestant, but the matter of faith had been presented to him as memorizing catechism, staying physically clean, and attending both school and church faithfully. That is to say, if you did what people said you should do, then it was an accepted fact that you were a Christian. Should he be upset that the Nazis were desecrating and taking over churches? Should he be angry that old people and children were being turned out into the street? And it came to him that he had wanted to leave Germany for a long time now. He shrugged and caught a glimpse of his father-in-law walking down a field in the distance. He owed the man a great deal, even as he owed the soil. Kneeling down, Otto crumbled black earth between his hands. It trickled down between his fingers like water.

When Emmy went into a neighboring village on her bicycle the following week to visit a friend and to see if she could find a shop which would sell her some material for a skirt, she heard more about the matter of Münster. It was apparently well-known that Count Galen, the Bishop of Münster had sent a letter to Adolf Hitler himself protesting the requisitioning of church buildings and the expulsion of the people. As well, Count Galen had sent letters to the chief of the Gestapo himself, Herr Himmler, and to Herr Lammers, head of the Reich Chancellery.

"Even if Count Galen could wait forever," Emmy's friend said, "he wouldn't get an answer to his letters."

Rudi came by the following week to tell them more, visiting in the barn.

"I don't know if I want to hear what you have to say."

Hermann was up and out of the barn before Rudi could stop him.

"You can't hide your head in the sand, man," Rudi yelled after his retreating figure, "every good German citizen should hear about this."

Otto came and stood in front of Rudi.

"You can tell me," he said.

"You know," Rudi answered, "as far as that goes, you're not even a German citizen, so why should you care? But even those who are not German citizens should know."

Otto did not move away but stood quietly and said, "Why? Why should I know, Rudi? Is it more important than the farm work?"

"That's right, son," Hermann added, suddenly reappearing in the open barn door, "Tell him how busy we are . Tell him we have more important things to do."

Then he left again, stomping heavily down the barnyard towards the house, carrying a broken harness.

"If you care for your wife, your home and your soul, Otto, you'll want to hear," Rudi carried on unperturbed. "That's all I can say. And that's all I will say because as of today I won't visit here anymore if I'm not welcome."

"You are welcome, Rudi. Don't be silly. Now please tell me what happened in Münster."

And Rudi sat down on a bale of straw and told him.

"There is a big church in Münster, Otto. It is a church that has stained glass windows, high ceilings, and images everywhere."

"Like the *Frauenkirche* in Munich?"

"Well, not that big. Anyway, I sat down in the back of this church. I was late for the meeting and the church was very full. I mean, it was packed. The Bishop walked in – very impressive. Nice gown, gold staff – you know, the works. He mounted the pulpit and began to address the people in the church in a booming voice. I'll say this for him, he did not appear to be in the least afraid. I looked around for some Gestapo uniforms, but didn't see any."

"So what did he say?"

Otto was curious. Rudi took a paper out of his coat pocket, unfolded it and read aloud:

"I, bishop of Münster, have voted against Hitler. For one single man cannot in peace, and much less in war, bear the sole responsibility for the fate of Germany. The authoritarian system is the system of the police state. I come of old German family stock. Thirty-one members of my family have fallen on

the battlefield. I am a German patriot and it is as a German patriot that I speak to you today. I accuse the secret police, which I call Germany's most dangerous enemy. Confidence and security under the law are necessary requisites for a country's strength. In Münster there is no justice for people who have lived all their lives according to the law and in love of their neighbor."

Emmy, who had walked into the barn just prior to Rudi's reading of the Bishop's speech, took Otto's left hand and squeezed it. He glanced at her and was surprised to see a dark red flushing her cheeks.

"The innocent have been expelled without reason. To my letters of protest I received only one answer from Minister Lammers. What does that mean, except that the accused sit in judgment over us? Let us pray for the innocent victims of the Gestapo."

A shaft of sunlight shone in through the barn door. The ray of light extended the width of the barn. Deep within himself, Otto longed for the courage and faith which the Bishop of Münster seemed to possess. Looking up, he searched the barn roof. Was God there – above, beyond? Did He allow things like this to happen so that...? So that what?

"What happened afterwards?" Emmy asked as Rudi folded the paper back up and returned it to his vest pocket.

"He was arrested."

"Arrested?"

"Yes, as soon as he left the church. The Gestapo were waiting for him. I didn't see them in church, but someone must have been listening in the foyer. He was not taken to jail but to his own home. That's where he's being kept under detention."

Rudi left and Emmy returned to the kitchen. Otto stood on a hillock just outside the barn and searched the horizon. To the far left he could see a train passing. It was traveling north. Trains passed often, quite often, and Rudi told stories about the trains as well.

The next day, before he got up to do chores, Emmy snuggled against Otto in bed and told him that she was expecting a baby.

"Oh, Emmy!"

It was all he could manage and then Emma cried and cried for a long time while he just held her.

"I have prayed for it," she finally managed, "Oh, Otto! I did very much want to bear you a child. God is so good to us, isn't He?"

Otto didn't know. He truly didn't know. Over her shoulder he contemplated the leather glove on his right hand, a glove which he also wore at night. But if he had not had the accident, would he have met Emmy? His arms tightened around her.

"When, Emmy?"

"In about six months. I didn't want to tell you until I was three months along."

She stopped and then continued.

"It's just, you see, that other women are always talking about that if you pass the first three months, then there's less chance of a miscarriage."

"So that would make it September?"

"Yes, September."

The summer passed without too much change on the farm. Only Emmy's stomach grew and grew even as the sugar beets, the rye and the oats and the vegetables grew. And many evenings when they huddled together in the safety of the farmhouse cellar, Hermann prayed with more conviction than Otto had ever heard him pray before.

"Heavenly Father, if we live through the war, I will witness to this child as a Christian grandfather should witness to a grandchild; and I will build a chapel on one of the fields so that others can worship here also."

"We should all leave," Otto said for the umpteenth time, after the 'Amen' had sounded firmly from Hermann's lips. "I really mean it, we should all leave Germany."

"Otto. Please!"

139

Emmy looked at him, eyes round with apprehension. But Otto continued even though he knew that Herta and Hermann would totally ignore what he said.

"I have heard Rudi mention guides who take people across the border to Austria and from there to Switzerland."

"But what would we do there?"

Emma was the only one who responded.

"Live," Otto answered, and repeated, "Live. Because we cannot continue to live here."

In September the baby was born. And it died as soon as it was born. Otto briefly held the tiny body that his mother-in-law brought out from the bedroom into the kitchen. He saw a small, wizened face cushioned by a yellow blanket. Taking the little body from his arms, Herta asked him to go into the bedroom to see Emmy. He did so on brown-knit stocking feet.

Emmy lay with her eyes shut. She didn't open them, even when he kissed her cheek and stroked her dark hair. But she whispered to him.

"You are right, Otto. There is no God."

"I didn't say that there was no God, Emmy, only that I...."

He stopped. In spite of himself he was shocked. Emmy was always full of faith, always cheerful and always full of hope.

"But He is not there, Otto."

Emmy's whisper was more like a whimper and then she opened her eyes. He was cut to the heart to see the light gone from them.

"And if He is not there," she went on, "then there is nothing, is there? Nothing at all."

Herta came and stood on the other side of the bed.

"It's time for Emmy to sleep, Otto."

He nodded and quietly, on his brown-knit stocking feet, he tip-toed out of the room.

Together with Hermann, Otto dug a grave in the south field. It had not been hit by any shells and the soil was moist and easy on the shovel. Hermann opened the Bible he had taken with him.

"I'm not sure about what to read," he said, as he opened it, "but I remember that Psalm 137 is about weeping."

Otto was silent and looked at the little mound of soil in front of them.

"By the waters of Babylon, there we sat down and wept, when we remembered Zion."

Remembered? Otto could hardly remember something he had held only for a moment. But he did remember Emmy's face as she was carrying the child in her belly. She had been so beautiful as she had bent over the little garments she was sewing.

"On the willows there we hung up our lyres. For there our captors required of us songs, and our tormentors, mirth, saying, 'Sing us one of the songs of Zion!'

Yes, singing was something one did not do when there was sadness. And yet within his heart great volumes of sadness wanted to cry out, to cry out in a huge lament - to wail with the agony he felt within himself.

"How shall we sing the Lord's song in a foreign land? If I forget you, O Jerusalem, let my right hand wither! Let my tongue...."

"I'm going for a walk."

Otto interrupted Hermann's reading abruptly. Startled he looked at Otto.

"What if there is a raid? You won't be able to get to the cellar!"

Doggedly Otto repeated his words and Hermann, still holding the Bible in his hands, watched him go.

Otto walked south, south through the field where he had just buried his child. Then he continued south over a neighbor's field and then another adjoining neighbor's. For some reason he could not fathom, he was making straight for the railroad. He often heard trains pass at night on their way towards Munich and beyond. Rudi said the trains carried prisoners. But who knew? His feet sank into the earth and he climbed a fence to keep his course straight – straight south to the railroad. It took him more than an hour to reach the tracks and when he did, he stopped short. What now? Here he was, but why? He sat down heavily against a tree stump and waited. He didn't know what he was waiting for, and suddenly he wept. The bark of the tree stump against which he leaned dug hard into his back. His body heaved and he heard his voice crying out and wailing up to the clear sky.

"Why, God? Why!! Why do You give only to take?!"

He shook a leather fist up at the stars. In the distance the unmistakable sound of a train could be heard.

"You can have the hand," Otto shouted, "but give Emmy a child!"

The train came closer. Otto felt rather than saw the lights approaching from the distance. And his voice mixed with the hollow echo of the train.

"Tell me why!" he shrieked at the heavens.

The noise of the nearing train grew. When it grew louder than his voice, he stopped shouting. But he did not stop speaking.

"You have interrupted my life from all quarters," he said through the roar, "but I cannot hear what You say."

The train, now only a few seconds away, thundered towards him. The noise was deafening. And then car after car after car passed. Until there was nothing – nothing but a still, small voice. The voice of a baby crying.

At first Otto thought the sound was only in his mind. He sat very quietly, pushing his back up straighter against the tree stump. He sat that way for a full minute. And unmistakably the mewling sound of a baby reached his ears again. It traveled towards him from the left and on all fours he crawled towards a thick clump of bushes on that side, stopping every few seconds to make sure he was still heading in the right direction. Stones cut into his knees and branches scratched his face, but still he crawled on towards the pitiful whimpering. And then he held it. He held the noise. He held the small mewling sound, wrapped up in a cocoon of blankets. He cradled it and dandled it and sang to it, until it stopped crying.

Early, very early in the morning hours, he laid the child, a newborn, into Emmy's arms. It was a baby girl. Then he went and stood next to his mother-in-law at the foot of the bed.

"Where," began Herta, "did you...?"

He put a finger over her lips. Emmy was weeping, but even as she wept she sat up and held the child against her breast. The baby began to suckle. Emmy turned a tear-drenched face to Otto.

"I dreamt," she said, "that the baby died and that all the windows in the house were closed. But she didn't die, did she?"

"No," replied Otto, "she didn't."

The child, remarkably, looked very much like Emmy. Dark, curly hair, big eyes like chunks of coal and a lovely olive complexion graced her little face. They named her Hope. Neither Hermann nor Herta ever pressed for information as to where Otto had found the child and Emmy firmly believed the baby to be her own. And once begun, little Hope began to grow. True to his word, Hermann began reading the Bible for a devotional time each day, addressing Hope specifically in these readings. He read Genesis and explained Creation to her in detail until Emmy, laughing at her father, told him that the baby couldn't possibly understand.

"No, but you can and so can Otto," he said, "and if I teach you, I also teach her. I did not do it enough when you were a child."

Emmy merely looked at him and then, after she put the baby down into his lap, she kissed his stubbly cheeks. And outside the shells fell from the sky and pitted the fields just a bit more.

Little Hope grew into a sturdy toddler. Dark, abundant hair crowned her head and Emmy often tied it back with a red ribbon. She was a precocious child and the apple of Otto's and Emmy's eyes.

Hermann and Herta as well, doted on her. The war was not going very well for Germany. Rudi kept them well-informed and he also warned them that Commandant Heinrich Von Schwer was rounding up any suspicious people in a last-minute fanatic fit of patriotism to support the Reich.

"Keep Emmy and little Hope indoors," he told Otto, "Did it never occur to you that they look Jewish?"

"Jewish?"

"Yes, and if truth be told, and Hermann should have told you, Herta's grandmother was Jewish."

"Was she?"

Otto was perplexed and stood up straight. He was cleaning out the gutter next to the stalls and Rudi had come to take some beets and potatoes back to Munich.

"Yes, and if I know this, who knows what von Schwer might know as well, and who knows what he might do in these last days. A losing boxer sometimes comes alive with a last well-aimed punch."

Otto laughed but Rudi wagged a finger at him.

"Be cautious, Otto! Be cautious."

It was not even a full month after Rudi's warning that the SS drove up to the farmhouse to requisition a beef. They materialized from time to time and Hermann generally let them have what they wanted. When they arrived Emmy and little Hope happened to be in the barn. The soldiers admired the child. In their bright, green uniforms they strutted about the farm as if they owned the place. They were almost like schoolboys allowed out for recess, boys wearing high, black boots and dark wide belts with the inscription *Gott mit uns*, (God with us), in the center. Heinrich von Schwer, who was in charge, sauntered over and stood in front of Emmy.

"Motherhood becomes you," he said, running his hand along her arm.

She stiffened perceptibly at his touch and picked up little Hope who held onto her hand. Otto walked over from where he was standing.

"I think we have a cow that will suit Herr Commandant very well," he said, taking care to keep his voice polite.

"Your child is very dark, isn't she?" Heinrich said, never taking his eyes off Emmy for a moment while he spoke, "You'd almost swear she was a gypsy."

"A gypsy indeed," laughed Otto, "Come, Herr Commandant, this way."

"I will be back, *fraulein*."

Heinrich clicked his heels together, stiffly saluted Emmy with a 'Heil Hitler' and followed Otto. Emmy took Hope inside and did not come out again until Heinrich was gone. She worried Otto with questions that night. What could Heinrich do? What had he meant? And did Otto think they should cross the border now perhaps?

But it was neither Emmy nor little Hope who were picked up by the SS. The next morning, as Otto was working one of the south fields, three men thundered up on motorcycles. They immediately advised Otto that he was under arrest. Not allowing him to return to the house to tell anyone of his leaving, they roughly pushed him towards their vehicles.

"*Schnell! Schnell laufen*! Walk quickly!"

Ordered to ride in the side car of one of the officers, Otto found himself standing in the foyer of Heinrich von Schwer's Gestapo headquarters before the noon hour.

Otto was not the only person who had been arrested that morning. There were a dozen or so people pressed against the wall in the ante-room outside the interrogation section. Soldiers guarded the door, rifles slung over their shoulders. Otto recognized some of them as soldiers who had been in the barn the previous day. One by one people were called in to be questioned and again and again Otto heard Heinrich von Schwer's high-pitched, harsh voice penetrate the walls.

"Filthy dog! Did you think it would escape notice that you were disrespectful to the Reich!"

Screams were frequent and eight times Otto saw men taken out past him to the courtyard where they were shot. A woman next to him tried to pray but could not get past *Vater unser,* Our Father." Her whole body shook so with fear that Otto patted her arm.

"Don't worry," he whispered, "it will be all right."

A soldier strode over from the door and kicked Otto in the groin. He doubled over in pain but not before he recognized the perpetrator as the waiter who, years and years before, had advised him to visit the Frauenkirche.

"Silence! You are not to speak to each other."

Otto did not speak again, but he clearly remembered, as pain flooded him, the pillars obscuring the church windows. But the windows had been there behind the pillars. He did not know why, but the thought of the windows somehow made him feel superior to the man who had kicked him. The woman was called in next and ten minutes later was marched out again into the courtyard. He did not hear any shot and hoped that she had been permitted to live.

"Otto Haak! Schnell!"

As Otto entered the office, Heinrich von Schwer was gazing out the window. Turning sharply, he eyed Otto with disdain.

"So here is the hard-working Dutch farmer turned German."

Otto did not reply but noted that Heinrich's Gestapo uniform was not as immaculate as it usually was. It was crumpled, crumpled as if the man had slept in it. As well there were stains on the sleeves and Heinrich's face was unshaven. The sound of planes could be heard in the distance and Otto detected tiny pinpricks of fear in Heinrich's eyes.

"You have lost the war," he suddenly heard himself say and regretted it the next minute when he saw the fear replaced with intense hatred.

"And you have married a Jew," Heinrich replied, "and I believe you are aware of what we do to Jews."

Otto stayed quiet, his hands at his side. Heinrich pointed to his right hand.

146

"I don't know why she married you, cripple that you are! It must be that Jews cannot choose well, that their brain functions at a lower level."

The sound of the planes grew in volume.

"Your wife and child," Heinrich continued uneasily, turning his head to glance at the window, "will be picked up tomorrow and shot before your eyes."

"God will punish you."

Again the words were out before Otto realized it. Heinrich got up, strode towards him and struck him squarely in the face with such force that Otto staggered backwards, tripped over a footstool and fell over.

"God will not punish me before I punish you," Heinrich hissed, "Swine!! Cripple!"

Wiping the blood off his mouth, every fiber in Otto's being wanted to jump up and strike back. But the whistle of bombs dropping nearby, suddenly brought Heinrich to his knees as well, face to face with Otto.

"Punish me then, but please don't kill my wife and child," Otto replied.

His voice was hoarse and he wished there was some way he could send Emmy a message to warn her that she must hide – that everyone must hide – that everyone must leave the farm.

"Please don't kill my wife and child," he repeated slowly, not knowing if he was speaking to God or to Heinrich.

His face still close to Otto's face, Heinrich mimicked his voice in a clownish fashion and laughed hysterically even as they heard nearby explosions in the neighborhood.

"What can I do," whispered Otto, "to make you...."

"Make me?"

Heinrich hit Otto in the face again and got up unsteadily.

"You can't make me do anything, you cripple hand."

Slowly and carefully, Otto got up as well. Heinrich walked back to his desk and sat down, folding his hands in front of him. He smiled at

Otto with a certain amount of cunning. He opened a cigarette case, took out a cigarette, lit it and took a deep breath.

"All right. Just to humor you and to let you see that I'm not an unreasonable man, I'll give you a chance. Let's see if you can make me release Emmy even before she's been arrested."

He pushed back his chair, took a puff of his cigarette and considered Otto as he stood before him even as he continued.

"All right," he said again, "This is the condition – that you grow hair on that crippled hand of yours. That you grow hair on it right now."

Heinrich laughed loudly as if he had told an uproarious joke. Otto felt weak. For a moment he heard the retreating sound of the train by the railroad track and within himself her remembered the still small voice afterwards. Then he walked over to Heinrich's desk, undoing the clasp on the leather glove as he walked. Pulling it off, he bent over and lay his scarred, right hand, palm down, on the desk. Then he turned it up. The palm was covered with black hair.

"How...?" Heinrich began, his face twisting into a grimace of disbelief and fear.

A bomb exploded several houses away. Heinrich began to shout hysterically.

"Get out of here, you devil! Leave me! Get out! Go! Go!"

Otto needed no prodding. All things seemed to work together for good. Without bothering to put the glove back on his hand, he walked out. The way was clear. The pillars had dissolved.

5: I Was a Stanger

Then the King will say to those on his right, "Come, you who are blessed by my Father, inherit the kingdom prepared for you from the foundation of the world. [35] *For I was hungry and you gave me food, I was thirsty and you gave me drink, I was a stranger and you welcomed me,* [36] *I was naked and you clothed me, I was sick and you visited me, I was in prison and you came to me" (Matt. 25: 34-36)*

God is our refugee and strength, a very present help in trouble (Ps. 46:1).

The dominee, familiar and black-robed on the high wooden pulpit, preached with dedication and zeal as he alternately gazed at his notes and at the flock in front of him. The church was crowded to capacity. It had been crowded for a number of Sundays. And although most of the people had their eyes on the dominee, a great many had their thoughts elsewhere.

"God loves His people with an everlasting love. This is something we cannot always fully grasp with our finite minds. But, dear people, we can understand, and indeed we are specifically told, that He dwells in His church – that He dwells in you and me – by His Spirit. If then He dwells in us His people, and if then our present rather bleak circumstances are brought before Him through the intercession of His Son, how can we think that He ever loses sight of us – ever forgets us?"

Someone coughed, and several others followed suit. The sound echoed.

"The truth, I fear," dominee Raadsma continued, bending over the edge of the lectern, "is not that He forgets us, but that we forget Him."

It was quiet now. The dominee paused – paused for a long time.

"There are a host of things to think about these days," he finally continued, "a host of things. What we must strive to remember is that in everything that happens, whether that be good or ill, it is for us to say with conviction, 'The Lord is in this and He is in control for our good and for His glory."

Again he paused before repeating, "The Lord is in this and He is in control for our good and for His glory. Amen."

Most Dutch people were taken by surprise when the Nazis invaded their country. Perhaps that is because ordinarily most people do not like to think of or contemplate the worst. The neighbor is the one who is diagnosed with cancer; the person across the street is the one whose wife leaves him; and Germany, although it had undeniably attacked Poland, would never attack Holland. Indeed, the Germans would respect Dutch neutrality, even as they had done during the First World War. This was a commonly held sentiment and one most devoutly hoped. Consequently, the sentiment became an almost truth. But an almost truth, sweet as the word truth may ring, remains a lie. Within a week of the initial German onslaught, on May 10, 1940, after a devastating and horrible bombing of the city of Rotterdam, Dutch resistance collapsed.

In contrast to their neighbor, Belgium, and not at all in conjunction with the country across the border, France, where only military occupation prevailed, the Netherlands almost immediately experienced both military and civil control by the Nazis. Five German commissioners were appointed as quasi-ministers to supervise five different departments of the Dutch administration. All these departments were headed by the wicked and cruel Austrian, Dr. Seyss Inquart.

Diestadt was a medium-sized village of about three and a half thousand people. Among its inhabitants lived some one hundred Jewish families. They were devout families for the most part. They were families who faithfully attended a solid wooden synagogue every Friday night, each Shabbat morning and the occasional time when someone wanted to make a minyan during the week and the quorum of ten was met for that service. There was also cheder, an elementary Hebrew school, for the Jewish children. It was open from four to six every weekday. In other words, the synagogue and its members were an accepted part of the landscape. No one thought much of it either one way or another. A great number of the people of Diestadt were staunch Calvinists with little tolerance for scandal or the unusual. May 1940 rolled in as thunder rolls across the sky. But once they had absorbed the shock, the population of Diestadt realistically contemplated the events as the beginning of a horrible storm. Indeed it was a wicked storm. Most of the people, however, did not take the necessary precautions to sit out the storm. Perhaps that was because initially there seemed to be no serious repercussions for the Jews. Initially.

Several streets over from the synagogue, Cornelis Goedhart ran a grocery/dry-goods store on Rechte Weg. By nature a cheerful, talkative man, he loved his wife and three children dearly. Each morning, swinging his thin, pyjama'd legs over the edge of the four-poster bed he shared with Dora his wife, his first thought was: "Good-morning, Lord. Thank you for another day in which I may praise You." And praise God he did by singing much. Sometimes, in the estimation of his beloved Dora, he sang too much, hummed too loudly, and gave away too many candies to neighborhood children. Both of Nelis' and Dora's two boys were married and out of the house. The only child still living in the family home was their youngest daughter, Tilda. Tilda had turned seventeen in January of

1940 and was the apple of her father's eye. To say that she was a beautiful girl was an understatement. Brown hair curled naturally around a sweet-looking face, a madonna-like face. Great greenish-brown eyes, a flawless complexion, high cheekbones and a gentle smile, all made people look at her twice. She carried herself straightly, almost regally. Nelis often reflected as he watched her, that she seemed like a princess. Then, a few seconds later, he would grin at his pride and ask God to forgive him.

It was over the counter of his grocery store, a counter more informative than the local newspaper, that Nelis heard that violence had erupted in the Jewish quarter of Amsterdam. A number of Jews had defended themselves against attacks by one of the members of the N.S.B. movement. Himmler, head of the SS, reacted swiftly. On February 22, 1941, four hundred and twenty-five Jewish youths were picked up randomly, beaten brutally, and shipped off to camps.

"Camps?" Nelis asked, bewildered, eyes wide, "What camps?"

"I'm not sure," his informant answered, "But I don't think they'll come back."

"But...."

"Oh, Nelis! Don't be so naive, man!"

Rabbi Heyman frequently stopped by the grocery store to purchase one thing or another for his wife. A short, squat man, in his early forties, he got along well with the thin, wiry Nelis.

"Shalom, Nelis."

"Shalom, Rabbi Heyman. What can I get for you today?"

The rabbi looked sad, or perhaps grave was a better word.

"A piece of freedom," he said, and then smiled at the absurdity of his request.

Nelis smiled back and a moment later reached under the counter coming up with a piece of gingerbread.

"A piece of friendship," he answered, "and that goes a long way towards freedom."

The rabbi smiled again, took the gingerbread, turned and walked out of the store without buying anything. Nelis began to sing. Singing usually calmed him. He knew with a sickening feeling that the piece of gingerbread would do nothing to really help the rabbi and his family. It would not procure a radio for the man; it would not take care of the increasing number of signs appearing on more and more buildings reading, *"Jews forbidden"*; it would not erase the yellow star which he and his family were forced to wear; and it would not take away the fear of the deportations, news of which was becoming more and more distressing each day. Nelis increased the volume of his singing. Instead of calming him, however, the emptiness and sadness reflected in the rabbi's eyes echoed through the notes, flattened the harmony, and finally gave way to silence.

As the months went by, the wider selection of goods rapidly disappeared from Nelis' grocery shelves. Items were simply becoming unavailable. Clothes and shoes and food were rationed. It was all part of the German control system. Ration books were distributed from a Distribution Office. There were coupons for everything: bread, meat, sugar, clothes, shoes, oil, gasoline, coal, and tobacco. In order to get these coupons a citizen had to register. And once a person or household was registered, the Nazi authorities had access to their names and addresses. Jewish ration books were stamped with a large 'J'.

"I intend to maintain," Dr. Seyss-Inquart had broadcast in a speech, "Dutch laws as far as possible and to work with the Dutch civil administration, and I guarantee the independence of the judiciary. We have no desire to enforce a foreign ideology on the Dutch, but, of course, we do not consider Jews to be Dutch."

By the end of 1941, the N.S.B was the only political party allowed in the Netherlands.

Adept at bartering, Nelis had established a system with a number of local farmers, two of whom were his sons, in which he traded goods such as cloth for flour. It worked – for a while – but the future worried him. And it was not only the emptying shelves which worried Nelis. Late in 1942, Tilda worried him as well.

"I don't want to go to church anymore."

"Why not?"

Nelis countered the rebellious words spoken within the privacy of the Goedhart living room, quietly.

"Because...."

Tilda stopped, seemingly unable to continue.

"Because?"

Nelis cautiously repeated the word.

"I just don't want to."

There appeared to be an indecision, an apathy, in the girl's words, an underlying mystery which Nelis could not grasp. Consequently, when cleaning his depleting shelves, he could suddenly stop singing in the middle of a psalm.

"What is it Nelis?" customers would say, "Why did you stop?"

But he would only shake his head, unable to explain the nagging fear in the pit of his stomach and in the core of his heart.

It was also on a day late in the fall of 1942, as he stood with his back to the door working his shelves, that the customer bell clanged noisily. Turning away from the shelf he had been stocking with some flour, some eggs, and some potatoes which he had just carefully bartered from a farmer, he faced his daughter – his daughter accompanied by a lanky youth.

"Vader."

Tilda's voice was nonchalant with a touch of bravado in it.

"Tilda."

"Vader, this is Dolf. He walked me home from Tante Klara's."

"Yes?"

For Nelis the 'yes' was a question. Dolf who? and why had he walked Tilda home? Actually he knew why. After all, was not his daughter beautiful? But the 'who' was more troublesome. There was something about the boy which immediately struck him as unwholesome.

"Dolf's father, Marinus Wilman, runs the accounting business on Walen Street."

"Oh?"

Tilda's information, openly given, struck a chord of remembrance. The boy, tall and awkward in length, strode up to the counter after her words, strode up with an air of self-assurance and offered his hand. Nelis considered for a moment before he extended his own.

"How are you, Dolf?"

"Fine, thank you, sir."

The lad's grasp was hard, almost too hard, too cocky. Nelis withdrew his hand first.

"Your father, I think, is the town clerk. And now he also owns the accounting business on Walen Street?" he questioned slowly, "Wasn't that the business run by Karel Winter?"

"Yes," Dolf was quick to answer, "but my father bought him out last month."

It had come to Nelis, via the grocery counter, that Karl Winter, who was a Jew, had been forcibly liquidated before being deported.

"I see," he answered and gave the boy a thin smile, absently turning back to his shelves.

"Vader!"

Tilda's voice was irritated.

"Yes, child."

Nelis did an about face.

"Dolf came in to buy some coffee. Didn't you, Dolf?"

The boy nodded.

"Coffee," Nelis repeated slowly, "You know, that's a much-wanted commodity and I'm sorry to tell you that I'm all out right now."

He turned back to his shelves and heard the customer bell clang angrily behind him. And he began to sing.

There was an underground in Diestadt – a strong underground. Nelis' two sons were members and he himself was also involved. Hands-on sabotage, smuggling, and falsifying identification papers – these things were outside of his realm but he helped in other ways. The underground group often met in a hidden room beneath the store and he allowed them to keep a printing press there. Forbidden pamphlets were stacked neatly against the wall until they were distributed to the people of Diestadt and the surrounding district.

Rabbi Heyman visited the store less and less frequently and when Nelis did chance to see him on the street, his friend and neighbor seemed to have shrunk – shrunk into a small, almost invisible, black-coated figure whose yellow star nevertheless screamed identity. It was in the early days of December in 1942, that the rabbi came into the store one last time. Nelis was startled to see him. He had expected that the rabbi and his family would be gone, gone as most of the Jews of Diestadt were gone, gone somewhere safe. Standing with his black-coated arms at his side, Rabbi Heyman told Nelis that his wife was expecting again.

"Mazeltov, rabbi," Nelis responded automatically, supporting his chin on his hand as he leaned on the counter, "and how is she feeling?"

"Tired."

The answer itself sounded tired and bedraggled and the rabbi stroked the yellow star of David on his black coat as he spoke.

"And how many...."

He did not have to finish his question.

"Six, friend. It will be baby number six."

"Well," Nelis commented thoughtfully, stroking his chin, "you will have three more than I have. Children are a blessing from the Lord God."

Then, feeling he was being much too glib with his words and wishing to interject a more personal comment, he added, "And how do the other five children feel about having a baby brother or sister?"

"Miriam, your Tilda's age, is not home right now. She has gone to stay with... with relatives. So have Rachel, Aaron and Job. There is only our little Rosa left to us now."

"Ah," Nelis breathed, "only Rosa."

"Yes, only Rosa. We were to go away very soon ourselves... to... relatives but...."

"But," Nelis encouraged.

"But they will not take us with the new baby due in the summer."

The rabbi's black coat rose and fell with agitation. His hands were clenched. The tendrils in his black beard trembled and he eyed the door behind him furtively.

"I see."

Nelis did see. Reaching under the counter he took out a package of tea. It was the last one he had left.

"Here. For Anna."

"I did not come here to beg for food, for drink. But beg I do. I came... I came to ask...."

He stopped and looked directly into Nelis' eyes.

"I know, old friend. Let me think on it."

Nelis did think on it. He spoke at length that very day with Dora, with his sons, and with the other leaders of the resistance. It was true. Not one of the addresses in their district, or surrounding district, was presently willing to harbor a Jewish family expecting a baby. A newborn baby meant extra risk.

"But Nelis," Dora said, "we really cannot do it either. You know that the Germans come into the store often. They know who lives in this house. And then there are the underground meetings. We cannot... Surely you see."

She was right, his Dora. Too many of the enemy visited his store, chatted around the counter and eyed everything going on about his house. This was encouraged by the underground. Often Nelis could pass on information that some loose-lipped German soldier had dropped. But it was already a tricky business and to add to it would be foolish and would jeopardize the underground meetings in the basement. At least that is how everyone viewed the situation. Dora, straightening out imaginary creases in her blue-checkered apron, gave Nelis a kiss on his cheek. He smiled at her. She was not a coward, his wife, and often ran risks by carrying messages, as well as illegal newspapers, to a number of homes.

"It will turn out, Nelis. Don't worry. God will provide."

"God helps those who help themselves," he answered.

In the days that followed, his sons, particular his oldest son Frans, reinforced their mother's refusal.

"She is right," Frans said, "there would be too much risk involved for all of us. Besides that, we actually just found an address that is willing to take the rabbi and his wife and Rosa. Willing to take them immediately."

Nelis was extremely relieved and sang more than usual that day, until Tilda walked in, arm in arm with Dolf.

"Hello, Vader."

"Hello."

He had spoken with her at length about not seeing the boy anymore. Dolf's father had predictably metamorphosed into an outspoken member of the local N.S.B. and had been responsible for rounding up a number of Dutch patriots who had since disappeared from the face of Diestadt. Dolf himself showed every sign of following in his father's footsteps. He was reported to be frequently looting, in the company of German soldiers, the homes of those who were arrested. Nelis could not understand what his Tilda, his once so sweet and kind daughter, saw in the fellow. Looking from her to the boy, he could not help the feeling of loathing that overpowered him. The sight of Dolf's arm, now possessively draped around Tilda's shoulders, made his blood boil. Through the open coat, he could see that the boy was wearing the blue shirt and black pants that the youth branch of the N.S.B. party doled out to its members. The astrakhan cap with the emblem of a stormy petrel, was perched jauntily on his head.

"I heard you were down on Tweede Straat last week, Dolf, helping the SS soldiers ransack a home that belongs to Willem Parelman."

"Ransack?" Dolf repeated, dropping his arm from Tilda's back.

Underneath the coat, his blue shirt rose and fell in agitation.

"Yes, ransack," Nelis repeated as well, his voice quiet and steady, his gaze never leaving the boy's face.

"I was certainly there when the empty home of Willem Parelman was being checked out and I am proud that I can help the ruling authorities in this city," Dolf answered stiffly, "if that is what you mean."

"No, that is not what I mean," Nelis continued, oblivious of Tilda's warning eyes, "Windows were broken in the Parelman home, books were burned, and I recall being told that soldiers urinated on the furniture. There seemed to be no one taking the part of those who were gone. The Jews are helpless, at least that is what some people like to think, as life becomes more difficult and more intolerable for them."

He paused for breath, his cheeks turning red. Dolf took the opportunity to interject a reply.

"You are the father of a girl I really like, so I will not report what you have said," he parried rather smoothly, "and as for the Jews, they are guilty of many crimes and do not deserve to continue living in our city."

Those words were too much for Nelis.

"Not deserve? Out of this store, boy! Out before I kick your...."

Stepping threateningly from behind the counter, Nelis moved towards Dolf as he spoke, rolling up his sleeves at the same time.

"And remember that there is a God in heaven Who sees everything."

Dolf walked backwards towards the door. There was a glint of fear in his eyes. Tilda still stood where he had left her in front of the counter. Her hands were twisted together.

"Goodbye, Tilda."

Dolf's voice registered a slight squeak.

"And by the way," Nelis said as the boy turned to open the door, the bell clanging noisily over his head, "you are forbidden to see my daughter ever again."

After Tilda had gone up to her room without saying a word to her father, he remembered, remembered how she had that previous spring confessed her faith; how she had stood in front of the church in a dress especially sewn for the occasion by Dora - a pale red dress.

"Do you, Tilda Goedhart," dominee Raadsma's voice had boomed resoundingly as he read off the questions, "heartily believe the doctrine contained in the Old and New Testament?"

She had looked very frail, but also very strong. What a contradiction! And that was the nub of faith, wasn't it – strength in weakness.

"Do you confess that you seek life not in yourself but only in Jesus Christ, your Savior?"

She had worn a brown hat, a brown hat on top of her brown curling hair. It had been a shame, actually, to cover that pretty hair.

"Do you declare that you will forsake the world, mortify your old nature, and lead a godly life?"

Nelis remembered Dolf's arm around Tilda's shoulders and swallowed with difficulty.

"Do you promise to submit to the government of the church and also, if you should become delinquent either in doctrine or in life, to submit to its admonition and discipline?"

She had answered 'I do'. She was eighteen years old and what did she know, he had thought at the time, of delinquency in doctrine or in life. But her answer had rung clear as a bell and he knew, that is to say, thought he had known, that she meant it – meant it with all her heart. Dominee Raadsma had then given her a text, as he had given everyone in the class a text. It had been from Matthew 25.

"Verily I say unto you, inasmuch as ye have done it unto one of the least of these my brethren, ye have done it unto me."

She had been so happy that Sunday, had exhibited an inner delight that in turn had delighted himself. But he was mystified now and did not know what to do with his thoughts.

Hans, the second oldest of Nelis' and Dora's sons, dropped by that evening. It was not easy to visit in the evening. Curfew was early and sneaking around the streets of Diestadt after curfew presented its hazards. Hans patiently listened to his father's bristling tirade of what Dolf had said, what danger Tilda was in, and how he wished the war was over, not interrupting with even a single word until Nelis had completely vented his grief and anger.

"Marinus Wilman, Dolf's father," Hans offered by way of information, as he sat in the living room of the grocer's shop, "who, as you know, is also the town clerk, has been ordered to compile a list of all the men in Diestadt born between the years of 1897 and 1924. Birth dates and complete addresses have to be handed in to the Nazis within a week."

"Why?"

Both Dora and Nelis stared at Hans.

"So that the Germans can call up anyone they would like and ship them over to Germany for employment in factories, mines, or wherever they fancy."

"I'm sure that Marinus Wilman will be happy to comply with his overseers."

Nelis spoke dryly and absently ran his hand along the edge of his chair. Dora nodded in agreement.

"Well," Hans smiled, "we're going to make it a little difficult for him to do that."

"How?"

Dora's voice was just a trifle shrill.

"The card index system, the system that Wilman will need to compile the names, will possibly end up in ... well, maybe in the belly of a stove."

"He's not going to give it to you for use as firewood of his own free will."

"No, he won't."

Hans grinned and added, "Well, don't worry about it. And don't worry about Dolf either. He's just a young boy and I'm sure that after this dressing down that you gave him, he won't come back."

"I sincerely hope so."

"And before I go," Hans said as he stood up, "why don't I go up to Tilda's room and talk to her for a bit. Maybe she's willing to take advice from an older brother."

The rest of December passed peaceably enough, and there was fervent hope in everyone's heart that 1943 would see an end to the war. Then, early in January of 1943, all of Diestadt was suddenly abuzz, not with the news of the recent raid on city hall, but with the news that both Marinus Wilman and his renegade son had been found dead in a field south of the city. There was much speculation as to who had committed the murders. Some suggested the underground, as it was widely known that Wilman was N.S.B and had been involved in many shady deals with the Nazis. But others thought that perhaps the Nazis themselves had turned on the man and his son. Nelis' grocery counter heard it all, and he was silent, not commenting but just listening. Most of the folks that came in were curious, well aware that Nelis' daughter had been seen 'stepping out' with Dolf. Tilda herself had taken the news quietly, but her green-brown eyes had been suffused with a sad light. Nelis had longed to take her in his arms but could not bring himself to walk across the room to do so. And when the paralysis that had seemed to creep into his bones finally disappeared, it was too late. She had left to go up to her room where she stayed for most of that day and the next and the next.

"Does she eat?" Nelis asked Dora.

"Some," Dora answered, looking at him, he thought, rather strangely.

"Do you think she'll get over it?"

"That remains to be seen."

Dora spoke rather sharply and Nelis sought retreat in the store.

"Women," he commented irritably a little later, furiously cleaning the counter before turning disconsolately to his mostly empty shelves, "who can understand them."

He could not tell when he first suspected that Tilda was pregnant. But suddenly it seemed quite apparent to him. The clothing worn looser, the lack of appetite, the listlessness – all those things added up. It gave him an infinite sadness. He did not speak of it to Dora, but he knew that she also knew. Indeed, he felt that she had been aware of this development much longer than he had. He pondered about it. And then it seemed to him that everyone knew, and the whispers and innuendoes reaching his counter became myriad.

"When... when is the child due?"

"The beginning of July, or thereabouts."

Dora spoke rather loudly, almost cheerfully, Nelis thought.

"Is she... is Tilda all right, do you think?"

"She seems to be fine, Nelis."

He sighed.

She turned to him, and took his hand.

"You know, Nelis, I think it would be a good idea if Tilda went to stay at Frans' and Hilde's farm until the confinement. She wouldn't be subject to as many eyes as she is here and they still have lots of milk and eggs."

"Away from us?"

"Well, we could easily visit her. They don't live far. But the country air would be good and... and she can come home after the baby arrives. What do you think?"

"Does she want to go?"

"I think she does. She gets along well with Hilde and she can help with the children and the chores on the farm."

He nodded. It would be a solution of sorts. It was the beginning of March now. There would be some time to think of what to do later – what to do with the child after it was born. But what was he thinking? It would be his own grandchild, a child related to him by flesh and blood, even as the other grandchildren were. But there was no denying that it would be a traitor's grandchild as well. The idea tortured him. It took his sleep. It ate at him. And all the time the days crept by.

Before Tilda left to stay at the farm, dominee Raadsma came for a visit. No elder accompanied the dominee. He remained closeted privately with Tilda for more than two hours. Nelis had offered to be part of the discussion, part of the strong admonition which he was certain his daughter would receive. But dominee had shaken his head.

"No, Nelis, I think I had better speak to her by myself. You need not worry. But I think this is best."

That was all he had said but Nelis did not reckon those words enough. What exactly it was that he had wanted dominee to say, he could not rightly define. And then life went on.

After the birth register disappeared from city hall, a new ruling was implemented by the Nazis. Cards called 'Ausweisen' became available. People were told that if they possessed such a card, they would be exempt from being sent away for forced labor in Germany, as well as being pronounced safe from the ongoing house searches. To obtain an Ausweis, one simply had to go to city hall, fill in an application with one's name and address, and wait.

"It's not true!" Frans exclaimed heatedly to his father, "It's just a ploy to get more people's names and addresses. I hope you haven't applied."

"As if they don't know my name or where I live," his father replied.

Frans looked at the furrows on his father's forehead and walked over to him.

"Hey, Tilda is fine. You needn't worry about her. Dr. Verstar has promised to come by when the time comes and Hilde looks after her very well."

"But later," Nelis responded, looking at his son, "what about later?"

"Well, don't you want her back home?"

"Yes," Nelis answered hastily, "of course I do, of course I do."

And so he did. Only, not with the child – not with the ill-begotten child.

Nelis and Dora were notified by Frans on June 24, that a child had been born and that mother and baby were doing well.

"What is it?"

Dora's curiosity knew no bounds and Nelis thought her enthusiasm a trifle unbecoming regarding the situation. She was virtually dancing with excitement, her eyes sparkling and her mouth beaming a broad smile.

"It's a boy, Moeder. A healthy boy, 6 pounds and 3 ounces."

"What," Nelis said slowly, "what is she going to name the child?"

He had been thinking about that question for a long time. If the circumstances had been normal, he might have longed to have a namesake, a little Cornelis. So far, after all, all the grandchildren were girls. But circumstances were not normal and he knew that he did not want the baby named after himself. Frans, who was bringing them the news, laughed at the question.

"It's going to be called Johannes, father."

Johannes was a beautiful name. As a matter of fact, if Tilda had been a boy, they would have called her Johannes. He nodded at Frans. Dora was full of questions.

"And Tilda, how is she? How long was the labor? Was the doctor there in time?"

"Hold on, Moeder. One question at a time. Tilda is fine. The labor was quick - I think about three hours in all."

"Three hours?" Dora interjected, "That's very quick for a first baby. And was Dr. Verstar notified right away and did he come before she delivered?"

"Yes, Dr. Verstar was there in time and he and Hilde delivered the child together."

"And what does Johannes look like? Does he have hair?"

"He is a very dark baby. Looks like you, Moeder."

It was true. Dora had a dark complexion and black hair. Nelis often teased her that she had been smuggled into Diestadt with the gypsies.

"Like me?"

Clearly Dora was pleased. No, that was not the right word. She was delighted.

"Well, you will have to come and see for yourself tomorrow, Moeder. Then you can hold the little lamb in your own arms and ask all the questions you want."

"Yes, we'll go tomorrow, won't we Nelis?"

"Well, I don't know, Dora. You can go, certainly, but I should stay in the store."

"But hardly anyone comes to buy anymore, Nelis. We have so

little stock left. Surely you can lock up for a few hours?"

He stubbornly shook his head and refused to look at his wife. Instinctively he knew he had to get used to the idea of Johannes, had to let it cool down like his Sunday bowl of soup before he took a first spoonful.

So it was the next day that Dora, arms full of baby things on which she had been working every evening since Tilda left, departed for the farm and Nelis stayed behind the counter of the store.

"Gutenmittag."

It was one of the German officers. Officers often came to the store, checking whether or not Nelis had any surrogate coffee, or bread, or even fish. From time to time Nelis bartered his wares for some local fish caught by anglers. Today, however, his shelves were naked.

"I hear," the officer went on, "that you have become an Opa."

He laughed and extended his hand by way of congratulations.

"Güssman," he said by way of introducing himself.

Nelis took the hand. Since the Wilman debacle, the Germans, some of them in any case, had made sympathetic comments to him. Too bad about Dolf, they said, laughing and smirking simultaneously. Nelis took the comments. He was, after all, part of the underground and heard a number of things at his counter which he could pass on to contacts. It was best not to spoil relations even though his heart was not in it.

"Yes," he answered curtly.

"The baby, what is it?"

"A boy."

"A boy? *Wunderbahr. Wie heisen sie*? Wonderful. What is his name?"

"Johannes."

"A good name. Yes, I like it."

Nelis nodded and wished the fellow would leave.

"I have a son. He is called Wilhelm."

The officer leaned his elbow on the counter.

"Too bad this boy will not know his *Vater*. Is this not so? Poor

166

Dolf!"

He left off speaking. Nelis turned his back on the man and began dusting the shelves, even though there was no dust.

"You have seen this baby?"

"No, I haven't."

"Ah."

The man sighed deeply as if commiserating with Nelis before continuing on with his comments.

"It is this *krieg*, this war. Soon perhaps it will be over and we can go back to our *heimat*, our home. I will again see my children and you...."

Nelis turned. He now contemplated the soldier with some compassion but could not bring himself to speak.

"Well, I will go again."

He extended his hand and Nelis shook it once more.

Two weeks later, Tilda came home. Nelis had not been out to the farm even once. He was ashamed of himself. But he simply could not force his legs to walk the distance – the long distance of acceptance. He made excuses. He had a headache; he was busy; and, in the long run, Dora stopped asking him. Tilda looked well. Rosy cheeks, shoulders straight, and a determined look on her face which gave her, Nelis thought, a maturity which neither he nor anyone else could fathom.

"Hello, Vader."

"Hello, Tilda."

She carried the child. She carried Johannes in her arms. He walked over slowly and stood in front of her.

"Would you like to see him?"

He swallowed but said nothing. A small mewling sound erupted from the blanket.

"He is hungry."

"Oh."

It was all he could think of to say. Behind him, Dora laughed.

"Go on, Nelis. Take the baby. He's such a good boy."

Slowly his arms reached out and Tilda placed the blanketed little heap within the contour of his outstretched limbs.

"There you are then, Opa."

Suddenly she gave him a smile. And all his hard-fought animosity almost melted within that smile. Johannes made another sound, a small sound. Nelis sat down in the nearest chair and moved aside the blanket. A tiny face peered up at him. Coal-black eyes intensely scrutinized him.

"Hello, Johannes," Nelis said hesitatingly, thereby gingerly wrapping the gurgling child into his heart.

1943 continued on quietly without any fanfare. People tended to stay home more and more. Blackouts were enforced. Fall and winter evenings were spent with curtains drawn and folks going to bed earlier to ward off the cold while snuggling under their blankets. Coal was not easy to come by and it was better to keep it for the day. Johannes thrived. He gained weight, slept well at night and was quite content if he was but fed and dry. Tilda did not feed the baby herself but used goat's milk. Frans or Hilde brought it over, or Tilda herself would walk over to the farm and come back with a few liters.

"You shall have enough goats' milk for your food, for the food of your household, and the nourishment of your maidservants."

Dominee Raadsma visited the Goedhart's early on in 1944, and smilingly quoted the Proverb to Nelis in the store. Nelis smiled back in a half-hearted manner. Although he could not deny that he was fond of Johannes, he was still not very comfortable about speaking of him to others.

"How is Tilda doing?"

"Well. She is doing well."

"Make sure she goes out regularly with the child. I understand that someone has given you a *'kinderwagen'*, a baby carriage?"

"Yes," Nelis answered stiffly, "it was a gift from some of the German officers who said they wanted to give it in remembrance of Dolf. I have no idea where they got it, but it's a solid carriage and we may as well use it."

As a matter of fact, he had wanted to refuse the carriage, or use it as firewood, but Dora had stopped him.

"Don't be silly, Nelis," she had said, "We can use it. I don't have our old carriage any more, and the baby has to be taken out sometime. So what if it comes from the Germans. If they want to be generous about Johannes, let them. They've taken away so much that belongs to other people."

Dora had sighed as she added that sentence, finishing with "and we should feel no compunction about taking something from them in return."

The dominee coughed, and Nelis was brought back to his surroundings with a start.

"The baby," dominee said, "should be baptized, I think."

"Yes."

Nelis did not commit himself to any other words.

"Well, I was thinking," the dominee went on, "in light of the fact that Tilda is a single mother, and in light of the fact that some people have expressed hostility, it might be best if it was a private occasion."

Nelis felt relief flood through him. The days had passed and he had not spoken of baptism to either Dora or Tilda. But he had thought of it. He had been contemplating going to church, walking down the aisle, encountering a host of curious faces, condemning faces, faces eager to see both the child and the mother. Tilda had not been to church since the baby had been born. He had not spoken to her of that either.

"When?"

"Well," dominee spoke slowly, as if he were weighing the matter, "perhaps in a week or so. We will, of course, announce it to the congregation. We will simply announce that Tilda's baby will be baptized."

"What will you say if they ask you why it will not be baptized publicly?"

Dominee smiled.

"I'll think of something," he said, "Yes, I'm sure I'll think of something."

So it was that two weeks later, with a cold January frost settled on the windows, that Tilda, with the baby bundled up warmly in the carriage, left for church. Dora was about to follow her. Nelis said that he would come shortly.

"You are coming, Nelis?" Dora said with a half-worried frown on her face as she was doing up the buttons of her blue winter coat.

"Yes, yes, of course."

"Well, Frans and Hilde will be there with their children and so will Hans and Tina."

He nodded and she walked out the front door. He proceeded to the living room window and looked out from there. He saw Dora overtake Tilda who had already manipulated the carriage down the garden path and onto the street. She companionably put her hand onto the carriage handle in liaison with Tilda. Nelis felt a twinge of jealousy as he peered at them through the pane. He then went to the back to lock up the store and find his coat. He would, he feared, not have been a good father for the prodigal. But he was not the prodigal's father, was he? He was actually a prodigal himself. Dominee had once preached a sermon on it. His arms struggled with the sleeves of his coat, but then the coat was on, and he was ready. But he waited a few more minutes before he finally ventured out the front door himself.

The air was crisp outside. He breathed it in deeply and began to stride purposefully towards the church. It was not far, only some five blocks.

"Hey, Nelis."

It was Jan Pot, the local shoemaker, appearing out of nowhere and running to catch up with him.

"Hey, Nelis, where are you off to, man?"

"To church," he answered shortly, not in any mood for conversation.

"To church? You've got your days mixed up. It's only Wednesday."

"Yes, it is. But I have some business at church."

170

"Business?"

"Yes."

He wished the man would go away. Not only was Jan Pot a gossip, he was also thought to be a collaborator, although he had not, to anyone's knowledge, joined the N.S.B.

"Well, I'm going that way as well. Mind if I walk with you?"

Nelis did mind, but he did not say anything, only stepped up his pace.

"Cold, isn't it?"

Nelis did not wish to talk. He murmured assent and left it at that. But Jan Pot was bound and determined to chit chat.

"How's the new grandchild? Nice to have a boy, isn't it? But it must be hard, knowing where the child came from."

Nelis shrugged.

"What do you think actually happened to Wilman and Dolf? I mean, what do you really think happened to them?"

Nelis shrugged again.

"What do you think of the possibility that the Nazis themselves killed them? After all, Wilman and his son knew a lot of things that were going on at Nazi headquarters, if you know what I mean. Do you agree?"

Why was the man so persistently talkative? Nelis studied the ground, his shoes, and shrugged once more.

"Well you must think something about it, Nelis!"

Jan Pot was gesticulating now, his hands coming perilously close to touching Nelis' face. The church was visible, its spires rising in a gesture of worship.

"Well, what do you think?"

"It could be," Nelis said, just to stop the man from asking again.

"What could be?"

"It could be that the Nazis killed the Wilmans."

Jan Pot stopped short in his tracks. His small, almost yellowish eyes shone with a secret triumph.

"Nelis Goedhart, I am making a citizen's arrest. I am arresting you for accusing the Nazis of willfully killing two of their most ardent supporters."

"You are what?"

Nelis stopped as well and looked at Jan Pot incredulously.

"And you will come with me to the police station at once. If you resist, it will only make matters worse."

"What matters?"

The man was crazy.

"Matters of ... matters of security and of importance to the city. Matters which will be of interest to the police of this city."

"You are out of your mind, Jan Pot."

Nelis began walking again, but Jan Pot put a hand on his shoulder.

"We will pass the police station before you get to the church, Nelis. Do you want me to shout and make a scene so that someone will hear? That wouldn't be good for your business, would it? And it wouldn't aid your already tarnished reputation in Diestadt."

It was true that the police station stood kitty corner to the church. They could see it as well as the church from where they stood. Nelis could also see, within his mind's eye, a little group of people gathered around the baptismal font, a little group waiting for him to arrive. He could see Tilda with the baby in her arms, and Dora standing next to her anxiously eyeing the door.

"Well, Nelis, are you coming quietly, or do I shout?"

"You are an extremely irritating little man," Nelis began, "and I don't want you to waste my time any longer."

"The police are already aware of the fact that you accused them of murdering the Wilmans."

"And who told them that?"

"My wife."

"Your wife?"

Jelle Pot was a thin, small lady, always coming into the store asking for things that she knew he didn't have. She was forever complaining, haggling over prices and never satisfied with what he did have in stock.

"Yes, my wife. She went into the station this morning and told them that you had informed her that you knew that the police was personally responsible for murdering the Wilmans. And also that you were spreading this rumor to every customer that came into your store. Now will you come quietly into the station, or must I run for a policeman to come and follow you into the church."

"Your wife is a liar, Pot," Nelis began, adding, "Are you looking for some sort of reward, Pot? Is that what you're up to? It's dangerous to play with the enemy."

"The enemy?"

Jan Pot rubbed his hands together and smiled gleefully, before continuing.

"That's another phrase the police will be happy to know you are in the habit of using."

Nelis sighed. He might as well go into the station. He knew several of the officers and hoped that someone familiar would be on duty. Better straighten this silly matter out rather than have Jan Pot and some SS ruffian disrupt the baptism. He could explain later.

"Fine, we'll go and speak to someone at the station."

There were two officers seated at the front desk when Jan Pot and Nelis walked in. Jan Pot began speaking almost immediately upon entry, putting his right hand on Nelis' shoulder by way of introduction.

"This is Nelis Goedhart, the man my wife told you about this morning. He runs the local grocery store on Rechte Weg."

"*Ja*, yes, I know him."

To his great relief, Nelis recognized one of the officers as Güssman, the man who had stopped in the day that Johannes was born, the fellow who had a son called Wilhelm.

"How is your son, Wilhelm?"

The words were out of his mouth before he knew it. But Güssman smiled cordially and responded warmly.

"I had not heard for a month, but just last week I had a letter. Wilhelm was well then, as was his mother."

"This man," Jan Pot, interrupted, "this man has accused the police of murdering the Wilmans. He has accused you of ...!"

Güssman waved his hand to stop the flow of words coming out of Jan Pot's mouth.

"You have proof of this?"

"Yes, he told me just now as we were walking along the street. As well, last week he spoke of it to my wife when she was in his store."

"It is just your word and your wife's?"

"Well," Jan Pot stuttered, disappointed there not more immediate reaction on the part of the officers, "you told my wife this morning you would look into it."

The second officer, who up to this time had said nothing, stood up.

"You will both sit down and wait while we confer."

The men left and both Jan Pot and Nelis sat down on the chairs lined up against the wall. Nelis did not take a seat next to Pot but left a few spaces between them. He was disgusted with the man. About half an hour later, the officers returned.

"I understand," the second officer said, "that your daughter is the mother of the little baby boy – the child of Dolf Wilman?"

Nelis looked up at him and stood up. Almost imperceptibly he nodded.

"The death of young Dolf was most unfortunate."

Nelis waited. He said nothing. At precisely that moment the door opened and Tilda walked in, a crying baby in her arms.

"*Vader*," she called out even before her feet were over the threshold, "We waited and waited. Then finally we heard that you were... that you had been taken...."

She stopped, confused. Slowly making her way over to Nelis, she stood next to him. The baby continued its wailing. She rocked her arms back and forth and both officers watched her. And all the while Johannes hiccupped his distress, Güssman had a sympathetic look on his face.

"I think you should both go home," he said, adding, "and quickly, as it is beginning to snow."

It was true. Small snowflakes were falling past the window pane and the sky was growing dark.

"Thank you," Nelis said, and taking Tilda's elbow, steered her towards the door.

Jan Pot got up as well, but he did not get further than a few steps.

"We would like to question you further."

"But...."

Both officers held up their hands.

"This way please."

Nelis opened the door and let Tilda exit first before venturing out into the falling snow himself.

"*Vader*."

Tilda's voice was small, almost as if she too was ready to cry. He glanced at her, saw tears rolling down her cheeks, and took her arm.

"Shall I carry the child for you?"

She handed him over even as she whispered, "What happened, father?"

"At home, Tilda, I'll tell you everything at home."

Later, as they were gathered in the living room, he apologized for not being present at the baptism and then related what had happened with Jan Pot.

"It is ridiculous really," he finished, "absolute poppycock and I don't know what the man means to gain by it."

"Still," Frans commented thoughtfully, "you'd better be careful. The SS kill at will and a friend today maybe a foe tomorrow. Lie low, Vader, don't go out and maybe you should close the store for a while and stay with Hans and Tina – you and Moeder both."

"Nonsense," he said, "I've done nothing wrong. Even if the truth is that I think they probably did kill the Wilmans."

The next few months passed peaceably enough. Winter passed into spring, and the spring became the summer of 1944. People were thinner. Food was becoming scarcer and scarcer. Still Johannes drank goat milk and grew. Dora baked bread made from dried peas and rationed it to one small slice per meal – two on Sunday. She planted a garden at the back of the house, hoping for some beans and carrots to can for the winter. Clothes were not to be had anywhere, and Nelis fixed the holes in the shoes that he, Dora and Tilda wore by cutting up an old leather handbag. Dora unraveled one of her sweaters and knitted a new sweater for Johannes, a green one. Nelis' store was permanently closed now. There were no more goods to be had.

On sunny days that fall, Tilda used to walk out with Johannes in his carriage. He was a friendly baby, one who smiled engagingly and dimpled for anyone who happened to look his way. It was on one of those late fall days in 1944 that Nelis, listlessly gazing out through the front window, saw Tilda approaching down the street pushing the carriage in front of her. She appeared to be walking quite fast and then he noted with some alarm that a group of school-aged children were following her. They seemed to be pelting her with something. He stood up from his chair in front of the window.

"Dora," he said, "Dora, look."

She absently got up from her chair, still half-absorbed in her reading, and stood next to him.

"What, Nelis?"

He could feel her tense up. Then, as Tilda came closer, they could both see that the children were throwing stones.

"I don't believe it."

His cry was intense and he felt pain in his stomach. He was out on the walkway, out on the street, before he knew it. In his haste he had forgotten to put on his shoes, and was running towards his daughter on his stocking feet.

"Tilda," he called out, "Tilda."

She was bleeding from a cut on her temple, but was not crying. Johannes had been totally covered with a blanket. He was protesting this indignity loudly and moving about as much as he could in his limited space. Because he was tied in with a harness, he could not fall out. Nelis put his right arm about Tilda, and took over the pushing of the carriage with his left. The children, seeing him, ran off.

176

"Has this happened before?"

"No... well, yes, a few times."

"Well, from now on, I will go with you when you take Johannes for a walk."

She sobbed then, wearily, as if she had been fighting for a long time. His arm tightened about her and he swallowed. Reaching over, he took the blanket off Johannes.

"Boo," the small boy said, thinking for a moment it was the game they often played with him before he went to sleep.

Dora stood waiting at the steps. She clucked at the blood on Tilda's face, but then calmly took her hand and led her into the house. Nelis was quite certain a lot of the neighbors were watching through their curtains. If this had happened before, why had no one told him? Mrs. Meester, their closest neighbor, was waiting for word on her husband who had been sent to Germany to work in an armament factory. Mrs. Geest, on their other side, was waiting to hear from her husband as well. Only he was in a concentration camp. Did they identify Tilda with the oppressors? Did they feel the same hatred for her as they felt for the Germans? Nelis sighed. He undid Johannes' harness and lifted him up out of the carriage. The child laughed and grabbed his cheeks.

Inside, Tilda was weeping on Dora's shoulder. Dora looked at Nelis and motioned with her hands that he should take the baby somewhere else. Nelis nodded and took Johannes with him into the empty grocery shop. He played with the boy. He sat on the floor and then lay down, letting the child crawl all over him. Johannes, excited by the individual attention, roared with laughter every time Nelis tickled him. There was a knock from the outside door. Nelis, flat on his back, Johannes on his belly, sat up. No one ever came to the shop door any more. A very clear sign was posted reading "Not open for business." But persistently, the knock intruded again. It was a very decided knock. Nelis put Johannes down and got up. Cautiously opening the door just a crack, he saw Mrs. Pot's face close to his own.

"Yes, can I help you."

"No, you can't," she said, "but here's a neighborhood petition signed by many of your neighbors, asking you to move away from here."

She slid a piece of paper through the crack. He took it and before he had a chance to reply, she had gone. He sat down on the floor next to Johannes. The child tried to grab the paper from his hands, but he held it up in the air with his right hand. Then, reaching for the glasses in his shirt pocket with his left, he read:

To the Goedhart family:

We, the undersigned, would prefer it if you all left the neighborhood. Though you have been a good neighbor for a long time, we cannot tolerate the presence of your daughter, someone who collaborated with the enemy. It would be for Tilda's own good if she just left these parts. The end of the war will be here soon and then what will happen to her? This note was written to let you know that traitors will be punished sooner or later.

Twenty names were affixed to the bottom of the letter. Nelis stared at the names and stared and stared. Then he ripped the letter up into shreds.

"You can move in with us, Vader," both Frans and Hans said.

But neither Dora nor Nelis wanted to do that. To run away from the neighborhood where they had lived since they were first married did not sit well with them. Besides that, they did not believe that everyone on the list had actually signed. Perhaps, they argued between the two of them, most of the names on the paper had been forged there by the Pots. But that there was a growing animosity of people towards Tilda could not be denied. The girl was unable to walk the streets any longer by herself. It had happened several times now that she had been pushed and shoved by total strangers, people who seemed intent on physically harming her. Dominee Raadsma visited and encouraged. Sometimes he talked to Tilda privately and always she came away from these meetings happier and more hopeful. And Johannes grew and thrived throughout that difficult autumn and even throughout the hunger winter and spring that followed.

There were air raids at night now and sometimes during the day as well. Nelis, Dora, Tilda and Johannes spent many sleepless hours huddled together in the storage room underneath the shop. More and more German troops passed through Diestadt, retreating back into Germany, carrying German equipment with them. Nelis, as well as all the inhabitants of Diestadt, often saw allied airplanes overhead flying in V formation. They were on their way to Germany where they would drop bombs. Farther out, close to the next town, it was reported that the Germans were starting to dig foxholes, were getting ready for the Americans and the Canadians. It became dangerous to walk out on the streets. The Germans were constantly patrolling, shooting at any and everything. Far away in the distance, the sound of machine guns rattled and rattled and rattled.

"I've seen an allied soldier. Actually, I've seen at least a dozen of them."

Frans was excited. He sat on the floor of the shelter with his parents and talked non-stop.

"But none of you should venture out yet. It's definitely not safe."

"What about you."

"Don't worry about me. But...."

He stopped suddenly, eyeing his sister with a certain amount of trepidation.

"Make sure Tilda, that you do not go out alone either," he said, "Wait for either Hans or myself before you go out. Do you promise?"

Tilda nodded, giving her word readily.

"Good."

He smiled at his parents before he went on.

"There are Belgian, French and Polish soldiers about. They're all part of the American, British and Canadian forces. The streets in the next town are filled with tanks, trucks, and jeeps. And one of them gave me some chocolate."

He pulled several chocolate bars from his pocket and handed them to his family. Tilda ripped one open and broke a small piece off for Johannes. Opening his mouth wide, he was delighted with the taste and clamored for more. They all laughed.

"I have to go again, but remember what I said. Tilda do not, under any circumstance, leave this shelter until I or Hans come to get you."

"I won't," she agreed again.

"Good," Frans repeated, leaving them savoring the chocolate bars.

The next evening, dominee Raadsma came to the house.

"I've spoken with your sons and I'd like Tilda and Johannes to stay with my wife and myself until things have quieted down," he said.

"Why?" Nelis asked, but he knew within himself that it might be a very good idea.

"The Germans have all but left Diestadt now and the next few days could be rather difficult," dominee answered, "No one will bother my wife or myself or even think to come to our home to look for what they conceive to be collaborators."

"But she did not...."

Nelis stopped. Did she not? Tilda looked down at the floor.

"Go and pack a few things for yourself and the child, Tilda," dominee said, "and I'm sure we'll get to the parsonage safely under the cover of darkness."

Tilda got up and left with Dora in tow. Nelis nervously began to tap his fingers on the edge of the table.

"Will things be all right, do you think, dominee? Will people forget?"

"Time will tell, Nelis. Time will tell. Make sure that you and Dora attend church this Sunday morning."

"Yes, dominee."

It was strange for dominee to say this. Nelis pondered the words within his heart. After all, he and Dora never missed a service. Why should they miss one now? He watched as dominee walked away down the garden path towards the road. Dominee had his arm around Tilda, who was carrying Johannes on her hip. It was dark out and the wind shook the leaves of the trees they passed. And then he could not see them any longer.

Church was packed that Sunday. The ushers had to bring chairs and place them in the aisles, beneath the pulpit and next to the walls. Everyone was wearing their best, and many people were wearing something orange as well. Dora and Nelis had arrived early. They watched the sanctuary fill up with church members as well as with people they had never seen before. Although thin and undernourished, there was no doubt that everyone was overweight with heavy smiles. The organist began the prelude and rich tones swept through the church. There was an air of expectancy, of keyed-up joy – a joy that was just waiting to be released. But there was an infinite sadness within Nelis. He wanted more than anything else for his Tilda to be sitting by his side. He wanted to glance at her face, as he had done so often in the past when she had sat next to him in the pew. He wanted to see the eager anticipation on her face as she listened to the minister preach. But there was no Tilda, not yet anyway, and he did not think in his heart of hearts that dominee would deem it wise to bring her to church.

The consistory filed in. One by one the men passed through the aisle with the minister last of all. And, lo and behold, Tilda was walking at Dominee Raadsma's side. A murmur ran through the congregation. It was a low murmur – neither approving nor disapproving. Nelis reached for Dora's hand and she squeezed his fingers hard as if to say, "It will be all right, Nelis. Don't worry." The last elder, as was the custom, stopped and shook Dominee Raadsma's hand and then, much to everyone's surprise, he also shook Tilda's hand, before taking his place in the elder's pew.

Dominee Raadsma, stepping back, motioned that Tilda should precede him onto the pulpit. She walked up the steps, her back straight and tall, looking every inch, Nelis thought, like a royal

181

princess. He smiled at himself. How often had he thought that in the past. And now, of all times, he was caught in pride again. Tilda had reached the top of the steps. Dominee Raadsma was close behind her. He indicated, when he reached the top as well, that she should sit in one of the chairs behind the pulpit and she did so. It was breathlessly quiet in the sanctuary. No one made a sound. No one.

Dominee Raadsma walked over to the chancel.

"Dear people of God," he said, "dear liberated people of God."

Nelis felt a shiver go down his back. What a blessing it was to be liberated. Not just from the Germans, but from sin. Yes, what a mighty blessing! Just behind the dominee, he could see Tilda's dress. She was wearing the light red dress that Dora had made for her for the confession of faith Sunday.

"What a blessing it is to be here this Sunday! What a great, great blessing!"

It was still eerily quiet. Everyone had their faces turned towards the dominee. Everyone wondered, speculated and listened.

"Before we begin our service," dominee went on, "I want to tell you a story."

Dora squeezed Nelis' fingers again. His hands were cold and he felt sweat pour down his armpits.

"A few years ago, a young girl made profession of her faith in this church. She was young but wished with all her heart to serve the Lord."

Dora squeezed Nelis' hand once more and he glanced at her. Tears were running down her eyes.

"Examined by consistory, this girl was found to be pure in heart and earnest in her desire to profess her faith. I gave her a special text to carry with her throughout her earthly life. The text was *'Verily I say unto you, inasmuch as ye have done it unto one of the least of these my brethren, ye have done it unto me.'*"

Now a tear slid down Nelis' cheek.

"You all know, of course, that I am speaking of Tilda Goedhart, daughter of Nelis and Dora Goedhart. And you anticipate that I will ask all of you to forgive her for the indiscretion you believe she committed by bearing a child – the child Johannes."

It was deathly quiet.

"However, I do not ask that."

Dominee paused and looked down at the congregation.

"As a matter of fact, I ask something entirely different."

He turned and looked at Tilda.

"Tilda, will you come and stand next to me?"

Very slowly, Tilda rose from the great chair which had enveloped her all the while the dominee had been speaking. She came and stood next to him and he put an arm about her shoulder.

"I ask her instead to forgive you."

The hush was palpable now.

"Back in the winter of 1942, one Jewish family in this area was desperate for an address – for a place to hide from the infamous razzias that took so many of their countrymen to camps – camps from which they never returned. An address for this family, sad to say, could not be found. Many people were asked but all were afraid to take this couple who only had one child with them. The reason they were afraid to take the couple was because the woman was pregnant with another child. People felt that to take a Jewish couple with a baby due to be born meant extra risk – and no one was willing to take that risk."

Nelis had trouble breathing. He remembered. He remembered.

"Tilda took the text she had received at her confession of faith, seriously. She came up with a plan, a plan to safeguard the coming child. She offered to be a surrogate mother to that child – offered her own body to protect it. She had been seeing young Dolf Wilman, at the request of the underground, in order to gain information and a plan was born in her heart after Dolf was killed. And so, as I said just now, she offered to be a surrogate mother to the little Jewish child. She offered even though she knew that in pretending to be pregnant with this child, she would suffer the consequences of scorn and derision from her friends and neighbors."

Dominee paused for a moment before he went on: "I ask that Johannes Heyman now be brought to the front of the church."

Mrs. Raadsma calmly stood up from a back pew and came towards the front carrying the child. Johannes was solemn and quiet, contemplating all the faces he passed. But when Mrs. Raadsma mounted the pulpit steps and the child discovered Tilda, he crowed with delight. And a smile passed through the congregation. And Mrs. Raadsma gave the baby to Tilda, who kissed his forehead.

"May I now ask Rabbi Heyman and his wife to come up here as well."

Again, from the back, two people, hand in hand, moved quietly through the center aisle and climbed the pulpit steps. Nelis now wept openly, as did several people around him. Tilda walked towards them and gave Johannes to Annie Heyman. Baby Johannes, fond as he was of faces and beards in particular, grabbed the rabbi's beard in passing. Then Tilda began to weep, and the rabbi embraced her and kissed her.

The organ began to play – softly at first, but increasing in volume as the lines flowed.

Hallelujah! Praise the Lord!
In His house, with one accord!

People began to hum, to sing along. And on the pulpit Tilda still stood in the embrace of the rabbi.

Praise Him in the wide extent
Of His spacious firmament;
Sing and shout His praise uprightly.

First one person and then another, stood up. And the volume of their singing swelled the rafters.

His unbounded greatness praise
And extol His wondrous ways;
Praise Him for His deeds so mighty.

6: The Fallen Lines

The LORD is my chosen portion and my cup; you hold my lot. The lines have fallen for me in pleasant places; indeed, I have a beautiful inheritance (Psalm 16:5-6).

Possibly someone could argue that experiences, things that have happened both in the past and in the present, are like suitcases which people lug about with them. The suitcase gets heavier and heavier with age as more and more events are added. Sometimes people are crippled by the burden they attempt to carry and in the long run, the weight might rip the suitcase open. Consequently, past and present events cascade out onto the ground in front of them and behind them. Amazingly, these events, if studied carefully, spill out into a straight line.

Berend Verbond immigrated to Canada from Holland approximately two years after the Second World War. His father was a farmer - a diligent and dedicated farmer - but one with relatively few holdings. There were two children in the Verbond household, two healthy boys. Berend was the youngest and second child. Even though farming coursed through his veins and he dearly loved the country in which he had been born, he knew that the prospect of acquiring his own property and running his own place were less than bleak. The truth was that Holland had been left with a surplus of men eager to till the soil; and another truth was that after the retreating German soldiers had destroyed the dikes, much of the Dutch soil lay flooded. Besides these truths lay the fact that even if Berend were to give up on the dream of farming and somehow manage to get a reasonable job somewhere in a Dutch city, there was also the matter of a rampant housing shortage. Many homes and factories had been bombed. Consequently, even with the best of intentions, Berend could not imagine a future for himself in Holland.

When a Canadian immigration officer was sent to the Netherlands in late 1946 to resume a pre-war immigration program, Berend applied and was accepted. As well, at this time, he proposed marriage to Hannie Mathijs, the pretty daughter of a nearby neighbor. Actually, Hannie had been the one who had informed and urged him on towards immigration. She had fed him exciting stories of family members who had crossed the ocean and who now lived on large farmsteads; of friends who had left Holland for Canada and who now breathed in wide open spaces and who tilled their own rich earth. She, and her father, had fired his imagination and Berend could literally see himself plowing fields, could visualize himself as the owner of many acres. But during this time of burgeoning desire to leave his native land, he had apprised neither his mother nor his father of the rather monumental steps he was considering. When he did finally speak to them, he had been surprised that they were more upset by the announcement that he was marrying Hannie than that he was leaving his native country for Canada. Hannie did not belong to any church.

"Berend," his mother had spoken softly, after his father had not minced words about being unequally yoked with an unbeliever, before leaving the house to tend to the cows in the barn, "Berend, son, she is not a Christian."

"Oh, Moeke," he had replied, "She's a good girl, a hard worker, and her parents sometimes go to church."

"Are you hoping to ..." his mother had paused, searching for words and starting again, "Are you hoping that she will become a Christian? Because in the long run, God willing you should have children, she will be their mother."

"Sure, she will," he had answered the question rather glibly and easily, as if he were smoothing out inedible lumps in the morning porridge, "Sure, I think that in time Hannie will come to believe what I believe. She is a good girl, mother."

His mother had smiled. It had been a wry smile. A smile that implied that she knew he was not considering the matter seriously. She had responded to his statement with another question.

"What do you believe, Berend?"

It startled him, that question, and he pushed it away, deep within himself. And he had not answered.

"You like her, don't you, Moeke?"

"Yes, I like her. But that's not the point, Berend. The point is whether or not God approves of you marrying Hannie."

He had not told his mother or his father, at this point, about the baby - a baby that would be born in Canada.

Hannie had accepted his offer of marriage very quietly. It had puzzled Berend. Didn't she want to go with him; didn't she want to begin a new life as his wife in Canada? He attributed her reticence to the finality of the plans, plans which they had only talked about in the past. It was difficult to think about leaving - leaving for always. He did not like to dwell on it too much himself. Although Hannie's own mother and father, when they were told of the firmed-up immigration plans, confessed that they would miss Hannie very much, they did not protest.

It actually almost seemed to Berend as if they were relieved she was leaving. But then, he reasoned within himself, they did have four other daughters who would be staying in Holland, four other daughters for whom they had to provide. It only made sense that they welcomed this match. It was one less daughter about whom to worry. Neither did Hannie show any special compunction about leaving her family. She had never, to his knowledge, harbored sick feelings in her gut about saying goodbye; about the prospect of traveling to another country.

Together Berend and Hannie had decided that because the date of farewell was so close at hand, they would not tell their parents about the pregnancy before they were well-settled in Canada. Deep within himself Berend knew that this was cowardice on his part and he felt shame. This shame prevented him from speaking to his father about the hopes he entertained for the future. He avoided his parents as much as he could and was astonished when his father, mere days before Berend's and Hannie's departure for Canada, had quietly given him an envelope containing a cheque, a substantial cheque.

"Part of the inheritance," he softly said one evening after supper, his rough hands shaking as he handed it over, "But this," he added as he pushed a Bible across the table towards his youngest son, "this is the bulk of your estate."

At one point Berend had secretly worried that his father might possibly evict him from the house before he left. Now as love unrelentingly kissed him on the cheek, he felt remorse. His father studied him carefully for a long moment, studied him almost as if he were weighing him, before going on to say, "May God ever be your guide, Berend."

He added softly, "Do not forget whom you are, son. After all, a good name is rather to be chosen than great riches."

Then he sighed deeply and repeated almost dolefully, as if he believed Berend had already forgotten, "Never forget whom you are."

Hannie had informed Berend shortly after his proposal, that her father had a second cousin who lived in Ontario. This cousin had recently written to them explaining that he was sorely in need of a hired man with experience in milking. Brian Niks milked fifty cows, a mixture of Jerseys and Holsteins, and owned about two hundred and fifty acres. A house would be provided for whomever landed the job. Hannie's father had immediately telephoned cousin Brian and it seemed this distant relative was willing to take Berend and Hannie on, sight unseen. There was, therefore, no need for them to worry about where they might live. As well, the pay this cousin Brian was willing to offer seemed more than fair. Hannie clapped her hands after she told him before soundly kissing him on both cheeks.

"Oh, Berend, isn't this just what we need! What amazing luck! And my father's accepted the offer for us and has told him that we were coming."

Glad that she was excited, but feeling slightly awkward to be relying on Hannie's family, Berend was, nevertheless, relieved that the unknown future seemed to be playing into their hands. Yet he knew better than to relegate circumstances to 'luck'. There was, after all, no such thing as luck; there was only providence. And he would explain this to Hannie when the right time came. No need to preach yet. Was there not a whole lifetime ahead of them? - hours and days and years and ages? So it seemed in any case.

Before long Berend and Hannie waved emotional goodbyes to their families and to all their friends as they stood on the deck of the large liner taking them away from Holland - taking them across the ocean to Canada. They had been married at the city hall the previous day. The minister of Berend's church had refused to marry them, repeating father Verbond's words, 'You shall not be unequally yoked to an unbeliever." Berend had felt a pang of unprepared-for sharp pain in his stomach at the quiet resignation on the faces of his parents during the small ceremony at city hall. He recalled it now, even as he stood between all the passengers on the crowded deck of the ship, even as an excess of laughter, crying, yelling and cheering surrounded him. Leaning over the railing, he stared long and hard at the receding small and smaller figures of his mother and father on the pier. He knew his mother had been crying and saw that his father's arm was around her waist. He took Hannie's hand and squeezed it. They would do well. This was the right decision.

The two-week-long voyage was a daily adventure for Berend. It had cost a little over 600 guilders per person and he felt that at this price he ought to enjoy every minute of the crossing to the fullest. Hannie, however, subject to severe seasickness, was not able to make it up to the deck. He sorely missed her. She was delegated to sleeping in the women's quarters and he had little access to her as she kept to her bunk most of the day. He himself was quartered in the men's section of the boat but spent most of his days and evenings traversing the length and breadth of the ship. The crossing was deemed rough and so the decks were empty a good deal of the time. Berend strode about freely, exploring, enjoying the feel of the wind blowing in his face. He contemplated that, even though he would not have anticipated this voyage a year ago, surely the lines were falling for him in pleasant places. Surely the Lord was with him. Mesmerized he stared at the coast of Greenland, beheld pods of dolphins, and gazed up at the vast sky as he walked past the ship's railing in the evenings. The rather tempestuous swaying of the large boat rocked him to sleep at night and he considered how small he was! But how vast the opportunities before him. There was both excitement and contentment within him as he daily beheld the white, curling waves swelling about the vessel. And then the trip was over. Canada was in sight.

Pier 21 in Halifax, Nova Scotia was the designated landing point for many immigration ships coming to Canada. An immigration depot for thousands of newcomers arriving by boat in Canada, it fairly pulsed with new life. The office of Customs and Immigration was housed in a brick building on the harbor front - a brick building through which everyone coming off the boat had to pass. Consequently, Pier 21 was a busy place. The immigration annex was connected to the ship by an overhead walkway through which Berend and a pale-faced Hannie walked, together with hundreds of other passengers, towards the customs. There was no hold-up. Their papers were in order, the customs officer was friendly and pointed them in the direction of a restaurant-dining room where they were able to buy a meal for fifty-five cents. From there it was possible to advance towards a ramp which connected Pier 21 to the railway station.

Hannie was still shaky from the long voyage and not very hungry, but Berend was ravenous. He began to eat her sandwiches as well as his own and felt uncommonly happy.

"We're in Canada, Hannie," he announced, his mouth full of bread, but smiling as he chewed, "We're in Canada, little wife. We made it. We've arrived in our new country!"

She returned a wan smile to his exuberance only to begin crying the next minute.

"What's the matter?"

Awkwardly, he put his right arm around her shoulder, swallowing the bread in his mouth.

"I don't feel well," she sobbed, "I think it's the baby."

"The baby?"

"Yes," she managed to whisper, "I'm bleeding, Berend."

"Bleeding?"

"Yes, and I have cramps too. Cramps in my stomach."

Berend lay down the sandwich he still held in his left hand and studied Hannie carefully as she sagged rather heavily against him. Her color was not good. He remembered seeing a Red Cross station on their way to the dining room. Rising abruptly, he left the half-eaten slice of bread on his plate. Staring up at him, Hannie's face was tear-stained. Compassion flooded him. He had not taken very good care of his new wife.

"Can you walk?"

She nodded and to prove it, stood up, leaning on the table as she did so.

"Here, take my arm, Hannie."

Slowly he guided her through the crowded restaurant, past the tables, back through the waiting room teeming with people, towards the place where he had noticed the sign of the Red Cross. A nurse, standing in the entrance, saw them coming.

"Is your wife ill?"

The woman spoke English, but he understood.

"Yes, she is ... she is ... having a baby."

A starched arm reached out for Hannie's other arm, guiding them into the station. There was a waiting room with some chairs. As well there were two closed doors behind which Berend supposed there were examination rooms. It was through one of these doors that the nurse led Hannie. He was asked to stay behind. Sitting down on one of the chairs, he wondered if Hannie would be all right. Then he wondered if they would miss their train and then he berated himself for even considering this. Supposing the examination would take a while, he stood up and wandered back into the dining room, to the table where they had been sitting, picked up the half-eaten sandwich and returned to the Red Cross station. Eating the bread slowly, he decided that their crate - a crate which held all their belongings - would have to be held back from being put onto the train. But he could not presently leave again. What if the nurse came out and he was not here? To his relief the door opened shortly thereafter. He stood up.

"Mr. Verbond, can you step inside."

She beckoned him with her finger as she spoke. He strode over. Hannie was laying on an examining table. Her eyes were closed.

"How is my wife?"

He enunciated the English words carefully.

"She will need some medical intervention."

The nurse was middle-aged. She looked to be a kind woman and indicated that he should sit down on the chair next to the examination table, next to Hannie.

"Your wife has had a miscarriage, Mr. Verbond."

"A miscarriage?"

He repeated the words slowly, but understood them.

"Yes, and she will need to be hospitalized for a small procedure. So I'm afraid that your plans for boarding a train will not take place today. Perhaps tomorrow, but I strongly advise some rest and no strenuous activity the next few days."

Berend could not follow everything the nurse said, but he grasped the general drift of her conversation. The words hospital, miscarriage, rest, and train were all jigsaw pieces and he built them into a picture. He reached for Hannie's hand.

"How are you?"

"We lost the baby, Berend."

"I know, but we'll have others."

In a strange way, he was relieved. There was no need now for subterfuge with his parents; no need to send them a letter about a premature baby; no need for anything like that at all.

"Berend?"

He looked at Hannie. Her face was so white that his heart overflowed with deep concern for her well-being.

"It will be all right, Hannie. Don't worry. Before you know it we'll be settled on your cousin's farm and we'll...."

He stopped. Hannie's eyes were full of tears and they coursed down her cheeks. She made no noise. But she looked at him through her tears and stared at him so intently and so sadly that he became uncomfortable.

"Hannie?"

Then she closed her eyes and he let go of her hand.

There was, in all, a three day delay before Berend and Hannie could continue on to Ontario. Cousin Brian, who had been notified of their situation by telephone, proved to be very sympathetic. Telling them not be concerned about traveling to his farm from the train depot, he assured Berend he would meet their train at Union Station in Toronto. And that's how matters proceeded - proceeded smoothly and as planned. Hannie was listless and tired during the train journey, sleeping and dozing as they travelled, but Berend told himself that this was to be expected. She would soon perk up once they were settled in their new home. Fascinated, he watched the vast landscape fly by. He pointed out the magnitude of the horizon to Hannie and was rewarded with a few smiles - weary smiles they were - but still smiles.

The soul of solicitude, cousin Brian was kind from the moment Berend and Hannie stepped off the train. The little house waiting for them at the end of Brian's laneway, after several hours of driving, was furnished comfortably. The pantry was also stocked with many food items and they were told to feel at home.

"Tomorrow," Brian had smiled and spoken to them that very first day, in broken but very understandable Dutch, "you sleep late, and when you are feeling rested, then we will begin to talk about what you will do here on the farm."

But Hannie and Berend had been too nervous and too excited to sleep that initial night, although eventually they had drifted off. There were so many new things, so many stimulating and wonderful things to think about. That first morning on the farm Hannie had gotten up at daybreak, and Berend had found her in the living room, touching and stroking the colorful throw on the couch, simultaneously staring at the reproduction of a Vermeer painting on the wall behind the couch. The painting was one of a woman wearing a blue smock, a woman who was heavily pregnant. The blue-smocked woman was reading a letter and behind her, on the wall, Berend could see a map. For a moment he wondered what the woman was reading and what part of the world was depicted on the map, but then Hannie moved away from the painting towards a rocking chair by the window. She touched its back and it gently rocked forward and backward, forward and backward. Just the hint of a shadow passed over her face before she turned to face him.

"Oh, Berend," she had said, "I can't believe that this is our home, our very own home. If only...."

Not wishing to put a damper on the beauty of this first day, and full of boundless energy, Berend stretched his tall frame, almost touching the whitewashed ceiling of the living room. How very well everything had all turned out in spite of his father's misgivings, and in spite of the miscarriage. As he stretched, he pushed away the vague feeling of discomfort that lay deep within himself. For there was little doubt in his mind that had his father been in his place, he would at this time have sat down at the sturdy wooden kitchen table with folded hands, and that he would have said, "Let's thank God for all the blessings that have come our way, Hannie. Let's thank Him for the safe travel, for your restored good health, for the kindness shown us by cousin Brian and for the wonder of a home all our own. Let's thank Him for all these things before we do anything else." In the space of a single second during his stretch towards the ceiling, Berend knew that this was exactly what his father would have done and said. Sighing, he dropped his hands to his sides, and then defused the feelings of guilt building up in his heart by quietly thanking God through a quick prayer offered up in his own heart. No need to burden Hannie with any religious points of view yet. She was much too vulnerable right now. Time enough in the future.

There was much to learn in the weeks and months that ensued, much to absorb, but Berend was a hard worker and a willing learner. Nothing was too difficult for him or too hard. He put all his zeal, and most of his time, into repairing fences, helping to enlarge the barn and digging out a pond. The pond was an innovative thought cousin Brian had brainstormed and Berend had enthusiastically supported the idea. The pond was spring-fed. It provided water to clean the cows before milking and it was also used to clean the barn after the milking. A pump drove the water through pipes, and both Berend and Brian grinned at one another the first time they used it. The cows produced about twelve cans of milk each day, milk which was faithfully trucked to the nearby dairy.

Cousin Brian was in his late fifties and he was a rugged, tanned man. In spite of his apparent health, however, he tired easily, and often Berend would espy him sitting down on one of the bales of hay piled up against the side of the barn. During these moments he seemed to have trouble breathing. Berend noted the problem with growing concern but felt uneasy about saying anything. After all, cousin Brian kept up with the work, laughed heartily but encouragingly at Berend's broken attempts at English and was always in good spirits. That surely indicated good health! The only negative aspect about cousin Brian was that when he was excited, or frustrated, he would use God's name in vain. It made Berend uncomfortable, but he never commented on it. He reasoned to himself that he was on cousin Brian's property, and that it was cousin Brian after all, who swore, and what did that have to do with him! But he realized innately, although his mouth was hesitant to articulate it into so many words, that it was not because cousin Brian was the owner of the farm that he did not confront or correct him, but that it was because he did not want to put his job, his livelihood, into jeopardy. At the same time, he was very fond of the older man. Consequently, the next time cousin Brian took a rest on one of the hay bales, coughing so loudly that it drowned out the cooing of a mourning dove far away in the distance, Berend felt a keen sense of foreboding. He liked the sound of these Canadian mourning doves. Half-glad, half-sad their cry was, as if they nostalgically remembered how sweet life had been to them, but also as if they knew that they would die soon. Cousin Brian stood up and returned to work with vigor and Berend was glad of it.

There was a lot of adjusting those first few days and months. Hannie rested each afternoon, as she had begun to do after the miscarriage. Both Berend and cousin Brian had told her to stay out of the barn, had insisted that her duties lay within the home. Truth be told, Berend only saw Hannie at mealtimes, if then. There was always so much to do - so much work to accomplish, and so much to learn. But Hannie appeared happy enough when he did see her and she was quite willing to cook and clean house both for themselves and for cousin Brian. The odd times that Berend came into the house during the day and found her gone, he assumed that she was taking care of things at cousin Brian's house.

The greatest adjustment to life in Canada was a strange one. Cousin Brian, as they had been wont to call him from the beginning, called them into his living room one evening that first winter. It was just a week before to Christmas.

"I hope you are feeling at home," he said, after they were all settled comfortably.

Hannie's dark blue eyes shone towards their benefactor and Berend remarked within himself that she was very beautiful and that he was very glad he had asked her to marry him. Dark shoulder length hair curled about her face, and her red cheeks glowed with renewed health. It was uncommon for Berend to think much about these things. Usually his thoughts were directed towards farm work, usually they were entangled in the chore of the moment. But Hannie had told him only that morning that she was expecting once more, that they would have a baby early on in the summer. He had been thinking about that most of the day.

"Oh, cousin Brian," Hannie now exclaimed with heartfelt sincerity, "we are feeling very much at home. Thank you again for your kindness."

Berend could tell by the way the older man smiled at his wife that he was truly touched by her words. Cousin Brian had been in Canada for decades and for a good many of those years he had lived alone. A hard-working farmer, he and Berend got along famously - both in the barn and out of the barn.

"I want to ask you both a question," Cousin Brian continued, "and I want you to think on it carefully, very carefully."

He paused, took out a handkerchief, and wiped his face.

Next to Berend on the couch, Hannie moved a little closer to him, a strange rather inscrutable look on her face.

"I want to ask you to legally change your last name to mine."

No one said anything for the space of almost a minute. The fire crackled in the hearth and the smell of coffee permeated the room. Berend didn't have the foggiest notion what cousin Brian's words implied. So, after a long pause and after clearing his throat, he asked.

"What exactly do you mean?"

"I mean I'm asking if you will visit a lawyer with me and if you will change your last name from Verbond to Niks."

"Why?"

Cousin Brian stood up and began to walk back and forth, back and forth in front of them.

"As you know, I came from Holland a long time ago. It was tough here in the beginning, but I worked hard and, in time, I married."

Hannie nodded and her eyes automatically traveled to the china cabinet where a photograph of a young cousin Brian, arm around a white-clad bride, prominently stood in view. It filled her with amazement that on this ordinary cabinet a piece of human life should be so displayed. But life was over for the bride. Would she herself stand on a china cabinet someday, smile fixed, eyes gazing blankly at some unknown object in the background? She twisted her hands on her lap and sighed. Cousin Brian followed her gaze and walked over to the cabinet. Taking down the picture, he brought it over to them. Almost reverently, Hannie took the photo from his gnarled, work-worn hand and stroked the glass. There was a small crack in the right hand corner. She was suddenly filled with sadness, as if something was passing her by and, even if she wanted to, she would not be able to stop it. It was time. She knew it was time.

"She was beautiful, my Lena."

"Yes," Hannie agreed, "she was very beautiful."

"You look a little bit like her, Hannie. I don't mean just in the way you look physically, but also in that you are kind and sweet, just like she was."

"Oh," Hannie replied, blushing and at a loss for words.

For a moment she again beheld herself behind the glass of the photograph, tucked away in the corner of a desk or a bookcase. She shivered.

"We never had children - children that lived, that is. They died before they were born."

Hannie laid a hand on her belly and sighed deeply, putting the photo back into cousin Brian's hand.

"Lena, she died too. We were only married for eighteen years."

Cousin Brian stopped talking. He returned to the cabinet, gently arranging the photograph next to a china plate. Then he plodded back to his chair and sat down again, sinking heavily into the cushioned softness. His breathing was labored.

"I'm sorry," Hannie offered.

He shook his head in reply and studied the carpet for a long while. Berend cleared his throat. He didn't know what to say. His father would know what to say. Perhaps something about eternity, about the passing of time and about God. Of course, about God. He cleared his throat again searching for words, but his heart had delegated such phrases and sentences to a shadow corner and he could not read them because the light was too dim, much too dim. Suddenly Cousin Brian began to speak again.

"The church people," he began, in a low tone, "they wouldn't ... that is, they weren't ... they weren't very friendly to my Lena. Lena had a German name you see."

Then cousin Brian swore. Hannie looked startled and Berend patted her hand. She pulled it away.

"Cousin Brian," she said, "you know that I love you and that I am so grateful you put us up here and gave Berend a job."

She stopped for a breath. Berend was surprised. Hannie was usually quiet, not speaking much in company. But she went on and he listened.

"Well, cousin Brian, you shouldn't blame God. And you shouldn't say His name like that, I think."

She stopped and then fell silent, looking down and studying the carpet. To Berend's surprise, cousin Brian did not react with anger.

He only smiled at her and repeated, "You speak like my Lena. But to go on with what I was saying. My Lena had a German name and that is why people were not so friendly."

"I see."

Glad to be able to say something, Berend responded this time and indeed, he did see. Had he not been in the Resistance during the war and did he not even now feel antipathy towards all things German?

"But my Lena was from the United States not from Germany. She could not even speak German. Her grandparents had come from the

Black Sea and Volga River regions of Russia. They immigrated to America. But that was long before she was born. "

Cousin Brian breathed in deeply and continued.

"I met Lena because she worked for a farming family to the north of here and I was delivering some fence posts to that farm. When I saw her for the first time...."

He stopped obviously moved by the memory. Hannie stood up and walked over to where cousin Brian sat. She knelt on her knees by the older man's chair.

"Cousin Brian," she said, her eyes earnest, "Cousin Brian, I think you probably made her very happy. I think that you had a very happy marriage."

He smiled down at the face in front of him.

"Yes," he answered, "we were both happy, Hannie. But we had no children. No children that lived, you see."

"We are going to have a baby," Hannie said, "It is growing now in my belly. And if it is a girl, I think I would like to call her Lena."

Cousin Brian took Hannie's hands into his own. His eyes filled with tears.

"That is very good of you, Hannie," he whispered, "It's very kind."

Berend cleared his throat once more. Back in the shadow areas of his heart, he latched onto what cousin Brian had said previously.

"But the suggestion you made," he said, "about the... about the name change. What do you mean by that?"

Dropping Hannie's hands, cousin Brian now gave his full attention to Berend. He did not answer the question directly but began to speak of his health.

"My days here are numbered. I have a heart condition. The doctor has told me this. So when I knew you were coming, I thought...."

"Oh, cousin Brian," Hannie interrupted, pupils wide, not letting him finish, "is there anything we can do?"

"Yes, you can."

He sat up straight and again looked directly at Berend, who shifted uncomfortably on the couch. He knew instinctively that his response to what Cousin Brian was about to say was of vital importance. That it would change his life.

"I have no children, as I said," the usually sturdy voice quavered now, "but I would like to see the farm settled on family."

"But how would I... I mean...."

Berend could not quite fathom, did not want to grasp the significance of the request. His name was Berend Verbond. This had been his grandfather's name. He had loved his grandfather.

"You have to submit certain documents," cousin Brian went on, "this is what the lawyer told me. But this is not difficult. I will pay the legal fee that is required. And, the whole matter will take some time, because you have to live in Ontario a number of years before you can become a Canadian citizen. And then, when you are a Canadian citizen you can change your last name. For the moment I just want you to promise me that you will do that."

"I see," Berend responded slowly.

And it was his father's face he saw. For some reason he saw his father's face as he had gazed at him just prior to his departure.

"May God be your guide, Berend," he had said and he had also said, "Do not forget whom you are."

For a split second Brian thought that perhaps he had forgotten whom he was. After all, he and Hannie had not been to any church as yet. On Sundays the chores needed to be done as well as on other days and usually Berend was dog-tired and took a huge nap after lunch. He excused this lapse of church attendance by reasoning that the Sunday gave him a little more time with Hannie and that she needed this time. But he also saw in that split second that they had lived in Canada longer than half a year and as the months passed it became increasingly more difficult to change habits that were solidifying around him like a shell.

"Can you promise me that you will do that?"

Cousin Brian repeated his question. But Berend was quite lost in thought. Had he ever spoken with Hannie about his faith? Did he actually have faith? He remembered what his mother had asked him.

"What do you believe, Berend?"

He had not answered her. In his heart he knew that he had not answered his mother because he didn't really know what he believed. His father was a good man. Even though he had been angry about his marrying Hannie, he meant well. Berend knew that and his stomach heaved. He tasted bile in his mouth.

"Your name is Berend, like your grandfather. Your grandfather was a faithful man, and I hope you will be a faithful man also."

These were the words his father had solemnly pronounced when he, Berend, had made profession of faith.

Cousin Brian's living room spun and now, suddenly, he was a little child walking out with his father in the cow pasture.

"We have a special surname, Berend. Did you know that?"

"No, father."

"Verbond means covenant. Do you know what covenant means?"

"No, father."

"It means something like pledge or agreement."

Here father had paused, had leaned over a fencepost staring out at the horizon."

"God made a covenant with us, son. He has promised to save us from our sins. You are little, but you have many sins, Berend."

"Yes, father."

The memory of having taken several candies without asking, of having kicked the rooster, and of keeping back the penny he had been given for the collection plate, had confronted him right there in the cow pasture. He repeated his words.

"Yes, I know, father."

"But if you ask God to forgive you, each time you sin, for Jesus' sake, well then, it will be alright again between you and Him. He has made a covenant with you, as He made with all His children. And you are a special child, for your last name is Verbond. Never forget that name, son.

"Yes, father."

Berend almost mouthed the two words before the living room swam back into focus. Cousin Brian was regarding him intently.

"So you want me to promise," he spoke slowly and changed his position on the couch as he spoke, "that I will become Berend Niks at the time that I become a Canadian citizen. And that all my children will carry the surname Niks?"

"Yes, that is what I want you to promise me."

Safe for the ticking of the grandfather clock, it was quiet in the living room. Hannie stood up from her position on the floor next to cousin Brian's chair, and came back to sit next to Berend on the couch. She tucked her arm through his arm and smiled at him.

"I will leave you the farm - lock, stock and barrel - everything here will be yours. If only you will do as I ask."

"You will leave us the farm, the entire farm?"

Berend's voice squeaked a little and then he was silent. He was at a loss for words. Hannie squeezed his arm tightly. He had never dreamt that he would own a farm of his own so relatively quickly. In the far-off distant future perhaps, after he had saved his wages for a number of years, then perhaps he might possibly have enough for a down payment on one of the farms around here. But he knew that was years away, many years. And this farm was so much bigger than the farm on which he had grown up. And by working it hard, as he had been doing, he was beginning to love it as his own. How proud father.... Here his thoughts stopped. But surely father would want him to have this farm. His mother certainly would also. He smiled as he imagined his mother's face if she ever should come to visit. He could see himself leading her around the yard, showing her the house, pointing to the cows, to the ducks, to the sheep, to the chickens, to the machinery, to the pond.... Then her face faded. Hannie shook his arm.

"Berend."

He turned his eyes towards her. Her cheeks glowed, and she was smiling radiantly. He smiled back, slowly, uncertainly.

"I will think about it."

It was all he could manage. It was all he could say at the time. But apparently satisfied with that answer, cousin Brian smiled.

"That is fine. And I'm sure you will come to the right decision."

There was a decision of sorts to which Berend did come that very evening.

"We are going to find a church, Hannie."

"A church?"

"Yes, I should have done so earlier, but...."

He stopped not really knowing what else to say. He was actually surprised that he had verbalized what he had been feeling during the conversation with cousin Brian.

"Perhaps we can go to a Christmas service somewhere in a few days," he went on uncertainly.

Hannie smiled.

"That would be nice, I think. My parents liked to go to church at Christmas also. And maybe we'll meet some people."

Berend felt a pang of guilt. Hannie had not complained, but he knew that she missed her parents, her friends and her sisters. He never took her anywhere.

"I've actually been asked, Berend... I've been asked by a neighbor to come to church."

He was startled.

"A neighbor?"

"Yes, I was getting the mail one day and a lady, that is to say, a girl my age, walked by. She stopped and talked to me. Her name is Joanne and she lives down the road from us."

"And she asked you to come to church?"

"Well, she asked me over for coffee first. And I... well, I went to her house."

"To her house?"

Hannie's 'yes' in answer to Berend's question was soft, apologetic almost. In contrast, Berend's voice was tinged with irritation; irritation that there was something Hannie had done about which he had not known.

"When was that?"

"Well, you are gone a lot. Sometimes after I clean and cook, I go for walks. Anyway, she does not live far away and I can walk there quite easily."

"Joanne? Her name is Joanne."

Hannie smiled.

"Yes, and you know what! She is Dutch and can speak Dutch and in her church they still have a Dutch service once a month."

Berend frowned. He did not like to be informed of things after the fact. He wished that she had told him sooner about this Joanne. But he did not really know what difference it would have made.

"How are you feeling?"

"I'm feeling fine."

But her smile faded even as she spoke and her words had a certain amount of flatness to them. It baffled Berend. Only a moment ago she had been happy. Was she worried about this pregnancy? Was she afraid that she might lose this baby too? They were sitting up in bed. Hannie was paging through a magazine and he was perusing a farm article. Not one for many words, he took her hand and stroked it. She turned her face towards him. He winked at her. It had been a wink which had caught her attention the first time they met. He had thought her so pretty but had been shy about speaking to her. So he had winked when she had glanced at him. She'd marched right up to him and winked back. It seemed like a long time ago, a very long time. But it wasn't really. Actually it was only just last year - just last year. But Hannie didn't wink back now. As a matter of fact, she began to cry. He took her in his arms and patted her on the back. Women were sometimes so passing strange!

"Do you love me, Berend?"

"Of course, I do."

"I'm glad we're going to go to a church."

Again, there was a strange pang which penetrated his heart. A pang which told him he had been falling short, far short of what he should have been doing.

"Do you think we should change our last name, Hannie?"

She didn't answer, only sniffed sadly and then blew her nose into the edge of the bedsheet.

"You know, Hannie," he said, patting her on the back, and staring at the wall in front of the bed, "You know, it's really amazing. Cousin Brian's offer to give us the farm is nothing short of a miracle."

"A miracle?"

"Yes, I think so. If we do change our last name, we'll have a farm of our own. We'll be able to expand it a bit in the future maybe. We've already saved a bit of money. Cousin Brian is paying me a good wage... and... well, I think that probably we should do it. We'll still be the same people, and what's a name, after all."

His voice had increased in volume. Perhaps to drown out his father's voice. Perhaps to drown out his mother's question.

He repeated, "What's in a name, eh? And this is so... well, it's so amazing."

He stopped. Next to him, Hannie sat up straighter. She adjusted the pillows in her back.

"Are you really feeling all right, Hannie?"

He repeated the question and was relieved that she nodded even as she again began paging through the magazine. He persisted.

"Are you afraid? Afraid that maybe you will... that you might lose...."

He was treading lightly, feeling his way carefully around what she might be thinking. And he suddenly wanted to know what exactly it was that she was thinking. Lately he had seen her standing underneath the Vermeer painting again, staring at it. It was almost as if she were becoming the woman in the painting, reading a letter of which he knew nothing.

"Did you feel sadness, Berend?" Hannie asked, laying down the magazine on the blanket, and beginning to pluck at the woolen softness of the covering.

"Sadness?"

He did not follow her train of reasoning.

"Yes, sadness about..., you know, when the first little baby...."

"Oh, is that what you mean."

He could sense, as his arm still encircled her back, that she was tensing up. Was she still mourning the loss of this last little baby, a baby conceived in Holland?

"Of course I was sad," he said, feeling rather like he was lying, because, truth be told, he had never spent much time in thinking about the child.

He had actually felt a sense of relief, he shamefully recalled, a sense of gratification that he had not been forced to write his parents that he had failed them in more ways than one.

"You never said," Hannie continued, "you never once said to me that you were sad."

"I'm sorry."

The words hung over the bed lamely, as if they had no strength. And indeed, they had very little impact on the conversation.

"Before I met you," Hannie's voice also increased somewhat in volume, "there was a...."

She stopped and he could see that whatever it was she was trying to say, it was very difficult for her.

"Yes," he encouraged.

"Berend, I love you."

He smiled.

"I love you too, Hannie. And if this little baby is a girl, I hope she is just like you. Cousin Brian was right when he said that you were kind and gentle and...."

To his surprise, she began to cry again before he could finish. To avoid her using the bedsheet once more to blow her nose, he got up, took a hankie out of the back pocket of the pants lying on the chair across from the bed, and gave it to her.

"Here, blow your nose, sweetheart, and then I'll give you a big hug."

She did blow her nose and smiled at him rather tremulously.

"Berend, I want to tell you something."

He climbed back into bed and put his arm around her once again. She didn't begin immediately but pulled up pieces of wool from the blanket, rubbing them between the thumb and index fingers of her right hand.

"Would you have married me if... well, if I hadn't been expecting a baby?"

"Of course."

She sighed deeply and continued.

"I've been talking to Joanne, Berend, you know the neighbor girl I told you about. She's been... well, she's been reading the Bible with me."

He felt slightly miffed. Hannie's fingers kept twirling the wool, and she kept on talking.

"I ... I've been lying to you, Berend."

"Lying?"

Berend didn't quite understand where Hannie was going with this conversation.

"Joanne is a good friend to me, Berend."

He nodded, trying hard to ascertain the gist of what was being said.

"She told me that you deserve to know. I have already told God."

She stopped and there was a long pause.

"What have you told God? What do I deserve to know?"

"Just before I met you, Berend, a friend of my father's visited us. He had gone to school with my father and his son came along. The son was my age. He took me out and...."

"Stop," Berend said, and repeated, "Stop."

Hannie's hands ceased from plucking the wool.

"I can't stop now, Berend. I have to tell you. I have to...."

"I don't want to know."

"The baby was not yours, Berend. I'm sorry! I'm so sorry! I made a mistake!"

Berend could see snow falling through the space in the half-open curtains. It was a thick snow, a heavy snow. He'd have to shovel tomorrow - shovel a long path to the barn. He wished he were in the barn now so that he could think. Everything in his brain seemed twisted about. He removed his arm from around Hannie's neck.

"My father said," Hannie whispered in a low voice, "that you were a good man."

"Your father knew?"

She nodded.

"How could he...?"

He didn't finish.

"You seemed so remote," Hannie's voice went on tremulously, "after the miscarriage. Almost relieved, I think. And in a way, I was too. I thought that I would really never have to tell you about this. I thought I could bear the sadness myself."

There was a pause again and Berend eyed his pants. He could possibly dress quickly, go out now and do some shoveling, check on the cows and....

"But I couldn't stop thinking about ... about the baby. I thought that perhaps it was my fault that it died. I felt I was ... I was bad, very bad."

Berend's feet were over the edge of the bed. He wanted to be gone, to be someplace where it was quiet, to be someplace where he could put his thoughts in order.

"Joanne said," Hannie went on, her voice spilling out onto the floor next to his shoes, "that if I confessed what I had done to God, and if I was truly sorry, that He would forgive me."

"Were you sorry?"

Berend's voice was hoarse. It did not sound like his own voice. It did not sound like himself.

"Yes, I was very sorry, Berend."

Hannie stopped pulling at the wool and raised her eyes, her big, dark-blue eyes, to his face. They were shiny with tears and he knew that she was telling the truth. But there was a great anger within him.

"You would have given that child my name."

It was not a question but a statement.

"Your name?"

Hannie's voice was surprised and then she continued.

"But you are going to give your name away anyway, Berend."

It was a logical statement. Then Hannie swallowed and went on.

"Will you forgive me, Berend?"

He did not answer.

"God forgave me. I know that He did because He sent Jesus to die for my sins. Joanne prayed with me and ... and I don't know how to explain it, but ever since she did, I'm...."

"What? What are you?"

Berend voice was still thick - thick and hoarse. He could hear himself speaking but he did not recognize the sound.

"Well, it's like I'm the woman in the picture in the living room. You know, the woman in the blue top who's reading a letter."

"So?"

"Well, the letter is from God, you see," Hannie's voice quivered, but went on, "and it says, 'Hannie, I love you. I will not condemn you. You are my child now and your name is Christian. And I'm giving you another chance, another baby.'"

Berend didn't know what to say.

"Will you forgive me, Berend?"

Berend got up, dressed quickly and left the bedroom without a word. He spend the next few hours shoveling and after he had cleared what seemed like mountains of snow, sought refuge in the barn. His thoughts were jumbled. His own voice echoed and re-echoed off the rafters, mingling with Hannie's voice.

"You would have given that child my name?"

"But you are going to give your name away anyway, Berend."

Eventually he sat down, put his head in his hands and wept. Then he stretched his body out on a few bales and slept.

His mother shook him.

"Berend, Berend, it's time to wake up!"

She was small, his mother, not four foot three. But she could shake you awake, that was a fact, so that you were out of bed in a trice.

"Moeke?"

She looked at him for a long time before she spoke.

"Berend, son, Hannie is a Christian."

He was awake now and the hay he was lying on was hard and uncomfortable.

"Oh, Moeke," he said.

It was all he could manage, for her face would not let him go. He wanted, more than anything else, to stand up and move towards her, to throw his arms around her neck. But like two heavy pieces of wood, they were dead weights by the sides of his body.

"She has become a believer and she is going to be the mother of your child. This is what you hoped and what you prayed for, is it not, Berend?"

Struggling to reply, his mouth was wired shut. Berend's mother smiled a wry smile. A smile that implied that she knew he had not really been in the business of praying for the conversion of his wife. Berend's tongue was now glued to the roof of his mouth and he could not answer her a word. Her eyes would not let him go.

"What is it you believe, Berend?"

He groaned. It was a deep groan and came from his soul.

"You were angry with Hannie because she would have given your name to a little baby that knew no better. Yet you yourself are willing to take the name of someone who takes God's name in vain."

Cows mooed in their stalls, and a goat bleated mournfully. Berend's whole being roiled within himself. It seemed as if the weight of his life was too heavy and something broke within himself and spilled out onto the ground.

He woke up on the stable floor- and he saw that the stable lantern was casting a straight line towards the door which the wind had blown open.

7: The End of a Thing

Better is the end of a thing than its beginning; and the patient in spirit is better than the proud in spirit (Eccl. 7:8).

Our village in northern Holland had never been very large, but those first few years following the second world war, it seemed especially small and shrunken. A number of men had died at the hands of the Germans; others had died of starvation that last hunger winter of 1944; and still others had moved away to cities and to jobs. With the exception of a large hospital just on the outskirts of the village, a hospital which served a large surrounding district, there was nothing unusual about our village. Like many other villages, it was a little world within the world. Everyone knew who everyone else was, what they were doing and what they were going to do. And why shouldn't they? Most of them belonged to the same Protestant church, except for the few Roman Catholic families scattered here and there. Children attended the same school; parents went to the same grocery store; and the baker baked the same sort of bread for all of them. When it rained or when it did not rain, when someone was ill, got married or died, or when a child left to attend university in the big city, it was a community affair.

It was a long time ago, but a tiny incident stands out in my memory. I recall walking down the main street of our village one day when I was about twelve or thirteen years old. I was part of a bevy of girls, all of whom stopped suddenly because one of the girls in our group noticed that the 'for sale' sign in front of the Lander house was gone. Bert Lander had been a retired farmer who had built a monstrosity of a house in the middle of our village back in the 30s. He had not had the pleasure of living in it for a very long time, because he had died of a massive stroke only a year after he moved in. His wife had not long outlived him. The children, none of whom had become farmers and none of whom wanted to live in our village, had rented the house out to various people, most of whom had been lawyers, doctors and other studied people. For some reason, the house was never occupied for a long period. At any rate, it had recently been put up for sale, and now the sign was gone. Unashamedly, we girls walked up to the windows and peeked in. There was nothing to indicate life. Whoever was to move in had not yet arrived.

A few days later a moving van drove down Main Street and parked in front of the house. Again we traipsed over and watched as the furniture was unloaded. A black, shining baby grand piano brought sighs, and a couch meant to drown owners in its puffy opulence, left us breathless. And so it went on. Whoever it was who had bought the place, was wealthy, extremely wealthy. Our curiosity was piqued and we chattered excitedly. But when we tried to satisfy curiosity by once more peeping through the windows the next day, the curtains had been drawn and we were left with no information.

The following week, however, a new girl stepped into our school classroom. She did not bother to knock, but opened the door as if she was the headmaster. Walking straight, head held high, she did not seem the least bit intimidated by the fact that she was facing a room full of inquisitive students. For I have to admit that we all stared at her most unashamedly. She made her way to the front, stopping short next to our teacher, Mr. Kits. He rather took the moment in stride.

"You must be Sanna Klok," he stated calmly.

There was not much that upset Mr. Kits. He was in his fifties, balding and ate tiny little diamond licorice candies out of a small blue tin underneath his lectern throughout the day. We conjectured that this was because his wife would not give him any sort of sweets at home. She was a very thin, anorexic-looking woman and rumor had it that she had food hidden in the attic just in case the Germans came back.

"Class, please welcome Sanna," Mr. Kits continued.

"Welcome, Sanna," we repeated rather parrot-like, never taking our eyes off Sanna and her blue velvet dress, a dress with pleats and a white lace collar.

Our classroom was arranged into four rows of desks, desks which housed two to a seat. Mr. Kits pointed to the only available empty seat in the class – the one next to me. Sanna made her way through the second aisle. I sat in the last row. Initially my place had been in the front row but that had changed when Marcus Rook had been diagnosed with myopic vision, something which had sounded very romantic but which simply meant he was nearsighted. He was assigned my seat and I was assigned to his. Sanna, everyone noted as she walked towards the back of the classroom, had a small snub nose, dark blue eyes with very long black lashes, a pale complexion, and blond, shoulder-length hair that curled at the edges. The boys gaped and so did the girls, truth be known. Before she sat down, Sanna took a long, hard look at me. I suppose I passed muster, because she permitted herself a small, stiff smile. I smiled back trying to appear indifferent to the fact that everyone was turning around looking at us, and helped her find her place in the various subjects we studied that morning.

At recess, all the girls crowded around Sanna. But she gave away very little, safe for the fact that her father was a business man, that her mother had died when she was born and that she had no brothers or sisters. It rapidly became apparent that first week, that Sanna was a wizard in most subjects. She spoke fluent English, French, and German, and literally danced her way through the rigors of Algebra.

"Tutors," she explained her incredible talent away, "I've always had tutors. My father wants me to do well."

No one at school had ever had tutors. The girls in class eyed Sanna with an almost reverential awe, an awe which had begun when they noted with a certain amount of incredulity that her fingernails were polished and that she applied an almost unnoticeable amount of lipstick to her two small round lips. I sometimes bit mine to make them red, but I had begun to hide my short fingernails under books whenever the discrepancies between our hands became too obvious.

In the month that followed, Sanna formed a friendship with Anne, the daughter of the greengrocer. Anne was a lamb, a follower. That is to say, she slavishly swallowed any attention given to her and generally speaking, always did what someone else told her to do. A nondescript girl with brownish hair and a few freckles on her cheeks, she wore clothes that had been handed down to her by three older sisters. Why Sanna had chosen her of all the girls in class to chum around with, was a source of wonder. But she seemed to love going to the grocer's house, often waiting for an invitation to stay for supper. She had to be told at times, Anne's mother told my mother, to leave. Sanna also marked me with her graces, especially on Sunday. She would often walk up to our pew, smile at mother and sit down next to us.

Perhaps this was because father was the minister and possibly she felt there was some sort of spiritual significance to hobnobbing with me on that day. Her father rarely came along to church. He was often out of town on business. Mother, who encouraged me in this friendship, pointed out frequently that Sanna, after all, did not have a mother and had to contend with a housekeeper to teach her manners and to give her affection. She often said this when she tucked me in at night and I spilled out some grievance that I had been harboring most of the day.

There was a middle-aged woman in our town, a Mrs. Smit, the local seamstress, whom Sanna, for some inexplicable reason, disliked. Whenever she saw Mrs. Smit walk across the street, and the woman had a slight limp, she would mimic her. I never once saw her come close to the woman, never saw her engage her in speech. But from a distance she would make fun of her and I don't know how Anne, who was usually with her, could stomach the mocking. Perhaps she was just too naive. Mrs. Smit was a gentle woman. I liked her. She had made me a green dress the previous summer, taking the time to measure carefully and to compliment me on the fact that I was growing taller. Yes, I liked her. No one was exactly sure where she hailed from and it had been the subject of many lively discussions. She had only lived in the district for some three years. Long enough, though, to win the respect of a great many mothers whom she helped with this and that.

"Dorcas," my mother said, "her name should have been Dorcas Smit."

It was nearing Easter and Mr. Kits had graphically related the Bible story about Thomas, disbelieving Thomas. For being a quiet man, Mr. Kits was an avid and very descriptive teller of tales. It was almost as if he came alive each morning when he explained and retold Scripture in his own words. His eyes glowed and his hands moved about as he searched for and found just the right phrase to emphasize a point. He usually had the entire class in the palm of his hand.

We had all been struck with the horrible dismay and mortal fear Cain had felt after God spoke to him of his misdeed; we had all sweated along with Noah in the construction of the ark, a much more difficult building to construct than farmer Blom's newly erected silo; and we were all convinced that Abraham had probably looked somewhat like Mr. Korman, the butcher, whose long beard was a source of curiosity. It was very quiet in the class as Mr. Kits spoke of the doubting disciple.

"Thomas was not there the first time that Jesus appeared to the other disciples. But he was one of the twelve. He should have been there."

Mr. Kits looked at us over the thin gold rim of his spectacles as if we were all Thomases and as if we had all somehow missed the opportunity that Thomas had thrown away.

"Consequently, Thomas did not have peace. He was miserable and down-cast. He had no rest within himself. And this was even though the other disciples kept telling him 'We have seen the Lord, Thomas. We know He lives.'

Next to me, Sanna fidgeted. She was uncomfortable. I could sense it. It was a palpable emotion. As I saw her staring fixedly out through the open window, I wondered if she heard anything that Mr. Kits was saying.

"If we miss something that God puts on our way, and other people tell us about it, we should never be so stubborn as to not listen."

Sanna sighed. It was a big sigh rolling straight down the second aisle, breezing through the window and cascading onto the street. Everyone heard it and heads twisted around. Mr. Kits stopped his discourse.

"Miss Klok, perhaps you would be kind enough to tell the class what has been said these last five minutes?"

Sanna's head turned. She looked at Mr. Kits, but there was a faraway look in her eyes. I knew she didn't really see him.

"What you said?" she repeated dully, "Yes, I can tell you that. You were talking about Thomas, doubting Thomas. He did not believe that Jesus had really come back. And he should have believed."

It was very quiet in class. Sanna spoke in a monotone, as if she were reciting a lesson. She went on.

"But I don't blame him for not believing. I think that Jesus should have showed him in some other way that He was still alive. Maybe

Thomas missed out because he was locked up somewhere and couldn't get out. Maybe he just couldn't make the meeting with the other disciples through no fault of his own. I think you should put that into your story as well. That's what I think."

It was very quiet in the classroom. Everyone digested what Sanna had said. Mr. Kits tapped his fingers on his lectern.

"I'm happy to know that you were, after all, listening, Miss Klok," he eventually responded, and then he continued on with the story as if there had been no interruption.

That day, Sanna ran away across the playground after school and even Anne, the greengrocer's daughter, was left to walk home alone.

That following Sunday, putting her arm through mine after we had shuffled down the center aisle at the end of the service, Sanna pulled Anne and myself into the bathroom behind her. It was a small bathroom, only boasting a tiny sink and two small toilet cubicles.

"I thought the sermon would never end," she sighed, as she pushed a thick blond lock over her right shoulder and eyed herself in the mirror.

There was a noise in one of the cubicles, warning us there was someone else present, but Sanna payed no heed. I flushed at the comment. Not that I listened to sermons as attentively as I should, but it was my father, after all, who preached them. Anne giggled nervously, simultaneously making big eyes at me rather apprehensively. Squashed against the wall, she waited patiently to be told when it was time to leave.

"Did you see Mrs. Smit's coat?"

Sanna's voice was derisive. She pulled an old blue towel off the towel rack, draped it around her shoulders and pranced around. Not that you could actually prance around in the small space permitted but she did seem to manage it.

"How anyone can wear something so outdated and moth-eaten is amazing! Don't you think so, Anne?"

Anne nodded half-heartedly.

"And then," Sanna continued, "the woman sits in one of the front pews where everyone is forced to look at her in that awful, awful coat."

"Well," I interrupted, running the tap and beginning to wash my hands as I spoke, "she is a little hard of hearing and being close to the front helps. Besides that, I rather liked her coat."

The noise of the tap-water hitting the sink, cushioned my words somewhat.

"That's silly, Nelly," Sanna bit back at me, "And what do you know about fashions anyway? The truth is, Mrs. Smit's coat dates back to the year zero and she and the coat both smell like moth-balls."

"Well," Anne said, biting her nails and then looking up, "I think I have to go. We're getting company for lunch and Ma said I should be home shortly after the service."

She moved towards the door and if my hands had not been wet, I would have slipped right out the door with her. But as it was, I grabbed the towel off Sanna's back just as Anne threw a 'good-bye' over her shoulder. Sanna grinned at me, and followed Anne out the door.

"Maybe I can go there for lunch," she sang out before the door shut.

The toilet flushed in the cubicle and to my horror, Mrs. Smit walked out.

"Hello, Nelly," she calmly said, as she moved towards the sink.

I dried my hands and hung the towel back up on the rack.

"Hello, Mrs. Smit," I responded and then, without another word, I also walked out.

When I came home from school on Monday, mother told me that the Kloks would be joining us for supper that evening.

"Why?"

I threw the word out rather angrily and mother looked at me as if I were a stranger. She didn't know I half suspected that someone had told her about the Mrs. Smit fiasco. I had not seen Sanna at school that day and that had been fine by me.

"Go and do your homework, Nelly," was all the reply I got.

When the supper bell rang, I slow-footed it down the stairs and walked into the dining-room. Mr. Klok and father were already seated and mother called me into the kitchen to carry in the salad.

"I didn't see Sanna," I said as I picked up the yellow salad bowl.

"She wasn't feeling well today and is staying home with Mrs. Appel.

Mrs. Appel was the housekeeper and a very jolly lady she was too. Round like a dumpling, you disappeared into her bosom when she hugged you.

"Oh," I replied and felt a trifle more comfortable about the next hour.

Supper went well. Mr. Klok was a nice man. Sometimes I wondered why, because she was surrounded by such admirable people, Sanna had turned out to be such a domineering child. We had brussels sprouts that evening. Not my favorite and Mr. Klok, who sat next to me and saw me poking at the green little cabbage mounds on my plate, took several sprouts onto his own plate while mother was not looking. I suspect father saw, but he didn't say anything. After Bible reading and prayer, as mother got up to clear the table and as I also pushed back my chair to get up and help, Mr. Klok asked her to sit down again.

"I can't stay long," he said, "but I just wanted to say this. I do so appreciate the friendship that you have shown, both to me and to Sanna."

Father began to reply, but Mr. Klok waved his hand to indicate that he was not done speaking. "I want to tell you," he said in his rather deep voice, "why I came here. To this village, I mean, and why I didn't settle in some other part of Holland."

Mother sat down again and I stayed where I was. My chair was pushed out just a trifle behind Mr. Klok's chair so that I could look at him as he spoke.

"You didn't know," Mr. Klok went on, "my wife. That is to say, when I use the past tense it sounds as if she is... well, as if she has died. And I don't know whether or not that is the case."

"But," I interrupted quite rudely, "Sanna said...."

An immediate look from both mother and father stopped me.

Mr. Klok paid no attention to the interruption. He ran his hand through his thinning, reddish hair and then put his elbows on the table, resting his cheeks on his hands. He had long hands, an artist's hands and his nails were quite a bit cleaner than mine. I remembered Sanna's manicured, polished nails and inadvertently glanced down.

"I met my wife in the late 1920s."

Mr. Klok was now speaking to the wall opposite the table.

"She worked in one of the stores with which I regularly did business on my travels. She was a couturière and was very good at what she was doing."

"Couturière?" I repeated slowly, earning me more stern looks from my parents.

But Mr. Klok turned around and smiled at me.

"It's a hard word, isn't it, Nelly? It means someone who designs, makes and sells clothes, fashionable clothes."

"Oh," I said and repeated the word in my mind several times over.

It sounded sophisticated and lovely.

"We fell in love and were married."

Mr. Klok put his elbows back on the table and continued his story.

"It was not too difficult at that time yet to marry a Jew."

"She was Jewish?"

This time father interrupted.

"Yes, she was. My wife was a Jewess. But not a practicing Jewess. She converted to Christianity when she was a child. Her parents, who both died while she was a teenager, were members of the Lutheran church."

"Hmm," was all my father permitted himself to say.

"We had no children. That is to say, Sarah was very delicate. Her health was not good. After we had been married about three years, she was diagnosed with tuberculosis."

Mother clucked. I wasn't too sure exactly what tuberculosis was, but I had seen the little tents in our village. Tom Vlietman had been in one for about a year and then he had died. So had Leny Olster.

"I sent her to a sanatorium. Our doctor recommended a very good one in Switzerland. It cost a lot of money but I was able to manage. I visited her regularly. It was a hard time, a hard time for both of us. Just prior to Christmas 1934, the doctor told me that humanly speaking there was very little hope – that Sarah could not possibly live another year. 'She wants to come home for the holidays,' he said, 'and I don't see why she can't spend a few days of what will likely be her last months, in her home surroundings.'"

Mother's eyes were riveted on Mr. Klok's face. I knew she was close to tears. Mother always empathized wholeheartedly with everyone. That's why all the people I was acquainted with, including the milkman, were always ready to tell her whatever his or her troubles were. I'd certainly told her mine many times.

"It was a wonderful Christmas. It was so special."

Mr. Klok's voice broke but then he continued.

"After a few weeks back at the sanatorium, it came to light that Sarah was pregnant. She was expecting our first child."

Mother smiled. It was a slow smile. I wondered what Sanna thought of this story.

"Everyone at the sanatorium was furious with me. 'Poor Sarah,' they said, 'one foot in the grave and now she is pregnant as well'. They wanted her to give them permission to abort the baby but Sarah, my sweet, defenseless wife, became a lioness. She would hold her hands over her belly and rock as if she was already holding a little one. There was no arguing with her. She would keep the child and that was that."

"Good for her," father said and mother nodded.

"And the strange thing was," Mr. Klok went on, sitting up straight and pounding the table as he repeated, "the strange thing was, that what the doctors and nurses had not been able to accomplish by any sort of nursing or medicine or diet, this God-given pregnancy accomplished. The growth of tiny Sanna in her belly, pushed up her rib cage and healed her."

Mother's smile grew broader and I grinned.

"That is amazing," she said.

"God was good to us," Mr. Klok continued, "but then things became very difficult in Germany, as I'm sure you know."

"Yes," father said, 'but how is it that a Dutchman like yourself, was situated in Germany?"

"Well, I wasn't really," Mr. Klok replied, "it's just that some of the companies I dealt with were located there. And then, because Sarah had been born in Germany and had a nice apartment, we decided to stay there after we were married and after Sanna was born. I still traveled around to different places. Sarah stayed home and was much taken up with the child. They had a very special relationship, the two of them."

He sighed and continued.

""For a number of years I was able to continue in my business. We had obtained identity cards for Sarah and Sanna – Aryan identity cards. But somehow, and I don't know how, someone pointed a finger at Sarah. One day I came home from a business trip to find her gone. The Gestapo had taken her away."

He stopped and wiped his hands on his pants. There was sweat on his forehead. I could see it glisten under the lamp. He blinked nervously and mother offered him some water.

"No, thanks. Please forgive me. Always, always when I come to this part in my thoughts, I think that perhaps I should have done something else; that I should have moved back to Holland sooner; that maybe if I had acted differently, she might have been kept from suffering."

"Did you find out where she was? Where the Gestapo had taken her?"

The question popped out of my mouth before I realized it. 'Little girls should be seen and not heard.'. I could hear the unspoken phrase loud and clear. Didn't I know it? I looked down at my lap to avoid father's gaze. Mr. Klok turned around to look at me.

"No, I could not find this out, Nelly. It was as if she had never been. But little Sanna... I found little Sanna in a hiding place we had fashioned together behind a partition in the bedroom wall. The child was terrified, and would not speak for a long time."

"Then why does Sanna tell everyone that her mother died when she was born?"

"For a while she was afraid to tell people that she was half-Jewish. She saw so many people beaten up and taken away never to be heard from again."

"What happened after you came back home, after Sarah, your wife, had disappeared, I mean?"

It was mother who asked the question this time. Mr. Klok turned his eyes toward her.

"I exhausted my resources in trying to find out where Sarah had been taken, but I met with walls everywhere. Either people were afraid to speak or they would not. After a few months I took the child, I took Sanna, and left Germany. It was still possible and I had to get her, in any case, to a safe haven. Then, after the war, when people began to trickle back from concentration camps, I heard rumors that Sarah might have survived – that some people thought they might have seen her."

"And had they?"

Mr. Klok turned again and smiled at me.

"I think they had and the Red Cross said that possibly a woman who fit the description of my wife Sarah, had traveled to England and from there seemed to have gone on to Holland, to the northern provinces."

"Does Sanna know that you are looking for her?" mother asked.

"Well, yes and no. Yes, she knows that perhaps her mother is still alive and also that I make it my business to search out people who might have some tiny bit of information regarding her whereabouts. And no, she does not seem to be interested. She does not want to speak of her mother or of the time past."

"Was she ever mistreated?"

"No, not really. That is to say, she, of course, spent many hours alone and has not really had these last years the benefit of a mother's love, a mother's care."

I almost felt sorry for Sanna, until I remembered how unkind she had been to Mrs. Smit. There was no excuse, was there?

"She, my Sarah, had a small birthmark on her left wrist. Actually it was a bit higher than her wrist. She used to say that if I would see only her arm, I would always know her."

Mr. Klok pushed his chair back abruptly.

"Well, I just wanted you to know. I'm aware that people are saying that Sanna has not got a mother, and this might be true. But I must, you understand, I must continue in my search for Sarah. It was perhaps my fault that she was taken. I should have moved out of Germany sooner, but I never thought... I just never thought...."

He stood up and the serviette which had lain in his lap, fell to the floor. I bent over to pick it up and he patted my head.

"You are a good girl, Nelly. Thank you for being friends with Sanna."

I flushed and put the serviette on the table.

"That's all right, Mr. Klok."

A week later, father called me into his study.

"Close the door behind you, Nelly," he said, as he sat behind his desk partly hidden by his typewriter.

I closed the door a little apprehensively. Father sounded very serious.

"I spoke with Mrs. Boon this morning."

Mrs. Boon was the greengrocer's wife and Anne's mother. I felt myself growing more apprehensive.

"It seems that Mrs. Boon heard from Anne that some girls made fun of Mrs. Smit last week Sunday. Is that true, Nelly?"

I looked down. I had thought, because nothing had happened up to this point, that the incident would pass without notice. That is to say, I had hoped that it would. I had not expected Anne to talk to her mother, but had rather wished that she would talk to Sanna convincing her to go and apologize for her rude words.

"Well, Nelly?"

"Yes, it's true."

"Do you want to tell me about it?"

I began to fidget with my hands. I'd rather not tell father about it actually. What his question really meant was, 'You have to tell me about it.' So there I was.

"Sit down, Nelly."

I walked towards the desk and sat opposite father. He took a puff of his pipe, put it in the ashtray and folded his arms.

"Before you tell me," father said, "I want you to know that yesterday Mrs. Smit had a minor heart attack. She's in the hospital. I think she will be all right, but...."

"I'm sorry."

I looked up and met father's intent gaze head on.

"I am sorry, father. Honest."

"Well then, why don't you tell me exactly what happened."

The upshot of the whole matter was that father went to speak to Mr. Klok and that Mr. Klok, Sanna and myself were on our way to the hospital within the hour.

My shoes made a lot of noise on the tiles of the hospital corridor. Sanna's shoes must have had rubber soles, because she made no noise at all. She walked on the other side of her father, and he held her hand. I had mine stuffed into the pockets of my coat.

"What do I have to go too? I wasn't rude to Mrs. Smit."

"Because you didn't speak up enough, Nelly. And that is a sin of omission. What if someone had said something nasty about mother, or about me?"

I flushed, remembering what Sanna had said about the sermon.

"All right, I'll go."

The corridor was long and the place smelled as if no one ever fried potatoes or made apple pie. They were my favorite dishes and no one made them like mother.

"Yes, how can I help you?"

We were at the nurses' station, and Mr. Klok let go of Sanna's hand.

"We are here to visit Mrs. Smit."

"Mrs. Smit? Umh, yes, room 244. Up the stairs on your right. But children...."

"I'm fourteen," Sanna divulged with a certain amount of pride.

Looking at her as she stood defiantly in front of the desk on her rubber soles, I did not see how the nurse could refuse her. But neither did I understand why Sanna would want to be allowed to go to visit Mrs. Smit. After all, she had antagonized the woman.

"Well," the nurse hesitated.

"Both these girls are good friends with Mrs. Smit. It will do her so much good to see them," Mr. Klok intervened. "And I understand she has no other relatives. So please let them go up."

"Well, all right. But you must promise not to stay long."

We walked up the stairs one at a time. It was a thin stairs, a disagreeable stairs, and one which could not abide the pairing of people. Sanna was in the lead. I followed close behind her and at my back Mr. Klok trudged up. He looked tired and I could empathize. I was tired too - tired and nervous. I had no idea what I would say to Mrs. Smit. Sanna, on the other hand, did not seem the least bit intimidated about what was to come. The brown door at the top of the stairs had a small, rectangular window. I peeked over Sanna's shoulder and saw a hall much like the one we had left on the first floor.

"All right, Sanna. Keep on moving, love. Open the door."

Over my shoulder, Mr. Klok nudged his daughter. Sanna pushed the door open. It creaked ever so slightly. The first door on the right was numbered 239. There was no one in the hall. We walked slowly. My shoes squeaked again and I tried to walk on my toes for a few moments. The doors to most of the rooms were shut. They were all brown doors and they all had a small window, just like the door at the top of the stairs.

The door to room 244 was half open. Sanna suddenly stood stock-still.

"I've changed my mind," she whispered in a very small voice, "I don't think I want to go in after all, father."

Mr. Klok halted as well.

"You should go in, Sanna," he said, "and Nelly will be right there with you, won't you Nelly."

I nodded. What else could I do?

"I'm sorry I said that about her coat," Sanna continued in a whisper, addressing her father, "and Nelly could tell her that, couldn't you, Nelly?"

Mr. Klok put his hand on Sanna's shoulder and gave her a small shove towards the open door.

"Go on, Sanna," he said firmly, "Get it over with."

Reluctantly Sanna's rubber soles made their way across the threshold. My squeaking shoes followed. Just before I went in Mr. Klok spoke.

"There's waiting room down the end of the hall. I can see it from here. That's where I'll be when you're done."

There were two beds in room 244. A curtain of sorts hung between them. The woman in the first bed was lying down flat, her face turned away from us towards the curtain. A cream colored sheet covered her entire body although her hands were visible on the coverlet. She lay so quietly, it appeared as if she was not breathing at all. Sanna, after a small look to see if I was still behind her, walked over to the side of the bed. There was a chair there and she sat down in it. I stayed at the foot of the bed.

"Hello, Mrs. Smit," Sanna began, "I'm sorry that you're in the hospital."

She paused and studied her fingernails. I noted that they were polished a light, cherry red.

"I guess you might remember me. My name is Sanna Klok."

I cleared my throat and she glanced at me, slightly irritated at the interruption.

"I've come to visit you," Sanna continued, "because I guess I'm sorry about what I said to you the other day. And because my father made me come. But you know what...."

She suddenly sat up straighter and her voice grew louder.

"You know what? Actually I'm not really sorry at all! And why should I lie about that!"

I gasped at this revelation and Sanna looked at me again as if to say, 'Be quiet, and don't interrupt me.'

Sanna stood up.

"You know the first time I saw you, which was the first week that we moved here, I already began to dislike you. Do you want to know why?"

The breathing which had been almost imperceptible underneath the cream-colored sheet, became agitated.

"I disliked you because you looked so much like my mother... like my mother used to look."

I stared at Sanna.

"My mother was a liar. She lied to me. She promised me that she would stay with me. That she would unlock the door to the cubby-hole that we had made in the wall. That she would never, ever leave me. But you know what. She did leave me. She left me to go to strangers and she never came back."

I stepped to the opposite side of the bed. The rather asthmatic breathing troubled me. Sanna took no note of my moving. She continued to speak.

"And you hit me. You hit me in the face. I know it was because I wouldn't climb into the cubby-hole. We could hear the police coming. But wouldn't it have been better for them to take me as well as you? Wouldn't it have been better if both of us had been taken? And you hit me so hard, so hard that everything went black. And then when I came to...."

"Sanna!"

My voice was urgent. I interrupted her flow of words and repeated her name again, and she stared at me with a dazed sort of look.

229

"Sanna, this woman is not Mrs. Smit."

"What!?"

Disbelief tinged her voice and for the first time since I knew her, I felt a faint compassion for her stir my heart. What if my mother had hit me, had left me somewhere and then had disappeared out of my life forever?

"Well, then who is she?"

"I don't know."

The woman's eyes were closed and she seemed to be in a heavy, sedated sort of sleep.

"Sanna."

This time it was not I who spoke but the second woman in the room, the woman hidden behind the curtain of the other bed.

"Sanna, come here."

Sanna froze in her chair.

"No," she said softly, "No, no, no. I will not come."

"Why not?" the voice asked.

I stood between Sanna and the voice. It is hard to describe exactly how Sanna seemed to shrivel up, how she seemed to be disintegrating before my eyes.

"Because it cannot be. Because I do not believe it. That's why I cannot come."

The curtain parted slightly and a hand extended through, a small slight hand. The white hospital gown did not quite cover the thin wrist. A tiny red birthmark colored the skin upon the wrist. And I remembered the Thomas story.

8: Forming Adam

The wind blows where it wishes, and you hear its sound, but you do not know where it comes from or where it goes. So it is with everyone who is born of the Spirit (Jn. 3:8).

In the craft of sewing things are often joined together with stitches. There are a great many different types of stitches: the ladder stitch, the running stitch, the blanket stitch, and the feather stitch, to name but a few. The straight stitch is the most common stitch used in sewing. Thread is pushed through two pieces of fabric and pulled until the end knot catches and the cloth comes together. Straight stitches are used to form unbroken lines.

Even so in the craft of predestination, the great Creator of the universe breathes threads of events through lives so that creatures will be drawn tightly to Him; so that they will be conformed to His image in an intricate, but straight pattern. God's children are indeed fearfully and wonderfully made.

****

There was no more butter to be had anywhere. Vegetables had become a forgotten commodity. And who could remember the color of cheese? Meat coupons, coupons which had been rationed out to everyone in the small villages of western Holland, were not worth the paper they were written on, and the bread allotted to the skeletal townsfolk walking about was a mere 1,400 grams a week. The grim winter of 1944 had set in and its cold was colder because bodies were so much thinner. Roads were closed. Railroads were not functioning. Nothing moved. There was no food, no fuel and many families were beginning to burn their furniture and their books in order to keep warm.

Luit Adriaan had stopped shaving, had for the most part stopped talking, and had acquired a lifeless hue in his eyes. His older sister, Ellen, regarded his stubbly, half-bearded face with a certain degree of anger.

"You have given up," she said, even as she bent over a pan of water mixed with four grated tulip bulbs, stirring both angrily and persistently as though her very life depended on it.

She had handled and peeled those bulbs as if they were precious cargo; had cut them into halves; and had carefully removed the little yellow core at the center that everyone knew was poisonous. And perhaps her life did depend on this work because the tulip bulb mixture cooking in the pan of water together with a single browned onion and a little salt, would be the main and only course for supper that evening.

Besides having given up on shaving and talking, Luit Adriaan had also stopped trudging about on the roads, had given up on knocking at farm doors asking for handouts. People often shut their door, even locked it, when they saw him coming. Even more difficult to take than this refusal was the fact that very few people smiled at him. He knew why. It was not because there was absolutely nothing left on farm pantry shelves, but it was because during the early months of this year his brother, Lux, had been exposed as collaborating with the

Nazis. Caught and shot by the underground as a traitor, the surname Adriaan was steeped in shame. There was more than one person in the village who attributed the death of a dear one to Lux. Luit sighed deeply leaning his face on top of his hands. There was something in the dull expression of his eyes that both angered and grieved his sister.

"You must not give up!" she repeated, her words now a command.

Behind her the kitchen door opened and Nelleke, her sister-in-law, walked in. Nelleke's belly, which should have been as round as a melon at harvest time, barely dented her apron and made the dark blue maternity dress underneath that apron seem several sizes too large, ill-fitting and clownish.

"There is some tea," Ellen Adriaan breathed the words softly, even as she moved away from the stove and pulled out a chair from behind the table for Nelleke.

Actually it was not tea but a concoction of sugar beet juice. She poured the purplish liquid into a teacup and placed it in front of the girl.

"Drink," she ordered, "You must drink a lot."

Nelleke obediently lifted the cup to her mouth and slowly sipped. The hot liquid stained her lips. Then she put the cup back down onto the saucer.

"Luit," she said to her husband, "Luit, we haven't talked about it but what shall we call the baby if it is a boy?"

Luit somberly regarded his wife from his place across the table. His eyes softened for a moment.

"Norbert if it is a boy. Norbert for father. Father," he added softly, taking his eyes off his wife and addressing his sister for a small moment, "was a good man."

Feeling that the sentence was an accusation of sorts, Ellen turned her back on him.

"And if it's a girl?" Nelleke asked.

"Nora."

Nelleke lifted the teacup back to her lips and took another sip. The kitchen door opened again and Adam walked in. Adam was nine years old and wavy brown hair, very like that of his Oom Adriaan, fell over his forehead. But unlike his uncle, his eyes were alive. On thin but purposeful legs, the child proudly walked over to his Tante Ellen, pulling three dilapidated carrots out of his pocket.

"Meneer Ganzeveer gave them to me for you."

His voice was eager, rather as if he expected a pat on the head, an approval of sorts. But she had no comments and did nothing to show the boy that she was pleased with his acquisition.

"I think he rather likes you, Ellen."

Luit gave his opinion in a half-joking, half-serious manner, adding, "But I think you should be forewarned that he might be a dangerous man. He reminds me of Lux."

Ellen treated his comment as a joke and grimaced, for she secretly admired Mikkel Ganzeveer even though he was suspected of dabbling in the black market.

"Sit down, Adam," she said, taking the carrots from her nephew's hands, depositing them on the counter as she spoke, "and you can have some tea too."

Adam pulled out a chair next to his Tante Nelleke, who laid her hand on his shoulder and smiled at him when he slid into place. He smiled back at her.

"Soon your baby will be born," he said in a shy whisper.

"It will be your baby too, Adam," she answered, "and I'm sure it will love you."

"You will have a small cousin," Luit added, "and that means you will have a great deal of responsibility."

"Responsibility?" Adam questioned.

"Yes," his uncle said, "because if Tante Nelleke or myself are not there, it will be up to you to take care of the baby."

"Not here? Up to me?"

"Yes," his uncle answered, his eyes looking straight into Adam's eyes, "up to you."

After a few seconds, he added persistently, "Do you promise that you will look after this baby if you have to, Adam?"

His sister made a derisive sound with her tongue. She liked not this talk. It was defeatist and it also, she innately realized, put her down.

"I promise," Adam said, unable to look away from his uncle's gaze.

That night Nora was born. She weighed very little, and only mewled a pitiful birthing cry. And God pulled the stitch of that cry straight through that night so that even when it appeared to be a given that the child would not see the light of day, it turned out quite differently. Tucked away between wool blankets, eyes wide open in a paper-thin, blue-veined face, Nora stared up at her Tante Ellen. It was so cold in the bedroom that the water in the wash basin had frozen solid and Ellen Adriaan, although she applied all her midwifery skills, could not keep Nelleke from dying. Luit, hunched over on a chair by his wife's bedside, wept soundlessly, tears rolling down his cheeks. His hand would not release that of his wife, and his sister virtually had to pull it out of the dead woman's clasp. And then Luit died, his head resting on the bed next to his wife's hand. It seemed almost as if he had waited on the birth before stopping to breathe.

Adam was shaken awake by Tante Ellen as he burrowed deep underneath his blankets. He was dreaming of red apples and yellow pudding and had no wish to be roused. But Tante Ellen's voice intruded, pushing away the food.

"Adam," she whispered urgently, "Adam, you must dress quickly and...."

Adam was half-asleep and did not comprehend the fact that Tante Ellen's words were hoarse and that the voice which summoned him away from the pleasures of longed-for food was weeping. But then he was awake as suddenly as if someone had turned on a light switch.

"Why?" he questioned, rubbing his eyes.

There was another sound besides the sound of Tante's voice - a sound that he did not recognize. Through sleep-blurred eyes he could make out Tante Ellen's form dimly in the semi-darkness of the room. She had set a candle on the dresser next to his bed and was holding something in her arms. That something was making the unfamiliar noise.

"This is Nora," Tante Ellen iterated, repeating in a strange, thin voice, "This is Nora."

He sat up, the blanket falling off him, and stared. The chill air brought out goose bumps on his arms.

"Nora?"

"Tante Nelleke's baby was born a little while ago," Tante Ellen went on, "and we must find someone who will feed her or she will...."

She stopped and the little bundle moved - moved tiny arms convulsively as if they were striking out at the world.

"Can't Tante Nelleke...?" Adam stuttered and then his thoughts halted.

He instinctively felt that something was very wrong, that Tante Ellen would not be here with the baby unless, unless....

"What about Oom Luit?" he whispered.

Tante Ellen stared at him for a long moment and then shook her head - shook it slowly before she spoke again.

"You must dress, Adam, and dress quickly and warmly. I know that Coen Jansen's wife had a child a few days ago. Her child died. Perhaps she will still have some milk."

Ellen Adriaan suddenly sat down on the edge of the bed. There was something dreadful in her eyes which frightened Adam. He pushed back the covers all the way and swung his feet over the edge of the bed. The cold of the tiled floor woke him thoroughly. He was dressed in a minimum of time and then, as if possessed by some inner knowledge, bent over and took the child from his Tante's arms.

"It's all right. I will take the baby to the Jansen farm."

He left his Tante sitting on the bed and walked down the hallway cradling Nora with one hand and carrying a flashlight with the other. She stared up at him, eyes dark and large in the tiny face. He made it to the kitchen and laid the child on the table while he put on his coat and boots. He then took his uncle's greatcoat off the rack and carefully wrapped the baby in it. Next he loosely tied a scarf around her tiny face. Picking up both the child and the flashlight, he softly opened the outside door, stepping into the night. There was a curfew, but he could detect no movement, no people anywhere. Sheltering Nora's body against his chest and shining the flashlight onto the road ahead of him, he bent his head and began the trek towards the Jansen farm. He reckoned that it would take him a good three quarters of an hour.

"Please Lord," he prayed as he walked along the snow encrusted ground, "help me find the way. Help me and Nora."

He was not a praying child. All the Adriaans were just barely nominal Christians. Lux, Adam's father, had taught his son very little with regard to faith or hope. He had rarely, if ever, taken him to church. But the words invoking God fell from Adam's lips as if someone had breathed them into his throat and had pushed them out, and the boy did not know where they had come from.

A gander honked somewhere in the barn when Adam finally reached the front yard of the Jansen farm. He was cold to the marrow and fearful that the baby might have died. Her face, even underneath the woolen scarf, had acquired a bluish hue and the dark eyes had closed. The transparent lids had an unearthly quality but they opened at the sound of the consistent honking. Her eyes peeped up at Adam and as she peeped up, she let out a tiny wail of distress.

He whispered down to her, overcome with a powerful emotion that had been growing in him as they walked along the road, "Shh, little one, shh! We're here. Don't cry!"

She stopped whimpering at the sound of his voice, crinkling her face before sighing deeply. He smiled though the action hurt him. The cold had so cruelly bitten into his cheeks, forehead and lips, that he felt any more movement might shatter his face.

"Who's out there?"

Adam was standing by the side door. He had been here before, asking for milk for Tante Nelleke. Vrouw Jansen was one farmer's wife who had always been kind. Perhaps she would be kind now, even though the hour was late and his request passing strange.

"It's Adam," he answered in a low voice, "Adam Adriaan."

"What do you want at this hour, boy?"

The voice was not unfriendly.

"I need some help."

There was a stumbling sort of noise and a moment later the door opened and Coen Jansen's face studied him in the dark.

"What do you need help with?"

Adam did not have to answer. Nora mewled, kicking within the greatcoat. Coen Jansen stared as he stood in the doorway in his longjohns. Then he bent over and peered down into the confines of the coat.

"You have a baby in there?"

"Yes."

"Your Tante Nelleke's baby?"

"Yes."

Is she....?"

"Yes."

"Come in, boy."

Coen Jansen led Adam into the warm kitchen, opened the stove, threw a piece of wood onto the smoldering fire of its pot-belly, and stirred with a poker.

"Sit down," he commanded before walking out into the hall, and Adam sank into a chair, holding Nora close and feeling exhausted. She was now making sounds, insistent sounds, and he drew back the scarf, regarding her intently.

"You have to make a good impression," he whispered, "so smile if you can."

Farmer Jansen strode back into the kitchen.

"My wife will be here in a moment," he remarked rather gruffly, "she wants to see the baby. What is its name? Is it a boy or a girl?"

"A girl," Adam answered, "and her name is Nora."

Coen Jansen sat down opposite Adam. His eyes were kind.

"Here," he said suddenly, "give me the child. You are frozen through. Stand next to the stove, lad. Warm yourself."

Adam stood up, handed him the baby and positioned himself next to the stove. From there he watched the farmer gingerly unwrap Nora from the heavy greatcoat that had been Oom Luit's.

"She is a tiny thing," was all the farmer said just as his wife walked in.

Hanneke Jansen was clad in a blue, cotton nightgown, and seemed rather frail with her hair falling down her shoulders in two long, brown braids. Thirty something, she looked younger, much younger. Her husband regarded her with a half-smile from his position in the chair, then shifted his gaze down to Nora.

"Here is your salvation, little one. Here is one who is able to feed you."

Step by step Hanneke Jansen inched towards her husband. Adam watched intently, momentarily forgetting that he was cold, hungry and tired.

"Her breasts are bursting with milk," Coen Jansen went on, still speaking to Nora but now eyeing his wife, "and the Lord has this day provided food for your little lips, food that will leave you satisfied."

A sob escaped from Hanneke Jansen's heart.

"Do you think so, Coen?" she asked.

"Yes," he said, and handed her the small bundle that was Nora as he spoke.

She took the baby from his arms and stood quietly, holding Nora without moving. From his place by the stove Adam could see that Nora's eyes were solemnly fixed on Vrouw Jansen.

"I will feed her," the woman finally said to no one in particular, "if she will take my milk."

"Ah," answered her husband, "and is this milk yours?"

She did not respond but turned and left the kitchen, dandling Nora in her arms as she walked out.

"Would you like some bread, Adam?" farmer Jansen asked.

Startled Adam nodded.

"Thank you."

Coen Jansen got up, speaking as he rose.

"You must not mind that my wife did not speak to you. She is still weak from losing our child three days ago. We lost two before that...

Yet... if she'd had proper care,... but no one was here at the time but myself... and so...."

He left sentences dangling. Whether he spoke to the boy or to himself was not obvious. Adam nodded sagely, but farmer Jansen was not looking at him but busy opening a breadbox as he was speaking and taking out a loaf of bread. The boy left off nodding and stared. He'd not seen a loaf of bread for as long as he could remember. When Coen Jansen placed a plate with two thick slices in front of him, his hands trembled with eagerness to bring the food to his mouth. The first bite was pure joy and he chewed slowly and carefully for he wanted the moment to last and last. There was nothing at all in the whole world, he knew with great certainly, that he desired more than this particular mouthful of bread. Farmer Jansen watched him.

"You haven't eaten for a while, have you?"

Adam, did not answer until he had swallowed that first bite.

"No," he shook his head as he answered, simultaneously letting his hands tear off another small piece.

The knowledge that he could chew and swallow all of the bread on the plate in front of him was exquisite.

"How would you like to work for me for a while, Adam?"

Adam's hand, which was lifted halfway to his mouth, stopped short.

"Work for you?"

"Yes. Work. Work such as clean out the stalls, sweep, and what have you."

"And Nora?"

"Well, she is too small to be working," Coen Jansen joked, "but I'm fairly certain that my wife is going to want to keep her for a while."

And the thread of fabric weaving both Adam's and Nora's life, pulled tighter now, pulled tighter into what was the beginning of a straight line.

Ellen Adriaan had no objections whatsoever to her nephew staying and working at the farm especially when he occasionally brought home some food. As for Nora remaining with Hanneke Jansen, she shrugged indifferently.

"I cannot feed her," she said, "and with Luit and Nelleke gone, she is better off somewhere else."

Each time he came home Adam dutifully reported on the progress Nora was making. But Tante Ellen never appeared to be listening and neither did she ask questions. Nor did she put forth any effort to see her niece, somehow irrationally blaming the little girl for the deaths of her brother and sister-in-law. Eventually Adam stopped talking about Nora when he came home. But it was really not a home for him any longer because Mikkel Ganzeveer had moved in and married Tante Ellen as soon as was decently possible after the double funeral.

Then the war was almost over. In the spring of 1945, April 29, to be exact, RAF aircraft took off from England to take part in the first of several missions to drop food on the starving people of Holland. This operation, which was referred to as 'Operation Manna', was explained to Adam by Coen Jansen as they cleaned out the barn together.

"Do you know which Bible story speaks about bread called manna dropping down from heaven for God's people?" he asked the boy.

Adam shook his head. He was not too familiar with any Bible stories, although he was becoming more acquainted with some of them as Coen and Hanneke Jansen faithfully read the Bible out loud after each meal. Adam liked listening and thought a great deal about what he heard. Had the manna been wrapped in paper and put in packages - packages like the planes dropped? He knew that the Allied planes flew at very low levels for the food drop-offs because the amount of silk required to make parachutes for the parcels was not available. The planes simply opened their bomb doors and free-dropped the food over designated areas.

Thousands of people saw the food parcels drop. They were supposed to watch from the safety of their homes, from behind their windows. This they had been instructed to do by the authorities. But tremendously excited at the prospect of food and irregardless of the orders, many people ran outdoors to see the food dropped firsthand

and they cheered up at the airplanes from their places in the streets and in the fields. Adam thought about the Dutch people's disobedience to the authorities and he superimposed it on the story of the Israelites and their journey through the desert. Coen Jansen had recounted the story to him several times now and he believed everything Coen told him for he had begun to love the man who continued to be most kind to himself and to Nora. Adam wondered if the Israelites had scanned the heavens for food and speculated whether or not they had been overcome with excitement as multiple packages descended on them - packages containing bread and meat. Coen had actually not mentioned whether the Israelites had been allowed to watch and to cheer. Or whether they had only been allowed to peek out from behind tent flaps?

Adam went on to consider whether or not God had also been personally responsible for the food parcels which had landed in the cities of Leiden, The Hague, Rotterdam and Gouda. Surely if God had sent manna to hungry people in the desert, He could also have sent food to people in Holland. After eating the gifted food, the Israelite people had not been very grateful, if Adam understood the matter correctly, and things had not ended well for all of them. Should he therefore thank God for these packages dropped by the air force? - packages of dried eggs, milk, beans, meat and chocolate? Just in case? He distinctly remembered his heartfelt prayer to God on the night he had taken Nora over to the Jansen's. God had heard that prayer. Or would he have gotten to the farm safely anyway without the prayer? Life was full of questions. Overriding all of them however, was the fact that he was happy at the Jansen farm; that he was thankful that his little cousin Nora was thriving; and that he did not miss Tante Ellen in the least.

After the war, neither Adam nor Nora moved back to live with Ellen Adriaan, who was now Ellen Ganzeveer. Mikkel Ganzeveer had carefully pointed out to his new bride that the advantages the children would receive by staying on at the farm overrode the disadvantages that would arise should they come back. He smoothly asserted that the Jansens appeared to be happy with Adam and Nora. With no children of their own, it would be cruel to take them away. Besides that, food was still in short supply and Adam and Nora now had access to both food and fresh country air. There was logic in what Mikkel said and the truth was that Ellen wanted nothing more than to put a great distance between herself and that which had taken place during the war. Adam was part of that. His surname was Adriaan, a name spit upon by many local people, and a name Ellen wanted erased from her past and her memory. And so the children stayed on at the Jansen farm.

At the end of the summer, at the onset of the school year, Coen Jansen sent Adam, who had turned ten in August, to the local school, a Christian school.

"School will be good for you," he said to the boy, "you have to learn many things if you ever want to run a farm of your own."

He added softly, "and that is what I would want a son of mine to do - to go to school and do his best."

Adam had nodded solemnly and obediently. He had always liked learning and had a quick mind. Punctual and cheerful in the farm chores Coen assigned to him, he also faithfully watched out for his little niece whom he loved devotedly. Ever mindful of the promise he had made to his Oom Luit, he played with Nora, sang to her and often rocked her to sleep. The only crack in Adam's existence was that he did not get on with the grade five teacher.

Mr. Legaal was a middle-aged man, short of stature, temper and patience. He knew, as most of the townsfolk did, that Adam's father had been a collaborator. But Mr. Legaal, unlike most people, held it personally against the boy. Not a single child in the classroom blamed him for that. Behind hands it was whispered that Mr. Legaal's oldest son had been killed in a Nazi raid - a raid in which Adam's father had supposedly been involved.

There were Bible lessons each day. Mr. Legaal paced back and forth in front of the class flicking a wooden ruler against the side of his right leg as he told stories from Scripture. He was a good story teller. Every now and then he stopped to ask questions. He often singled out Adam and Adam knew this was because he usually did not know the answer to the questions and was thus made to look foolish.

"Who was the first man, Adam?"

"Adam was the first man."

All the children were aware of Mr. Legaal's prejudice against Adam and they had, for the most part, taken the teacher's side. After all, who didn't hate the Nazis?!

"What happened to Adam?"

"He... he fell into sin."

Unfamiliar with Biblical phraseology, Adam was hesitant. To fall was to trip, to slip. You slipped on the stairs, you slipped in ill-fitting shoes and you fell on the ground. Was sin in the ground? But he knew from past experience, even as these thoughts passed through his mind, that this was the answer Mr. Legaal was looking for.

"What is your name, Adam?"

"My name is Adam, sir."

"Have you fallen into sin as well?"

From where he was standing in the aisle, Adam looked down at his desk. He peered into the deep, black recess of his inkwell. You always had to stand up when speaking to the teacher. He knew Mr. Legaal expected him to answer yes, but he did not totally understand why the answer should be yes. So he did not answer. Mr. Legaal walked down the aisle and stopped in front of him, his ever-present ruler mechanically slapping the side of his grey trousers. He went on speaking.

"Often those who sin do not repent of their sin. Do you know what happens to those who do not repent of their sin, Adam?"

Adam could feel his cheeks flush but he still did not answer, concentrating his gaze on the ink well. You could write good things with black ink. How curious was that? The boy in the desk behind him snickered.

"I think that any student in this room could easily give the answer to this question, Adam. Those who do not repent go to hell."

The ruler stopped tapping the pant leg and Mr. Legaal turned around, away from Adam, to stride back towards the front of the class.

"I think it would be good for you to reflect on the judgment of God, Adam. I want you to stay after school and copy out a Bible passage I have marked out for you."

Adam sighed. Hanneke Jansen, or Tante Hanneke as she wanted to be called, would once more be waiting in vain by the school playground with Nora sitting in the stroller. And he would not be in time to help Coen in the barn.

The text which Mr. Legaal deposited in front of Adam in clear, concise handwriting, and which he had to copy twenty-five times, read: "For I the Lord your God am a jealous God, visiting the iniquity of the fathers upon the children to the third and the fourth generation of those who hate me."

As Mr. Legaal sat at his desk correcting work, Adam mechanically wrote out the words, wrote them out over and over. A jealous God? Of what was He jealous? And how did one visit iniquity? He used to visit Tante Ellen regularly, but she had never been happy to see him. He missed his Oom Luit. Oom Luit had been a good man, a man he would have followed had he been a soldier. Adam's thoughts scratched about in his head even as the nib of his pen scratched the paper. There was really no one now to whom, or with whom, he belonged. There was Nora, of course. She crawled after him and overtop of him on the kitchen linoleum when he played with her after supper each night. And Coen and 'Tante Hanneke', he grimaced as he addressed her this way in his head, had never given him cause to doubt their affection for him. It was just that 'Tante Hanneke' sounded a lot like Tante Nelleke. Tante Nelleke was not there anymore either and she had truly loved him. Coen Jansen had told

Adam that he would be pleased to be on a first-name basis with him. Adam smudged the word 'fathers', the ink making a dark spot. He sighed. Mr. Legaal would be sure to comment that he had been careless and there was no doubt but that he would tell him he must write it out again. Consequently he added a twenty-sixth line to the second page of his remedial homework.

"Are you ready yet, boy?"

"Yes, sir."

He stood up and trudged up the aisle, his footsteps sounding awkward and hollow in the empty classroom. Laying the papers on the desk in front of his teacher, he waited.

"You've blotched a word here, Adam."

"Yes, sir."

Mr. Legaal slid the papers across the desk back to the lad.

"Write it out one more time."

"I already did, sir. You can count it out. There are twenty-six lines on the sheets."

"Read the text for me, Adam."

And Adam read: "For I the Lord your God am a jealous God, visiting the iniquity of the fathers upon the children to the third and the fourth generation of those who hate me."

"Do you think your father hated God, Adam?"

"I don't know, sir."

"You don't know?"

"No, sir. He never spoke of it."

"Hatred or love comes out in what we do, Adam. Do you not know what your father did?"

Mr. Legaal's voice was even and unemotional, but his eyes, cool and grey, contemplated Adam with disdain. And Adam remembered with a certain amount of pain in his stomach, that his father had never spoken to him of anything that he did or did not do; that his father had never included him in any conversation; that his father had only had conversations with him when ordering him to do something such as 'Get me a drink' or 'Clear the table' and 'Go to bed'. Only Oom Luit and Tante Nelleke had been kind. But now they were both gone.

"He...," the boy faltered, seeing the demanding face of his father metamorphose into that of Mr. Legaal, "My father... he went out and I don't know what he did."

Mr. Legaal smirked, "Fine father he was."

Adam looked down at the floor.

"You may go, boy."

And Adam went.

Coen and Hanneke did not ask why Adam had to stay late or why he had to write lines. The truth was that they guessed things were not very easy for Adam at school but they hoped that time would show his classmates that the boy was earnest, well-behaved and kind. And Adam told no one his problems but the gander that Coen kept in the barnyard. It was a wild greylag and Coen had successfully domesticated it as a sort of guard dog.

"Geese," he had told Adam, "have a loud call and are sensitive to unusual movements. He'll let me know if anyone or anything comes on the property. That's how I knew you were there the first night you came to us."

'Really?" Adam had asked rather doubtfully, eyeing the proud animal as it waddled around the yard, orange beak lifted up as if it owned the world, adding hopefully, "Wouldn't you like a dog to do that for you?"

"Tante Hanneke doesn't want a dog," Coen answered, "A dog sat on her once when she was little and she just doesn't want one."

"Oh," Adam answered, a trifle disappointed.

But for some reason Hugo, the gander, took a grand liking to Adam. It sought him out when the boy crossed the farmyard and inexplicably followed him from place to place. The bird even tolerated Adam's hand as he stroked the greyish-brown plumage, often emitting loud honks if the boy sang songs he had learned in school.

"I think Hugo either feels you have bad taste in music or he thinks you are a gander too," Coen joked.

"He won't migrate, will he?" Adam asked.

"No, I've clipped his wings. He'll stay the winter."

It was late fall, moving towards winter and Adam had seen large flocks pass overhead as they flew southward. Their flight calls, a loud series of repeated deep honking, was audible for miles and Hugo's brown eyes, it seemed to Adam, were forlorn at such times.

"Does he want to go?"

"I think not. He has it far too good here. His own small pond, lots of feed, and he has you."

"Will you ever get a female goose for him?"

"Perhaps next year," Coen said, "Who knows."

On Sundays there were, the closer the days edged towards Christmas, advent sermons. Usually Adam went along to one of the two services in the church which Tante Hanneke and Coen attended. He did not understand much of the sermons, but liked sitting in the bench with Coen, sharing a peppermint or two and feeling a sense of peace. But if someone had asked him, he would not have been able to put this feeling into words. The second service he babysat Nora, and Coen went to church with Tante Hanneke. Nora was growing, almost walking, and her favorite word, much to Adam's delight, was 'Adah' - a word she spoke frequently. The child was beautiful and resembled Nelleke. Black ringlets framed an oval face; huge, blue eyes sparkled underneath curling eyelashes; and two dimples appeared whenever she laughed, which was often. Tante Hanneke, Coen and Adam all doted on her.

Late one evening, Adam woke up with a great thirst and got up to get a drink of water. Passing Tante Hanneke's and Coen's bedroom, he could not help but overhear.

"We have to take steps for adoption."

It was Tante Hanneke's voice and Coen's reply, in a lower timber, was almost impossible to discern. Adam shuffled on in his slippers, towards the kitchen. Adoption, what was adoption? He looked it up in the classroom dictionary the next day and read: 'Adoption: formal legal process to adopt a child.' He went up the page to the word 'adopt' and read: 'to raise a child of other biological parents as if it were your own, in accordance with formal legal procedure.'

During the ensuing school hours Adam thought much about the adoption definition and what it could mean. He thought so much that Mr. Legaal gave him lines. "I must not daydream" was copied fifty times during recess. But when he sludged home that day through the thin, wet skiff of snow that lay on the ground, he continued to wonder. He wondered if Tante Hanneke had been speaking about Nora or about himself, or about both of them. It would make more sense if her words had referred to Nora. Nora was, after all, only a baby and she didn't know any better but that it was Coen and Tante Hanneke who were her parents. She was already calling Tante Hanneke 'mama' and Adam found that he did not mind that in the least. It was clear to him that Tante Ellen did not want Nora. Neither did she want him. Not that he minded. Tante Ellen made him increasingly uncomfortable by totally ignoring him when he saw her. He slid on the snow. Geese flew overhead. He stared up at them. Geese were free. He had read once that geese mated for life. Loyalty seemed a beautiful thing to Adam. Hugo, if he ever got a mate, would stay true. Geese were loyal. He'd reached the farmyard now and Hugo, silhouetted against the barn door, honked and waddled over towards him.

That evening Coen Jansen began reading the Gospel of Matthew after the meal. Nora sleepily hung back in her highchair, eyes half-closed. It was warm in the kitchen. Adam yawned behind his hand. He scanned the room and remembered the first time he'd sat down in the leather chair next to the stove. He could see himself sitting there even as Coen was reading the genealogy - names and names and more names. Adam saw the names floating around in the air as if they were music notes. All these names must have had faces at some point - faces and lives.

"... the father of Jehoshaphat, and Jehoshaphat..."

What a strange name that was. His mother must have had some time calling him in for chores. 'Jehoshaphat! Come here!'

"... the father of Jeconiah and his brothers, at the time of the deportation to Babylon."

"What's deportation, Coen?"

Adam knew he was allowed to interrupt to ask questions. Coen had made that very clear at the onset of his stay here.

"Deportation is," Coen began, furrows lining his brow as he formulated the answer, "being sent away from where you live."

"Oh," Adam responded, "you mean that I was deported from Tante Ellen's house."

He noted that Tante Hanneke threw Coen a look. The look was almost angry.

"No," she said, "No, it's not like that at all."

Adam appeared slightly puzzled and she went on a bit irrationally, went on even as color rose in her cheeks.

"Well, you weren't sent away from your home. You must not think of it like that. You just have to remember that we really wanted you to stay with us. The deported people Coen was reading about were disobedient and God punished them by sending them away. You were not...."

She stopped abruptly and smiled at him before she added, "Do you see?"

"Yes," Adam replied, although he did not really see, but he told himself that he would think about it.

Coen went on reading, after exchanging another look with his wife.

"And after the deportation to Babylon, Jeconiah...."

Nora began to whine. Tante Hanneke lifted her up out of the highchair and settled the child on her lap. Thumb in her mouth, Nora smiled a drooly smile at Adam. He grinned back.

"... and Jacob the father of Joseph the husband of Mary of whom Jesus was born...."

Jesus, that was the Son of God. Jesus, that was in whose name Coen always prayed and was teaching him, Adam to pray. You must say 'for Jesus sake', Adam, at the end of every prayer. So he did. It was enough for him that Coen said so. Coen never lied.

"... Now the birth of Jesus Christ took place in this way. When His mother Mary had been betrothed...."

"What's betrothed, Coen?"

"Betrothed is like being engaged. You know that time when a boy gives a ring to a girl because he wants her to be his wife."

"You have to give a ring to a girl if you want to marry her?"

Coen and Tante Hanneke smiled simultaneously.

"Well," Coen said, "that's usually what's done."

"Did Tante Ellen get a ring from Mikkel Ganzeveer?"

"Probably," was all Tante Hanneke would answer.

"When his mother Mary," Coen repeated, turning back to the Bible, "had been betrothed to Joseph, before they came together she was found to be with child of the Holy Spirit, and her husband Joseph, being a just man and unwilling to put her to shame, resolved to divorce her quietly."

"Where did the child come from?"

There was no answer for a few moments. There was only the crackling of the wood in the stove and the wet sound of Nora noisily sucking her thumb.

"The Child," Coen began, "that is to say, Jesus, came from heaven."

"You said," Adam interposed, "that heaven is a good place. You said last night that it was better than any place on earth."

"Yes," Coen nodded, "that's true."

"Well, then," Adam went on, "why did Jesus leave it?"

"He left it so that you and I could go to it."

Adam's face was blank and Coen continued.

"Well, we can't go to heaven if we are dirty, that is to say, sinful. Remember that we talked about sin the other day? God can't abide sinfulness. So Jesus left heaven to make us clean. He became a human being like you and I; He lived the perfect life that you and I could not live."

They were just so many words to Adam. He understood that he did bad things. He knew that deep within himself he was not good.

He didn't know why this knowledge was in him, but it was. Falling into sin, that's what Mr. Legaal had spoken of in the classroom. But for Adam the discussions were more or less like falling into a sea of words and drowning in their meaning without being able to come up for air. It was too much.

"Why didn't God just make our sins go away," he responded, "Wouldn't that be easier than leaving heaven and besides that, He can do anything, can't He?"

"Yes, He can," Tante Hanneke came into the conversation, "but He chose to do it this way. The Bible tells us that He took on our flesh. The Word, that is Jesus, became flesh and lived among us. He became a baby, and grew into a child, who grew into man, Who died for us. This way we can see Him more clearly as one of us, and we are impelled to follow Him."

"Impelled?"

"Well, that means we have to. We just can't help it."

"Became like us?" Adam said, "But why would He want to come to a place like our town where so many people are mean...."

He didn't finish. He never divulged the painful moments at school; never spoke of the secret kicks, the snide remarks, and the multiple snubs that were his daily fare. Coen closed the Bible.

"If He hadn't come to earth," Tante Hanneke repeated, patting Nora on the back, "the disciples wouldn't have seen Him, and then they wouldn't have been able to tell us about Him, and then we would not have been able to follow Him."

"But why couldn't we have followed Him without Him coming here?"

Coen cleared his throat, preparing to answer, but no words came out

"I wouldn't have come to earth if I were Jesus," Adam finished, "and that's the truth."

Suddenly embarrassed that he had said too much, he shrugged and stared at Nora pulling a silly face. Nora took the thumb out of her mouth and laughed out loud, dimples showing. Then she began to cry and Tante Hanneke motioned that Coen should finish off by praying, it was time for bed.

A few days later, on a Sunday afternoon walk through the woods with Hugo by his side, Adam noticed that someone or something, was following closely behind him. There were noises like branches breaking and it seemed that the trees overhead were whispering. He turned sharply at one point, only to see two boys run to hide behind a bush. He stood still for a minute but they did not come out and he resumed his walk at a quicker pace. Hugo trotting in and out of the bushes, picked up speed as well. Then a rock hit the back of his head just above the nape of his neck. It hurt and he did not know if he should stop, stay his ground and have it out with his pursuers or keep on walking. If he stayed, the boys might hurt Hugo. On the other hand, Hugo was a good fighter. He had seen the gander hiss and snarl and spread his wings at the goat when the animal had playfully butted too close for Hugo's comfort. It began to snow, and Hugo, unaware of any danger, honked his contentment. He delighted in cold weather. Adam reached his right hand up to gingerly touch his head where he could begin to feel the swelling of a bruise.

"Hurt you, did we, boy?"

It was the taunting voice of Herman, a boy in his class. Adam recognized it. He decided to stop and turned around. Herman was not alone. Kees Legaal, the son of Mr. Legaal, was with him. Kees was also in Adam's class. There was a rock in Kees' hand and in a swinging motion he lifted it above his head, making as if to throw it. Hugo had halted as well. The bird, sensing the tension in Adam, suddenly stood up straight next to the boy, puffing out his chest, and spreading his wings.

"Hey, look at that dumb goose."

"It's a gander," Adam replied, "and he's not dumb."

"Oh, no? Well, watch him fall down."

Kees threw his rock, but the missile went awry as Hugo simultaneously streaked towards the boys, hissing in a frightful manner. Reaching them, he began to peck and bite, going for legs, arms and bellies. For a moment Adam was transfixed with pride. Hugo was protecting him. Then he called out.

"Hugo. It's all right. Hugo, come home with me."

The gander, after a few more seconds of nipping sharply at his prey, stood still. His frightened quarry turned tail and ran. Kees ran helter-skelter down the road but Herman disappeared to the left. The left turn was a mistake. Crashing through several layers of bushes, not watching where he was going, he ran headlong into Zonnemeer, a small but deep pond covered with a thickening but treacherous coating of ice. Adam could hear Herman falling; could hear the sound of ice cracking; and then he heard the sound of water splashing, water swallowing. Next to him, Hugo was nibbling on some snow, looking remarkably unconcerned and innocent. Losing no time, Adam followed the boy's trail, until he reached the edge of the pond. Herman's head was visible where he had fallen through in the ice and his eyes looked shocked and scared. There were several feet of unbroken ice between the edge of the pond and the spot where he had fallen through. Although Adam's first instinct was to run out onto the ice to help, he was extremely conscious of the treacherous instability of the surface of the pond.

"It's all right, Herman," he shouted, "stay calm."

The boy began to cry and Adam prayed, and he prayed out loud, "Please God, let me help Herman so that he will be all right, for Jesus sake."

A calmness came over him.

"Lift your elbows out of the water," he said clearly, remembering what Coen had told him to do should he ever fall into one of the many ponds in the area, "and rest them on the edge of the ice where you fell in, and breathe in deeply and slowly."

He took off his woolen scarf, a red one that Tante Hanneke had knit for him, and measured it. It was a long scarf and would perhaps do the trick if he would be able to get just a little closer to Herman. He gingerly stepped out onto the ice. It held him and appeared solid. Herman never took his eyes off Adam even as Adam tied a loop at the end of the scarf. Perhaps if Herman's hands were too cold to hold the scarf, he could put the loop around his elbows. Prepared to throw the red rescue line, he heard the snow behind him crunch. It was Kees who had come back to see what happened to his friend. Panicking upon seeing him in the pond, he stood rooted at the edge.

"Herman," he shouted, "don't drown."

"If you want to help," Adam said, "hold my hand while I throw the scarf out to him."

Kees nodded and slid onto the ice behind Adam. Adam held out his left hand and Kees took it. The whole scene felt surreal to Adam, almost as if he were dreaming. And perhaps, he reasoned within himself, he was dreaming and in a few moments would wake up in his bed at the Jansen farm. But Hugo honked from the pond's edge, and he supposed that such a loud honking would never take place in a dream. He felt Kees' stiffen at the approach of the gander.

"It's all right," he reassured the boy, "Hugo won't hurt you. He's just watching to see what I'm doing."

Kees didn't answer. He merely nodded and shivered. Adam carefully took aim and threw the scarf across the ice towards Herman. Herman had closed his eyes now.

"Herman," Adam called out, "open your eyes and try to get hold of the scarf. We're going to try and pull you out of the water."

Herman opened his eyes and slowly reached for the scarf with his right hand.

"That's it," Adam shouted encouragingly, "reach just a bit further. You almost have it."

Herman seemed to be moving in slow motion. His hand was almost on top of the scarf and then his fingers took hold of the wool. Clamping down on the red, his other arm rose out of the water and followed the first.

"Good," Adam called out, and Kees joined him, "That's good Herman. You can do it. Grab it with both hands."

Herman managed the feat and both of his hands were now wrapped up in the wool.

"I'm going to pull slowly but will need both my arms," Adam cautioned Kees, "so let go of my hand but hold on to my coat."

Kees did as Adam instructed him and Adam began to strain as hard as he could. At first there was no movement although Herman's arms were now flat on the ice in front of him grasping the scarf. But then his body began to shift upward. Slowly the boy emerged from the water. His eyes were closed again. As soon as his belly slid onto the ice, Adam was able to step back.

"Here," he said to Kees, "help me pull now. You can let go of my coat and grab the scarf. Pull as hard as you can. We'll get him out together."

All this time Hugo was waddling back and forth on the land behind them, honking fiercely every few minutes. Kees took hold of the scarf as well, and began to lend his weight to the taut line. And bit by bit Herman was drawn closer, finally reaching the shore. His clothing was sopped through and through. Adam took off his own coat and undid the buttons on Herman's coat.

"Help me, Kees," he said, "Help me take his coat off and then we have to get him to walk, or run, so he doesn't...."

"I know," Kees responded, and knelt down beside his friend.

Together they managed to take off the boy's coat and get Adam's coat wrapped around him.

"Stand up, Herman," Adam said, "You have to walk now. I know you feel tired but you have to walk."

He slapped Herman's face. The boy opened his eyes.

"I'm so cold," he whispered.

"I know," Kees answered, "and soon we'll be home and we'll get you totally warm by the stove. But you have to get up and start walking or...."

To their surprise, Herman sat up and attempted to rise. Kees and Adam both put hands under his armpits and helped him up.

"Good," Adam said, "very good work, Herman. Now walk with us."

Herman obeyed - obeyed as if he were a robot - and the three began their trek back to the village.

"My house is closest," Kees said after they had been walking for some five minutes which seemed like five hundred, "so we should stop there. I'm afraid...."

They reached Kees' house after another ten minutes walking. Herman had ceased to talk. He just mechanically moved his legs forward. His eyes were shut again. Kees ran up to the front door and yelled for his father. Adam had both arms wrapped around Herman who was leaning heavily against him. Mr. Legaal appeared in the door. His eyes took in the situation and he immediately told Kees to start warming hot water bottles, as well as call for his wife to get some hot drink ready. Meanwhile he ran outside on his stocking feet, positioned himself on the other side of Herman and helped guide him towards the door, towards the warmth of the house. Mr. Legaal said nothing to Adam during this time and Adam spoke no word to him. Hugo was still on the road, honking dejectedly. When they got to the door, Mr. Legaal finally broke the silence between them.

"You can go now," he said to Adam, "I'll take care of Herman."

And Adam, after a final look at Herman who was still wearing his coat, went.

The wind had picked up in force and miniscule ice pellets fell. It would be Christmas on Wednesday. Adam loved the songs that Tante Hanneke hummed as she prepared meals and as she went about the house. He also loved the songs he was learning in school. To take his mind off the stinging ice that hit his face, he tried to sing one after leaving Mr. Legaal's house. But his voice would not obey his thoughts. His hands were numb and reaching for the pockets of his coat, remembered that he was not wearing a coat. He stamped his feet as he walked. Hugo had half-flown, half-waddled ahead of him down the road. He was trailing his right wing but seemed set on going home quickly. Adam watched him until the bird disappeared around a bend. There was a loneliness settling within him. It was like the frost that had cruelly nipped at his cheeks the night he had carried Nora, only this cold was tugging and nipping at his heart. The Jansen farm was ahead and he was glad of it for he did not think he could keep walking much longer. Tante Hanneke would ask where his coat was and what would he say? He had begun to shiver and although he tried very hard not to shiver, he could not help the uncontrollable shakes that seized him every few seconds. If he could just sit by the stove for a bit, just for ten minutes or so, with no one speaking to him, it seemed to him that he would be all right. The door was in front of him and he stared at it, unable to reach for the handle.

"Adam."

It was Coen's voice and it came from behind him. He moved his head to see where exactly Coen was, but then everything went dark and he slid down, down into a pond of treacherous ice, blackness and night.

When Adam opened his eyes, he was lying in bed and Tante Hanneke was sitting in a chair by his side. She was knitting, knitting something red - perhaps another scarf? He closed his eyes again and wiggled his toes in delicious warmth. How good it was to be wrapped up within a house, within a bed and to have someone sitting by your side who loved you. He reopened his eyes and this time Tante Hanneke stopped her knitting and laid it down in her lap.

"You're awake, Adam?"

He smiled a weak smile in agreement.

"That's good. You had me very worried for a while. You have quite a lump on the back of your head. Where have you been?"

There was no reproach in her voice. It was just a question. He smiled again trying to remember where he had been. He vaguely recalled the walk with Hugo by his side. And there were boys - Herman and Kees. And there was the pond. He closed his eyes and sighed.

"I was," he began, and to his own surprise, he could not continue, but started to weep.

Tante Hanneke laid her knitting on the floor and sat on the edge of the bed. She took his hands in her own and rubbed them gently.

"Never mind," she said, "it doesn't matter. What matters is that you are home safely and that I love you."

"I'm home," Adam whispered, and then he fell asleep again.

When he awoke for the second time, it was because there was noise of some sort in the hallway. There were voices. He recognized the voices but could not put a name on them. A minute later the door to his bedroom opened and Tante Hanneke walked in. She was followed by Mr. Legaal who was followed by Coen. They all looked serious. Adam wished he could put his head under the covers, but his whole body felt paralyzed. Tante Hanneke smiled reassuringly at him, and sat down on the edge of the bed.

"You have a visitor, Adam."

She spoke the words even as she took hold of his right hand.

"Hello, Adam."

Mr. Legaal mouthed his greeting in a clipped manner, and Adam half expected him to produce a ruler and begin hitting his leg with it. He did not answer. His mind might have woken up but his voice was still sleeping and unwilling to awaken.

"I came over," Mr. Legaal went on, "to tell you that I'm very thankful you brought Herman to my house this afternoon. It was a good thing you did, Adam."

Behind his teacher's frame, Adam could see Coen smiling cheerfully. But his own mouth would not smile back.

"You know, Adam," and Mr. Legaal's voice became rather low, as if he was having trouble enunciating words, "I made you copy out lines at the beginning of the school year, lines from Deuteronomy five."

Tante Hanneke raised her eyebrows and looked at Coen, who shrugged behind Mr. Legaal's shoulders.

"The words were," Mr. Legaal hoarsely went on, "For I the Lord your God am a jealous God, visiting the iniquity of the fathers upon the children to the third and fourth generation of those who hate Me."

Both of Tante Hanneke's hands now enclosed Adam's right hand and she sighed.

"But," the teacher continued, as his eyes now fully met Adam's, "I neglected the second part of that text which reads, 'but showing steadfast love to thousands of those who love Me and keep My commandments.'"

It was very quiet in the bedroom. Adam could hear his own heartbeat and felt it pulse in his temples.

"You are one of the thousands, Adam, and I am sorry if I...."

Mr. Legaal turned sharply, almost bumped into Coen and, passing him, made his departure.

Coen cleared his throat. Tante Hanneke cleared hers as well.

"Your teacher," Coen began, "told me what happened this afternoon, Adam."

Adam nodded. He was weary and actually wanted to go to sleep again. But he did wonder if Hugo had come home. He did not remember seeing the bird in the farmyard when he came back from his walk. But then there were a number of things in his head that were fuzzy.

"Hugo?" he asked.

"His right wing is a bit sprained. I've put him in a pen by himself for a few days. He's fine though, or will be in a day or two, and he is as bossy as ever."

Adam smiled and drifted off again.

Though he was pampered for the next few days, Tante Hanneke did not judge him quite well enough to go to the special Christmas Eve service. He protested, albeit weakly, that she should not worry and that he felt up to the walk, but she would not hear of it.

"It looks like snow," she said, "and I want you to stay nice and warm inside. And that's an order."

"I don't want you to miss the special service for me," he said, "so I'll stay home only if you go to church."

Coen had nodded in agreement.

"Adam is right, Hanneke," he said, "He's well enough to watch Nora and the two of us can go together."

Tante Hanneke had not truly wanted to leave him, but she had conceded battle. Dressed warmly the two of them had left for church after supper.

It had begun to snow ever so lightly. After he put Nora to bed, Adam stood by the kitchen window and watched the flakes dance. They illumined briefly as they swirled past the glow of the lantern swinging from the front porch. It was fascinating and for a long while Adam felt unable to take his eyes away. Then the flurries grew thicker and the wind picked up, faintly howling through the trees. Adam shivered, pulled the curtains shut and sat down in Coen's big chair. How different things were now as compared to last year. He could see himself standing in front of the stove, could see Coen take the baby from his arms, and he could see Tante Hanneke walk through the kitchen door in her nightgown, braids hanging over her shoulders. And now he lived here - now this was his home. Yawning contentedly, he leaned back and closed his eyes. There was only the one thing, just one thing, which worried him now. And that was the concern he saw reflected in Tante Hanneke's eyes when he prayed at night.

"Do you believe, Adam," she had asked him but the day before yesterday, the day that Mr. Legaal had come, and the day that he had been so tired and despondent, "that Jesus came down from heaven to save you?"

There had been a pleading in her brown eyes, and he had been tempted to say, "Of course I do."

But he was unable to bring the words forward for they were not in his heart.

So he had answered her with "I can't," only to see a sadness diffuse her eyes. He added, trying once more to explain his dilemma, "I don't know why Jesus would come here and become human. Why would He want to be like us? Why would He have to do that if He truly is God?"

She had replied, as she had done before, "Because He loves us. Because He knew that we would follow Him more easily if He became one of us. "

Then she turned away but he could hear her softly murmuring, "The Word became flesh and made His dwelling among us, full of grace and truth. We have seen His glory, the glory of the One and Only, Who came from the Father, full of grace and truth."

It was a verse Adam had memorized in school this last month, but had not quite understood. He opened his eyes again. He wished that God would knock at the door and explain it to him. He wished the answer would come to him in the lantern light with the snowflakes. Nora half-whimpered in her bedroom and he got up. But when he reached the crib, she was sleeping, thumb in her mouth, curls askew on the sheet. He gazed at her for a long time, remembering his promise to Oom Luit. Stroking her cheek, he caught himself humming a Bach melody - a melody which Tante Hanneke called a Christmas lullaby.

"*O Savior sweet, O Savior mild, Who came to earth a little child.*"

Adam felt confused by the words. He stopped humming and tip-toed out, making his way back to the chair.

As he settled in, pulling his sock-feet up and snuggling against the leather side, there was a loud thump against the window. Then another. Instinctively he slid out of the chair and lay flat on the ground. It was a reflex movement, a movement left-over from the war. There were more sounds outside, but they were not the sounds of airplanes overhead, sounds he still heard in bad dreams. Slowly sitting up, he crawled over to the window on his knees. Past the curtain's edge the yard was veiled in white and barely visible. The snowfall had become much heavier. Through the periodic gusting, his eyes met a very strange sight. A number of geese were wandering around the pathway leading to the door. Then squalls of white obliterated them from his sight. Adam rubbed the window-pane, trying to see more clearly. Where had these geese have come from? Had they been on their way south and had they been disoriented by this sudden storm? He spotted two of them close to the window, flapping their wings rather wildly and aimlessly. They were running around in circles. He wished Coen and Tante Hanneke were home but, because of the weather, maybe it would be very late before they would be back. Should he go outside and help the birds? He rubbed the pane again and strained his eyes. Between the paroxysms of the wind coughing the snow past the window, Adam thought he could count at least seven geese. Was Hugo with them? No, Coen had put Hugo in a pen. Perhaps if he opened the barn door, the birds might go in and find shelter instead of flying about in such a haphazard fashion.

Before venturing outside, Adam went to the bread board and cut off several slices of bread. He doubted whether scattering the bread would make the birds follow him, but just in case.... Carefully dividing the bread into small pieces, he stuffed them inside his pants pocket. Then thinking for a moment, he went to his bedroom and took the flashlight out of the drawer next to his bed. Then he walked back to the kitchen, put on his coat, his red scarf, his boots and then his mittens. Listening intently for a moment to satisfy himself as to whether or not Nora was still asleep, he stepped into the hallway and opened the door to the yard. Honkings and hissings swirled with the wind and whirled about with the snow. Quickly stepping outside, he closed the door behind him. Oh, to be Hugo for a moment and convey to these birds in goose language that they could follow him. Treading out a path on the snow with his boots, he dropped bread pieces and made his way to the barn. Would they follow? Initially it seemed not. Then one of them picked at a piece of bread and nosed forward for another. But the next moment a particularly heavy blast of wind blew him and a number of bread crumbs out of Adam's sight and when he could see again, the bird had wandered off in a different direction. Reaching the barn, he opened the door and turned on the flashlight, shining it into the doorway. Not one bird in the entire gaggle paid any attention. He walked back into the middle of the group.

"Follow me," he pleaded, "there's lots of straw and I can give you some chicken feed too."

Although honkings and flappings encircled him, none of the geese even came close to his outstretched hands. They were wary of him and afraid. He was not one of them.

"Perhaps if I carry Hugo outside," he spoke to himself, "they might follow him. After all, he is a real goose and I'm not."

Trudging back to the barn, it took him a few minutes to locate the spot where Coen had placed Hugo's pen. The gander sat quietly, brown eyes wide open, watching him. Adam felt a pang of conscience that he had not come to see him earlier.

"Hello, Hugo," he said, "how are you?"

The bird honked softly.

"I'd like you to do me a favor," Adam went on, "There are a lot of geese outside, lost in the snow. I thought you might show them the way to the barn because you, after all, Hugo, are a goose just like them and they will follow you."

He opened the pen door and Hugo waddled out, making straight for the open barn door.

"That's it, Hugo," Adam encouraged, "That's it. You're doing fine!!"

Hugo turned for one second at the door, dark brown eyes shining, his right wing hanging limply by his side. Then he turned his grey head and walked on, disappearing into the white. Adam ran after him, and reaching the door, initially could see nothing but heaving snow. Then something half-flew, half-darted perilously close past his head into the barn. It was Hugo, fan-shaped tail dragging wearily behind him. Following Hugo's lead while honking wildly and flying in a straight line, the seven geese streaked past him as well.

Turning on his flashlight, he stared at the grey birds, some of whom were already tucking their beaks under their wings. Bulky bodies, thick long necks and greyish-brown plumage were all huddled together on some straw. Hugo had retreated back into his pen. His orange bill emitted a soft 'Gaa', and Adam smiled. He heard the wind blowing outside. He did not know where it had come from or where it was going.

9: I Have a Sonne Seven Years Old

By this we know love, that he laid down his life for us, and we ought to lay down our lives for the brothers (I Jn. 3:16).

Perhaps it is true that one's conscience is like a songbird warbling high up in a tree. Though you cannot detect its form, its notes are clear and touch your soul with their pureness and you cannot walk by for weeping.

September of 1953 was a hot month in the city of Toronto. As a matter of fact, the second day of that month was the hottest day of the year with the thermometer reaching a high of 98 degrees Fahrenheit. With a view to the temperature on that Labor Day weekend, it did not seem to me to be a very auspicious time to open school doors and neither did it appear to me be an auspicious moment to be a first-time teacher.

I had graduated from the Toronto Normal School earlier that same year. As far back as I could remember I had always loved the idea of becoming a teacher - of being with children and imparting to them knowledge, truth and fine ideals. But when I faced my mixed class of seventh and eighth graders that first week - a medley of twenty-seven faces, all wilting with heat in the muggy, crowded classroom, my courage and commitment somehow deteriorated into nervous tension. There were names to memorize, characters to unravel and temperaments to discern. Not that the children were rowdy or disobedient. It was just that there seemed to be so many of them and so few of me.

Consequently, at the end of that initial week I stood in front of the half-open classroom window gazing out at the silent playground. The students had been dismissed. Tired and not a little discouraged, I contemplated whether or not I should have opted for another vocation, such as that of mechanic or traveling salesman. Drumming my fingers on the sill and staring off into the horizon, I recalled the respect I'd had for teachers who had made an impact on my formative years. Mr. Kunstenaar, a history teacher, especially stood out in my memory. How that man had been able to tell stories! Absently I wiped beading drops of sweat off my upper lip. A few boys appeared on the playground. Though the weather was hot and humid, they were running and yelling.

There were four of them and the first was much younger than the rest. As they tore past, it became obvious that the boy in the lead was being pursued by the rest. The child was a good runner, but his small legs did not stand a chance against the longer legs of his opponents. By some providential quirk, if there is such a thing, the boy zigzagged back towards my window and reaching it, turned and stood with his back against it. The boys stopped their chase and picked up clumps of dirt from the ground where they stood. They then began to pelt the boy with the dirt, one soft clump striking the top of his head and breaking into a hundred small grains of black on his crown. Pity flooded my heart. Stepping forward to make myself clearly visible, I stood tall behind the boy. Though I did not think he saw me, his pursuers certainly did. Neither gesticulating, nor saying one word, I just stood quietly. And one by one the three boys opened their fists, dropped their missiles and disappeared. I don't know what the child thought of his attackers leaving. The back of his head pressed hard against my window. The hair I could almost touch was blond - very blond - a blond mixed with black. I had a déjà vu moment but could not place it. Then the boy turned and smiled at me. It was a warm and radiant smile. In that instant I knew I had made the right decision about becoming a teacher.

The following Monday morning the principal asked if he might speak with me if I could spare a moment.

"I'd like to take advantage of your bilingualism," he said, by way of beginning the conversation, "of your ability to speak Dutch."

"Oh?"

"This year there are three children, children of Dutch immigrants," he continued, "who are attending our school. They need help with their English. It occurred to me that you might be just the man to encourage them. Can I ask for your help in tutoring some of these students for a few hours each week if I provide some extra help in your classroom during that time?"

"I have no experience," I said, "in tutoring."

"It's just to see them through an initial awkward and difficult period," he went on, almost as if he had not heard my objection, "You see, because of their lack of ability to speak English, they have been put back a year in school, and if they are able to become more proficient in English, perhaps they can be moved up to the grade level in which they belong."

To a certain degree I felt cheated. It was clear to me that tutoring was something a teacher's aide should be doing; it certainly did not seem to be work for someone like myself who had just studied hard to earn a degree. Besides that, was it not obvious that these children would pick up English quickly by themselves, immersed as they were in the mainstrain of school life? The principal, sensing my hesitation, stood up and patted me on the shoulder.

"Mr. Anders," he said, "I assure you it would definitely help these children a great deal and it's just a few hours every week."

So it came about, beginning immediately, that every Tuesday and Thursday morning were set aside for instructing three children. From nine until recess, two sisters, eleven-year-old twins alliteratively named Tina and Tonnie, were taught the rudiments of English. Following recess, the boy with the blond hair came in, the boy who had smiled at me.

Providence is a mixture of wonderful, strange, and fearful. It was a truth wrapped up in seemingly discordant notes which fell onto my heart when the child told me his name.

"*Ik heet Nico*," he said, "*Nico Goudswaard, and ik ben zeven jaar oud.* My name is Nico - Nico Goudswaard, and I am seven years old."

Another vague déjà vu moment occurred.

"Nico," I repeated slowly, and again, "Nico."

"*Ja*, yes" the boy replied.

I sat down rather weakly and he came and sat down opposite me.

"What is your name?" he asked.

I did not answer his query instead asking him another question.

"Who is your father, Nico?"

"Well," the boy said, his clear eyes shining at me across the table, "that is a hard question to answer."

He looked down at the table for a moment as if thinking deeply. Then he looked up and smiled again.

"I do have a father though."

I did not know what to say to that and waited, for clearly the child was not finished. After thinking long and hard for another minute or so, hands folded on the brown tabletop, he finally added quietly, "Do you have to know who my father is to help me with English?"

I shook my head and grinned at him.

"No, but I would really like to know. Can you not tell me?"

"Well, you can't see my father. Not the way that other children can see theirs."

"Oh?" I said.

"Fathers are good," he continued, "When I ran to the window last week, then I pretended that you were my father. I only pretended for a minute," he quickly added, "because mother says that I must not do that - pretend that other people are my father."

"But you said that you did have a father, ...or don't you?"

"Well, mother says that my father is God in heaven and that He will look out for me always no matter where I am. I almost forgot that He was there when those boys were teasing me, but then I saw you and thought that...."

He stopped abruptly.

"How is your mother?"

Any adult would have looked at me strangely for asking such a personal question on such short acquaintance. But no one alive could have understood the absurdity of this present-day providence - even I did not understand it - this providence of me sitting at a table chatting with the child of a girl I had once known when I was a young boy.

"She is fine."

Nico had no trouble answering familiarities.

"Do you live close to the school?"

He nodded.

"Yes, I do. It only takes me fifteen minutes to walk to school."

Our whole conversation had taken place in Dutch. I took out a reader at this point and had him sound out simple words to ascertain his command of the English language. His English was actually far better than that of the twin girls. But my mind wandered continually as Nico was sounding out his words, wandered back to days long gone by. And when Nico left at lunch hour, I stayed behind in the small study room and thought, indeed, could not stop thinking, about the past.

There is no accusation which tastes as bitter as self-reproach. Others can accuse, often unjustly and unfairly. In those cases, the accused can rest in knowing he is innocent. But people who recognize the secret dealings of their own hearts, repeatedly cringe in shame and regret. So it was with me and I began remembering.

****

"'The White Book of Sarnen'," Jaap Kunstenaar said to the group of children facing him, and of whom I was one, "contains the earliest surviving record of the William Tell story."

We were in school, if you could call it school, for there was no bell, no principal, no heat, no recess and certainly no agenda of a list of subjects that we had to follow. There were some thirty children or so, facing Mr. Kunstenaar. They were huddled in their desks, students so skinny that ribs protruded and elbows jutted out of sweaters and they varied in age from eight to fifteen. I myself, Nico Anders, having just turned sixteen years of age, was the oldest boy there. The early spring of 1945, a spring which had followed a cold winter - was a death knell for many. Jaap Kunstenaar, a man who rapidly approached three score and ten years of age, was a retired teacher, and one who had offered to feed some history to the youth of our town two afternoons a week. We came, not because our parents forced us to come, but because there was not much else to do and because somehow, as we listened to Jaap Kunstenaar talk, we forgot the hunger pains in our bellies as we lived the heroic tales of the past.

I well remember the day that Mr. Kunstenaar told the story of William Tell for it was a day which marked a changing point in my life.

"The Book of Sarnen was accidentally discovered in 1856, and is believed to be a copy of a much older manuscript written in 1426."

Mr. Kunstenaar rubbed his thin and blueing hands together. The color of his hands indicated both the coldness of the room in which the pot-bellied stove had neither wood to burn nor warmth to throw, and his venerable age. Perhaps that's why he told history so well, because he himself was almost a part of history.

"More than 700 years ago," Mr. Kunstenaar began, and we all listened, already fascinated because of the intensity of his baritone voice.

"More than 700 years ago," he repeated, "a local farmer and well-known hunter hailing from the canton of Uri, strode through the market square of Altdorf. A crossbow hung over his shoulder. In all of the surrounding cantons, there was no one who could climb mountains as sure-footed and as quickly as could this man William Tell, and there was no one as skilled in the use of a crossbow as William Tell."

I could certainly use a bow and arrow myself. My father had taught me how to aim carefully and how to unfailingly hit the mark from the time I was old enough to hold a bow. 'My father taught me,' he told me, 'and I teach you. And, God willing,' he added with a twinkle in his eyes, 'you will someday teach your son.' We hunted rabbits and quail together, my father and I, and grandfather had shown me how to skin the rabbits and how to pluck the quail.

"Altdorf was one of the many small settlements in the area which we now call Switzerland. Its market square was no doubt very similar to the market square we have in town here. People strolled through it; they conducted business there; and they sat on the benches erected along its sides. But the freedom of walking through the square had been curtailed. This was because the town of Altdorf, as well as the surrounding cantons, was occupied at that time, even as we are occupied today, by an enemy. For Switzerland at the time of William Tell in the early 1300s, the enemy was Austria. Today, for Holland in this year of our Lord, 1945, it is Germany."

He paused dramatically and we all breathed deeply anticipating action before he continued. And why should we not? Stories that paralleled our situation were stories which gripped our hearts; stories with which we could empathize. Tales about the Spaniards occupying our country, for example, during the Reformation times, fascinated us and episodes of heroism encouraged us. Mr. Jaap Kunstenaar was a wonderful well of information, and we leaned forward in our desks listening eagerly, for a while forgetting our worries, aches and trials.

"The enemy agent for the Hapsburg Duke of Austria was a bailiff by the name of Hermann Gessler. He was the Austrian Duke's henchman. Strangely enough, Hermann Gessler sounds ominously like Hermann Goering, who, as you all know, is Hitler's henchman."

We all nodded vigorously for we were very familiar with the name of Hermann Goering, a top Nazi, and a hater of the Jews.

"Gessler was a proud man, a cruel man, and one who sadistically punished the Swiss people without reason. One day, overcome with pride, he placed his hat on a pole in the center of the Altdorf square and announced that anyone passing this hat would have to bow to it on pain of death. Shortly after his announcement, William Tell, a Swiss patriot and one not easily frightened, strode through the square. He refused to obey Gessler's ridiculous command, nonchalantly passing by the cap, totally ignoring it. And he passed by it walking upright, holding the hand of his young son, Walter."

We all laughed, the younger as well as the older children. We were enormously pleased that William Tell had not saluted the cap, for it seemed so obvious to us all that to salute a hat was extremely foolish and who would do such a thing? And the laughter we brought forth was shrill, almost as if we had forgotten how to do it. But we were hungry you see, and our voices had grown weak because of the severe lack of food. I clearly remember thinking that the red ribbon in the hair of the orphan girl Nienke Jongsma, in front of me, looked good enough to eat, even as we guffawed at the audacity of William Tell. And I remember thinking at the same time of the potatoes in Friesland, where Nienke had come from, potatoes which lay rotting but which were not allowed to be sent from that province to the other western provinces desperately in need of food. All the while during that thought, Tom Jansen sitting next to me, shook with mirth. And Ina De Wit in front of Tom, put her hand in front of her mouth to hide squeaky giggles. And fifteen-year-old Lieneke, my good friend Lieneke, with the beautiful blond braids and whom I loved with all the innocent passion of my teenage heart, had a wide grin on her face, showing all her pretty white teeth. Strange that such a sweet and pretty girl was the daughter of a suspected Nazi sympathizer. Mr. Kunstenaar waited until we had settled down before he continued.

"Loitering nearby in the center of the square were several guardsmen. When these guardsmen noticed that William Tell had not saluted Gessler's hat, they immediately arrested him. Shortly afterwards Gessler himself rode into the square surrounded by a hunting party.

"Why is this man in custody?" he demanded from the great height of his white stallion as he loosely held the reins, "And who is he?"

"He refused to salute your cap," the soldiers answered, "and his name is William Tell, a fellow who by all accounts, seems to be a remarkable marksman. He is said to have the ability to shoot a straight arrow at a great distance and not miss his target."

Gessler remained quiet and thoughtful for a few moments. Small Walter, Tell's son and proud of it, began to boast and his words rang through the square, stopping in front of Gessler on his high horse.

"My father,' he called out in his childish voice, interpreting the soldiers' claim in his own words, "can shoot an apple from a tree at a hundred yards!"

Gessler sneered: sneered from his high perch on the horse; sneered at the boy; and sneered at all the bystanders.

"Can he indeed?" he scoffed, "Well then he shall prove his skill to us here. Place an apple on the boy's head. And we shall see if he never misses."

I confess that the thought and mention of the apple in the story brought saliva to my dry mouth. That is to say, I almost drooled and I believed that if I had been in the place of Walter Tell and the apple had been placed on my head, I would have taken it off my head for a moment and crunched into it for one bite - just one bite. I could almost taste it - a much superior taste to that of the sugar beets which the town council was beginning to ration out sparingly to the families in town. We had heard of food packages being dropped out of planes flying over Amsterdam, but we had received no such luxuries.

"Walter was led to a tree at the far end of the square, and an apple was placed on his head. Quite a crowd had gathered in the square by this time. Everyone was horrified. Outwardly calm, William Tell took the crossbow from his shoulder and fitted an arrow to his bow. Walter stood very still and appeared not to be afraid. The child had an unconditional faith in his father's skill. William Tell took careful aim. The arrow left the shaft, whistled through the air, and found its mark in the center of the apple splitting it into two parts."

We all sighed collectively. And then Mr. Kunstenaar quoted an old Northumbrian English ballad. He quoted it with great emotion and I have retained it in my memory.

"I have a sonne seven years old;
He is to me full deere;
I will tye him to a stake -
All shall see him that bee here -
And lay an apple upon his head,
And go six paces him froe.
And I myself with a broad arrowe
Shall cleave the apple in towe."

It was quiet and we could all literally see the cleft apple lying on the ground in front of the boy Walter, who, no doubt, had a huge grin on his face.

"William Tell sprinted towards his son, and as he did so a second arrow fell from his coat. Gessler, puzzled, asked him why this second arrow was necessary. And Tell replied: 'That second arrow was for you, if the first had wounded my boy'."

We were all delighted with Tell's bravery and gleefully visualized the look of helpless anger on Gessler's face.

"A conversation," Jaap Kunstenaar went on, "reported between a Swiss diplomat and a German in 1939 at the onset of the Second World War, went thus. The German said, 'You Swiss are so proud of

274

your militia of 500,000 men. But what will you do if a German army of 1,000,000 comes marching across your border?' The Swiss diplomat calmly replied, 'That's easy. Each of us will shoot twice and go home.'"

We roared with laughter, at which point Nienke Jongsma fainted and Mr. Kunstenaar and some of the older girls, did everything they could to revive her. It took some time and after she was sitting up again, pale and hollow-eyed, as indeed we all were, Mr. Kunstenaar decided that it was time to go home.

"What happened to William Tell after that?" Jan Bezem asked as we filed out into the hall and from there into the street.

"He led a rebellion against the invaders."

"Did he win?"

"Yes," Mr. Kunstenaar smiled and patted Jan on the head, "and I'll tell you about that some other time."

I didn't go straight home as the others did, although I did pass by our house to pick up an old baby carriage from our shed. I had been instructed by my father, who came home under the cover of dark and then only once a week or less, to walk to Farmer Dikkens after four. It was close to four at this time and the two packages of cigarettes plus the two chocolate bars which my father had hidden in the false bottom of the baby carriage were to be used in bargaining for some wheat and potatoes. Farmers didn't take kindly to people coming any more. There wasn't much left of anything for people to barter with. But father had said that Farmer Dikkens would be expecting me. So I went, albeit reluctantly, because I knew that my bargaining powers were less than spectacular.

We lived on the east edge of our town. Its name is inconsequential. I lived there with my father, when he was home, and with my grandfather. My mother had died the first year of the war and I had no siblings. There were just the three of us. We had no other living relatives as both my father and mother had been only children. At this time we also had living with us a Canadian pilot who had shown up a few weeks ago sporting a bad burn to his right arm as well as a cut in his right leg. We doctored him as best we could. He spoke a decent amount of Dutch as his mother had been born in Holland and consequently our communication was good. Sometimes he stayed with father in his hiding place, and sometimes he came to the house. He was the one who had given us the cigarettes and the chocolate.

"Nico," father had said, "these cigarettes may very well be the saving of our lives; God-given they are."

So I prayed before I came to the farm.

"Dear God," I said, not out loud but within my heart, "please let Farmer Dikkens be generous so that I can come home with some food for grandfather."

It was quiet outside. The fields were bare and during my half hour or so of walking, I saw only one German soldier and he paid no heed to me, a skinny boy pushing a baby carriage. If only he had known that the carriage had a false bottom and that my father and I had hidden chocolate and cigarettes there. The Germans, very edgy now that the end of the war was indelibly written on the horizon, had dug holes the size of small rooms by the side of the road. In case of an air attack, they would have somewhere to hide. These holes appeared like graves to me, although, had a plane appeared overhead, I would have jumped into one without any hesitation. My walk that late afternoon was a lonely trek and I felt the atmosphere heavy with danger.

Miraculously Farmer Dikkens, a big man with a pot-belly and large jowls, was agreeable. An admiring smile on his small lips, he held the cigarette packages in his hand, turning them over and over, in his fleshy hands.

"What do you want for them?"

"What are you willing to give?"

I inwardly congratulated myself on this answer.

"Fifteen pounds of wheat."

"I think not," I answered, "there are others who will...."

He did not let me finish.

"All right, then, twenty-five pounds and that's my final offer."

Sliding my hand into one of my pockets, I produced one of the chocolate bars and put it on top of the cigarette packages in his hands, saying nothing. He studied me with piercing eyes, suddenly wary.

"You're not in cahoots with the Germans, are you?"

"You know my father," I answered, "How can you ask such a thing."

In the end he gave me thirty pounds of wheat and fifteen pounds of potatoes. His wife, it turned out, had been addicted to chocolate before the war and would be very pleased with the treat.

I walked back home as quickly as I could. It was a trek against the wind. To make things ever more difficult, the carriage wheels, which had no rubber rims, kept digging into the many ruts in the road. There was a gnawing worry within me. Grandfather had been very tired lately. His thin frame rarely got up from his chair any more although sometimes he surprised me. Pushing the carriage past an abandoned house, I noticed some scrap pieces of wood by its door. Our woodstove had not been burning this last month. Wood was very scarce. People had one night, months ago, cut down many of the trees lining the center road in town. I'd heard that one man who had no axe had fanatically hugged a tree tearfully claiming it as his own, refusing to let go. In the end, a neighbor lent him an axe and they compromised on sharing the wood. Others had jumped up and grabbed low-lying branches, breaking them off, pulling the branches behind them to their homes. There was no brushwood left close to the town. Out in the country there were still woods. But few dared to go and cut these trees down because the Germans had issued an order after that night, saying that anyone caught cutting down any more lumber would be arrested.

Leaving the carriage on the road, I ran up to the entrance of the abandoned house. Picking up the scrap pieces, I decided there was just enough wood for one good fire - a fire that would surely cheer grandfather's bones tonight. As well, I would be able to concoct, I thought, a meal that would taste better than the pancakes I had been making out of mashed tulip bulbs and other bits of left-over food.

And the remaining chocolate bar still stashed in my pocket could be our dessert.

In rather high spirits, I pushed the carriage back into our shed. Who knew but that the war would be over next week. I prayed again, quietly inside my heart.

"Thank you, Lord, for this food. Thank you, Lord, for this bit of wood."

Leaving the wood in the shed, I carried the potatoes under one arm and the bag of wheat under the other. When I pushed open the front door, it creaked horribly. One of the first things I would do after the war, was oil its hinges. No familiar call of welcome hailed me from the living room. Perhaps grandfather was sleeping. He slept much and sometimes, or actually very often, was rather befuddled about the situation we were in. I could see his head resting sideways against the back of the chair. It faced the east window from which place he could see the fields. Very likely he was dozing.

"Grandfather," I called, but there was no answer.

I walked through to the kitchen and deposited my bargaining trophies on the counter. Then I walked back into the living room, approaching grandfather's chair.

"Napping, are we?" I joked, "and that at a time when your favorite grandson is bringing you not only a good supper but also a warm-bellied stove for the evening."

Moortje, our black cat, was sitting on his lap. We never fed him any more as there was no food. Although thin, the animal was wiry and did an admirable job catching mice and rats on his nightly raids. Moortje was inordinately fond of grandfather. No wonder, for the black creature received innumerable scratches behind his ears, under his jaw and along his furry back from grandfather. As I came closer, Moortje stood up and began to meow, at the same time licking the top of grandfather's hand - a hand, I now noted, that hung slack over the edge of the chair. Suddenly afraid, I pushed the cat onto the floor and nudged the still figure. But even as I put out my hand, I knew. I knew that my grandfather had died before I could make the room warm;

before I could boil the potatoes and before I could make some sort of pancakes out of the wheat. Undeterred by my gesture, the cat jumped back onto grandfather's lap, and began butting his black head against the unmoving chest. I knelt down on the floor in front of the chair, resting my head on the still lap. The cat half-sat on my head and began purring. I vaguely took in the familiar smell of grandfather's pipe, for even though it had been a few years since he had last smoked, the odor of it had permeated his clothes. I did not weep, but was overcome with a weariness so great that all my limbs felt as if they had turned to jelly.

Perhaps I sat there for an hour or so. I cannot say and I did not have a clock. But eventually I heard the front door creak open. Then there were footsteps and Paul came into the room. Paul was the Canadian pilot.

"Nico?" he said in a surprised voice at seeing me on my knees with my head in grandfather's lap.

I stirred but very slightly.

"Yes," I answered softly.

"Nico," he repeated, and there was something in his voice that made me raise my head and look at him.

"What is it?"

"Your father," he answered, and then there was a catch in his voice which gripped my heart with fear.

"My father?"

Standing up I repeated his words mechanically. The cat jumped to the ground and ran past Paul's legs. A minute later we could hear the door creak as Moortje had the uncanny ability to somehow paw it open on her own. All the while Paul stood still and I knew again, for the second time within a few hours, that something devastating was going to occur.

"Is your grandfather sleeping?" Paul asked.

"Yes," I answered, reasoning within myself that he was asleep, for were not the dead asleep according to the Bible?

"Somehow," our Canadian pilot continued, beckoning me over to the kitchen where he was heading, "somehow the Nazis became aware of your father's hiding place in the woods."

I trailed him to the kitchen, not able to say anything.

"This afternoon," he slowly spoke on, leaning his left arm on the counter next to the potatoes and the wheat, his voice low and showing no emotion, "they raided it and your father...."

"My father," I regurgitated, feeling surreal and hearing my words as if someone else had said them.

"He was killed, Nico."

"No one knew where he was hiding," I protested then, "no one at all. There was just grandfather and myself who knew."

But within me I was aware that there was another person. And my heart pounded with the knowledge that I had confided in one other person where my father was hiding and that person was Lieneke Goudswaard - Lieneke with the blond, honey-colored braids. I stared at Paul. His eyes were full of compassion.

"We'll not wake your grandfather," he said, "not yet, anyway."

"But he," I stuttered, "he is dead too, Paul. He is dead too."

A half-scream, half-groan erupted from my heart and from my belly and Paul's arms encompassed me until I stopped. I was quiet afterward but could speak no words; neither could I weep. A great weariness overtook me again as I gazed at grandfather sitting in his chair, head tilted to one side while the potatoes and the wheat stood upright on the kitchen counter. And then things went black.

I awoke on my bed later that evening, and I awoke because the door creaked. My head was fuzzy and it was hard to immediately remember what had happened. But the realization of death, loneliness and betrayal returned full force as soon as I sat up. Candlelight shone in from the living room. Swinging my feet over the edge of the bed, I peered through the small hall. I could just make out the figures of three men standing in the living room, one of them holding a candle, standing around grandfather's chair. They were Piet Winter, Hugo Enkel and Klaas Boks - all part of father's team, all part of the underground. I must have made some sort of noise, because all three simultaneously turned to find me looking at them.

"Ah, Nico," said Piet, "I'm sorry, son. I'm deeply sorry about your father and," he added, "your grandfather."

The others murmured agreement and I nodded, not trusting myself to speak.

"We're going to bury your father tonight," Piet went on, "and we thought perhaps it might be a good thing if we buried your grandfather and your father next to one another."

I nodded again. Klaas, a big man, lifted grandfather's body out of the chair and began carrying it towards the front door. It could not have been a difficult task for him because grandfather was light as air, so thin he had become.

"Where," I asked, "will you bury them?"

"In the church cemetery, next to your mother," Piet said, "we've already had some men dig the holes. We can't wait, Nico, because the liberation is coming closer each day and the Germans are getting so nervous that we're not sure what they'll do. But we're pretty certain they won't take the time to dig up graves. Do you want to come?"

I walked towards him rather unsteadily.

"Let me come with you afterwards too, Piet," I pleaded, "I've got nothing left here."

He said nothing, but held out his hand and I took it - me, a grown boy of sixteen years, hanging on to someone as if I were a toddler.

When we reached the churchyard several people emerged from their hiding places behind some of the larger tombstones. One of them was the dominee. No one spoke. As one body, we all moved forward silently towards the west side of the church. This was where my mother was buried. Had I not visited it with my father just last week? And now, in the moonlight, I could see that two yawning hollows had been dug next to her grave. I watched silently as my father's body and my grandfather's body were lowered into those black mouths. There had been no wood for coffins for a long time now. *There are three things that are never satisfied, four that never say enough! The grave....'* Like arrows from the bow of a hunter, the words from Proverbs found their mark straight into my heart and a great anger overcame me so that I turned away from the small group bunched around the grave site and ran blindly away between the markers. Reaching the metal gate, I lifted the latch eventually finding my way home. And all the while I was thinking about what I would do next; all the while I was scheming how I could avenge; and I did not leave the end up to God.

Paul came to the house sometime later. He always came and went, had become part of this and part of that. I did not know the full extent as to how he was involved with the underground, but I could feel him bend over my form as I lay in the bed feigning sleep. He whispered my name but I did not answer. Then he went to my grandfather's room and I knew he would sleep there for the night. But I did not sleep.

Even before the morning light touched the horizon, I was up and into my clothes. My bow and arrows were stashed away in the shed under an old wheelbarrow. I checked them carefully before I headed out in the direction of Lieneke's house. It had rained during the night. Puddles lined the road but there was a sweet south wind - a warm wind - and I thought of how grandfather would have enjoyed this day. He might even have sat behind the house if the sun would prove to be warm enough. No one was about. Certainly a year ago, or even a half a year ago, I could not have walked out as freely as I did now or as I had done yesterday on my way to farmer Dikkens. The Germans badly needed man-power and randomly conscripted men and young boys off the street. But the war was almost over now, or so it was said, and Germans could be seen leaving our town. Every day we saw small groups of soldiers walking through our streets and heading north-east. No matter though, on this particular pre-morning hour there was quiet and not a soul was about. Lieneke lived on the western edge of town and upon reaching her home, I stood for a long moment under the window which I knew held her bedroom. Then, taking the few pebbles I had collected from the roadside, I began to toss them gently and steadily, hitting her pane with a soft ping each time. It would not do to waken her father who would not take kindly to seeing me. Before long the curtains parted slightly to silhouette Lieneke's form. She opened the window and whispered.

"Is that you, Nico?"

"Yes," I answered, making my voice bland, giving away none of the emotion which roiled around inside me.

"What is it?"

"I'm going for a walk. Will you come?"

She was silent, and for a few moments I was afraid that she would not come. We had often gone on walks together, she and I, and had been able to talk about many things. What these things were, I cannot recall now - only that our rapport had been excellent. The reality of the bow and arrow under the wheelbarrow in the shed, lay heavy on my heart. Birds began to sing for the hour was so early that their songs had not yet begun prior to this moment.

"I'll be there in a minute, Nico. Wait by the road."

I breathed in deeply. She would come then. Slowly I sauntered back to the road. Spring, though late, had come and almost gone. I could smell it. Ragged robins, marjoram, and wild balsam flowered - flowered while people died.

"Here I am, Nico."

She had come up behind me so softly that I was startled.

"Lieneke."

"Where shall we go for a walk?"

I did not answer but began to lead the way back in the direction of my house.

"I'm sorry about your father and grandfather, Nico."

There was something within me, something which pushed all other emotions away except for the overriding sense of...of something I did not know how to define. Lieneke's hand gently stole into mine. It was a very thin hand and I could feel the bones.

"I am truly sorry, Nico," she repeated.

No response found its way to my lips and my right hand roughly pushed her hand away. She did not seem overly hurt by the gesture, supposing that my bereavement entitled me to rudeness. Blackbirds whistled their songs in fields, mingling their voices with those of finches. A lark rose up high above our heads, strong and proud, flying straight up to heaven. It was almost morning - almost. We walked without speaking for a long while, and eventually came to my house. I turned in, walking towards the shed.

"What are we going to do, Nico?"

I said nothing, simply holding the door open for her. She slipped into the semi-darkness of the interior and sat down on a broken chair propped up against the east wall. The earliest sun rays faintly fell through the cracks in the wall, shining on her blond braids. I noted that she had not taken the time to comb her hair. It was slightly disheveled with strands of it escaping from the thick plaits. But it did not look unkempt to me, rather it gave her an aura of being totally caught up in my welfare. I was not happy with that thought and forced myself to visualize my father being lowered into his grave. I sat down as well, on the dirt floor straight across from her, and took a deep breath.

"Someone," I began in a neutral voice, "betrayed my father. Someone informed the police where my father was hiding."

She nodded, her blue eyes fixed steadfastly on my face.

"There was no one," I continued, "no one except myself, my grandfather and you, who knew where he was hiding."

Her eyes became clouded, worried and then tears formed. I could see them pooling, then overflowing and finally falling down her cheeks.

"Oh, Nico," she whispered, "you don't think that I...."

"It is a fact," I said, "that there is no one else who knew."

She said nothing but just looked at me. Tears ran down her face. I wanted a denial, a strong denial, and hot anger flooded my being.

"You," I pushed out vehemently, "You're a traitor, just like your father! You wicked girl!"

I stood up then, balling my hands into fists. Backing out through the shed door, I knelt down on the wet ground and picked up a pile of dirt. Packing it into a ball, I stomped back in. Lieneke still sat in the same spot. She hadn't moved. It was as if she were frozen. I hesitated but only for a moment. Slowly coming up to her, never taking my eyes of her face, I heavily deposited the huge clump of dirt on top of her head. Part of it oozed down, down past the honey-colored hair, onto her cheeks, mingling with the tears; but most of it stayed on top of the blond pile of hair. Walking backwards, I took my bow and arrow from under the overturned wheelbarrow. Fitting the arrow into the shaft, I aimed at the apple of dirt on Lieneke's head.

"Why did you tell them?" I cried the words in agony.

My fingers trembled. She did not contradict me but sat so still that she could have been a painting. The sound of loud, raucous laughter traveling up from the road surprised me - surprised me so that my fingers let go of the arrow. It whistled and struck Lieneke's left cheek, narrowly missing her eye. She flinched and her hands flew up to her face at the same time as the door behind me opened revealing Paul.

"Nico! What are you doing?"

I could not answer. For suddenly it was as if the dam of grief within me had burst its bounds and the waters swept me away so that I no longer had any control over my body. Paul was at Lieneke's side in an instant, speaking as he moved.

"There is a German patrol coming down the road. I do believe they're totally tipsy. But neither of us had better be here if they decide to check on the house, or search this shed."

"Run! You must run!"

The words were Lieneke's and through my tears I saw that she had stood up. Blood trickled down her left cheek even as she spoke. What had I done?

"I think you are all right," Paul said, addressing Lieneke, and then coming for me, he added, "Nico, we have to make a run for it. Those Germans will shoot us on sight."

"But what about...?"

My words slurred and I could not stop looking at the blood running down Lieneke's face.

"I will be fine," she spoke rather woodenly, the wet dirt on her head continuing to seep downwards to mingle with the blood on her left cheek, "and as you know, most of the Germans in town are acquainted with my father."

She lifted one of her hands in a mock salute, a hand wet with her own blood as she added, "So you need not worry about me at all."

Rooted in my spot, Paul had to push me alongside him towards the shed door, talking to Lieneke as he did so.

"Go to the house and wash that wound," he instructed, looking at her over his shoulder, "Don't let any of that dirt infect it."

Opening the door, and peering around the corner, he next pulled me out with him and we began our escape. Our house was built on a slope and the field behind it curved downwards towards a small stream. Even now I remember the shouting, the loud voices calling us to halt. We did not halt. Miraculously the shots that were fired missed us. Slipping and sliding, we reached the water, and all the while Paul dragged me behind himself. He dragged me until I lost consciousness. It was then that he carried me.

When I awoke, I was lying on a cot in a small room. Paul was sitting at a table, as were some other men. I recognized Piet Winter and Klaas Boks, but there were others I did not know. Shifting slightly, the movement alerted them to the fact that I was awake. Paul stood up and sat on the edge of the cot.

"So how do you feel?"

"Where am I?"

"That doesn't matter. What matters is that you're safe."

"How long have I been here?"

"Well, you've been sleeping for about two days now."

"Two days!"

He nodded and smiled. I was struggling to remember everything that had happened and closed my eyes at the immensity of the memories that hit me. My father and grandfather were gone. There was no one at all now except for Lieneke and she....

"How is ...?" But I could not bring myself to say her name out loud, and repeated, "How is...?"

"First I want to tell you that we know whom it was who told the police where your father was," Paul said in a low voice.

"Who was it?"

"It was your grandfather."

Paul uttered the sentence softly. He knew the words would hurt. The men at the table had gone back to playing cards, to speaking quietly among themselves.

"How could he? How could grandfather?"

"He did not mean to. The Gestapo came to your house that afternoon. Only they were not dressed like officers. They were dressed like ordinary folks. They questioned your grandfather and led him to believe that they were loyal Dutch citizens and that they were friends. They promised to bring some food for himself and for you if he would only tell them where his son was. They said they had an urgent message for your father from the queen."

"The queen?"

"Yes, and your grandfather believed it and was more than willing to point them in the direction of your father's hiding spot."

Paul stopped for a moment and eyed me compassionately before he continued.

"Your grandfather was suffering from aging, Nico, and did not quite know what he was doing or saying the last while. Surely you know that."

I did know it. I remembered clearly how he had talked out loud to the cat as if she was my mother. And I also recalled that he had told me only a week ago that Prime Minister Gerbrandy had come to call, asking for his help in fighting the Nazis.

"How do you know for a fact that he really told them?"

I asked the question with a sigh and moved my feet under the thin blanket covering my form.

"Because one of the German officers told Hendrik Jansen. The officer thought it was a huge joke. Hendrik is one of our men, but the officer didn't know that."

I knew Hendrik Jansen. He was Tom's father and I'd gone to school with Tom for a long time.

"So it was not Lieneke?"

Paul shook his head.

"No, Nico, it wasn't her at all.

"How is she? Is she hurt very badly?"

He replied rather indirectly, and I vaguely sensed that he was keeping something back.

"The wound on her cheek was not very bad, just a scratch really."

I sighed again, partly in relief this time, but when I wanted to get up, dizziness overtook me. Paul pushed me down.

"Sleep, Nico. Sleep."

Two weeks later the war was over. So was my life as I had known it. Our house had been burned down to the ground. There was nothing left. There were only the three graves in the cemetery and I could not bed down there for the rest of my life. But I had no other family except for those three. It was Paul who provided me with a solution of what I ought to do.

"Come back to Canada with me, Nico."

"Come back with you?"

"Yes," he said with a warm smile on his face, "my mother and father would love you. After all, it was your family, your father and grandfather and yourself, who saved my life."

I talked with the dominee, and with Jaap Kunstenaar, both of whom encouraged me to accept Paul's offer and go with him to Canada. I also tried very hard to see Lieneke, but every time I knocked on the door of her home, no one answered. The windows had been boarded up and the property appeared untended, unkept. The neighbors raised their eyebrows when I asked them about Lieneke and would tell me nothing. Neither was dominee or Jaap

Kunstenaar able to relate anything to me as to the whereabouts of the family Goudswaard. To tell you the truth, I was ashamed to tell anyone what I had done to Lieneke the day after my father and my grandfather had died. Paul was the only one who knew. And so I left my village without saying goodbye to someone who had never shown me anything but kindness.

But now here was the mystery. Lieneke was in Canada. Not only that but she was in Canada with a child. That child was seven years old, born the year after the war was over. So he had been conceived during the war. Echoing, loud laughter in the hallway reminded me keenly of the loud, raucous, crowing laughter of the drunk soldiers coming down the road - coming down the road that morning when the birds had just begun to sing. And it came to me that Lieneke had offered herself as a substitute - offered herself so that Paul and I could live. I groaned out loud.

Someone knocked at the door. Still absorbed in the past, I stood up and opened it. Little Nico Goudswaard faced me, or was it Lieneke? His grin sang at me.

"I came back because you forgot to tell me your name."

"Nico," I answered, "my name is Nico, just like yours. And," I added, "I think that I would like to ask your mother...."

I didn't finish the sentence. I couldn't because I was weeping.

Glossary

Ausweis - an ID card showing the official identity of the wearer

Dominee - pastor

Fraulein - title of address for an unmarried German woman

Goudswaard - gold worthy

Gutenmittag - good afternoon

Heimat - home, or homeland with specific connotation to German culture and society.

Kinderwagen - baby carriage

Krieg - war

Meneer - mister

Moeder - mother (Dutch)

Moeke - mom

Niks - nothing

Normal School - Teacher's College

N.S.B., (Nationaal Socialistische Beweging), the national Socialist Movement, was founded by Anton Mussert in 1931. Mussert studied civil engineering and became a chief engineer in Utrecht until dismissed in 1933 because of his membership in the N.S.B. State employees were forbidden membership in that party. A swastika was not used as an emblem. Instead, to convince the Dutch of the party's patriotism, a lion on a shield of horizontal orange, white, and blue was used. The party greeting was 'Hou Zee', that is to say, 'Hold steady', a sailor's cry. Mussert was a friend of the Germans but opposed to German take-over. His so-called three pillars were: 1. Faith in God, 2. Love of nation, and 3. Willingness to work. Initially not opposed to Jewish participation in the N.S.B. party, he had to yield to pressure to prohibit their membership. Mussert used strong-arm squads and published a newspaper.

Oom - uncle

Opa - grandfather

Razzia - hostile raid with the intention of capturing those in hiding

Tante - aunt

Vader - father, dad (Dutch)

Vater - father, dad (German)

Verbond - covenant

Weg - road, way

Alongside and Within

Further Reflection
for
Individuals, Book Clubs and Classrooms

1: I have Called You by Name

1. What are your thoughts on Job's taking the letter he has received and spreading it out before the Lord? Should decisions be made without laying situations before Him? Discuss. Is there a Biblical precedence for this?

2. Are any of the names in the story significant? Why/not? Are there Trinitarian references?

3. Was Els Deken's decision to take the place of her sister, correct or incorrect? What would you have done? Have you ever been in a situation where you had opportunity to give someone else a chance to repent?

4. Can you consider this story an allegory? Why/not?

5. Can a person, (Aafke Roos, for example), escape justice in the long run? What do you think of War Tribunals? - bodies which have the jurisdiction to prosecute individuals for the international crimes of genocide, crimes against humanity and war crimes. Who sits in judgment on the Last Day?

2: Any Fool Can Sing in the Day

1. Historically it is a fact that the town of Geel in Antwerp, Belgium took in and protected mentally disabled persons. How do you feel about an entire city doing such a work together?

2. Can suffering, cruelty or abuse ever serve as an excuse for atheism?

3. All things are in God's providential hand - also things such as cruelty and abuse. Discuss and apply to the story.

4. Father Christophe was an appealing and generous character. However, where your treasure is, the Bible says, there your heart is. Where do you suppose Father Christophe's heart was?

5. What was it that Paulus understood in the end?

3: The Drawing

1. Would you consider this a story about faith? What is faith?

2. Is it true that things seen, material things, are, in the long run, more real then things not seen? Why/not?

3. When Jesus says to His disciples in John 16:16 "In a little while you will see Me no more, and then after a little while you will see Me", what does He mean?

4. Is there a parallel between the art of drawing and being chosen, or drawn, by God? Consider the verses of Psalm 139:15-16 as you ponder this.

4: When You Open Your Hand

1. A skin graft is skin used to cover an area where the patient's skin has been lost due to a burn or an injury. The most effective grafts involve moving the patient's own skin from one part of the body to another. What part of the body do you suppose was used as a skin graft on Otto's palm?

2. Is there such a thing as a heart graft? Consider Ezekiel 11:19.

3. There are references to windows throughout the story. Is that significant? God's windows can release both good and bad. Search out Gen. 7:11 in the ESV and look up Malachi 3:10 in the NKJ or the KJV. Comment.

4. What might the pillars signify in the story?

5. Does it often take a providence to make us see the caring nature of God? What were the providences displayed in Otto's life?

5: I Was a Stranger

1. Is humility one of the most difficult and yet one of the greatest of all virtues? Why/not? How is this illustrated in the story?

2. If you had lived in Diestadt, would you have condemned Tilda? Have you ever condemned someone on hearsay?

3. How hard is it to do a good deed without telling others? Do John's words in John 3:30 apply to him only, or also to us?

4. Comment on the title of this story.

5. Although the name and the place of the city are fictional, the story is based on a true event. With which character can you identify?

6: The Fallen Lines

1. Would you consider the first paragraph of the story an apt description of providence? Why/not?

2. How and why are names significant in this story? Compare Berend's and Brian's surnames.

3. Berend had an intellectual belief, but his conscience although pricked from time to time seemed inactive. A godly conscience is directly connected to life, behavior, lifestyle and speech. Why is this true or untrue?

3. Psalms 23 speaks of goodness and mercy following David all the days of his life. Hebrews 9:14 talks about God cleansing our consciences from acts that lead to death, so that we may serve the living God. Does God, at some point, take Berend by the nape of his neck, so to speak, and nudge him with goodness and mercy?

4. How does the last paragraph of the story connect to the first?

7: The End of a Thing

1. Are people often shaped by their past or by what has been done by someone else in the past? Explain.

2. In some ways living in the past might preclude the present and the future. In some ways looking to the past might strengthen your present and give you hope for the future. Do you agree/disagree, and why?

3. Is what has been done to us or our family in the past ever an excuse for a complaining temperament? Are phrases such as 'if only I had been given' or 'if only I had been shown', feeble excuses that deny providence? How so? May we ever use such excuses?

4. Was it wrong of Sanna's mother to strike her child in order to hide her in the secret place? Does God ever strike His children in such a way as to save them from harm?

8: Forming Adam

1. Ephesians 1:4 tells us that God chose us in Him before the creation of the world. Is it necessary to understand salvation? Why/not?

2. Considering both the first and the second Adam, how was Adam Adriaan formed?

3. Can you empathize with Mr. Legaal. (Note that the word 'legal' is translated 'legaal' in Dutch.) Is there a bit (or a lot) of a legalist in all of us? Explain your reasoning.

4. Can and does God ever use extraordinary means to grow faith?

5. What does the last line of the story indicate to you?

9: I Have a Sonne Seven Years Old

1. Do we often condemn people using human logic? How and why did Nico condemn Lieneke?

2. After a wrongdoer is forgiven, should restitution be a part of his/her life? Is our legal system set up for restitution? Read Exodus 22:1-15.

3. The tale of William Tell encouraged the school children during the war and gave them hope for victory and peace. Are there godly stories which can be given to encourage believers so that they can look forward to heaven? Ought we to speak to one another, to encourage one another, about the end of time? Can you support that Biblically and how would you go about doing that?

4. Can you point to instances of grace in the story?

Printed in Great Britain
by Amazon

17952279R00172